LETHAL ALLIANCE

Lethal Alliance is the second book in the
Lethal Legacy series.
Lethal Legacy, the first book, is out now on Amazon.

Sign up at www.fehupress.com to be the first to read new work.

LETHAL ALLIANCE

PAULA WALSHE

FEHU PRESS

OFELIA

"Ofelia!"

Mama's voice, thin and full of fear, comes through the smoke and chaos of the ballroom explosion. "Ofelia, is Masha with you?"

The smoke is so thick I can barely see in front of me. I'm pushed up in a corner, in between the stage and the back wall, and somehow, miraculously, I'm not hurt.

Was that a bomb?

"'Felia!" Masha squirms underneath me, and I grip my little sister tightly.

"She's here, Mama." I hug her small body close. "Are you hurt, Masha?"

"No." She shakes her head against my chest. I gulp breaths of air, trying to make order out of the broken stone and chaos. My ears are still ringing from the explosion. I feel weirdly insulated, like there's an invisible layer cutting me off from the people screaming and crying all around us. Masha clings to me. She's the only reality in the insanity that, only moments ago, was the best night of my life.

Barely meters away, Matvei is lying face down. He's not moving.

We were dancing. I can remember it, his arms around me, the way he was looking at me. *I thought he was going to kiss me . . .*

Someone grips my arm, not gently. "I've got them, Inger," he says to my mother.

I recognize his voice, although before tonight, I'd never met him.

It's the same person who pushed me and Masha into the corner, right before the world exploded.

"Wait." I struggle feebly. "We have to help Matvei—"

"There's no time." The man speaks with a thick Russian accent. "You're in danger."

"Get them out of here!" Mama sounds terrified.

Is she hurt?

I have to get it together.

"No!" I fight against the hand holding me. "Mama!"

"I'm fine, Ofelia. Uncle Nicky is with me. His friend is going to help you and Masha, okay?"

"Listen to your mother." The man is trying to make me stand up. "Nikolai will take care of her."

That's why I don't know him. He's one of Uncle Nicky's men.

"We need to get you out of here." The man presses his earpiece. "Roman says you need to come with me. We're under attack."

Roman. Just hearing my godfather's name reassures me. *Roman is okay.*

I think of him, and Lucia. *What would they want me to do?*

I need to pull myself together. To be strong for Masha.

"Okay." I clutch Masha by the hand, trying to steady myself as the man pulls us to our feet. He has his gun out, and he's looking around warily. I don't remember his face, but he's big, and he has an earpiece. He looks just like all of our normal security guards.

"This way." The man pushes Masha and me through a hole in the wall, and suddenly we are outside. The night air is fresh on my face, and I inhale it gratefully. "Hurry," the man urges us.

We stumble across the rubble toward a waiting car. The door is open, and another man is standing beside it with a gun in his hand, talking into a radio. "Quickly," he orders, bundling Masha and me into the back of the car.

"What happened?" Masha stares up at me, blood trickling down her face from a cut on her forehead. "What happened, 'Felia?"

"I don't know, *myshka*." I hold her close, trying not to think of Matvei's still body, of the horrible blast that seemed to shake the air itself. "I think somebody set off a bomb."

The doors on either side of us lock automatically, and the car takes off. We're alone in the back seat, with a window in between us and the driver.

"Hey." I knock on the glass window. "Where are you taking us? Where's my brother, Mickey? Are Lucia and Roman okay?"

There's no answer. I press the button on the intercom and ask again.

"Everyone is fine," the driver answers. It isn't Bryce or Dimitry or any of our usual drivers, and like the man who took us out of the ballroom, he speaks with a thick Russian accent. "I'm taking you to a safe house. Roman and . . . *Lucia* will meet you there." The smart-ass way he says Lucia's name tells me he knows it's not her real one.

Something isn't right.

I hear Roman's voice in my head: *"I want you to always be thinking for yourselves, to be smart and accountable for your own safety . . ."*

I press the button again. "Can I use your telephone, please? I want to call Roman."

The first security guard answers this time. "Roman's busy. You can talk to him when we get to the safe house."

My unease increases. I don't have a phone with me; mine was in my purse, which I left on the table when I was dancing with Matvei. I shudder when I think of his inert body lying in the rubble.

I don't think Matvei is okay.

I have no idea where Luce and Roman are.

And nothing about this feels normal.

"'Felia." Masha looks up at me, her lip quivering. "Where are we going?"

"I'm not sure, *myshka*." I hug her close, trying to reassure her with my touch.

"Will Mickey be there?"

"I hope so."

I stare out of the window, trying to work out where we are.

Somewhere near the airport. I can see planes coming in to land.

The car turns off onto a side road and then passes through a security gate. The driver flashes some kind of pass, and the man waves our car through without looking in the back. The area around us is dark except for the colored ground lights that guide planes in. We're not at the main airport. This is smaller, and there's no big terminal, only a small hanger lit by fluorescent lights.

The car comes to a halt beside a private plane with the stairs down. Our car door is pulled open. The driver and security guard stand on either side of it, automatic weapons hanging from their hands.

Why are their guns out?

Our guards normally keep their guns hidden.

Then again, I try to tell myself, *there's nothing normal about tonight.*

One of them holds out a phone. I snatch it out of his hand. "Hello?"

"Ofelia." Mama's voice is shaking but clear. I grip the phone, closing my eyes in relief.

"Mama! What's happening? Where's Roman?"

"There was an attack, darling. Some of Roman's men have been hurt, and we're worried there are people looking for you and your sister."

Okay. I nod. *That makes sense.*

"Roman wants me to take you to stay with my family in Miami, until we know it's safe."

Yeah—that makes no sense at all.

"Deda and Baba Melnyck's house?" I try to act like that isn't the weirdest damn idea ever. "I thought Roman said it wasn't very secure there?"

Masha makes a face. "I don' like Deda and Baba's house—"

I squeeze her hand warningly, and she subsides.

Inger's voice rises slightly, like she's arguing. "Roman has men who will meet you there, Ofelia."

"What about Mickey? And Lucia? Where are they? Are they okay?" I hold Masha's hand tightly, staring around at the barren airfield, shivering despite the mild night.

Something is very wrong.

"They're fine." Inger's voice is shrill and hurried. "They're just with the police now, giving a report."

I don't like this.

"Can I talk to Roman, please?"

Inger covers the phone, but I can still hear her muffled voice. "She wants to talk to Roman."

I need to work out a plan.

A moment later Nikolai's voice comes down the line. "Roman has gone after the men who set off the bomb. I know you want to talk to him, but you need to listen to your mother. Spain isn't safe for us anymore. We're taking you to stay with

Deda and Baba Melnyk in Miami until Roman gives us the all clear."

How do we get out of here?

I shake my head slowly, eyeing the men with the guns. I don't like the way they're looking at me. "I want to talk to Lucia."

Nikolai makes an impatient noise. "Her phone was lost in the blast. She'll call you as soon as she can. Can you give the phone back to the security guard, please, Ofelia?" His voice sounds strained. The guard with the gun takes the phone from my hand before I can answer.

"*Da,*" he says curtly. He listens for a moment, then his mouth curls unpleasantly. "I don't take orders from you." He hangs the phone up without speaking again and nods toward the stairs. "*Bystro,*" he snaps. *Quickly.*

"'Felia?" Masha is staring at him, her mouth set in an obstinate line. "Don' like him."

I don't either.

Roman's men never make us feel unsafe. Even Nikolai's men always treat us with respect.

The man said he doesn't take orders from Nikolai. But if he's Roman's man, he should be treating us a lot differently.

"No." I try to make my voice sound certain, like Lucia does when she gives orders. "I want to speak to Roman before we go anywhere."

The man smiles unpleasantly. "Not going to happen." He steps closer, and I move away, pulling Masha with me. He laughs, then nods at the other man. "Get them on the plane."

"Wait." I pull Masha against me, but they're herding us toward the stairs, the muzzles of their automatic weapons pointing directly at us.

There's no way this man works for Roman.

We have to get out of here.

Surely they won't shoot us, if they're talking to Inger and Nikolai?

I squeeze Masha's hand. She looks up at me, and I flick my eyes toward the edge of the airfield. Masha nods solemnly.

We break and run at the same time, Masha holding my hand.

We make it about thirty meters before Masha screams, a high-pitched sound of terror that cuts me to the bone. Her hand jerks out of mine, and I stop and turn, but it's too late. One of the guards has her firmly in his grip. The other one tackles me, and I hit the ground hard enough to knock the wind from my body, the guard on top of me. I struggle, trying to push him off, and he laughs, thrusting his thigh between mine.

He puts his mouth close to my ear. His breath smells like cigarettes and old alcohol.

"Keep struggling, little *blyat*. That's just how I like it." A long blade comes up, right next to my face, the metal edge gleaming in the airport lights. He puts the tip of it against my skin, right next to my eye. "Now tell your sister to calm the fuck down."

I turn my head uselessly on the ground and see Masha, her legs kicking frantically, in the grip of another guard.

"'Felia!" she screams.

"Do as I say, and I won't cut her." The guard on top of me thrusts his hips obscenely into my groin then pulls me to my feet. He turns me around, holding me roughly against him, his knife still against my face.

"Do as they say, Masha." I try as hard as I can to keep my voice steady.

My little sister stares at me, her eyes wide and furious, her legs still kicking. "Let 'Felia GO!"

"Sounds like she needs a little more encouragement." The guard pushes the tip of his knife into my temple and drags it down the side of my face, opening my skin in a flash of white-hot, searing pain. Masha's shrill scream gets higher.

"Shut up," snarls the guard holding Masha, "or we'll make your sister hurt even more."

Masha's scream cuts off midair, and she stares at me in horror. Blood drips into my eye, obscuring my vision.

"Looks like we got her attention," the guard murmurs in my ear. I can hear the excitement in his voice. "Maybe one more cut, just to drive the lesson home—"

"What the fuck are you doing?"

The cold, hard voice cuts through the night, stilling the knife hand of my attacker.

The guard swings around, aiming his rifle at the newcomer, his knife still at my throat.

I try to blink away the blood streaming into my eyes so I can see clearly.

The man facing me is the most frightening I've ever seen. Dressed entirely in black, he's as tall as Roman, with a patch over one eye. His good eye is a hard, arctic blue, staring at the man holding me with an expression so flat and cold it sends a chill through me.

It's like he's dead already.

"What are you doing here?" The guard with his knife at my throat snarls the question. "You're supposed to be on the boat—"

"A boat you idiots made fucking sure every coast guard in the country is currently chasing. Quite the oversight in planning, it seems." He walks toward us slowly, without an ounce of fear for the guns currently pointing at him. "Or perhaps," he says silkily, "it wasn't an oversight at all. Either way, I'll be taking it from here."

"You can't do that. We don't take orders from Orlov's mad dog." But the guard's eyes are moving around uneasily, and even I can hear the fear in his voice.

The man's lips curl contemptuously. "You do now." He nods, and a group of men emerge from the darkness, their automatic weapons pointing at the guards holding us. "Put your guns down," the man says coldly, "and let the girls go."

The guards look around warily, but they're outnumbered ten to one. They release us and put their guns on the ground.

Masha runs to me. I hold her tightly, looking for an escape, but I already know there isn't one. Men surround us, but at least now their guns are pointing at our original attackers, not at Masha and me.

The guard who cut me glares at the man with the eye patch. "You're making a big fucking mistake, Petrovsky."

Petrovsky?

I know that's Lucia's real family name, just like I know the Orlovs are the people chasing her. Mickey might not tell me everything he knows, but he's told me that much.

I feel a nervous flicker of hope. One that fades almost as soon as it rises.

Petrovsky's hard face has none of Lucia's warmth. And his lone eye is terrifyingly blank, like an icy abyss.

"A mistake, huh?" Petrovsky's voice is cold as winter. "Not nearly as big as the one you just made, friend." He smiles, a chilling sneer that doesn't reach his eyes, and holds up his right hand in a clenched fist. A red sparrow, vivid as blood, is tattooed on it. The red ink gleams in the lights of the plane. "Vilnus Orlov thanks you for your service."

His hand drops, and two shots ring out in quick succession.

The guards who took us fall to the ground, their blood spreading across the tarmac.

I push Masha's face into my leg to stifle her scream. I stare at the dead men, my own scream stuck in my throat.

Blood from the wound on my face drips onto my gown, turning the material a dark purple. I can't even feel the pain anymore.

I can't feel anything at all.

The man with the eye patch turns to us.

"My name is Alexei Petrovsky." He tilts his head politely at the stairs. "Please board the plane." His voice is chillingly calm.

This time, Masha and I go.

Alexei Petrovsky isn't our friend. He isn't anyone's friend.

He's a killer—and now he's our kidnapper.

2

DARYA

Darya—

I know you are planning to run.

I'm not going to stop you. But I want you to be safe, and I want you to know the truth.

First, your safety.

Inside this envelope you will find a passport, more than enough money to get you out of Spain, and a card with the name and address of someone who will help you disappear.

You cannot take your father with you, not this time. The Orlovs are too close. Sergei will remain here in my care. Trust that I will keep him safe.

And now for the truth.

My name—my real name—is Roman Borovsky. My father was Aleksander Borovsky, a famous safe maker and jeweler.

When I was a child, my father built a vault for a very powerful man. Until recently, I never knew this man's name. My parents thought that keeping me ignorant would keep me safe.

They were wrong.

The vault was built for your father, Sergei Petrovsky.

I don't know how or when the Orlovs learned it was my father who built the vault. But they did, because when I was ten years old, the Orlovs came for us. When my father wouldn't tell them how to access the vault, they killed him.

My father must have known they would come for him. He'd already sent my mother into hiding, and he made sure I got out before the Orlovs could get their hands on me.

The Orlovs hunted me for years. They believed I knew how to open the vault and stopped at nothing in their efforts to find me. Despite the danger, I stayed in Miami, hoping my mother would return.

She never did. I must assume that she, too, is dead, and my father's secrets with her.

Given their relentless pursuit of you, it seems the Orlovs' determination to open that vault has not lessened with time.

I should have told you the truth long ago, but you of all people might understand how difficult it is to drop the habits of a lifetime. Let me just say that it took me longer than it should have to trust you, and for that, I can only apologize.

Which brings me to our current situation.

I understand your loyalty to your brother, and his to you. I believe there is nothing Alexei will not do to keep you safe and guard your family's legacy. I understand that. I can even respect it.

Except that it seems Alexei is planning to trade with the Orlovs for your freedom—and his bargaining chip is a project I have spent many years creating.

I can protect what is mine, no matter who comes for it. But I can't protect you if you run to Alexei now.

I know your brother will never stop trying to get you back, just like I know the Orlovs won't ever stop trying to get into that vault, no *matter what he offers them. I won't allow you to be a pawn in their games.*

I'm asking you to trust me, Darya. Trust that I will care for your father and do all I can to keep your brother safe. But to do that I need to know you are safe, too. And that means asking you to disappear again, somewhere your brother can't find you. There's more than enough money in the account to run as far as you wish. If you need a new identity, the man I've named on the card will help you do that.

When I have won this war—and I will win, Darya—I will find you again.

You may not wish to see me. That is a chance I have no choice but to take. I will respect your wishes whatever you decide.

I meant it when I said I loved you. Even if I never see you again, I want you to know that I am

Yours,

Now, and always.

Roman.

I FOLD the letter with shaking hands. I wonder when he slipped it into my clutch.

When he had me naked in a darkened office?

When I lay beneath him in the aftermath of the explosion?

Either way, it was before he thought I'd betrayed him.

I stare blindly into the stored baggage locker at Malaga Airport. My satchel is sitting inside it, a lonely reminder of the life I've led, and the one I'm about to lead again.

A life of running. A life without Roman. Without the children. Without Papa or my brother.

I close my eyes, trying to still my churning stomach. But closing my eyes only takes me straight back to the ballroom in Malaga, and the bomb that has changed our lives forever.

Whatever Roman might have felt for me when he wrote this

letter is long gone. I saw the killer in his eyes when he told me to run. Roman believes me to be complicit in the explosion at the ball. He thinks I deliberately endangered his children. There's no coming back from that kind of betrayal.

The children.

I saw Roman's face. Whatever Dimitry whispered into his ear turned him from the man I thought I knew into a stone-cold killer. I can't imagine what news could have been that devastating.

Not the children. Please, God, please, not the children. Please let them be safe.

But even the thought that they might be hurt, even the slightest edge of that thought, is an abyss I cannot dare approach. That way lies utter madness, a loss of such horrific magnitude I can't begin to comprehend it.

I fumble blindly in the envelope that held his letter, needing to do something, anything, other than let my mind go down that dark road, and my shaking fingers pull out the passport and ticket he put inside it.

I read the name on the passport dully, without taking it in. It belongs to someone else, a name plucked from the ether by some anonymous forger. Just holding the passport, facing the prospect of yet another name, of years lost to the lonely darkness of running, makes me feel sick.

I clutch the edges of the locker, trying to breathe, to force my mind to function. It's been less than half an hour since I ran from the explosion. It feels like an eternity.

I'm no longer wearing my ball gown. It's stuffed behind a gas station dumpster half a mile from the ballroom, exchanged for a simple black slip dress made of thin enough material to fold into a tiny patch in my clutch purse. My elaborate hairdo has been replaced by a simple braid, makeup wiped off in a couple of easy swipes. My heels were plain enough to match both dresses. I got a taxi on the roadside outside a bar half a mile away from the ball. I feigned an argument with a nonexistent boyfriend as I climbed into it and addressed the driver in terrible, English-accented Spanish, telling him to take me to the airport so I could fly back to London. I cried the entire way to the airport to give my story credence.

The tears, at least, weren't fake.

My escape was made on autopilot. I'd thought it through, known that a solid plan was the only prevention against what I knew would be an emotional, not to mention dangerous, escape.

I just hadn't truly believed it would come to that. Some part of me had dared to believe there might be a solution that would allow me to stay without endangering those I love. Instead, it seems I waited too long, and endangered them all.

Not in my worst nightmares could I ever have envisaged the devastating reality.

I'd known the Orlovs were coming for me. And I know, better than anyone, the extent of their evil.

I still never expected a bomb.

A bomb my brother knew about.

The nausea hits without warning. I run to the garbage can at the end of the line of lockers, making it just in time to retch up the bare contents of my stomach. I can still feel the aftermath of the juddering blast, smell the acrid scent of it on my hair.

Who was caught in that blast?

Who died because of me?

I clutch the cold steel, resisting the urge to sink to the floor and cling to it like a life belt.

There are cameras in here.

I can't afford to lose it.

I force myself to turn and walk back to the locker. With hands that are ice-cold and shaking, I open the other envelope in my clutch. The one Alexei gave me.

I ignore the airline ticket and reach instead for the letter wrapped around it. Part of me wants to burn them both without even looking. But there's no time for theatrics. No time for the rage and hurt.

I know all too well that there will be time enough for both, in the lonely days to come.

Instead I breathe deeply to calm the nausea and fury churning inside me and force myself to read.

My sister,

I hope you are reading this somewhere safe.

When you arrive at your destination, go to the address written on the back of your ticket. A friend of mine will contact you there.

Don't be afraid. I wish I could explain it all to you in this letter, but what needs to be said is too dangerous to commit to paper. Please burn both the ticket and this letter as soon as you arrive.

Both, if found by the wrong people, will mean my death, and yours.

The rest must wait until my friend finds you. Please trust her and believe what she says.

Most of all, have faith.

We're nearly home safe.

I CRUMPLE the letter into a hard ball, trembling with anger and sadness.

If Alexei had truly wanted to keep the children safe, he would never have let them be in a ballroom with a bomb.

He used them to make me run.

Alexei knows that I would never allow the children to fall into the Orlovs' hands, and he deliberately played on that. He used the one threat that he knew would make me obey his instructions without question. He told me that the only way to keep the children safe was to run—and so I ran, just like he intended.

But that doesn't mean I have to run where he wants me to go.

I'm not the girl who fled Miami, blindly following the course set for me by my brother and father. I'm not the sister Alexei remembers, any more than he is the little brother I left behind.

It's been over six years since my brother helped Papa and me escape. I know that Alexei is changed. I saw it in his face, heard it in the harsh tones of his voice. He is no longer the teenage boy I tried so hard to take care of.

He's a man, one raised in the ruthless world of the Orlovs, subjected to God only knows what manner of torture. No matter how much I want to trust him, I can't. Not after that bomb. Not after he put the children in danger.

I look at the other passport, the one Roman gave me.

I can't use that either.

Roman has no reason to keep me safe anymore, no matter what his letter says. The man who wrote those words is gone. Whoever Roman was, whatever he felt for me, changed forever the moment that bomb went off. Now Roman is the killer he became long ago, determined to protect what is his.

That doesn't include me. Not anymore. And after reading his letter, now that I understand at least part of his story, I wonder that he didn't kill Papa the moment he learned our true identities.

Roman's own father died to protect my family's vault.

His mother was lost to him for the same reason.

My family is why Roman found himself orphaned on the Miami streets at ten years old.

Roman has no reason to love anyone named Petrovsky, and every reason to want us all dead.

I want to believe that Roman won't hurt Papa, but I can't know that. And despite what he's written, I'm not at all sure Roman hasn't been playing me this entire time, hiding me in the wings until the right time comes to use me.

Whatever the truth was before tonight, his final words left me with no illusions about how he feels now.

"So go on, then, Darya Petrovsky. Run. Run fast. Because if any harm has come to my children, I swear I'll hunt you down and fucking kill you myself."

I shiver, sick and cold inside.

I had thought myself alone during the years Papa and I ran from the Orlovs. Now I realize I never had any idea of what it means to be truly alone.

I can't trust my brother. The man I love is a killer who believes I betrayed him. One who might also have been betraying me all along.

Which means the only thing left for me to do is disappear.

I try to force my shattered thoughts into some kind of order. Alexei's ticket is in one hand, Roman's ticket in the other. Oddly enough, though they are for different flights, they are both for the same destination: Zurich, Switzerland.

I have no intention of taking either flight.

But those watching me need to believe I'm on at least one of them.

And they will be watching.

Roman may despise me, but sooner or later, he's going to want to know where I am. It's the kind of man he is.

As for Alexei—I have to assume that he, too, has ways of monitoring my movements. The ticket he gave me is booked under the name on my new passport, the one Papa's contact sent from Argentina. Alexei clearly knows a lot more than just how to find me at a ball, and that makes him dangerous.

From the ballroom to these storage lockers, my movements will be relatively easy to trace. This is the moment when it becomes more complicated, when I need to think like the fugitive I have been and must become again.

If it were just me running, I doubt I would even bother.

But it isn't just me.

My hand steals over my belly.

Roman's baby doesn't deserve to suffer for my mistakes. I don't have the right to risk the life of yet another child. I have to stay safe, not because my life is worth saving, but because the child inside me deserves the chance to live.

That thought gives me strength.

Think, Darya.

I can't take my backpack through international security. There's enough currency in there to set off every alarm in the place, even without the extra roll of cash from Roman.

But I need to board at least one of those flights.

I take the satchel, close the locker, and exit the luggage area, not hiding from the cameras scattered around. In the international terminal, I enter the ladies' bathroom and head for an end stall, where I change into jeans, a T-shirt, and sneakers and put my hair up under a cap. I exit from the opposite entrance to the one I came in and leave the terminal again, keeping my head down.

It takes me ten minutes to walk to the nearest airport hotel. I pay cash for three nights, using the passport Roman gave me for identification. In the room I remove everything I will need, including nearly all the cash, from the satchel. I stuff the empty bag with a towel and my cell phone. I put my slip dress and heels at the top, along with a small amount of cash. The bulk of the money and the rest of my belongings I wrap in clothing. I make the bundle watertight by using two garbage bags and stash it inside the toilet cistern.

I head back to the airport terminal with my satchel. I go into the bathroom, change back into the slip dress and heels, bundle the other clothes and money into a tight ball at the top of the satchel, and head for security.

I scan every face I pass, but I don't see any of the Orlov men

I know. Not that it means anything. They could be using anyone.

I also don't see any of Roman's men. But that isn't any surprise, even if it hurts.

I try not to look at the televisions in every room, all of which show endless images of the ballroom explosion that make my every nerve seize in painful anxiety and hurt.

Half an hour later I've used my passport to check into the flight Alexei booked for me under the name in my new passport. I enter a duty-free shop and pay cash for some perfume, then ask the assistant for a large carry bag. I linger behind a row of shelves and quickly move the bundle of my jeans, sneakers, and T-shirt from my satchel to the duty-free bag. I join the boarding line for my flight, trying not to look over my shoulder.

"Welcome aboard, miss." The stewardess gives me a bright smile, which I return with a wan effort that makes her frown in concern. "Are you unwell?" she asks, studying me.

"A little." I smile feebly. "I think I'll be okay."

The stewardess looks unconvinced and murmurs something to her colleague as I pass.

Good. She'll remember me.

I push my satchel far beneath the seat in front of me before either of my neighbors arrive, holding the duty-free bag on my lap, staring out the window at the walkway. I wait until I see the flight staff begin to close the doors before abruptly standing up. "Excuse me," I mutter to the woman in the seat next to me. "I think I'm going to be sick."

She moves out of the way immediately. The stewardess eyes me worriedly as I hurtle toward her with my hand over my mouth. I shake my head, gesturing frantically at the exit, and she doesn't stand in my way. I race up the walkway and thrust my head into the nearest bin.

Throwing up is the one thing I don't have to fake.

"I can't fly," I gasp to the staff on the desk. "I'm unwell."

No airport crew member will ever argue with that.

I head straight for the bathroom and change clothes again. Then I make my way back to check-in and repeat the entire process, this time using the passport and ticket Roman gave me. After I feign illness again, I make my way to baggage claim and wait.

Eventually I find what I'm looking for. A Moroccan woman, with my height and coloring, dressed in traditional djellaba and headscarf with large dark glasses pushed up on her head. She looks around nervously and hurries into the ladies' room. I enter after her, waiting by the sinks. When she emerges from the stall, I smile at her.

"*Salaam aleikum.*"

She looks up worriedly, her eyes darting this way and that.

"Don't be afraid," I say to her in Arabic. "I want to help you." She's running from an abusive husband and takes little persuading. Ten minutes and five hundred euros later, I exit the bathroom wearing her djellaba and headscarf, her glasses covering my face. My duty-free bag I leave in the bathroom trash.

It takes me less than half an hour to get back to the hotel, recover the package from the cistern, and hide it under the voluminous skirts of my djellaba. I take the fire escape, then a taxi to the ferry terminal. The ticket office is closed—it's past two a.m.—but the waiting room is full of Moroccans slumbering on striped plastic carry bags, waiting for their morning voyage back to Tangiers. I curl up on the plastic seats beside two older ladies, pull the hood of my djellaba over my head, and feign sleep, one eye open behind my large sunglasses.

The truth is that sleep has never been further from my mind. And I know that the moment my eyes close, the nightmares will come.

I want to know what happened. I'm terrified of knowing what happened.

The only thing I do know is that everything I loved is gone.

And if I think about that, I won't ever be able to save the only thing that matters anymore: the life inside me.

I stare at the chipped tiles on the floor, counting the cracks in them to stop myself from staring into the horrific abyss of my thoughts.

3

ROMAN

Several Hours Earlier

"It's Nikolai." Dimitry covers the phone with his hand. "Inger's badly injured. He's going with her to the hospital."

"Go, go." I wave my assent, focused on the carnage in front of me. The explosion has taken out one entire side of the ballroom, leaving a gaping hole in the wall and a mass of rubble on the floor. The worst of the victims have already been pulled from it, many by my own hands.

I needed to know for myself that Ofelia and Masha weren't among them.

Inger was standing somewhere near here, last time I saw her, before the bomb. I close my eyes briefly.

Before the bomb.

After the bomb.

My life is divided into two parts now, and forever more. The life I had before, and the shattered remnants of it now that everything I trusted has been blown to shreds.

I'm glad Nikolai is with Inger. No matter the bad blood between us, I would never wish her harm. But nor do I have the time, or emotional head space, to deal with Inger right now.

And I have no idea how to tell her the girls are gone.

Darya's face passes through my mind, white and stricken. I thrust it away with ruthless determination.

I don't even want to *think* about Darya Petrovsky. Ever again.

"Bryce has Mickey," Dimitry says. "I told him to get the boy out of here, like you said. He's got half a dozen good men with him."

"Good." I'm even less equipped to deal with Mickey right now. I just want him safe, and I want him the fuck away from here. "Are you fucking sure the Orlovs have the girls?" I ask Dimitry in an undertone, eyeing the rubble with a sickening feeling in my gut. "Because if they're somehow still under there—"

"They're not." Dimitry shakes his head curtly. "We've turned over every stone. You might want to ask him." He nods at Boris Obolensky, who's staring blankly at the rubble, his face ashen. "His grandson, Matvei, was dancing with Ofelia, right next to the blast. Boris got to him immediately after the explosion. Matvei was badly wounded, but he was also alone. And it seems Boris actually recognized the man who took the girls. But go easy," he adds, lowering his voice. "Boris's limo left for the hospital with Matvei inside it, minutes after the blast. The boy is in a bad way."

Christ.

"Find out what those useless fucks know." I snap my head toward the police, who've only just arrived. "Give them whatever they need, but make it clear I want to know every fucking thing they do. We've got men inside their ranks—use them."

"Done." Dimitry nods.

I approach Boris Obolensky's swaying figure with caution. Boris may be old, but he's always been tough. And watching his oldest grandchild get blown half to pieces in an attack that he surely knows is my fault isn't exactly a good footing for the conversation I'm about to have.

"Your grandson," I say in greeting. "I believe he's wounded. Is there anything I can do?"

Obolensky shakes his head slowly. His face is covered in white dust, his eyes red rimmed and distant with shock. "My wife." His voice cracks. "She was only inches away. She fell. I thought she was—" He takes a shuddering breath and passes a hand over his face, composing himself. "She's fine," he says, as if trying to reassure himself. "She's gone to the hospital with Matvei." His voice cracks again. Another breath. "There's nothing you can do," he says simply, looking directly at me for the first time. "He will live, or he will die." He speaks the last line in Russian, as if his native tongue can give him the strength he needs.

Perhaps it can.

Russia is built for this bullshit, inhales death as it does life. It's the world we were both born to, one it seems Russians can never escape, no matter how many seas we cross.

I grip his shoulder. "*Ne atchaivaisya.*" *Don't despair.*

I wonder who I'm saying it to, Boris or myself.

He nods slowly, then turns to me. "Before the blast," he says, still speaking Russian, "I saw a face I know. Two years ago he blew up a gaming room that belonged to a friend of mine. He is a specialist in these things." His face twists in distaste. "I was asked to track this man down and kill him. But he was a nephew of Vilnus Orlov, and at the time I deemed it too . . . controversial. Now I wish I had."

"My friend told me you believe this man took my daughters." I would usually be more diplomatic, but there's no time.

There's no fucking time.

"He was watching when your daughter danced with Matvei. I saw this man. I noticed him. He was standing by the sound equipment, over there." He nods at a corner just off the stage. It's a perfect hiding place, somewhere anyone could pass unnoticed, assumed to be part of the sound team. "I was coming to tell you, but then . . ." His voice trails off as he waves at the chaos in front of us.

"Is there any other reason you think this man took the girls, apart from the fact that he was watching Ofelia?"

"Masha was with her mother seconds before the blast, and they were standing very close to the sound equipment. After the blast I saw Inger in the rubble, with her friend leaning over her, but there was no trace of Masha or the man." He meets my eyes. "Ofelia was dancing with Matvei only moments before that blast, very close to where her mother and sister were. But when we found Matvei's . . . body, Ofelia was nowhere to be found. I am sorry, my friend." It's his turn to grip my shoulder. "I wish I had protected her better."

"That is not your job." I nod curtly at him. "You have done more than enough and suffered more than you should have. If there is anything your family needs—anything at all—come to me."

I turn away, sick with shame.

It was my *job. My job to protect them, my job to see danger before it happened.*

But I invited the danger into my home.

I took it into my bed.

The person I was trying the hardest to protect was *the danger.*

But that mistake ends now.

I'll fix this, no matter who I have to fucking kill to make it right.

Dimitry and four of my men appear at my side. "We were too late," Dimitry says grimly, holding out his phone. "The

Guapa weighed anchor half an hour ago. The Spanish coast guard are on the line. They need a reason to board."

"*Blyat.*" I snatch the phone out of his hand. "You need to board that fucking boat," I say in Spanish.

It takes ten minutes, a very heated conversation with a disgruntled Spanish minister woken from his sleep, and a sizable donation to an offshore account to get my point across. With every minute, I can feel the girls slipping further from my grasp.

"There's fuck all we can do here." I punch the end call button and stare around at the mass of paramedics, police, and crying families. "Leave two men here to watch the police investigation. We need to get to the lab."

"Pavel has already hacked into the footage," Dimitry says as we turn to leave. "He's got the whole tech team on it. They're tracing everything we can, from the *Guapa* to Alexei Petrovsky."

"That *mudak* can't have gone far. How the fuck did he disappear so fast? We had men right up his ass."

Dimitry doesn't answer. He knows it's a rhetorical question. Alexei was gone before my men got anywhere near him. His meeting with Darya in that corridor was a decoy. The bastard played us, pulled men away from the ballroom at the one time I needed eyes on it.

I dropped the ball.

I don't need anyone to tell me I fucked up.

The men acted on my orders. Orders I gave because I was watching the wrong goddamn target. I had everyone watching for a man with an eye patch, watching for anyone trying to talk to Darya.

I have nobody to blame for this but myself.

Myself—and Darya fucking Petrovsky.

And if I find her aboard that goddamn boat with her brother . . .

I close my eyes briefly, horrified at the effort it takes not to throw up everything in my gut.

What then? What the fuck am I supposed to do then?

Because even after all this, after her horrific betrayal, no matter how much I know I have to put a bullet between her eyes, I'm still not sure I'm actually capable of it.

And that weakness scares me almost as much as the thought of my daughters in the hands of a monster.

4

DARYA

At 5 a.m. the terminal begins to fill again. I stretch and yawn as if I haven't had my eyes open and heart thudding for the past few hours. I exchange pleasantries in Arabic with the women beside me, who beam and chatter away.

I can't help but wonder how long their smiles would last if they knew I was an unwed mother-to-be. Not to mention one who has a river of blood on her hands.

I feel a sudden, visceral longing for Roman, so savage it takes my breath away. The feeling isn't logical. It's just there. Like driving along a highway that hasn't yet been completed and discovering halfway across a bridge that there is no road ahead. Over the past months, Roman has become the road I travel. My direction, my destination, and my traveling companion. His body has been my lodestone, his soul a beacon for my own. Without him I am profoundly, devastatingly lost.

I shiver despite the mild morning.

I buy two tickets to Tangiers, one on the six a.m. ferry and one on the nine a.m. Out front of the terminal, I buy an over-priced knockoff Gucci bag, more pairs of sunglasses, and several designer headscarves from one of the African hawkers. I speak in broken French, using the Moroccan accent I became accustomed to during the months Papa and I spent there, waiting for a boat to Spain.

It seems like a lifetime ago.

The hawker has a friend who exchanges currency. He wakes the man up from napping on the floor, and I change a thousand euros into dirham, the Moroccan currency, explaining that I'm just about to travel home to my family. Then I join the crowd milling around on the docks, eyeing every face carefully, but again finding nothing to cause alarm.

I board the six a.m. ferry and go straight to the bathroom, where I change clothes yet again, this time into shorts and a T-shirt with sneakers. I go back through the crowd and down the gangway, waving my nine a.m. ticket at the bored crewman, explaining in badly accented Spanish that I'm a backpacker who boarded the wrong ferry by mistake. The ticket itself I give to a backpacker, who is delighted to score a free ride.

Another taxi, this time to the bus terminal. I shop in the cheap bulk stores nearby, buying the long embroidered shirts, loose trousers, and sequined sandals favored by Moroccan women visiting Spain. Another five tickets, each to different Spanish cities. A clothing change for each purchase.

I go into the disabled toilet, lock the door, and get changed for the final time, at least for today. When I'm done, the woman looking back at me is almost entirely unrecognizable as the one who fled a ballroom last night.

My hair is in a thick bun behind my head, covered by a neatly pinned headscarf with a discreet Yves Saint Laurent logo. Bright gold earrings in a delicate Arabic pattern hang from my ears. I'm wearing one of the loose, stylish pantsuits over sandals

I bought, carrying the large Gucci handbag and a single candy-striped plastic carry bag. I look exactly like every middle-class Moroccan woman straight off the ferry.

There's only one thing missing.

I grip the edges of the metal hand dryer and take a deep breath.

Come on, Darya. You've had worse.

Bracing myself, I slam my right eye into the corner of the dryer.

Giving myself a black eye isn't difficult. All I have to do is remember Roman's white-faced contempt when he believed I had betrayed him.

The pain feels justified.

It feels like less than I deserve.

The ferries both leave for Morocco without me.

By the time I board an afternoon bus to the Spanish city of Almeria, I look exactly like what I intended to become: a battered wife, escaping her abusive Moroccan husband.

I curl into the window seat, pulling the headscarf self-consciously over my eye, avoiding the sympathetic glances from other travelers. Nobody talks to me. Nobody wants to be part of whatever mess I'm running from.

Lucky them.

I close my eyes, readying myself for the nightmares I've barely managed to hold at bay since I ran from Roman's accusing eyes.

Twenty-four hours later, I'm sitting on the terrace of a small villa in Granada, a city eighty miles northeast of Malaga. Despite the short distance, I took countless buses, trains, and taxis to get here. I've left a labyrinthine trail behind me, one I doubt even Roman's investigators can follow.

I can't be found by anyone, and that includes both Roman and Alexei.

It was my father who taught me how to run, and Sergei Petrovsky is a master in the art of subterfuge. If the Orlovs didn't catch us in all the years we ran together, I'd like to see anyone try now that I'm on my own.

The woman who eventually paid cash for a run-down one-room apartment in the gypsy district of Granada looks nothing like either Darya Petrovsky or Lucia Lopez. The woman sitting on this terrace now wears a hijab and dark sunglasses to hide her bruises. She speaks fluent Arabic but only broken Spanish, and she paid for the villa in dirham instead of euros.

My black eye has swollen impressively. Every time I press my fingers against it I remember Roman's white-faced contempt as he told me to run. At least the shame I feel fits with my new identity.

The woman from whom I rented the villa took my money with gratitude, sympathy for the bruises, and no questions. I paid double the asking price, and she guaranteed discretion. I've paid for a week, but I'll only stay a day or two.

Keep moving.

I'm holding my two passports. Neither of them are of any use to me, not anymore.

I need to disappear.

For now, that means staying in Spain. After this, in Europe. Crossing borders on foot. Staying in private rooms that don't require a passport to register.

I open a pack of firelighters and crumble them into a bowl on the table in front of me. I wait until the flames have taken hold before I slowly feed first one, then both of the passports to the flames.

The fire takes them remarkably quickly.

I watch my face shrivel and melt, my two false names disappearing in a plume of foul-smelling black smoke.

I've read the letters from Roman and Alexei so often on the interminable bus ride here that the creases are worn smooth. Now I read each of them one last time, savoring each word, committing the contents to memory.

Then, when the passports are no more than ashes, I add the letters to the fire.

Part of me wants to keep them both. Despite what Alexei has done, he is my family. My blood.

And as for Roman . . .

There is no world in which I could ever not love him.

But I'm not sure that I can trust him again either. Roman lied to me about who he was. All this time that I thought I was safe in his care, he was biding his time.

Was our entire relationship a lie? Did he know who I was from the beginning and seduce me on purpose?

It's hard to believe he could have been so deliberately manipulative, not to mention such a convincing liar. But I'm not naive enough to not see the holes in his letter to me. What he didn't say shouts volumes. I don't know how much he understands about the vault, or whether he is planning to try to open it. I'd certainly understand if he felt entitled to whatever is inside it. But his letter says nothing about what his plans are. He says that the Orlovs hunted him for years, but he never mentions if he has what they are searching for. It's hard not to think that he is still keeping secrets, and that hurts almost more than everything else.

I clasp my hands over my belly and say a silent prayer for our unborn child.

Our Borovsky.

My choked laugh dies in my throat. I chose that name as a private joke. Not so funny, as it turns out. My baby really *is* a Borovsky.

And now he, or she, is the reason I have to stay alive.

Perhaps the only reason.

For years, all I've cared about is finding a way to open my family's vault. To use the reported treasure inside to reclaim the legacy that we lost the day Vilnus Orlov launched his coup.

But tonight, for the first time in my life, I wish that damned vault had never been built.

All I can see is that it's torn three families apart.

Mine.

Roman's.

And the family we might have built together. The family our unborn child will never get to experience.

The flames flicker in the growing night as the letters turn to ash. I'm no longer someone's sister, daughter, lover, or even surrogate parent figure, if that's what I was to Roman's three children only days ago.

I feel as empty as a burned-out husk. As if I, too, could disappear into ash on the wind with barely a touch.

A night bird caws overhead, a lonely, heart-wrenching sound. I sit in the darkness for a long time after the fire has died, silent tears running down my cheeks.

5

OFELIA

The flight to Miami takes twelve hours. Masha and I travel in a private suite at the rear of the plane, which has a large bed and a bathroom.

The door to the suite is locked, of course.

From the outside.

I clean up the cut on my face as best I can in the sink, but it needs stitches. I explain this to the guard who brings us a tray of food.

He ignores me.

I find some antiseptic and Band-Aids in the cupboard and do the best I can with those.

The only time we've seen Alexei Petrovsky since we boarded the plane is when he told us curtly that we are indeed flying to Miami. Since then he hasn't spoken to Masha or me at all.

"Are they taking us to Deda and Baba Melnyck's?" Masha

asks. She's huddled into my side, her eyes watching the door warily.

"I don't think so, *myshka*."

Unless Inger's parents are part of this, too.

It's the worst feeling I've ever known, not knowing who to trust. It makes me feel more alone than I ever have. I've been trying to work it out ever since I heard the guard tell Nikolai on the phone that he doesn't take orders from him. I've been trying to do what I think Roman would, trying to think through everything that happened at the ball and afterward.

In fact, I've spent most of the twelve-hour flight going over every single thing I can remember.

And no matter how much I don't want to believe it, the only possible conclusion I can draw is that Inger, *our own mother*, is the one who planned this.

Planned to have armed guards kidnap her own children.

It's an awful thought. One most people would probably not even consider. But more than either of my siblings, I've had a front-row seat to my mother's greed and selfishness for as long as I can remember. I've done my best to protect them both, to be the mother she never was, for any of us. To preserve at least a little of the illusion that she really does care for us all. But the truth is, I'm honestly not sure if Inger would really notice if any of us lived or died.

And now she's traded us to the Orlovs. For what reason, I don't know.

I'm not sure if Inger was working with them from the beginning or not. Perhaps she and Nikolai planned to kidnap us themselves. But they clearly had outside help, and somehow that help is connected to the Orlovs.

Why would Inger do this?

What possible motivation could she have for working with the same people Roman and Lucia are fighting against?

Darya. Not Lucia.

It seems important that I stop pretending, about even small things, to myself. The savage cut on my face is a reminder that there is no point in pretending. Not anymore.

I don't sleep for the entire flight, though Masha eventually dozes off. I can't sleep. I'm trying to think of a way out of this, of something I can do to alert Roman and Darya to where we are.

I try to think of what Mickey might do, but it's impossible to even imagine. Mickey's mind is a different world than mine. I don't have his skills, his insane genius brain.

Instead, I try to think of what Darya Petrovsky might do.

Ever since I found out the truth about Lucia, I've been kind of fascinated by her. Mickey wouldn't tell me much. Most of what I got out of him Roman had already told us or I'd researched myself on the internet.

I know that the Orlovs took Darya's family home in a coup, and that Darya and her father eventually escaped. Mickey said they'd been running for years before she came to live with us. Darya was so good at hiding that apparently not even Roman knew who she really was at first.

She managed to escape from the Orlovs.

And that means I can, too.

I just need to think like Darya. To be as strong as her. For Masha, as well as for myself.

I just wish I knew what being strong looked like.

We land on another private airfield and emerge to brilliant sunlight.

Several black sedans are waiting for us, all with tinted windows and armed men standing beside them. Alexei follows us down the stairs, his men behind him. He's clearly showered and changed on the flight, swapping the black suit he was wearing in Malaga for a blue shirt rolled to the elbows that reveals the tattoos on his forearms, over white linen trousers and leather boots. Aviator sunglasses cover his unsmiling face. His white-blond hair gleams in the sunshine, like one of the Vikings off that TV show.

He's huge. He's terrifying.

"The girls ride with me," he says curtly, nodding to the middle car. It's a limo, larger than the others.

One of the armed men spits off to one side. He has a fat face and thin, mean eyes. "I don't think—"

"You don't get paid to fucking think, Junior." Alexei doesn't so much as glance his way. "Your people nearly lost these two in Malaga. I'm not risking you fucking up twice."

When the other man looks like he might argue, Alexei's face twists into a contemptuous sneer. "My crew will stay here, so I'll be entirely without backup, if that makes you feel better. You can take it up with your father when we get there—if you have the balls for it." He stalks past the fat-faced man and opens the back door to the limo. "Get in," he orders us.

We do. Whatever my escape dreams might be, a private airfield surrounded by what seems like fifty guns is definitely not the time.

He enters behind us and closes the door. The men who were on the plane with us remain on the tarmac, silent and black clad, guns at their sides.

The interior of the limo is silent, the glittering sunlit world outside the windows like another planet. Masha clings to my side, watching Alexei with wide, unblinking eyes. The convoy takes off with us in the middle. Alexei's men watch us go.

He waits until we've left the airfield and turned onto the highway, then lowers the screen blocking us from the driver's seat, but only an inch.

"You swept the vehicle, Dima?"

"Yes." The driver's mouth barely moves as he answers, and in the rearview mirror I can see his eyes, covered by sunglasses, staring straight ahead. "It's clean. We're fifteen minutes out. You can talk until we hit the gate, then we'll have eyes on us."

"Good." Like the driver, Alexei stares straight ahead, his lips barely moving. He's clearly not taking any chances of being seen. "What am I walking into?"

"Orlov's nervous." The driver, Dima, says this in a matter-of-fact tone, like someone describing the weather. "But so far, I think you're good. Nobody knows you were in the ballroom."

"Got it." Alexei leaves the screen down, but he turns back to us. The car rounds a corner, and for a few moments, we're out of sight of both the car in front and the one behind. He raises his sunglasses. His lone eye looks at Masha, then me. "We don't have much time," he says calmly, "so I need you girls to listen closely, okay?"

Masha scowls at him. "Don' wanna listen to you." She tucks her head into my arm.

Alexei's mouth twists at the edge. It could almost be a smile. "I can understand that. But I need you to anyway, Masha." His eye shifts to me. "I especially need *you* to listen, Ofelia." I feel a queer jolt as his eye fixes on mine, as if he's staring straight through me and into my soul. It's an uncomfortable feeling. I have to force myself not to look away. "You're going to a very dangerous place." His tone is low and even. "But if you do as I say, you will make it out of this alive. Don't nod. Just say yes if you understand."

"Yes." My tongue feels thick and heavy in my mouth.

Masha looks up at me, frowning. "Shh, Mash." I squeeze her hand. "Just listen."

"Good." The rest of the convoy comes back into sight, and Alexei drops his sunglasses back down. "You're about to meet a man called Vilnus Orlov. He's not your friend, and he *will* hurt you. I think you already understand that."

"Yes." I fight the urge to touch the cut on my cheek. It's stopped bleeding, but it still pulses hot pain through my entire skull.

"He will make me hurt you." His calm tone only makes his words more horrifying. "He is not going to be happy that I got to you, and he is going to be suspicious. It's my job to convince him that I'm on his side. That means that no matter what story I tell him when we get there, you need to pretend it's true. It also means that when he sends me in with a knife, you need to appear terrified of me."

I shudder. *That's hardly going to be difficult.*

"The only reason I'm telling you this is to stop you doing anything stupid that might make this more dangerous than it already is. That means no sudden moves, and no argument with the story I tell him. If you work against me, I can't help you. Do you understand?"

"Why should we trust you?" My voice is a hoarse whisper.

"Because I am the only hope you have of ever seeing your family again. And you are the only chance I have of saving mine."

I swallow. "You said he'll make you hurt me. What did you mean?"

"Vilnus likes knives." His voice has not once altered from the same flat, cold tone, nor has he moved at all. "He will want me to use them on you, to prove my loyalty. If you trust me, I can make sure you are not scarred for life." His lips harden into a thin line. "Believe me when I say I've had plenty of practice."

He doesn't need to convince me. Up close, in daylight, I can see the thin silvery scars that crisscross his face. It seems there's barely an inch of his skin that hasn't been touched by the knife.

I shiver, huddling back into the seat of the limo, holding Masha close.

"I can do that. But if he tells you to hurt Masha—"

"He won't." Alexei's lips twist.

I frown. "Why are you so sure?"

He opens his mouth, as if he's about to say something, then closes it again. "Just trust me. He won't. But he *will* want to hurt you, Ofelia." He glances out the window. "We're nearly there. Once we're inside the gates, you don't ever talk to me like this unless I speak first and tell you it's alright to do so. There are eyes and ears in every corner of the compound. All it takes is one mistake. Remember, you're terrified of me. I was the one who cut your face back at the airport, and you're scared I'm going to do it again. I'm the most frightening man you've ever met."

Again, not hard.

"Are you going to hurt us?" Masha is staring at Alexei through narrow eyes.

"I have to." Alexei answers her flatly, without embellishment. He flicks up his sunglasses again so his lone eye meets Masha's. "Or at least, I have to pretend to. If you fight me, you will make it much worse than it needs to be."

Masha glares at him.

Alexei glances at me. "You need to make her understand," he says. "Fast."

"Masha." I cuddle her into my side. "Alexei is Lucia's brother. He won't hurt us."

Oh, you're sure about that, are you, Ofelia?

I swallow my own doubts. Masha needs to believe this.

"If we're going to stay safe, we have to play a game." I turn her face so she looks at me. "We have to pretend that Alexei is the man who cut me at the airport. We have to pretend we are very scared of him. If he uses a knife on me, you can scream and cry. But our secret is that Alexei isn't really hurting me with his knife. Even if you see blood on my face, it's all just pretend, okay? But nobody can know that. It's our secret. Yours, mine, and Alexei's. Nobody else can know, or else we will be hurt for real, like I was back at the airport. Do you understand?"

Masha's large blue eyes study Alexei with a scrutiny that might, under other circumstances, make me laugh. "Does Luce know the secret?"

Alexei's mouth tightens. He looks like he's going to argue. I glare at him over Masha's head. "Yes, Mash. Luce is part of our game."

Masha looks confused, and my stomach twists with guilt. *Better she believe the lies than give us away.*

Finally, to my relief, she nods.

"Good," Alexei says as the limo slows. He puts the screen back up, blocking Dima from view. "Because we're here. It's game time, ladies."

His face is hard and cruel behind his glasses, and I shiver.

Some game.

The gates open, and we drive through them.

MY FIRST IMPRESSION of the Petrovsky compound is that it's big.

I mean, as in *huge.*

The driveway itself goes on for what seems like forever, through lush gardens filled with exotic flowers and big old banyan trees, the kind that have loads of roots that go down to the ground. Through the trees I can see glittering water that stretches to the horizon.

There are worse places to be kidnapped to.

I give a hiccup of nervous laughter, and Alexei glares at me.

Or maybe that's just his resting gangster face.

Palm trees grow around a helicopter pad, which gives way to a dock.

That's one escape route.

There's no way I'm getting out through the front gate. The

walls on either side of the entrance are solid concrete, too high and smooth to climb, and covered in barbed wire at the top, like a prison.

The limo glides to a stop in front of a large fountain. It's made of colored stone and opens like a flower. Strange as it is to notice such a thing at a time like this, I can't help but think how beautiful it is.

The front of the house is nothing like any home I've seen before, though it is similar to pictures I've seen of palatial houses in Russia. It has strange curved edges and oddly shaped windows, with an intricate arch over the front entrance that almost looks like it belongs on a mosque. It's peaceful, some-how, despite the armed guards stationed at every point.

The door opens, and Alexei steps out, then holds the door for us. His face is stone-cold, with no trace of his earlier twisted smile. Part of me wonders if I imagined our entire conversation in the limo.

Armed guards fall in front of and behind us, leading us through the entrance and along a large marble corridor. It's like being inside a museum, with large paintings on the walls and an arched ceiling overhead. There's even a central court-yard like they have in Spain, with another fountain and scented plants all around it. We pass a huge old grandfather clock. Masha stares around her in amazement, clutching my hand.

Eventually we come to a set of double wooden doors with a big brass handle. Two armed men stop us outside and pat Alexei down efficiently.

The fat-faced man who tried to stop Alexei at the airport pushes past us, sneering unpleasantly at him as he goes.

"Let's see who's laughing after this, Petrovsky."

Alexei takes off his sunglasses and hangs them from his shirt, looking at the man with as little interest as he might give to an insect.

"Men will always laugh at you, Junior. You've just got that kind of face."

The two armed guards at the door smirk, then quickly compose themselves when the man called Junior scowls at them. He pushes open the doors, and we follow him inside.

There's a big, heavy desk at one end of the large room, which has bookshelves all around the walls and brown leather couches set around a marble coffee table at the other. The man sitting behind the desk has an even fatter face than the man Alexei called Junior. They're clearly father and son. They have the same narrow, piggish eyes and heavyset build, though the man behind the desk looks meaner than his son and is so fat his belly spills over his trousers. He's smoking, and from the smell of the room and the overflowing ashtray on his desk, it's far from being his first cigarette for the day.

He glares at Alexei, ignoring both Masha and me.

"Do you want to explain to me why two of my men are dead and you arrived on my plane instead of on the yacht I entrusted to you?"

"You're lucky that plane arrived at all." Alexei answers him with cool detachment and no hint of fear. "After the bomb you neglected to tell me about, half of Malaga's entire force of Spanish Guardia Civil were chasing the car with the girls in it. The authorities were just about to order your plane to be grounded when I turned up."

Okay, that's his first lie.

The fat man blanches. Alexei nods coolly.

"Now the Guardia Civil are busy chasing an empty yacht instead of your plane. But if I hadn't been listening to the police channel, or if I'd left it to your bunch of incompetent idiots, these two would already be safely back in their beds." Alexei roughly pushes Masha and me forward. I stumble, falling to my knees in front of the fat man's desk. "Your men had already given up their weapons when I turned up."

That's lie number two.

"I'm supposed to be in the middle of stealing a billion-dollar cyber project for you, and instead I had to drop everything to save our organization from being front-page news. Want to share why you got a second-rate pack of mobsters to set off a bomb, Vilnus, instead of just asking me to snatch these two for you?"

Vilnus Orlov. This is the man who Alexei told us about. *The dangerous one.*

This is the man who stole Darya's home and kept her captive.

And that's not all he's done.

I've known the name Vilnus Orlov since the summer I was ten years old, when my parents broke up for the last time.

Vilnus sneers at Alexei. "You forget your place in this organization, dog. I don't explain myself to you."

"I never forget my place." Alexei's voice is calm and even. "I kill who you tell me to. I torture when I'm asked to. I burn and sabotage and do any other form of shit job you don't want to dirty your hands with. Right now, I'm working night and day to steal a billion-dollar deal for you. If you wanted the Stevanovsky kids, all you had to do was ask." Ignoring the men standing either side of him with raised guns, Alexei places his hands on the desk, leaning forward so he's eye to eye with Vilnus. "You know there's nothing I won't do to get that vault open for you, just like there's nothing I won't stop at to steal the cyber project. I thought we were in agreement on both of those things. Instead, you set off a bomb that's put unwanted attention on all of us. Which has also started a war with Roman Stevanovsky, right when we are poised to destroy the bastard. How does any of this help us get what we want?"

"*We.*" Vilnus leans back in his chair and studies Alexei through slitted eyes, a half smile on his face. "You might have that sparrow on your hand, Petrovsky, but don't ever think that means I trust you. You say you can steal this cyber project, but we've only got your word that it even exists. You say that *if* you can steal his pet project, Roman Stevanovsky will definitely open the vault for us in return for getting it back. *If. Can.* I hear a whole lot of talking, but I don't see any real outcomes. Taking the Stevanovsky girls, on the other hand, gives us actual leverage." His lips curl unpleasantly. "Maybe you're right, that stealing this project will make Roman come running to open the vault. But I *know* that taking his children will achieve that. So you can look at it this way, Petrovsky: now, instead of having one thing to use as blackmail, we have two." He tilts his head to one side, regarding Masha and me lazily. "Or should that be three?"

Alexei shakes his head. "I think this is a mistake. We're not ready for a war—"

Despite being unpleasantly fat, Vilnus moves with a sudden, predatory speed that makes me jump back, leaping to his feet and slamming his meaty hands down on the desk in front of him, his face barely inches from Alexei's.

"And that, right there, is why I didn't ask you to get the Stevanovsky girls," he hisses. Droplets of spit hit Alexei's face, but I notice that he doesn't move. He doesn't even flinch. "How many times do I have to tell you not to think? You don't run your family's clan anymore, Petrovsky. *I* do. I have for a decade. You're nothing more than my dog, there to do as I tell you. No more, no less. You don't have a brain, except for the one in my head that gives you orders. Or do I need to take your other eye out to remind you of your place?"

Vilnus's head tilts to one side, as if he's actually considering this.

"No," he says eventually. "What good is a blind dog?"

His men snigger.

"*If* you deliver that project you keep promising me, and *if* you actually help open that vault, then maybe we'll talk. But until and unless both of those things happen, you're nothing more to me than the scum you've always been. The scum I'm going to make you be again, now that we have these two." Vilnus's eyes narrow unpleasantly as he nods at Masha and me. "You're going to be using your knife on these two. I've missed watching you cut into little girls, Alexei. Remember how much fun that used to be? You might have been reluctant at first, but you got the hang of it eventually, boy, didn't you? And it looks like you couldn't wait to begin on this one, no?"

He eyes the cut on my face with an almost envious expression. It makes me sick.

"Oh, well. That cut on her face should make the right impression when we give Roman a call. The sooner he launches whatever attack he's planning, the better." He smiles coldly at Alexei. "Don't tell me we're not ready for war, Petrovsky. I have plans you can't begin to imagine, with people powerful enough to bring Borovsky to his knees before you can say open fucking sesame." He stands up and comes around the desk until he's standing directly in front of me. He pulls Masha's hand out of mine and thrusts her to Alexei, who holds her small body against his legs and puts a hand over her mouth when she tries to protest. I nod at her, trying to convey reassurance. She stands still in Alexei's grasp, her wide, terrified eyes on me.

Vilnus smells of sweat and cigarettes. I have to force myself not to recoil. One large hand reaches out and grabs my breast, squeezing it hard enough to make me cry out.

"And when I'm done with that *mudak* Borovsky," Vilnus says in a low, insidious voice, "I'll make him watch while I fuck your sister in front of him. I've waited a long time to feel Darya Petrovsky's tight little pussy around my cock." Vilnus moves behind me, his hand still brutally clamped on my breast. Masha cries out and tries to run to me, but Alexei restrains her with one hand, his face entirely still.

"Then," Vilnus goes on, his hot breath foul on my ear, "after

I've fucked little Darya bloody, I'll make Roman Borovsky watch while I fuck his daughter."

Why is he calling Roman by a different name? Who is Borovsky? And what does he mean by Roman's daughter?

He releases me abruptly, pushing me with so much force that I fall straight into Alexei's body. It's like falling against a wall. Alexei doesn't move. In fact, he's watched the entire exchange with a face as still as a marble statue.

Vilnus glares at Alexei as he lights another cigarette. "Since you took it upon yourself to act without my orders, you've earned yourself babysitting duty."

He waits, as if he's expecting Alexei to argue, then, when the other man stays silent, his fat lips spread in a sneering smile. "Wise choice, Petrovsky. And it's not all punishment. You can still play with that knife you like so much. Just make sure to keep your games to parts of her body that are hidden—and make sure I get to watch."

Alexei grips my arm hard enough to make me wince. "What about the little one?" His voice is sickeningly eager, as if he can't wait to sink his knife into Masha.

It's a game, I remind myself. *It's pretend.*

Vilnus's mouth twists contemptuously. "You're a sick fuck, Petrovsky, you know that? But no. You know the rules. Nobody touches my daughters except me."

His daughters?

But I don't have any time to absorb what that might mean, because Alexei's knife tip is pressing into my side.

"Move." His lips touch my ear as he speaks, and he smells sharp and dangerous, like the cold edge of a winter night. I don't know whether to recoil or press myself against him for safety.

Instead his knife presses me toward the door, and I walk ahead of him, through the long marble corridors, then down a long set of stairs that lead to a series of underground tunnels.

I gulp the still air, trying not to let terror overwhelm me. Masha clings to me like I'm an anchor in a storm.

Finally Alexei opens a door and pushes Masha and me inside. We sprawl on the stone floor, hard enough to hurt.

The door slams closed behind us, and Masha and I are alone.

6

ROMAN

"Our men boarded the *Guapa* and searched it from bow to stern." Bryce delivers his report evenly and without losing eye contact.

Which takes no small amount of balls, given my barely restrained fury.

"Ofelia and Masha aren't aboard," he goes on. "There's no evidence they ever were. The Orlovs were smart. They knew we'd focus on the *Guapa*, and they got it into international waters fast and kept cruising at top speed. Between dodging the Spanish coast guard and flouting a dozen international maritime laws, we've wasted over twenty-four hours chasing a false lead."

I grip the edge of the long oval dinner table, staring blindly out the penthouse window at the distant sea. It was only recently that I had Darya bent over this table, naked and moaning beneath my hands, while the children slept peacefully on the floor below.

Now two of my three children have been taken, and Darya is gone.

It feels like an age has passed between those days and this one.

"Was Alexei Petrovsky aboard?"

Bryce and Dimitry exchange a wary glance. "No," Dimitry says reluctantly. "The *Guapa* has a hired crew aboard who are under instructions to get the yacht back to Miami ASAP. They know nothing other than the orders they've been given."

"*Khuy!*" I push off from the table and stalk the length of the room, fists clenched at my sides. I've never felt less in control in my life. The thought of Ofelia and Masha in the hands of the Orlovs makes my blood run cold.

That's not the only thing that terrifies me.

Darya is out there somewhere.

Probably running with her brother.

That thought makes me feel physically sick. I still can't reconcile the Darya I thought I knew with the ruthless bitch who deliberately endangered my children.

The Darya who allowed my girls to be kidnapped.

By the fucking *Orlovs*, for Chrissakes.

Pizdozh.

I can't think about Darya or the Orlovs. Both thoughts make me lose focus altogether, and there's no time for that. Not while Ofelia and Masha are out there somewhere, in the hands of the men who murdered my father.

"Boss." Dimitry comes to stand next to me, lowering his voice. The other men move to a discreet distance. "We need to find Lucia. We know that she spoke to her brother at that ball. She must know something."

"Darya," I snarl. "Her name is Darya Petrovsky. And she's a distant fucking last on my list of priorities."

"She would never hurt those children, Roman. You know it as well as I do."

"Don't." I drop my head, my fingers clenched hard enough on the table edge to turn the knuckles white.

That's the damned hell of it. I *did* know that. Or I thought I did. Now?

I shake my head slowly. "You didn't see her face."

"Bullshit."

I swing my head sideways and Dimitry meets my eyes, his own as blood-rimmed and exhausted as mine. "I saw her face as clearly as you did. Yes, Darya knew the Orlovs were planning something. But that doesn't mean she was complicit in it. You said yourself she was planning to run. What if she was running *because* she knew the children were in danger? Abby said—"

"I don't care what Abby said." Every word is like a sledge-hammer on the brick wall around my emotions. A wall I can't afford to drop now, of all times. I push back off the table with enough force to rock the marble slab. "Let it fucking go," I snarl. "There's no time for this."

"Mickey thinks—"

"I don't give a fuck what Mickey thinks!"

"Well, you fucking should." I swing around, frowning, to find a white-faced Mickey standing in the doorway. His face is gaunt, his mouth set in a particularly grim line.

"I told you to stay in your apartment." I try not to snap, but I'm close to losing my shit. Mickey's face is a constant reminder of my failure to protect his sisters. I've been unable to face him from the moment they disappeared.

"And I don't give a fuck what you told me to do." Mickey's eyes flash with hard anger. "I've been trying to talk to you for hours. It's my sisters the Orlovs have taken. I have as much right to help look for them as you. More. So you can listen to me, or you can watch me walk out the door and go to someone who will."

I stare at him across the room. He doesn't move. The months of boxing training, combined with a sudden growth spurt and the shock of his sisters' disappearance, has stripped the last trace of boyhood from his face. Not that Mickey ever was very boyish. Possessing genius-level intelligence has always lent him a certain gravity. But now, staring me down across the room in front of a dozen of my hardest *vor*, Mickey looks dangerous enough to match any of them.

I glance at Dimitry. "Give us a moment."

"Boss." He nods reluctantly, his eyes still reproachful enough to piss me off.

"And find out how Inger is." I rub a hand over my face, mentally cursing myself for the fact I haven't bothered to check in on her. Inger is Mickey's mother. He has to be worried about her, and I haven't even managed to make a phone call.

"Yeah. Sure," Dimitry mutters, casting Mickey a sideways glance as he leaves. He and the other men file into the elevator with their heads down, faces grim. They might not like Inger, but they all love the girls. This is as personal for them as it is for me.

"Dimitry is right." Mickey doesn't wait for permission to start speaking. "Darya would never hurt the girls, and you know it."

His switch from *Lucia* to *Darya* isn't lost on me. Mickey is done with the lies. "I know you want to believe that, Mickey, but—"

"But nothing." Mickey glares at me. "Darya ran because she found out who you are—and why you wanted her here."

I'm so taken aback that I'm momentarily silenced.

"And the Orlovs took Ofelia and Masha because they found out who *they* are."

"What?" Now I'm genuinely confused. "What the hell is that supposed to mean?"

Mickey puts his laptop on the table and twists the screen

toward me in a curt, angry gesture. "I told you I was helping Ofelia with a school project."

I stare at the tree graphic on the screen, my tired mind trying to make sense of it. I vaguely recall him mentioning something about helping Ofelia. I can't for the life of me imagine what on earth it has to do with getting his sisters back.

"Mickey—"

"It's a family tree." Mickey's tone is impatient. "Ofelia wanted to get extra points by including a section on DNA, tracing back our ancestry as far as she could. She asked if I could help her, and so I used the upstairs facility at the lab to run our DNA. Ofelia's, Masha's, and mine." He meets my eyes with a rather defiant look. "I took yours as well. And Darya's."

Oh, shit.

I'm starting to understand Mickey's dark looks lately. And DNA testing?

Khuy.

I'm starting to get a very fucking bad feeling about this.

"Mickey. Tell me you hacked the online records anonymously to get the results. Tell me you did it discreetly."

"Yeah—no." Mickey folds his arms. "I didn't realize there would be a reason to do that, you see. Maybe if someone had actually *told* me why it might be dangerous, I would have handled it differently."

Fuck, fuck, fuckety fuck.

"But you haven't asked why it's important." Mickey's eyes gleam with anger. "You're just worried because now you're on the radar, aren't you? Don't you even want to know why I got curious enough to test your DNA?"

"Why?" My voice is hoarse, the room swirling around me discomfortingly.

"Because when I first ran tests for the three of us, they came back inconsistent. As in, we aren't full siblings. None of us. We share the same mother—but we all have different fathers."

The room snaps back into focus. "What the hell, Mickey?"

"Look." He nods at the screen. I look at the tree again, but I can't make any sense of what I'm seeing. "Oh, for goodness' sake." Mickey points impatiently. "Ofelia's DNA came back as a perfect match for Inger on the maternal side. I took Inger's DNA when we were out the other day," he adds with a sidelong glance. "I didn't . . . mention it to her."

"Seems to be your modus operandi lately." I don't attempt to hide my irritation.

"Yeah, well, I learned from the best." His glare matches my own. "Anyway. I don't have Papa's DNA, so I used myself as a comparison. If we have the same father, we should have been a one-hundred-percent match. We weren't. Not even close." He glances sideways at me. "So then I took Masha's. Same thing. She's Inger's daughter, but no match to either Ofelia or me on the paternal side. However, when I ran her through the database, a match did come up." He meets my eyes. "Vilnus Orlov," he says quietly. "He was required to give DNA for a criminal trial ten years ago. It's on the public record. Masha is his direct descendant. Here, you can see for yourself." He points at a string of numbers and graphs on the screen, but they swim in front of my eyes.

"How the fuck," I say blankly, "can Masha be Orlov's daughter?"

"Well, that isn't all." Mickey is very pale, but his voice is strong enough. "I took Uncle Nicky's DNA too, after that. It wasn't hard. I just stopped by Pillars briefly the other day."

I shake my head, wondering how the fuck I missed all of this. Luis, the kids' driver, is going to have some damn hard questions to answer.

"I thought maybe I was—that maybe Nikolai was—" Mickey takes a sharp breath. "Anyway. He isn't my father." The relief in his voice is palpable. "But he is my uncle. So it's safe to assume that Papa really was my . . . papa."

Despite everything that is happening, all the hell that has been unleashed in our world, I can't help but realize the gravity of the moment, how much this has mattered to Mickey.

I grip his shoulder. "Of course you're Mikhail's son, Mickey." I meet the deep blue eyes, so like his father's. "I'd have to be blind not to see him in your face, particularly when you smile. You're so like him. Not just in the way you look." I put my hand on his chest. "Here as well. You've got your father's kindness, and his strength. Mikhail would be so proud of you."

Mickey swallows hard, furiously blinking away the sheen of tears. "Anyway." His voice is hoarse. "Ofelia wasn't a match to anyone in the database. Not Vilnus, not Papa, not Nikolai. Not anyone.

"Except one distant hit to a Colombian family name: Cardeñas."

He glances at me. "That was when I tested you. I remember you saying something about your mother being Colombian. And I thought . . . well." He shrugged. "When I ran your DNA, it came up as the direct descendant of an unsolved murder case twenty years ago. A man named Aleksander Borovsky."

Every word cuts through some part of me, crumbling me further.

"I looked him up. Aleksander Borovsky was married to someone called Rosa Cardeñas. They had one son: Roman Borovsky." He meets my eyes, his own shadowed. "And when I tested you against Ofelia, it was a one-hundred-percent match.

"You're her father, Roman. That's why the Orlovs took the girls, and not me. Masha is Vilnus Orlov's daughter. Ofelia is yours."

Mine.

My daughter.

My child.

Ofelia is mine?

Recollections pass through my mind like a disjointed slideshow.

Mikhail's resigned laughter when he learned Inger was pregnant: *"Must have happened the first damn night we slept together. Condoms should have a bigger warning on the packet . . ."*

Mikhail, the night Ofelia was born: *"She's a little early, but she's perfect, Roman. Her eyes are the same color as yours."* He'd looked sideways at me, but I'd ignored the unspoken question in his eyes. Said instead, *"She looks just like you."*

Had I known even then?

Ofelia, glaring at me with iron-hard cobalt eyes.

Ofelia placing herself between her siblings and every threat that comes for them.

No, I acknowledge to myself, *I didn't know Ofelia was my daughter.*

But maybe that was simply because I didn't allow myself to actually *see*.

And Masha. Did Nikolai suspect that Masha was Orlov's daughter? Is that why he was taking photographs of her?

Inger.

My fists clench, my gut lurching with sudden, horrible suspicion. Apart from Nikolai's phone call to say he was taking Inger to the hospital, I haven't seen or heard from either of them. For all I know, they could be anywhere.

If she's involved in this, I will fucking kill her.

I keep my face even with no small effort, dragging my attention back to Mickey, who is still staring at me accusingly, his eyes piercing my own.

"I spent the last few days reading all of Pavel's research and Lance Ryder's work," he says in a low voice. "The Naryshkin treasure isn't just a myth, is it? It's very real. And your father built the vault that holds it." He stares at me, but I don't respond.

I'm not sure any response I have will help.

"That's why you changed your name," he goes on. "Why you're so secretive about your past. The Orlovs believe that you know how to get into the Petrovsky vault." He shakes his head. "They didn't kill Darya or her brother when they had the chance, which means they must need them to open it, too. I imagine the Orlovs thought they hit the jackpot when they realized they had you and Darya in the same place. All the keys to the treasure they've been coveting for years, right on their doorstep for the taking. All they had to do was take the one thing they knew you'd trade anything for: your daughter."

His eyes harden. "That's what I think Alexei came to warn his sister about. I think he realized who you are—and why you wanted Darya in the first place. And you were waiting for him to come, weren't you, Roman? You wanted the same thing the Orlovs have all this time. To have control over Darya and her brother, so you could open the vault yourself."

I stare at him across the table, the air around me swirling and rearranging itself, coming in and out of focus so I feel vaguely nauseous.

"Is that what you think?" I barely manage to rasp the words out. "You think I deliberately hunted Darya down? That all of this has been some kind of elaborate plot to recover whatever damn bullshit is in that vault?"

Mickey's eyes narrow. "Isn't it?"

"No! Christ!" I shake my head in frustration. It's the same accusation Darya hurled at me at the ball. "She knew," I say, my tired mind trying to sift through the facts. "Darya knew the Orlovs were coming for the children. There's no excuse for that—"

"And she knew *why* they were coming for them." He cuts me off impatiently. "So she did the only thing she thought might keep them safe: she ran."

For a long moment we stare at each other, Mickey white-faced and breathing hard, me temporarily frozen as the pieces slowly sink into place.

They're forming a new pattern. One I didn't consider until now.

One I goddamn missed.

"I want my sisters back more than anything," Mickey says quietly. "But Darya is our family, too. You told us that yourself. You've been looking in the wrong place, Roman. We all have."

I stare at him, horrified realization dawning.

If he's right . . .

I'm reaching for my phone when the elevator dings and Dimitry steps out. "Boss. I'm sorry to interrupt, but—" He sees my face and halts. "What's happened?"

"Inger," I manage. My voice sounds like it's coming from someone else.

"That's what I came to tell you." His voice is resigned. "She's gone, Roman. You were right," he says, nodding at Mickey. "Mickey asked me if anyone knew if Inger had actually gone to an ER. None of us had bothered to check. And he was right. Inger never showed up at a hospital. She's not answering her phone, and there's no trace of her anywhere. It looks like it was her who took the girls."

I grip the table again, a slow, burning fury taking hold of me. "Inger was in the apartment. She had access to their passports."

"She took them." Mickey confirms what I already know. "I hacked the security footage from the apartment."

And I blamed Darya.

I think of my final words to her and wince.

I told her to run for her life. I told her that if my children were harmed, I'd hunt her down myself and kill her.

I rub a hand over my face.

I told her I'd kill her myself.

I think of her expression as she backed away from me

toward the exit. It was guilt, and I'd read that as confirmation that she was complicit in her brother's plans.

The truth is that Darya felt guilty that the Orlovs' relentless pursuit of her had put the children in danger.

Mickey was right. So was Dimitry.

Darya would never endanger the children.

I know that, just like I know Inger wouldn't hesitate to do so. Especially if she thought she would gain something from it.

And now Inger has my two daughters. Or rather mine and Vilnus Orlov's.

Not that I give a fuck what a piece of paper says. Ofelia and Masha are my girls. My babies. Now and always.

Inger, however, must have thought she'd hit the fucking jackpot when she'd found out about their paternity.

Darya.

Oh, God. She's out there alone. Afraid.

And she thinks I hate her.

Shame and a terrible, gut-wrenching fear twist inside me. The three girls I love most in this world are lost to me—and I've wasted twenty-four hours by being an idiot.

The elevator doors ding, and we all turn. Abby steps out, wild-eyed, her face crimson with fury.

"Oh, shit," Dimitry mutters. "Abby." He moves toward her. "I told you not to come up here."

"I don't give a single *fuck* what you told me to do." She twists out of the security guard's grasp. "And you can get your damned hands off me, Igor, or whatever the hell your name is." She turns fiercely to me. "What the *fuck*, Roman? I've spoken to Mickey and Dimitry, told them why Luce was planning to run."

"Darya," Mickey says quietly. "Her name is Darya, not Lucia."

Abby throws her hands up in frustration. "Darya. Lucia. Who gives a fuck what her name is. She's my *friend*, Roman. And I thought she was a hell of a lot more than that to you. You cannot be so stupid—"

"We have to find her." I interrupt Abby, barely managing to get the words out. "Darya. We have to find her."

Mickey raises a sardonic eyebrow that could just about match my own. "Oh, you think?"

Dimitry rolls his eyes. "Well, it's about fucking time."

7

DARYA

I sit with coffee on the terrace in the brilliant Granada sunlight and stare at the burner phone I bought from one of the illegal street traders.

Lesson one of running is to never look back. But I've barely slept for worrying about the children, and the news is giving me nothing. I can't exactly call the hospitals and start asking questions.

I don't know what, if anything, Papa might know. I doubt Roman is beating his door down for company right now. But I'm certain Papa would have kept his burner phone a secret, and dangerous as it is to risk calling him, he is the only link I have to everything I've lost.

I brace myself and hit the numbers.

The phone rings for so long that my heart sinks. *They must have found his phone.*

Then, miraculously, the call is picked up.

"Da?"

It takes all I have not to burst into tears. "It's me, Papa."

"Dayushka!" There's no hiding his relief. "Listen to me." He speaks before I can respond. "You must come back. Make Roman listen. He has it all wrong." Good as it is to hear Papa speak so fluently, I've never heard him sound so agitated.

"About what? What has he said?" More to the point, what has he done?

If Roman has hurt Papa . . .

I wince. I can't even imagine that. Surely, no matter how much he hates me, Roman wouldn't hurt an old man in his care? Is he truly capable of that?

"Come back, Dayushka. You both need to know the truth—"

"I can't come back, Papa. Roman—I can't come back." *Fuck.* It's so hard to know what I can and can't say. "I just need to know if the children are safe."

"The children?" He sounds genuinely bewildered. "Why wouldn't they be safe?"

I frown over the terrace, staring at the dull ocher walls of the Alhambra, pale in the early-morning brilliance. There's something calming about the sensual curves of the ancient palaces, a timelessness that lulls me into a false sense of security and makes the noise and terror of the explosion seem like a distant dream.

But it wasn't. The explosion happened. And the children were there.

"There was a bomb." I pick uneasily at a loose thread on my headscarf.

"A *what?* Why have I heard nothing? Ah." He pauses. "That is why they have kept me from the television."

"There was a bomb at the ball. And Alexei." My breath hitches, the words falling clumsily from my mouth as I realize I haven't even told Papa about my brother. "I saw him. He came to warn me, Papa, to tell me to run. He said the children were in danger if I stayed."

"Alexei?" Papa's tone sharpens. "Did he say why? What did he tell you? Darya." He continues before I can answer his questions. "You *must* come back. You can't be out there alone, and I need to speak to you both."

"The children, Papa." I keep my voice even with an effort. "Can you just ask one of the guards if they're okay?" I can feel tears beginning to form behind my eyes. It's something that happens more and more frequently lately.

Hormones, I guess.

"Yes. I will ask. But, Darya. Tell me where you are."

I shake my head. "I can't," I whisper. "Find out about the children." I hang up before the tears begin to fall.

I stare dumbly out over the valley at the growing morning. I have no idea what to do next.

Or for the rest of my life.

I feel none of the edgy excitement I did back when I ran from the Orlovs, nor any of the single-minded determination that has carried me through the lonely years that followed. I can't find the hard thread of tenacity that I've clung to, the certainty that one day there will be an end to this. All I see now is an endless road into nothingness ahead of me, a journey that has no end nor even the promise of one. Just a lonely string of days where I must live a lie—and raise my unborn child to live it with me.

What kind of a life is this for a child? To never belong anywhere, to have no past or family to call their own? To live with the constant threat that one day they may be found and held hostage to a legacy they don't even understand?

To never know their father?

I groan aloud, covering my face with my hands. I can't escape the memory of Roman's face when he believed I'd betrayed him. My own hurt at discovering his true identity is nothing compared to what I felt when I saw that implacable wall rise in his eyes. Anytime I think of our unborn child, that wall is all I see. A barrier to any possible future.

I stand up impatiently. I have to walk. I can't sit here all day, seeing Roman's face over and again. I saw it a thousand times on the journey here, every time I reread his letter. It's one of the reasons I burned it.

I have to put those memories aside now. Try to find the space to build something new.

Try not to imagine the lifeless bodies of the children.

I shudder, feeling another cold wave of fury that Alexei could have knowingly endangered them like that. My feet hit the cobblestones hard as I move mindlessly through the labyrinthine alleys that make up the Albayzin, the medieval part of Granada. The brisk pace and beautiful surroundings do nothing to ameliorate my anger.

My brother is as lost to me as Roman is. Though for different reasons.

While I have sympathy for what Alexei has suffered at the Orlovs' hands, I can't ever forgive him for that bomb. For knowingly risking the children's lives.

I even feel angry at Papa. He told me Alexei would only be in touch with our Argentinian contact in the event of an emergency. Yet Alexei knew the name on my new passport. The only way he could have known that is if the contact told him, and that means he's been in touch more than just in emergencies. I find it impossible to believe that Papa doesn't know that. Which means that he, too, knows more than he is saying. That my father and brother have been keeping me in the dark, planning together, just like they did back when we escaped the Orlovs and they didn't tell me that Alexei was going to stay behind.

I'm tired of the secrets and lies. Exhausted by what has taken place and all that I've lost because of it.

I walk up and down the steep, narrow alleys, stopping occasionally to buy a bottle of water. I have no appetite and I can't stop. Every time I stop walking, I'm swamped by emotions I can't handle. As dusk comes closer, I turn toward the steep road that leads up to and past the Alhambra, heading for the mountain above it, and the solitude of nothing but wind and birds.

ROMAN

"How the fuck can she just disappear?"

I grip the back of Pavel's chair in the lab, staring around at the tense faces of his whizz kids. "According to your research, Darya boarded two different flights to Switzerland, but didn't actually take either of them. Nor was she on the *Guapa*." I stare at my white knuckles on the back of the chair. "She can't have got far on land, and she *must* have left a trail."

I'm met by a roomful of downcast eyes and awkward shuffling.

"Fuck." I shake my head tiredly.

"On the upside," Pavel says cautiously, "we do know where the girls are. Or at least, we have a lead."

"Mickey told me." I stare unseeing at the bank of screens. "Private plane, landed at Miami–Opa Locka Executive Airport early this morning. Owned by an Orlov company. The passenger manifest was deleted from the record, but you pulled Masha's and Ofelia's passport details from US immigration, correct?"

"Only just in time." Pavel twirls his fidget spinner incessantly, and for once I don't react. He's worked nonstop since this began, as have his whole team. "Record of their entry was wiped barely moments after it was registered. The Orlovs aren't taking any chances."

"Mickey said you tracked the vehicle carrying the girls to the Petrovsky's Coconut Grove compound in Miami?" I try to keep my voice steady, but all I can see are the scars on Darya's back, and all I can hear are my father's screams. I know what the Orlovs are capable of. The thought of my girls in their hands turns my gut to water in a way no enemy ever has.

Pavel nods. "I'm guessing we'll get the Orlovs' demands any minute now."

"Their demands?" I'd laugh, but I'm pretty sure it would come out sounding deranged. "The only demands the Orlovs will be making will be for me to stop breaking their fucking bones."

There's a grim murmur of assent from around the room.

"I know how to deal with the Orlovs," I say coldly.

It's not a lie. I've thought of little else from the moment the bomb went off. To be honest, even before that. I've known this moment would come, although I never imagined it would involve my children being in danger.

"As soon as we've identified exactly where the girls are, we'll set up an attack. Meanwhile, we need to find Darya. We have to get her off the streets and into safety before any of this goes down."

I avoid looking at either Mickey or Dimitry. Neither has forgiven me for my initial hostility toward Darya. Going by the incessant buzzing of his phone, Dimitry is getting grief from Abby as well, which no doubt isn't improving his mood. Mickey has barely looked up from his screen since the night of the explosion. He's lost every woman in his life who means anything.

His sisters.

Darya.

His mother.

The fact that he loathes Inger doesn't change the fact that he's lost his mother. No matter what the outcome of the current situation is, Mickey won't ever trust Inger again, and I, more than anyone else, understand the scar that kind of loss leaves on a young heart.

"Wait." Mickey leans forward, frowning at the screen. "Have a look at this." He pauses a grainy CCTV feed from the Malaga bus station and points to a woman climbing onto a bus. She's wearing Moroccan clothing, with a headscarf and dark glasses, and she's carrying a large handbag. It's impossible to see her face clearly, and the voluminous Moroccan djellaba swamps her figure. Nothing, from her stance to her clothing, looks anything like Darya.

"What am I supposed to be looking at?" I try not to sound impatient.

"Have a look at this screen." Mickey has another feed paused. The same Moroccan woman, heading into a bathroom at the airport, approximately one hour earlier than the video footage taken at the bus stop. Only this woman has intricate henna patterns on the backs of her hands, starkly visible even in the poor-quality feed. Mickey points back at the first screen. The woman's hand is clasped around the handrail inside the bus door.

No henna.

I look back and forth between the two images. The clothing

isn't just similar, it's exactly the same. Same slight tear on the headscarf, same glasses. The only difference is the handbag; the woman at the airport has a large suitcase on roller wheels.

"Then there's this." Mickey fast-forwards the airport footage. A few minutes after the Moroccan woman enters the bathroom, a woman exits wearing jeans and a sweater that I immediately recognize as Darya's. Her black hair is in a long plait, and she keeps her face averted from the camera. From behind, she looks enough like Darya that I do a double take, until Mickey points out the henna pattern on the hand pulling the large roller suitcase.

"And after a few more minutes," he says, flicking through the footage, "there's this." Another woman exits the bathroom, wearing the djellaba and headscarf. She's carrying a duty-free bag, but not the satchel.

The satchel had already been left on a plane bound for Switzerland, with Darya's phone inside it.

"By the time she's at the bus stop, the duty-free bag is gone and she's bought a handbag," Mickey says. "Less conspicuous, I guess." I glance at Dimitry, but he's already got his phone out, giving low-voiced orders.

A lead. It's all I need. From here it's only a matter of time before I find her.

Even if I have to turn over every stone in Spain to do it.

I have a quick conversation with Dimitry and then put Darya out of my mind with no small effort. I know none of my men will rest until she's found. Meanwhile, I have a phone call to make, one that can't wait.

I go into my office in the Mercura secure room and pick up the telephone that only I ever use. It's safer in here than any government SCIF used for military purposes. The phone line is completely untraceable.

I pull out the thick cream business card and dial the gold-embossed number on it. The line rings once before it is picked up. I'm greeted by a smooth, coolly professional female voice.

"*Da.*"

"I need to get a message to Makari Tereschenko. It's Roman Stevanovsky. Tell him I'm calling in that favor."

ROMAN

Mickey folds his arms stubbornly. "I'm coming with you."

I run an impatient hand through my hair. "No, Mickey, you're not. I want you here."

"I'm the one who found her. I want to be there." He stares me down, something I'm becoming more used to than I might like. "I want Darya to know she has a family. She thinks we don't care." He gives me a rather hard look. "She should know that we do. That *I* do," he adds pointedly.

Christ. The kid hasn't let up on me for a second. "I'm beginning to regret letting you back into the lab," I say resignedly.

Mickey smiles tightly. "You need me, and you know it."

I shake my head. "You're turning into an arrogant little shit, you know that?"

He shrugs. "I learned from the best."

We both almost smile, then a computer pings, and we zero in

on the screen, all trace of humor lost. That's the thing, the last couple of days. There are moments, here and there, when I forget the hellish reality we're all living. Moments when Mickey makes me smile, or Dimitry and I fall into our familiar banter. But as soon as the moments come, they go again, and the darkness descends.

I still haven't heard back from Makari. And I still don't have a plan.

For once, I've listened to Dimitry and Mickey. And, yes, to goddamn Abby, though that girl pisses me off beyond recognition at times. They've all advised me to wait, to hear what Darya has to say before I make an attack plan for Miami.

Mickey has also suggested talking to Sergei, Darya's father. That's a conversation I'm not ready to have. I did send Dimitry there, to find out if Sergei knows anything about Darya's whereabouts, but I already knew before he went that the visit would be useless.

Darya's been running a long time. She knows her father is the first place I'd turn for information. She'd never risk telling him anything that might endanger him or betray her whereabouts.

Mickey's phone buzzes again. He holds it up, waving the screen at me. "It's Sergei again. You should talk to him, Roman. He's worried about the girls."

"Oh, I bet he fucking is." I don't give a shit how Sergei Petrovsky feels. No matter how much I might love his daughter, I doubt I'll ever forgive the man whose ineptitude got my parents killed and whose greed got my daughters kidnapped. He can worry all he likes, as far as I'm concerned.

"Come on, then." I tilt my head at Mickey and hold the door to the lab open. "If you're coming, get in the bloody car."

He almost takes my arm off in his haste to duck under it.

"You should take the chopper," Dimitry says, frowning. "It's quicker."

"It also draws attention." I don't mention the fact that I'm actually looking forward to the drive. I need some time to get ready for the upcoming encounter, to prepare myself for the fact that Darya just might not want to come back, not after what I said to her. She might not want to be found.

She certainly did a good job of running.

Without Mickey's eagle eye and insane skill at hacking cameras in places I never would have thought of, we'd never have tracked her. Even now, we've only narrowed her location down to a rough area in Granada. It will take a bit of footwork on the ground to pinpoint exactly where she is.

If I'm honest, Mickey is the right person for the job. A kid asking questions is a lot less obvious than someone like me asking them. But the thought of being alone in the car with him for several hours isn't quite so appealing. Mickey might have kept the worst of his opinions to himself, but his snarky asides and hard side-eye have spoken volumes.

He's pissed at me. Seriously pissed. He's also terrified for his sisters, and frustrated as hell at how long it's taking to get them back. I'm guessing this car ride is about to become an interrogation, one I'm not really looking forward to.

"WHAT ARE YOU DOING?" I glance sideways to where Mickey is tapping away on his laptop. Dusk is falling behind the mountains, purple and gold in the distance. The coast is fading behind us as we go further inland, through the steep passes and winding roads that lead to the ancient inland city of Granada.

"Still trying to hack into the security cameras at the Coconut Grove compound." He glares at the screen. "It's surprisingly difficult. And the connectivity up here is cooked."

"Doesn't Pavel have a whole team working on that?"

"I'm better." He hunches over the screen, his lips pressed hard together.

"Mickey."

"Hm." He doesn't look up.

"Mickey. Put the fucking laptop away." That at least gets him to turn my way. "The reception won't get any better until we're through the mountains, and that's at least one hour, if not two. Pavel has a team working on hacking the system, with all the lab's power behind them. You clearly have some things you'd like to get off your mind. Now's your chance."

I take the corners at a measured pace, watching him from the corner of my eye. After a while he closes the screen and half turns in his seat, so he's facing me. "I'm not sure you want to hear what I've got to say."

My hands tighten on the steering wheel. I relax them with an effort. "I'm not going to beg, Mickey. You want to talk, you don't want to talk—it's up to you. But don't assume you know what I do and don't want to hear. If I wasn't interested, I wouldn't ask."

"Okay, fine." I can feel his eyes boring into me. "Why didn't you ever tell us your real name?"

"I've never told anyone my real name, Mickey."

"What about Papa? Or Deda Yuri? Didn't you have to tell them when he adopted you?"

"We're bratva. We do things our own way, Mickey, you know that. I told Yuri there was no record of my birth anywhere, and that I didn't want to know where I came from. He respected my decision. Pulled strings, got the adoption pushed through without the regular papers. Cut through bureaucracy." I shrug. "Rules have never meant much to people like your Deda Yuri and me."

"What about Papa? I thought you were like brothers. Why wouldn't you tell him the truth?"

My hands tighten again. I flex my fingers, trying to work out how to answer him. "Firstly, because he never asked."

He snorts. "That's not an answer."

"Well, it kind of is, actually." I cut my eyes to him briefly and see the skepticism on his face. "Look. Your father and I were teenagers when we met. Not much older than you are now. We didn't sit around discussing our feelings, Mickey. Our conversations tended to revolve around work, partying, and women, more or less in that order." I shrug. "Your father wasn't one to push for answers, particularly on private matters. He always respected my right to keep my past to myself, just like your Deda Yuri did."

"But didn't you *want* to tell him? Weren't you curious about your past? About the vault and the Naryshkin treasure?"

"Woah." I hold up a hand to halt his flow of questions. "That's a whole lot of questions. Let me take them one at a time. No, I didn't want to tell your father who I was. I didn't want to tell anyone. I'd been on the streets since I was ten. I'd buried my past a long time ago, learned to become someone else. Those years weren't easy. I guess it was simpler to look ahead, rather than behind.

"As to being curious . . . well, that's different. I knew some things about my past, though next to nothing about the Naryshkin treasure. There's a hell of a lot that I still don't know. For a long time I didn't *want* to know. Lately—since the Ryder stuff came out—I'm more curious, yes. But I'm wary, too." I can feel his eyes searching my face as I talk, taking in every nuance in my expression. I meet his eyes in the growing dark. "My past was a dangerous place, Mickey. The fact that the Orlovs have your sisters now should be proof enough of just how dangerous."

"Then why didn't you kill them?" The bluntness of his question momentarily silences me. "You're not exactly a peacemaker, Roman. From what I've seen and heard, you've never hesitated to put a bullet through anyone who gets in your way. So why are the Orlovs still alive? If they killed your parents, don't you want them dead? Surely you've had the resources for years now to get rid of them, if you wanted to?"

I'm squirming in my seat. Not a metaphor. I'm twisting around like a fucking pretzel, and to be honest, I've never wanted out of a conversation more.

Christ, this kid. He knows how to ask the hard questions, the little prick.

"You're worse than a goddamn therapist, you know that?" I shoot him a slightly resentful look.

Mickey almost smiles. "I've been sent to enough of them over the years. I know the drill." His smile fades. "Is it because you want whatever is in that vault your father built? Is it true that it's full of Fabergé eggs and other Russian imperial treasures?"

I close my eyes briefly. For a moment I'm back in Switzerland, my heart thudding with fear and trepidation, waiting for the safety deposit box to open. Hoping against hope that what I find there will lead me to my mother.

Instead I find myself staring at a glittering jeweled egg.

Priceless, definitely. Useful, certainly.

But utterly fucking meaningless in any way that truly mattered to me, then or now.

"It's not about the fucking treasure." Even I hear the bitter note in my voice. "That vault has cost more lives than I care to count. I don't give a fuck what's inside it; I never did."

That was Sergei Petrovsky's obsession, not mine. But I'm not saying any of that to Mickey.

I clear my throat. "It's complicated. I have a lot of unanswered questions, about both of my parents. I guess I'd like those questions answered before I start taking out the only people who might know something."

"Then why haven't you spoken to Deda Juan—Sergei?" he

quickly corrects himself. "Darya's father. Wouldn't he have some of those answers?"

"Maybe." I keep my eyes carefully on the road ahead.

He shakes his head. "I don't understand you."

I snort. "If I had a dollar for every time a woman has said that to me."

"Yeah, well." My humor clearly missed the mark. "Most people would leave no stone unturned to find out their own story. Especially when that story results in children being kidnapped."

That hits me like a gut punch. "I'll get your sisters back, Mickey. I fucking swear it." I hate how inadequate that promise sounds.

"You'd better." I don't miss the lethal note in his voice. Again, I'm reminded that he's not a kid. Not after this. "Don't you mean you'll get your *daughter* back?" He folds his arms and raises his eyebrows at me. "And my little sister. Who just happens to be the daughter of your worst enemy."

"They're both my daughters, Mickey, just like you're my son. You'll always have your real father, but today, and for all the days to come, we're a family. I don't care whose DNA is whose."

"Are you sure about that?" He's watching me closely. "Because that's the next item on my agenda. You said you didn't know Ofelia is your daughter. But I imagine you *do* remember sleeping with my mother?"

I wince. "Jesus, Mickey." This car ride is worse than open heart fucking surgery.

"So? What's the story there? How long were you together?"

"Maybe you should talk to your mother about this."

"I don't ever want to talk to my mother again." His voice is chilling enough to freeze fire. "Inger took my sisters. She kidnapped them and put them in danger. I won't forgive her for that. Not ever."

I don't bother trying to argue with him. I know that kind of anger. It settles in your bones, deep and painful, and calcifies there. It isn't the kind of anger that is fixed by a cozy conversation over a kitchen counter. Inger has endangered the two people Mickey cares about most in the world, taken the only true family he's ever known, and held them hostage.

When he says he won't forgive her, I believe him. I also don't blame him. Fuck knows, I won't ever forgive Inger myself.

"They're my sisters." His voice is low, slightly unsteady. "They were my responsibility, Roman. My job to look after. I should have seen what Inger was up to. I was so stupid. It was right in front of my face. I *knew* something wasn't right about those pictures Nikolai took on the yacht, and there was something weird about the way Inger suddenly wanted us all to go to that ball. She's never wanted us around when she's attending those kinds of things. I knew there was something wrong, and I just—I didn't—" His voice breaks, and he buries his head in his hands.

I pull the car into the gravel and am out of it in an instant. I pull his door open and haul the lanky length of him into a hard embrace. For once he doesn't argue. He stands stiffly for a moment, then his head falls onto my shoulder. His sobs are not the hiccups of the child he was, but the broken, rasping tears of the man he is becoming.

"It's not your fault, Mickey." I hold his head, my voice fierce against his ear. "You hear me? None of this is your fault. It was me who failed. It's my job to protect you all, and I dropped the fucking ball. Don't you ever blame yourself for this."

His head twists against my shoulder, his whole body tense and shuddering. "I should have seen it." His voice is muffled, but the self-recrimination in it hurts me inside.

"You listen to me." I pull away and put my hands on his face, making him meet my eyes. "You hear this, once and forever. You. Did. Nothing. Wrong. This is all on me. I run the security in my organization. I do the risk assessment, and I take care of business. There's only one person who fucked up here, and it was me. You know me by now, Mickey. Do you honestly think I wouldn't tell you if I thought you'd messed up?"

I hold his eyes until he finally gives a slight shake of his head.

"Right. Do you think Pavel and his team would want to work with you if they blamed you for the girls being taken?"

This time his shake is a little firmer.

"Exactly. They all know, Dimitry included, that this is my fuckup."

I step back slightly and grip his shoulders, still holding his eyes.

"They also know there's no point talking about whose fucking fault this is. There's only one thing that matters now: getting the girls back. There isn't anything I won't do to make that happen. My people know that.

"I will fix this, Mickey. No matter if I have to get a whole army to Miami. I'll get the girls back. That much I swear to you."

He nods slowly. "Will you promise to let me help? Not keep me on the outside?"

I nod. "I promise I won't keep a single thing from you, Mickey. From now on, we do this as a team." I pull him into a rough hug.

Eventually he pulls away, and I let him go. I give him a half smile as I open the passenger door. "Does this mean you'll stop grilling me in the fucking car? I don't know if I can take another hundred miles of this shit."

Mickey gives a shaky laugh and wipes his arm across his face. "Truce," he says. "For now, at least."

I roll my eyes. "I suppose I should give thanks for small mercies." I pull the door closed and give his shoulder a final squeeze.

"Come on, then. Let's go and bring Darya home."

1 O

DARYA

I avoid thinking about Roman and the children by wandering the hills above Granada, gazing down at the peaceful gardens of the Alhambra, feeling the mountain breeze sharp on my face, tasting the traces of snow from the peaks above on the air. If I sit still, my mind plays horrible tricks. I need to be physically exhausted to get even a few hours of sleep.

It's also harder to cry when I'm walking.

The rustling of the ancient olive trees and haunting cries of the mountain birds are the only things that even slightly calm my soul. I walk back down toward the city, along the road that runs past the Alhambra, accompanied by the rushing of water from old aqueducts and stone sculptures that have stood for centuries. I know I need to leave Granada tomorrow, but I can't begin to think of where to go next. It's exhausting even contemplating it.

As I approach my apartment, tension begins to steal back into my body, the ever-present fear of discovery. I walk cautiously, pausing in the shadows and watching carefully before proceeding, but I can't see anything amiss. My windows are dark, and although I watch for a time, I can't see or hear any sign of a visitor.

Still.

I take my time climbing the stairs, careful to make no sound.

I turn the key in the lock and step into the darkened room. A quick scan of the shadows shows nothing out of place. I walk out onto the terrace, inhaling deeply. I might sleep out here tonight. Something in me is reluctant to relinquish the breath of fresh air on my face.

Or maybe it's just that I like being near the outside steps and an escape route.

I lean over the terrace and listen to the sounds of flamenco as the Granada night comes alive, trying to recapture the calm I felt on the mountain earlier.

"Darya."

Roman's voice comes from the shadows behind me.

I don't have to wonder who the voice belongs to. It's haunted my every moment, sleeping or awake, since the ball.

He must have been waiting out here, on the terrace.

Behind the door?

I think through the options with clinical detachment, automatically wondering where I went wrong, what mistake I made that led him to me.

But the truth is, I don't actually care. There's only one thing I care about, only one question that has tortured me from the moment I ran from that ballroom.

"The children." I grip the terrace wall, staring out over the valley, unable to face him. "Tell me what happened to the children."

"Mickey is here with me." I almost collapse with relief,

sagging against the wall. "Alive and well," Roman continues, "and currently testing the limits of the Wi-Fi in a restaurant just up the road. He insisted on coming to bring you home."

I bury my head in my arms, breathing deeply to brace myself for what he isn't saying. "The girls." My voice seems to come from very far away. "Tell me, Roman. Tell me they're unharmed."

His pause is too long. Far too long.

My heart seizes, then sinks. The dark nightmares that have tortured my every moment burst into terrifying technicolor. "No," I whisper, the word barely audible. "Oh please, God, no."

"They're alive." Roman's voice is rough. "But they're gone, Darya. Ofelia and Masha are gone. The Orlovs took them."

"*No.*" I grip the terracotta tiles hard enough to hurt my palms, my head shaking from side to side. I squeeze my eyes closed, as if I can block out the truth, as if when I open them the girls will be safely at home in their penthouse, instead of prisoners at the hands of the most sadistic bastard I've ever known. The merest thought of Vilnus Orlov touching Ofelia and Masha hits me with such horror that nausea threatens to engulf me entirely.

"It was Inger." I can hear the deadly fury beneath Roman's exhaustion. "She's been working with the Orlovs, for some time now, it seems."

"Inger!" I'm so surprised I turn around, which is a mistake. Roman in the flesh is more than I'm ready for. More than even my nighttime visions recalled.

He's even taller and more imposing than my memories, his bulk more daunting given his two-day stubble and a dark suit that does nothing to lighten the deep shadows beneath his eyes or soften the hard line of his mouth. Going by his gaunt appearance, he's slept even less than I have. His eyes are hard to read, but even in the dim light, I see them narrow when he notices my face.

"What the hell happened to you?" he snaps. "Who did that to your eye?"

My hand drifts up to touch the swelling I'd all but forgotten about. "I did it to myself. Battered wives tend to gain people's trust easier than runaway girls."

"No wonder your landlady looked at me as if I were the devil incarnate." Despite his levity, there's no humor in his voice, and he doesn't move toward me. I want more than anything to throw myself into his arms. But despite my passionate relief at knowing the girls are actually alive, followed by my utter horror at the knowledge of who has them, I can't quite lower my instinctive caution.

"How did you find me?" I wish I sounded more defiant. Instead, my voice has a quiet, defeated quality that makes me feel rather ashamed.

"You didn't make it easy." Roman folds his arms, leaning against the low wall, watching me. "Mickey found footage from the airport of you changing clothes with a Moroccan woman. It still took twenty-four hours and a hell of a lot of man power to track your movements." The reluctant admiration in his voice does nothing to make me feel any better.

"If you found me, then the Orlovs can, too." I'm astonished my voice still works.

"They won't if you come home with me."

Home.

Being in Roman's bed. Cooking in the kitchen with the children.

The children who aren't there.

Who are gone.

Because of me.

Longing snags painfully in my throat. "I thought that would be the last thing you'd want."

"Christ, Darya." For the first time I hear the exhausted rasp in his voice. "I was wrong, okay? I got it wrong. I never should have said the things I did. I never should have threatened you like that." He closes his mouth, abruptly cutting himself off.

Alexei's warning about Roman runs through my mind on a megaphone: *The Orlovs will take the children. How long do you think Roman will hold out when they start carving up those kids? How long will you?*

Roman isn't here for me.

He's here because I'm the only trade he can make that will get his children back. Any apologies are only to make me go with him.

You don't have to convince me, I think dully.

As if I could ever rest while I know the Orlovs have the girls. Alexei knew that. It was why he wanted me to run.

Roman doesn't need the contents of that vault. And there's nothing he won't do to save those girls, I know that. He'll open the vault for the Orlovs. The question is what will happen to me after he does.

Not that there's any point in asking him. Right now, he'll say anything, make any promise he needs to, in order to gain my cooperation.

But like I said, there's no need to convince me.

"We should probably get on with it, then." I try to keep my voice steady. I try even harder not to think about little Borovsky. That's one secret I will have to keep to myself. I'm not making this any more complicated than it already is.

Roman frowns. "Get on with what?"

"Whatever deal you've made with the Orlovs. I assume they want the vault opened in exchange for the girls' lives?"

Roman is still frowning. "I think it's safe to assume that is going to be one of their requests. They haven't actually made any demands yet."

"They will." I force myself to meet his eyes, trying to ignore the thud of connection when I do. "You and I both know what they're capable of. We need to open that vault. Give them what they're asking for."

Roman takes a step toward me, then halts. "Why run, if you were always planning to give in to their demands?"

"I was hoping that if I ran, they wouldn't have a chance to *make* demands." I hold his eyes, determined to say at least this much, even if he doesn't believe me. "I had no idea what they were planning, Roman. None. Alexei came to the ball. He told me the Orlovs were there. He said that if I wanted to keep the children safe, I had to run. I thought that if I did what he said, I'd remove any incentive the Orlovs had to take the children."

"I know." His answer is flat, his face unchanging except for a faint tick in his jaw. "I know you ran because you thought you'd keep them safe. But it turns out the Orlovs knew more than either of us could have imagined. They'd have taken the children whether you ran or not, Darya." He looks away, breaking eye contact. It's like being released from an invisible tie, both a relief and a strange feeling of being cut adrift. He rubs a hand over his face, exhaling sharply. "Did you read my letter?"

It's such an odd change of pace that I'm momentarily taken aback. "Yes. I read it."

Only a hundred times or so, but hey, who's counting?

"Your brother told you my real name, didn't he? You discovered who I am—not, as you said at the ball, because of the Borovsky safe in my apartment, but because Alexei told you."

I nod.

"Alexei also told you that I have the missing key to the vault at your home in Miami." It isn't a question. His eyes bore into me, stripping away the flimsy defenses I've been trying to muster since I ran from the ballroom. Roman lied to me. Even after he told me he loved me, he lied to me. And despite all that's happened, that still hurts.

"Do you have the key?" I want to throw the words at him, but they're little more than a whisper. "You suggested as much in your letter. You said the Orlovs hunted for you because they believed you could open the vault."

He frowns. "And so you think that I kept you in my home because I want to open the vault and take the contents for myself?"

"I did, at first."

"*Blyat*." His response is uncharacteristically harsh. Seeing my surprise, his mouth thins. "It's the second time today I've been accused of holding you to open that vault. Mickey came to the same conclusion." Before I have a chance to ask how Mickey knows about any of this, he goes on: "You said you thought that at first. What changed your opinion?"

The horrifying days of darkness when I thought I'd never see you again.

The truth is that believing I had lost Roman forever lent my thoughts the detachment of regret, causing me to read the situation without the overlay of my emotional investment.

"I know your wealth is vast enough that you have no need of what is inside the vault. After reading your letter, I think I understand why you didn't confide in me."

"Then why—" His voice cracks, and he spins away from me. His hands are on his hips, his shoulders rising and falling in deep breaths as if he's struggling to calm himself. "Why didn't you talk to me?" He remains turned away from me, his voice low and raw. "Or warn me? Divided loyalties I can understand, Darya. I knew you would want to help your brother. But the fact that you didn't try to warn me? About a *bomb?*"

"I didn't know about that!" I reel as if I've been struck. "How could you possibly think I knew the Orlovs were going to set off a bomb? Don't you know I'd have done anything—*anything* —to save the children, if I'd known?"

He still has his back to me.

He doesn't trust me, any more than I trust him.

The realization is as shocking as it is painful.

"Why do you think I'm here, and not on the plane my brother booked for me?" I force myself to speak past the emotion choking my throat. "Do you think I could ever trust Alexei again, after what happened? I love my brother, Roman. I always will. But if it comes down to helping him regain our family legacy or saving the children's lives, there's no choice. My God." I shake my head, utterly bewildered. "How could you ever, even for a moment, believe that I would risk their lives?"

He turns halfway through my speech, his face still shadowed as he watches me. "Alexei didn't tell you about the bomb?"

"Of course he didn't tell me!" I'm so appalled I feel sick. "Alexei told me that the Orlovs knew who you were and that you had the missing key to the vault. They already have Alexei captive. With you and me in one place, Alexei said the Orlovs would have all the pieces they need to open the vault. All they needed was leverage, a way to ensure we all cooperated. I ran because Alexei told me that the Orlovs were planning to take the children and use them as that leverage."

Roman doesn't speak.

"Alexei never said anything about a bomb." My voice is weak. I'm finding it hard to speak at all. "Or about Inger. He just told me that running was the only way I could save the children." My voice starts to shake, the sudden burst of adrenaline fading, leaving me shocked and utterly distraught.

Roman crosses the terrace in one stride, and when he reaches for me, I have no thought of refusing. He pulls me close, and I fall against the wall of his chest, inhaling his familiar scent, clinging to him as if he were the only solid rock amid a tornado. "I'm sorry," he mutters, holding my head against his chest, stroking my hair as his other hand pulls me close to him. "I'm sorry it took me so long to tell you the truth about who I am. And I'm more sorry than you can ever know that I ever suspected you of endangering the children. I said terrible things, Darya, things I can't ever take back."

"I don't care." I shake my head against his chest, the tears I've been trying to hold back all day streaming down my face, dampening his shirt. "None of it matters, Roman, not now." I pull back to say more, but before I do his mouth finds mine, and in that moment of connection I can feel all the pain and longing and fear that is haunting him, the regret and the long years of secrecy he's been forced to live. I hold his face as his lips move on my own, feeling the heat between us, but it's far more than that. This kiss isn't about passion or desire. It's a reminder to us both that we are home, that this thing between us, however strange and complicated, is the one real, strong foundation we can rely on. That no matter what is coming for us now, we have this. We have each other.

When Roman finally lifts his mouth from mine, I truly see for the first time the grim exhaustion in his face, the shadow of horror behind his eyes.

"The Orlovs have already won," I whisper. "They have the girls." I stare up at him. "Nothing is worth risking their lives. We can seek justice later. For now, we need to do whatever it takes to get Ofelia and Masha back. Give the Orlovs what they want. We have to open that vault, Roman, and we have to do it as soon as possible."

"I agree." His voice is husky with exhaustion. "There's only one problem."

"What?" I frown. I can't imagine what could possibly matter, when both of the girls are gone.

Roman's mouth twists. "I don't have the key to open that vault."

11

DARYA

"What do you mean, you don't have the key?" Darya stares at me in confusion. "I didn't even know there *was* an actual key, but Alexei said the Orlovs suspect you have it. Key or not, the vault can't be opened without your fingerprints. I should know." I don't miss the hard note in her voice. "Vilnus pressed my fingers against that damned vault every day for years trying to open it."

"It's complicated." I glance uphill, toward the restaurant where Mickey is waiting. "We need time to talk about this, Darya. But I'd rather do it while Mickey is with us." I almost smile. "I promised that I would include him in every step. I don't want to risk breaking that promise less than a day since I made it."

"Then let's go." She moves toward the stairs without hesitation.

"Wait." I gesture inside the apartment. "Don't you have anything you want to bring with you?"

She shakes her head impatiently. "No. I burned anything important. And we've already wasted enough time."

I lead her through the alleyways, trying to keep my shock hidden. *"I burned anything important."*

Darya wasn't just running this time.

She was disappearing.

In only a day or two more, she would have been gone entirely, across a border, somewhere harder for me to follow.

I could have lost her forever.

The impact of that thought hits me hard. It's a different shock to what I felt after the bomb and the girls' disappearance. That shock was visceral, an all-encompassing horror that still permeates every cell of my body, and will until I have my daughters home and justice for their suffering.

But the thought of Darya simply vanishing into a vast, anonymous sea of humanity in which she might so easily become invisible chills me to the bone in a different way.

That chill is a loneliness deep in my soul.

It's the sudden realization that I would never have been able to stop looking for her.

I'd have searched every crowd for her face for the rest of my life, always hoping against hope that I would find her again.

In those simple words, *I burned anything important*, that alternative future is revealed to me with devastating clarity. And I know, with every fiber of my being, that I don't want to be the shell of a man I see in that vision.

Whatever life brings to me, I need Darya by my side to face it.

Without her, I am not truly myself.

That truth is like an optical illusion, a hidden image inside a picture. Once seen, the picture can never look the same again.

I cannot be without Darya.

In a week of devastating realizations, this one is the most unexpected—and the one I am least able to articulate. Particularly now, when so much else is at stake. I tuck it away inside myself and force my rational mind to refocus.

The restaurant is twenty paces away, and with it, all that Mickey has discovered with his DNA testing. All that Darya doesn't know.

I momentarily wrestle with myself, torn between my desire to prepare her for what is coming and the knowledge that we don't have time to waste. "Wait." I slow my pace.

"For what?" She gives me an impatient look.

"There are some things you should know." But I never get a chance to finish. Mickey must have been watching for us, because he is already out the door and striding toward us, his lean face animated with relief. Darya breaks away from me with a small cry, racing toward him. They meet in the middle of a cobblestoned plaza, Darya enfolding Mickey in a tight, wordless embrace, her hand on his head as she presses her lips to his temple. Mickey clings to her, his tall body taut with relief.

"Thank God," she whispers when she finally pulls away, tears streaming down her face as she presses his arms, as if reassuring herself that he is whole. "Thank God you're alive."

Mickey nods, trying to smile, but his lips are pressed firmly together, and I can tell he doesn't trust himself to speak.

"Come on." I put an arm around his angular shoulders, aware of the curious looks our little reunion is attracting. "We can talk in the car."

Mickey gives me a rather hard look, and I sigh inwardly. I know there's no chance in hell he will hold back from telling Darya the truth.

Christ.

It's going to be a hell of a fucking drive back.

MICKEY DOESN'T WASTE any time. We've barely hit the highway when he drops the DNA bombshells.

"Wait." Darya turns sideways in the passenger seat so she can look directly at me. Even with my eyes on the road, her shock is palpable. "Ofelia is your *daughter*? And Vilnus Orlov is Masha's father?"

"Takes a bit to get your head around, huh." I keep my eyes firmly on the road, not least because of my desire to wring Mickey's neck. But even if it had been left up to me, I know it's impossible to withhold the truth now, under the circumstances. I also know there's no point in ordering Mickey to do so.

That should piss me off. I've always demanded utter obedience.

If I'm honest, though, I feel an odd touch of pride. Young he might be, but Mickey is already his own man. Something he will need to be if he intends to make our world his life. And whether I like it or not, I don't think he can escape our life.

Not after this.

Besides, Malaga is barely three hours on the freeway from Granada. As soon as we arrive, we'll be back in the thick of the hunt. I know there's no way in hell Darya will accept being on the outside of that investigation. Brutal as it is, there's no real choice other than ripping off the Band-Aid and getting this over with.

"So." Her voice has a brittle edge that doesn't bode at all well. "You and Inger...?"

She doesn't need to finish the sentence to make her meaning plain.

"A long time ago." I glance at her briefly, taking in the pale cheeks, rather fierce eyes, and hard-pressed lips with no small amount of trepidation. Admitting to a youthful affair is one thing. Being forced to admit it in a car to the woman I love and nearly just lost—not to mention Inger's son, watching my every damn twitch—is about the worst kind of purgatory I can imagine. I dodged Mickey's questions on the way here. I know there's no chance in hell of doing it twice.

Worse, this is Inger, who has repeatedly tried to humiliate Darya. Not to mention hurt the children, first emotionally, and now by physically endangering her own daughters. I brace myself to do something I really fucking hate: owning up to a mistake.

"Inger and I had a brief affair back in Miami, the same summer that I met Mikhail." I glance in the rearview mirror. "It was already over between us when she met your father, Mickey."

That isn't entirely true, but I figure some details are better left unsaid.

The truth is that the moment Inger realized who Mikhail was—or rather, that it was his father's yacht that was moored at the local marina—she dropped me faster than she had her panties.

"We were very young." I meet Mickey's eyes in the mirror again. "Not much older than you are now. I wish I could say that there was more to the story, Mickey, but honestly, that's about it."

I glance sideways, but Darya gives me nothing, just stares at me with those gleaming eyes.

Fuck. She's really not going to make this easy. I want to touch her, to cut the distance between us by restoring the sensuality that has always bonded us so closely, but nothing about the situation lends itself to physical intimacy. I clench the steering wheel to stop myself from reaching for her. It's paralyzing how much I want to.

"Mikhail turned up on your Deda Yuri's yacht shortly after it ended between your mother and me."

Actually, the two things happened on the same day, but who's counting?

"Inger fell for Mikhail as soon as she met him and never

looked back." That part is true enough. I figure Mickey doesn't need to know that it was the yacht, rather than Mikhail, that Inger fell for. Though by the way his mouth twists with distaste, I guess he's smart enough to have worked that much out for himself.

"Did Papa know?" His eyes in the rearview mirror are laser sharp. "About you and Inger?"

"Yes." At least I can answer that without hesitation. "Mikhail asked me right at the start if I minded, if I was serious about her. I wasn't, and I stepped aside immediately. We never really talked about it again. Two months later, Inger was pregnant. They married a few weeks after that."

An uneasy silence settles over the car. I can still feel Darya's eyes on me, but I can't sense her reaction to the story. I swallow uncomfortably. I'm not used to feeling ashamed. But I was, after Mikhail told me Inger was pregnant. Not because I'd defiled something innocent, which by then, I knew Inger certainly was not, but because I'd been almost pathetically grateful that it was Mikhail she had set her sights upon. I knew, then and there, that I was not remotely equipped to make somebody a husband or father. I took no satisfaction from having dodged what I already knew was a toxic bullet, but I did learn from it. Afterward, I became almost pathological about keeping my relationships strictly businesslike.

"But you must have wondered if the baby was yours. Papa, too."

Christ, the kid is relentless.

I shift uneasily in my seat, choosing to meet Mickey's hard stare instead of Darya's quiet scrutiny. She's still wearing the headscarf and Moroccan outfit. I want to tear both off and run my hands through her hair, make her mine again. This car ride is fixing to be the longest of my damned life. "Inger and Mikhail had been together all summer. Her parents were very traditional, and they'd already met Yuri."

"But—"

"We're Russian, Mickey." To my surprise, it's Darya who heads him off. She turns in her seat, giving him a quiet, reassuring smile. "Questions just aren't asked in such circumstances. Maybe in a less traditional world they might be, but not for us. Marriage would have been the only option, given the public nature of their relationship."

Mickey settles reluctantly back in his seat. "I guess."

I should be grateful for Darya's intervention, but I'm not. Especially given that she won't quite meet my eyes. Mickey might be more or less satisfied with my answers, but despite her coming to my rescue, something tells me Darya is nowhere near done. And a queasy sensation in my gut suggests that her questions are going to be a hell of a lot harder to answer.

In the brief reprieve that follows Mickey's questions, I sneak another look at Darya. Her face is closed, her arms folded protectively across her body. Everything about her posture fills me with unease. Even Mickey seems disinclined to continue his cross-examination. He, too, is watching her, clearly concerned about the impact of so many revelations. In the end, however, it's Darya who broaches the next question.

"What about Masha?" She looks between Mickey and me. "Did you have any idea about her? Did Mikhail?"

"I don't think so." It's my turn to frown. "I still don't know how the hell that connection happened."

"I do." Mickey's tone is flat and hard. We both glance at him. "It was when Inger left Papa." His jaw is set, his anger clearly visible. "I remember that summer. I was eight, Ofelia was ten. Papa said we had to go to Miami for the holidays and stay with Deda and Baba Melnyk. Inger's parents," he adds, for Darya's benefit. "We didn't want to go. Their house is really small, and it smells weird."

I can't help but grin at they way he wrinkles his nose. "He's right," I say to Darya, as an aside. "Inger's mother is a big believer in traditional cooking. That house has smelled of cabbage ever since I can remember. And despite all the money Mikhail gave Inger's parents, they've never moved."

"Baba always says that the best place for money is somewhere people can't see it," Mickey says. He meets my eyes and actually smiles. "Papa used to say, if that was true, then he didn't see why she couldn't invest in some air freshener, since it's invisible."

I give an involuntary snort of laughter at that, then, given the topic we're discussing, try belatedly to turn it into a cough. I'm relieved to see that Darya is smiling too.

"I know that smell," she says to Mickey. "Papa used to take us to visit some old Russian friends of his, and their house always stunk of cabbage, too. It's the soup they make."

"Yeah." He rolls his eyes. "Papa also used to say that he couldn't see why anyone in Miami would want to cook *fucking soup*, since the air is already the same consistency." That makes us all laugh, despite the fact that I should probably pull him up on language.

"I remember him saying that." It feels good to talk about Mikhail. I realize, with surprise, that I rarely do. I should. His children need to remember who he was.

That thought sobers me up immediately.

"Regardless of those tests, Mikhail was still a father to your sisters." I meet Mickey's eyes in the mirror. "Like I told you, Mickey, DNA doesn't mean shit. Family is family, and you were all Mikhail's children. Don't ever forget that."

"I think Papa might have known about Masha, though. Or suspected, at least." His laughter has disappeared. "That summer was awful. Inger was away nearly all the time, and Deda and Baba Melnyk are really strict, so Ofelia and I weren't allowed out much. We pretty much hung around in our rooms, on our laptops. I was more interested in gaming, but Ofelia used to search for articles about Inger all the time. She hid the screen so

I couldn't see, but I saw enough to know that it wasn't work that was keeping Inger busy. The online tabloids were full of pictures of her at parties and on yachts." His face is tense and pale again. "Ofelia and I didn't talk about it much. But there were enough photos of Inger with other men to make it pretty obvious what she was doing."

"Your father didn't want you to go to Miami. He only sent you there to keep you safe." I owe it to Mikhail to ensure his children know the truth. "Your Deda Yuri had just gone to jail, and there was a war between the Russian families. Your father and I knew we were facing a bloodbath. We both wanted you far away from it."

"Yeah." Mickey gives me a humorless smile. "Ofelia and I saw that online, too."

That shuts me down pretty fast. I, more than anyone, should know how much children see. But the truth is, I was too caught up in the war, in founding Hale and Mercura, to care about what Mikhail's children were doing.

"I'm sorry, Mickey," I say quietly. "Your father and I should have done a better job of caring for you."

"It's okay." He shrugs, but I don't need to see Darya's frown to know how insincere his denial is. I grip the steering wheel and, for the thousandth time recently, vow to do better.

Much better.

"Anyway," Mickey goes on, "Papa came to Miami a few times that summer, but he and Inger fought all the time. She wanted him to bring Deda Yuri's yacht to Miami for us to stay on, but he said it wasn't safe. In the end Uncle Nicky sailed it over anyway, which was actually pretty cool at first. Inger was away on a modeling contract. Ofelia and I liked the yacht way better than Deda and Baba's house, and Uncle Nicky took us out, did stuff with us. But then Inger came back to stay on the yacht, and they more or less forgot about us. We saw very little of either of them for the rest of the summer. Ofelia said that the only reason

Uncle Nicky came in the first place was because he had a crush on Inger."

Darya's eyebrows nearly shoot through the roof. "Are you serious?"

I cover her hand briefly with my own in silent warning, and she gathers herself quickly. "I mean, wow. That must have been tough for you guys."

"No shit," Mickey says flatly. "It was gross. Anyway, it didn't end well. They had a huge fight one night on the yacht. Ofelia and I were both there. Uncle Nicky accused Inger of sleeping with someone else—apart from him, that is—and then she burst into tears, saying she was in love with Papa and wished she'd never left him. Uncle Nicky screamed at her for hours. The next day he was gone, and Inger took us to stay with Babushka Vera in the London house. She and Papa got back together soon after that."

How the fuck did I know none of this? I'm having difficulty hiding my shock, and from the sideways glances Darya's giving me, she's equally horrified.

"I'm pretty sure it was Vilnus Orlov that Inger and Uncle Nicky were arguing about." Mickey seems oblivious to our shock, which makes it even worse.

No wonder the kids disliked me so much. They thought I knew all of this and just didn't care.

"What makes you so sure?" Darya asks.

"After I found out that Vilnus is Masha's father, I did the math, then went back and trawled all the online pictures from that summer. Vilnus and Inger were at all the same parties, and she's pictured with him at least a dozen times. One of those photos was taken on my birthday." He smiles without any humor at all. "Uncle Nicky took us out, because Inger said she was working. Later, he saw that photo of them together, which was what caused their argument."

"Oh, Mickey." Darya reaches for his hand and Mickey lets

her take it, but only for a moment. Then he folds his arms and forces a smile.

"We'd been back in London for a month or so when Inger told us she was going to have a baby. I was so happy that Papa and Inger were back together that I never thought about it. I think Ofelia might have, though. I think that's why she asked me to do the DNA testing in the first place. Maybe she overheard Papa say something. I don't know if Papa had heard rumors about Inger and Orlov, or what, but he and Inger fought all the time back then. He left for the last time just after Masha was born."

That hits me like a gut punch, and from the look on Darya's face, it's hitting her, too. "Does Ofelia . . . know? About the test results?"

"No." Mickey's voice is raspy with tiredness. He shakes his head, then yawns widely. "Not yet. I didn't want to upset her before I spoke to you."

Thank Christ for that. I almost slump with relief.

Mickey yawns again, rubbing his eyes. It's almost morning, and he's been running on empty for hours. Darya is staring out of the window, her face hidden. We're all exhausted, and the next time I glance in the mirror, Mickey has dozed off.

The silence that falls across the car isn't an easy one. The gulf between Darya and me is far greater than the disconnection of a few days apart. The electric intimacy that has always formed an unconscious, tangible bond between us was shattered by the blast, by the words I said after it, by the days when we both thought we'd lost one another. The caveman in me wants to reinstate that intimacy immediately, lose myself in Darya's body and make it my own again.

Given the awkwardness of that distance, in some ways Mickey's questions and story have been a welcome relief. I'm not quite sure when it happened, but at some point over the past few months, the children became Darya's and my safe space. When we are with them we both know our roles. We slip into a mutually supportive team. Those roles are a comfortable place. But they're also a mask, a place in which both of us have hidden our truth from the other.

Instead of truth, we've had desire.

We've avoided the secrets between us in the bliss of being naked and entwined, lost amid an all-consuming sea.

A bolt of longing hits me right in the abdomen, so fierce I shift uneasily again. I want to lose myself in that sea again. Not later. Not after we talk. I need it now, like I need to breathe. But Mickey's sleeping form in the back seat isn't the only reason that's a bad idea. Something tells me that the time apart has dug a gulf that will take more than just sex to breach.

But Christ, it would be a good start.

It's almost a relief when Darya breaks the silence. "Masha is six." She speaks quietly, almost to herself. "I was still in the compound when Inger and Vilnus were together. Not that I knew anything about his social life. I wouldn't have wanted to either."

I glance at her. "Do you think the two things are linked?"

"I don't know how they could be, if Vilnus only recently found out your real name." She shakes her head. "But it's a strange coincidence. Strange to think our lives were linked back then, even indirectly."

I don't argue with that. I've had exactly the same thoughts.

She sucks her lips in and exhales slowly. "And you never guessed that Ofelia was . . . yours."

There's a slight catch in her voice. I hunch over the steering wheel, unsure of how to answer her. What I really want to say is that the only time I've ever even let myself imagine having children was very recently—with Darya. And even then, I never really believed it could happen for me.

But I can't pretend that learning Ofelia is my daughter doesn't mean anything to me.

As for whether or not I suspected . . . I don't know how to answer that either. I'm scared that anything I do say will drive Darya even further away than I already have, and that is something I don't even want to contemplate. I'm still wondering how to answer when she speaks again.

"Are you . . . happy? Knowing she's your daughter? That you're a—a father?" Her voice trembles. She's looking out the window, her arms folded over her body in an almost protective gesture, as if she's trying to defend herself from some unseen attack.

"Right now, I'm just focused on getting both of the girls home." Unwilling to say anything that might hurt her more than I already have, I avoid the question. "I need to work out how to put the Orlovs down for good."

She shakes her head, still staring out the window. "I know Vilnus Orlov. He's a piece of shit, but he doesn't do anything by chance."

The uncharacteristic bitterness in her voice makes me wince. It reminds me of all she endured before I met her, which in turn makes me savagely terrified at the thought of Ofelia and Masha in Vilnus's hands now.

"Until you know exactly what he is playing at, you can't just go in there with guns blazing. He'll be expecting that."

I might have promised Dimitry that I will hear her out before making an action plan, but her doubt pisses me off. Not least because going in guns blazing is almost precisely what I'm about to order Makari Tereschenko to do.

"When it comes to war," I say stiffly, "I know what I'm doing, Darya."

She gives a silent huff of humorless laughter. "And when it comes to the Orlovs," she says quietly, "I know them better than anyone. I can't make you take my advice. But if you really want to put the girls' safety first, then you'll get all the facts before you do anything. If I learned anything from the years he held me, it's that Vilnus is one of the most ruthless men I've ever met. His allies are even more ruthless. And cunning."

She meets my eyes, and in the headlights of an oncoming car, I see the fathomless depths of old pain in hers. "I know how dangerous you are, Roman. But the difference between you and Vilnus is that Vilnus won't hesitate to kill the girls, even if you give him what he wants. Not even if Masha is his daughter. He is a man without honor, without heart. He betrayed my father, killed my mother, and I've watched him murder his own blood when they've disappointed him. Vilnus *enjoys* inflicting pain."

For a moment I'm standing outside my father's house again, watching Vilnus carve my father's flesh into pieces as he screams in agony. I flinch. "I know what Vilnus is capable of," I say roughly.

She nods slowly. "I know that he killed your parents, Roman. But knowing it is one thing. I lived it. Every day for years, I lived with his knives and his sadism. And believe me when I tell you this, Roman: whatever cruelty you're capable of, Vilnus can do twice over, without blinking."

12

OFELIA

"Eat." Alexei pushes the tray toward us with his foot.

"I'm not hungry." I huddle against the wall, holding Masha close.

The door behind Alexei opens, and Vilnus Orlov glares at us across the small room. "My dog told you to eat. Do as he says, or I'll let him play with that knife he loves so much."

I shudder and take a bread roll from the tray, nibbling the edge of it. Masha takes a bunch of grapes. She eats obediently, as she has with anything else Alexei has put in front of her. Masha has gradually thawed to Alexei over the few days we've been here, not that I really understand why. He never speaks, except to give us orders, and he rarely moves at all from his station in the corner of our cell, not even to sleep. The only times we have left the room is when Alexei has taken us to use the bathroom across the corridor. At least we've been able to wash in the sink there and been given fresh underwear. No clothing change, though. I'm pretty sure Vilnus plans to make us look as rough as possible for whatever ransom video he plans to make.

Apart from a few short breaks when he's used the same sink to wash or to change his clothes, Alexei hasn't left us alone for a moment.

He has, however, used his knife.

More than once.

I shift slightly and try not to wince. The cuts Alexei made are shallow, but they still sting. They're under my armpits.

"Cut her where the marks won't show," Orlov said. His voice comes through a speaker on the wall most days, but I know he's watching us from behind the smoked glass on the wall. The wounds bled a lot when Alexei made them, but oddly, I barely felt them at the time. I have an uncomfortable suspicion that he knows exactly where to cut for maximum blood and minimum pain.

I don't like to think about how a man might learn skills like that.

Masha, of course, believes it is a game. Which is why I have to pretend the cuts don't hurt and that the blood is fake.

A guard appears at the door and murmurs something in Vilnus's ear. He smiles, the unpleasant, leering smile I've come to dread, and nods. "Bring them here," he orders, and the guard disappears.

"Well, Ofelia." Vilnus's piggish eyes roam over my torn dress, lingering on my almost entirely exposed breasts. "It seems you're about to have some visitors."

In the corner, I notice Alexei stiffening.

It's an odd distinction, given that he barely moves at all. Being so close to him for so long, though, I've started noticing the smallest changes in him. The way his face shuts down before he cuts me, for example, his fierce blue eye going strangely dull, as if part of himself has disappeared. Or how gently he hands Masha the food he seems to know she will like the most. How he changes the instant one of Orlov's guards opens the door, becoming weirdly invisible, so it seems like they don't even notice him.

And then there are moments like now, when every muscle in his body seems drawn tight, like my piano strings when they're freshly tuned. He does this any time Vilnus Orlov or one of the guards is in the room. This time, he seems particularly tense, as if he can sense that what is coming is bad.

Which makes me more nervous than I've been since we got here, and that's saying something.

"Where are you taking us?" The voice is loud and injured—and I'd recognize that whining, childish tone anywhere.

A moment later, Uncle Nicky stumbles into the doorway.

He's still dressed in the tuxedo he was wearing at the ball. His eyes are red rimmed and exhausted, and there's dried blood from a blow someone has given him to the side of his head. His hands are cuffed behind his back, and he looks dirty and disheveled.

He glances at me briefly, then his eyes slide away and fix on Masha. "I want my daughter."

Oh, no.

Suddenly it's all starting to make sense.

Uncle Nicky thinks Masha is *his* daughter.

That's why he took photographs of her. And why he helped kidnap her.

Not that it explains why he'd want to take me as well. It isn't like Nikolai has ever even liked me.

But there's clearly something going on that I don't understand.

I've been trying to make sense of Vilnus's comments about daughters ever since we've been in this room. Some of them make sense now, but not all. I can hardly ask Alexei what they mean, not without upsetting Masha. It wouldn't make any difference if I did.

Like I said, Alexei doesn't speak.

Vilnus sneers at Nikolai. "No wonder Borovsky never trusted you with anything more than that pathetic nightclub."

Borovsky. That name again.

"You really are the dumbest Stevanovsky, aren't you, Nikolai?" Vilnus puts his face close to Nikolai's. "Masha isn't your daughter, Nikolai. She's mine."

Masha looks up from her grapes, frowning. "What that mean, 'Felia?"

"Nothing, *myshka*," I murmur, tucking her head against me and praying she can't feel the frantic pace of my heartbeat. "They're just talking, that's all."

"Bullshit." Nikolai turns his head over his shoulder. "Inger, tell him the truth."

Inger?

Mama is here?

I want to call out to her, but my voice feels strangled in my throat. Everything is strange, and none of it makes sense. If Mama and Nikolai helped kidnap us, why is Nikolai bleeding?

Then Inger stumbles into view.

She, too, is still wearing her ballgown. And just like mine, it's ripped and dirty. Her hair is a mess, and there's dirt on her face. She's looking around in confusion, and she's clearly not here willingly.

Just like that, all my suspicions about her disappear.

She's my mother, after all.

"My babies!" She lunges toward us, bursting into tears. A guard wrenches her brutally back, and she cries out in pain. He covers her mouth with his hand.

"Mama!" I jump to my feet, reaching for her. In an instant Alexei is on me, his hands binding me like steel clasps.

"No!" Masha clings to me, staring up at Alexei. "Let her *go!*"

Alexei looks down at her, his back to Orlov.

Pretend, he mouths.

Masha's eyes widen. Then, to my surprise, she stops struggling.

Uncle Nicky turns to Vilnus. "You're making a big mistake, Orlov. Roman is going to kill you when he comes for us." But he sounds more desperate than strong, and Vilnus just laughs.

I hate Vilnus's laugh as much as I hate his smile. Both are fake, and his mean eyes never change.

"Oh," he sneers, "you'll see Roman long before he comes for me. You're going to send him a little message for me, Nikolai. But first, let's get the truth out there, shall we? It's about time these girls learned who they belong to." He turns to Inger. "My guard is going to take his hand off your mouth. If you scream, if you say a single word except to answer my questions, I'll tell Alexei here to use his knife on you, like he has on your daughter." Mama's eyes widen in horror. She nods mutely, and the guard takes his hand off her mouth.

"Now," Vilnus says conversationally. "Why don't you tell Nikolai here who Masha's daddy is? The truth, now, Inger. It's too late for lies."

Her eyes dart left and right, as if she's searching for an escape. All of a sudden, I'm back in the summer when I was ten years old, on Deda Yuri's yacht, listening to her and Uncle Nikolai fight.

"WHY ARE THERE paparazzi photos of Vilnus Orlov with his hands all over your body?"

"It's none of your business who I go out with! You don't own me, Nikolai!" Inger's voice is shrill.

"Oh, so you can just fuck who you want now, Inger? What do you think my brother will say about that?"

"Don't pretend you care about Mikhail!" Something smashes

against the deck. "Or me! You only ever wanted me to spite your brother—"

"That's not true! I love you, Inger. I've always loved you."

"Well, I don't love you!" Her shrieking makes me shudder. I want to put my hands over my ears, but I can't seem to stop listening. Even Mickey is sitting up in bed, his face pale. "Vilnus Orlov has known me since I met your father. He's an old family friend. He's like a father to me."

"Oh, sure." Nikolai's tone is scathing. "An old family friend who just happens to have his hands on your ass. You can go to hell, Inger. And you better believe I'll be telling Mikhail about this—"

"No, please, don't do that." She begins to sob loudly. "I never should have left Mikhail. I love him. I'm going to ask him to take me back."

"You're unbelievable." Uncle Nicky's voice is fading. I look out the small window in my room and see him standing in the small tender we use to get to shore. He looks angrier than I've ever seen him. "Fuck you, Inger. Screw Vilnus Orlov as much as you want. I don't care anymore."

"YOU'RE MASHA'S FATHER." I stare at Vilnus Orlov, mentally matching his face to the paparazzi shots I poured over on the yacht. "You and Mama had an affair, the summer we were on Deda Yuri's yacht. I remember your face from the paparazzi photos."

He smiles, that horrible, oily smile that makes me feel sick. "See, Nikolai? Even the Borovsky bitch is smarter than you."

Borovsky bitch?

Nikolai pales, staring at Inger. "You swore to me Masha was mine."

She faces him, pale and shaking. "I thought she was, Nicky!"

But I know my mother. I've watched her lie before. I know the telltale signs, the darting eyes, the way she bites her lip.

She knew.

What else is she keeping secret from me?

The Borovsky bitch . . .

"Mama."

Inger's eyes swivel to me. Despite where we currently are, despite Alexei's arms locked around me like a vise, the whole world seems to slip away, so there is only Mama and me.

"Why is he calling me a Borovsky bitch? Who is Borovsky?"

"Ofelia." Mama's eyes are wide, her tone pleading. "Please. It was all a long time ago. I didn't know—"

"Yes, you did."

It's Nikolai who interrupts. He's staring at Inger as if he's seeing her for the first time and doesn't at all like what he sees.

"You knew Roman was Ofelia's father, and still you let Mikhail believe the baby was his." He says it slowly, like he's just putting the pieces together in his head.

Wait.

Roman is my father?

The room swims in and out of focus, the fabric of my world coming unstitched, then reforming in a new, unfamiliar pattern.

If that's true, then why are they calling me a Borovsky bitch?

Roman's name is Stevanovsky.

None of this is making a single bit of sense.

"I bet that happened the first time you saw our yacht, didn't it, Inger?"

The world snaps back into focus as Nikolai stares accusingly at Inger.

"Roman was just a street kid with nothing. Why would you take him when you could have the Stevanovsky fortune? I bet you dumped him so fucking fast he didn't know what had hit him."

Inger looks defensively between Nikolai and me.

But she doesn't deny it.

She doesn't even look guilty.

"And look who's finally joined the party!" Vilnus claps Nikolai on the shoulder, grinning like this is the funniest thing he's watched in years. "Glad you finally caught up, little Stevanovsky. Now, why don't you finish the story and tell Ofelia why all this matters so much?"

Nikolai scowls and turns away from Inger to look at me. "Roman's real family name is Borovsky," he mutters*Borovsky. Not Stevanovsky.* I'm still reeling. *But so what?* The name means nothing to me.

Roman is my father.

Roman Borovsky *is my father.*

"Oh, come on now, Nikolai. Tell her the rest." Vilnus is still grinning.

Nikolai casts him a resentful glance. "Roman's father built a vault here, years ago. For Darya's—Lucia's, that is—father. Vilnus wants to open it, but he needs Roman and Darya to do it. That's why he took you, to blackmail Roman." He looks at Vilnus. "That's right, isn't it?"

"Among other things." Vilnus's smile fades, the mean eyes settling on me. "I need your father to come here, Ofelia. The Petrovsky slut, too. Then, with my tame dog here"—he nods at Alexei—"they can open the vault, and I will finally get what I'm owed. But for that to happen, I need everyone to play their parts just right. And that means that our friend Borovsky needs to understand what will happen if he tries anything." His eyes flicker coldly to Inger. "And your mother needs to understand that she's only alive as long as I get what I want—and so are her daughters."

He nods at Alexei. In a sudden, lethal rush, I'm on my back, Alexei looming over me.

"No!" Inger screams.

"Spread her legs," Vilnus orders, and the sudden excitement in his voice makes me want to vomit. "Show me if she likes the knife as much as Darya did."

There's a sickening tear, and my dress falls open from groin to floor. The tip of Alexei's knife, cold and dangerous, slides beneath the thin fabric of my underwear, slicing it away at the hip. His boot hooks under my knee and pushes it slowly outward, then the other knee, exposing me to the whole room.

I want to close my eyes in shame. I don't want to see Vilnus and his guards staring eagerly between my legs, any more than I want to see the way Uncle Nicky's eyes slide sideways then back again, as if he just can't help but take a look, or Mama's pale face, staring accusingly at Vilnus.

"*Look at me.*" Alexei's voice is barely a whisper, a breath pushed through his lips, inaudible to anyone but me. I glance sideways. Masha is watching me, her face frozen in terror.

Alexei moves subtly, his body hiding my face from the group at the door. I hold Masha's eyes with my own and force myself to smile.

Pretend, I mouth.

Masha's eyes dart to Alexei. He gives her the tiniest of nods, and to my relief, the acute fear fades from her face. Suddenly she bursts into a fit of hiccuping tears, drawing the attention of all the watchers at the door.

If I hadn't seen her pull the same trick with at least a dozen nannies, even I would buy it.

"*Don't move,*" Alexei breathes under the cover of her tears.

I look up at him.

His eye hasn't gone dull, like it normally does when Vilnus makes him take a knife to me. Instead it blazes a furious, intense blue, boring fiercely into my own. Strangely, the intensity isn't frightening. It's strengthening, like being injected with some vital force that makes my blood thrum through my body. His hand slides up my thigh, higher and higher, so close to the most intimate part of me that I can barely breathe, then halts. I feel the chill touch of the blade, right at the juncture of my thigh.

"*Trust me,*" he breathes.

The flat of the blade presses against my outer folds, a strange, cold pressure that makes me suck in my breath. His eye holds my own, and I bite my lip as the point pricks my skin.

"*Scream.*"

I do, a high-pitched shriek that fills the room and somehow manages to override the pain as Alexei's knife slices the join of my thigh in a lightning flash of pain.

It's only when he steps away that I feel the sudden rush of blood down my thigh and see the sickening fascination on the faces of the watching men.

I shrink back against the wall, wincing as I fold my legs, trying to tuck the remains of my dress around them. Masha runs to me, and we clutch each other close.

"That's enough." Inger's voice is shrill.

"Oh, no, it isn't," says Vilnus silkily. "Nikolai is here to send a message, remember? Let's give him something to take back to Roman. A little memento, something to prove that we mean what we say."

Nikolai struggles against the arms holding him. "Don't you dare cut her again—"

"As you wish, Nikolai." Vilnus nods at the guard holding Inger, smiling unpleasantly. "Her, then."

The guard pushes Inger into the room, covering her mouth with his hand. Alexei moves forward, wiping my blood from the blade with a cloth.

"A finger is all we need, I think, Alexei." Vilnus's eyes flash with excitement. "Given Inger's history of infidelity, let's make it the wedding ring finger, shall we?" He kicks a chair toward the guard, who forces Inger down so her hand is splayed on it.

Alexei moves over to the chair, positioning himself so she's blocked from Masha's and my view.

"Leave her alone!" Nikolai roars. "Inger!"

"Aw, look at that." Vilnus's smile widens. "Even now, he still seems to care what happens to you. I guess that's what happens when you're a boy's first love. You picked the wrong brother, Inger. You'd have had this one following you around like a puppy forever."

"Nicky!" Inger shrieks, struggling in vain against the guard as Alexei grips her hand. "No, Vilnus, you can't do this!"

His smile doesn't falter. "Oh, but I can, Inger. And so much worse." He nods at Alexei.

I don't see the cut of the blade.

But the sound of it slicing through flesh and bone is a sound I will remember for the rest of my life.

As is my mother's scream.

13

DARYA

Roman doesn't speak for the rest of the way back to Malaga.

I know I've insulted him by implying that he's underestimating Vilnus. Maybe, if I'm honest, I wanted to insult him.

It's not fair. It's not rational. But knowing that Roman is already a father has shaken me more than I knew it could.

Not because I'm jealous, or envious of his relationship with Ofelia. Nothing could be any further from the truth. If anything, I'm thrilled for Ofelia that she has a living father, particularly one of Roman's caliber. In some unconscious part of myself, I'm not even entirely surprised.

Of all the children, Ofelia has always resembled Roman the most. Particularly in her nature, the way she intuitively protects her siblings. More than once, I've had my breath taken away by the opaque expression that is so much like Roman's, when she tucks her emotions away in some deep part inside her. It breaks my heart that they have been deprived of one another all these years, denied the relationship they both deserve.

No. It's not Ofelia's paternity that upsets me.

It's the way Roman talks about it.

He's entirely dispassionate, as if it's a story that happened to someone else. Not once has he expressed any emotion about the relationship or given any indication that he is excited—or even moved—by the discovery. He avoids any question related to how he feels about being a father, and it doesn't take a genius to see that he's telling me barely the beginning of the situation with Inger.

I despise Inger, not just for what she's done now with her own children, but long before that, for the many ways she let them down and used them for her own ends. I loathe her even more for depriving Roman of his daughter, and Ofelia of her father, for so long.

I know Roman can be an incredible father. Just watching the way he's opened up to the children over the past months is proof enough that he has the capacity to love and protect them, to be the father they need.

But is that simply because he's one step removed, a godfather who is legally responsible for them? Now that he knows he is Ofelia's father, will he suddenly change, put a distance between himself and her? I know better than anyone how hard it is for Roman to allow himself to care, to open up. Given how hard it has been for him to express emotion to me, how much more will he fear exposing himself and his heart to his own child?

And what about the baby inside me?

Will he be willing to take that next step, to be all our child needs him to be?

We've never even discussed marriage, let alone children. And given the way Roman has reacted to the news of Ofelia being his daughter, I'm not at all certain how he's going to react to my news.

Either way, now certainly isn't the time to tell him about it. Until we have the girls back, my news will have to wait.

I settle back into my seat, staring out the window, trying my hardest not to tremble at the thought of Ofelia in Vilnus Orlov's hands.

The thought makes me physically sick with fear.

I meant what I said to Roman, insulting as he might have found it. Nobody knows what Vilnus Orlov is capable of more than I do. Not even my father or brother know the depths of his depravity.

I close my eyes, trying to sleep, to push the nightmare memories down to the place I've kept them for years. I don't want to remember, but the news of the girls' capture seems to have opened the floodgates to the past. The images rise despite my will, sickening and close enough to smell on the late-night air.

"You should be engaged by now, Darya."

It's past midnight, and I'm alone in my room. The guards on my door belong to Vilnus and stand aside without question when he comes on these late-night visits.

Since I turned twenty-one a month ago, the visits have been happening more and more often.

"There are plenty of men who'd pay handsomely to marry Sergei Petrovsky's daughter." Vilnus eyes my body greedily. I wear thick flannel pajamas even in the Miami heat, precisely because of these visits. "We need to take you shopping. Such a beautiful body shouldn't

be covered up by those ugly pajamas. You need a man to teach you how to show it off."

His pudgy hand darts out, squeezing one of my breasts with sudden force. I bite down on my cry of pain, trying not to react. This is the game we play, where he tries to get a reaction, and I do all I can to deny him even the slightest flinch at his touch. Four years in his captivity have taught me about his obsession with inflicting pain, the way his eyes get feverish with excitement when he senses fear.

"If you and your brother would just open that vault, all this unpleasantness would be at an end. I could marry you off to a nice man, one who would give you children, a nice home. I could even marry you myself. Keep you here, in your own home. You would be a queen, Darya. Together we would rule Miami."

His hand tightens brutally on my breast. I swallow my gag reflex. This is another one of his favorite games. I don't know if he honestly believes in the sick fantasy he conjures up or whether it's just another way to torture and intimidate me.

Either way, it's terrifying.

"You think I wouldn't do it, don't you?" His eyes narrow to gleaming, predatory slits. "You think that because I'm fifty with a wife and children, you're safe. Well, a wife is easily disposed of. Mine has bored me for years. I don't enjoy fucking her anymore, if I ever really did. Not as much as I'd enjoy fucking you. And I would enjoy that, Darya. You would, too, believe me. I know how to make a woman scream.

"One bullet, and my wife is gone. As for children—well. My daughters have already been broken in. I did that myself, Darya. I'm not letting any man take what's mine by blood. I took them both after they first bled. Taught them how to please a man. Tell me, why I shouldn't do the same with you?"

I force myself to meet his eyes, to pretend his words don't fill me with revulsion and terror. "You won't do it to me because you know I'm too valuable."

Pretend I'm unafraid. Pretend I believe my own words.

"Your daughters don't hold the key to a fortune. I do." I force myself to stare him down. "And if you ever try to do to me what you did to your own flesh and blood, you won't ever get what you really want. Because you don't actually care about my body, do you, Vilnus? The only thing you care about is what is inside that vault. And I promise you this: if you force me into your bed, that vault door will remain closed to you forever. I swear it on my own life."

"Then tell me!" He yanks me toward him, pulling my face close enough to his that his spit sprays me when he speaks. "Tell me how to open it, Darya."

"I've told you. I can't open it. I don't even remember my fingerprints being taken. It was all done when I was a baby. All I know is that it takes three sets. I didn't even know that much, or who the third set belonged to, until you told me. I've told you a thousand times that I don't know how that vault works. Neither does my brother. And if my father knew, he would have told you by now."

"Then tell me why I shouldn't fuck you bloody!"

"Because you know that my fingerprints are one of the keys." I hold up my hands, rippling my fingertips. "I'll cut them off myself, Vilnus. I've told you already that I'll do it, if you force me. I might not know where this Borovsky boy is, but I do know that even if you find him, you still need Alexei and me to open it. Lose me, and you won't ever breach that door."

His breath stinks of cigarettes and alcohol, and his fingers dig into my breast hard enough to leave bruises even through the thick material. But after a moment, and a particularly vicious squeeze, he thrusts me away from him.

"I'll fuck you one day," he mutters, stumbling toward the door. "I'll fuck you until you know how little girls should scream for their men."

I lie awake for the rest of the night, trembling with fear, wondering how long I will survive before his patience runs out.

———

I JOLT to consciousness with a sickening lurch. I must have cried out, because Roman is staring at me.

"I'm fine." I push myself up in the seat, rubbing my face. I've clearly slept, because we're in the underground garage beneath the penthouse. Roman's phone lights up as he turns the engine off. He punches the answer button.

"*Da.*"

He listens intently for a few moments. "No," he says decisively. "It's only a few hours until dawn. You need to get some rest, Pavel, same with your team. I'm waiting for a call from someone, so I won't act before then anyway. None of us have slept in days. We know where the girls are. For tonight, there's nothing more we can do. Leave a team to keep trying to hack the security cameras on the compound, and make sure everyone else gets their heads down. We'll meet at the lab first thing in the morning."

Mickey sits up, rubbing his eyes and frowning. "Is that Pavel?" He reaches for the phone. "I need to talk to him—"

Roman hits the end call button and glares at him over the headrest. "You're going to get into that elevator, go to your apartment, and go to bed. Nobody, not even you, can work without sleep. I want your word that laptop will stay closed until you've had your head down for at least a few hours, or I'll fucking take it myself. Am I clear?"

"Fine." Mickey casts him a resentful glance. "But you have to promise to wake me if anything happens."

"If anything happens, you'll be the first to know."

"Hm." Mickey gives him a rather hard look, then switches his eyes to me. His face softens. "I'm glad you're home," he says quietly.

"Me too." I touch his arm and he gets out of the car, giving us both a half wave with his back turned as he gets into the elevator.

"That boy gives me more grief than the entire squad of tech

heads," Roman mutters, shaking his head. Despite all that's happened, I find myself half smiling. There's an exasperated familiarity in his exchange with Mickey, something oddly touching in the way he casts his eyes skyward and rubs a crease on his forehead as he speaks. I can hear the pride behind his words.

The paternal pride.

I swallow hard on the sudden rush of emotion.

Roman still thinks he has a choice about whether or not to be a father, but that choice was gone long ago.

The kids have chosen him. They chose him months ago, just like I did.

Roman is already a father. Not just to Ofelia. To all three of his godchildren.

He just hasn't really grasped it yet.

His long body uncurls as he steps out of the car and walks around to open my door. I force myself not to shiver as he takes my hand to help me out. I feel almost blindsided by longing for him, and guilty for wanting anything when he is so clearly devastated and exhausted. Some primal part of myself needs to feel him deep inside me again, to reassure myself that we are still us, even if our world has gone to hell. I want to crawl inside his body, to be skin to skin and mouth to mouth, lost and found as only he makes me feel.

But he drops my hand as soon as he takes it and stands a good foot away from me when we enter his private elevator. He hits the button for my floor, and I chastise myself for feeling disappointed.

Of course he's shattered.

It's selfish, not to mention childish, to want anything more from him amid the crisis we are living.

I fold my arms over my body again, the cold terror of the girls' absence like a hollow darkness inside me. Roman is a warrior, first and foremost. There will be time for us again, perhaps, when all this is over.

The elevator pulls to a halt at my floor, and the doors open. I stand dumbly, suddenly frozen in place.

Do I kiss him goodbye? Just say something like "see you tomorrow?"

What exactly is the protocol for saying good night to a man with whom you've shared the most intimate of moments, but who right now feels a million miles away?

"Darya." It's only one word, wrenched from him like pulling a rusted bolt from old wood, but the need in it tells me all I need to know.

I turn as he's reaching for me, and by the time he's punched the button for his penthouse, his mouth is on mine and I'm already lost.

———————

THE DOORS HAVE OPENED and closed multiple times on the penthouse floor when he finally breaks the kiss, but it's only so he can pick me up and carry me down the corridor. He pulls my headscarf off and drops it to the floor.

"I've wanted to do this from the moment I saw you." He tugs out the pins holding my hair, and it tumbles down. "I need you," he says hoarsely into my hair. "I need this."

I touch his face with my hand. "Me, too."

He carries me straight to the bathroom. "It's been the longest day of a hellishly long week." He turns the shower on as he begins to undress me. "I need to wash it off, and I need you here."

I want to be here. I want to stand under the tumbling jets and inhale the familiar citrus scent of the soap he uses, want to trace every scarred line of his body and make it mine once more. The warm water feels like healing, easing the weariness in my bones and the deep pain in my soul.

"I thought I'd lost you." His lips trace my collarbone as one soapy hand slides over my shoulder and down my spine, pressing my naked body toward his. "I never want to feel that way again, Darya."

I don't want to talk. Words feel too hard, too complex. I run my hands over the achingly familiar lines of his body, feeling the corded muscle in his neck tense, the hard globes of his ass clench under my touch. He's hot and hard, his need a throbbing urgency against my skin, but his hands on me are unbearably gentle. They stroke downward over my swollen breasts. "Christ." His voice cracks as he cups their new fullness. "The feel of you, Darya . . ."

His lips close over my nipple, and I give a sharp cry, my entire body reduced to that lone point. I arch into his mouth, my newly sensitized flesh enflamed by every touch of his tongue, heat licking through my body like a wildfire taking hold. I spread my legs and straddle his thigh, pressing my throbbing center against him. I ride his thigh hard as he takes one nipple after the other, careening toward orgasm like an out-of-control freight train. I grasp his cock and he groans, his shaft surging in my hand.

My head falls back against the tiles. "Get inside me," I gasp.

"No." He pulls me against him and takes my mouth again. "I don't want to rush this, Darya. I want you to know how much I—"

I hold his face. "I need you to fuck me." My body is a frenzied, turbulent mass of desire. I can barely get the words out. My hands slide back to his cock, gripping him hard enough to make him suck in his breath. He pulls back from me, eyes dark, lips pressed together as he fights for control.

"I should make this last," he rasps.

But the hollow loneliness of the past days, combined with

the passionate relief of having him naked in my embrace, has spawned a lust so potent it's almost savage.

I don't want to play.

I don't want a game.

I just want him, fast and hard.

I tug him toward me, one hand slipping underneath him to cup his balls. "Fuck that," I whisper in his ear.

Whatever thin line of control was holding him snaps. He pulls me up, his hands under my ass, my legs wrapped around him. He spins out of the shower and carries us into the bedroom, our mouths hot against each other's skin, devouring every inch like souls lost in the desert discovering water once more. His cock is a searing rod against my clit, and I'm bucking against him, grinding my body into his as his mouth marks my neck and breasts, his tongue teasing my nipples as his palm rests under my opening. He groans aloud as he feels the slick wetness seeping from me. His fingers dip inside and I clench around them, the first tremors of orgasm already twitching inside me.

"Fuck, Darya." His hands spread my opening wider, and his clever fingers drive inside me, but it isn't enough. It isn't even close to being enough.

I thrust down against his cock. "I need this. I need you."

He throws me down on the bed, and I spread my legs wide, arching my hips toward him. He enters me with a savage thrust. I revel in the hoarse cry he can't bite back, feeling an almost primal triumph as he fills me. My body feels unbearably full, as if every nerve is heightened. Each thrust opens me further, my body swelling and pulsing as he goes deeper and deeper. The orgasm that has been threatening since the moment he touched me is hovering on the edge, growing to such intense pressure that I angle my hips up, desperate for release.

He groans and his hands go under my ass, lifting me to the right angle as he drives right into me, hitting the places deep inside me that take me into orbit.

I scream and he surges home, roaring as he feels me exploding around him. His orgasm bursts into a hot, urgent stream inside me, and his mouth owns mine, our bodies rippling together as the mind-shattering release takes us both.

I WAKE BARELY an hour later to find him fresh from the shower. He's dressing in the corner, his back to me. A pale dawn threads across the horizon, but the day is still distant.

"You need sleep." I prop myself up in the bed, rubbing my eyes. My body is heavy with lethargy, the nausea that is fast becoming a daily trial churning uneasily in my gut.

"I need to get the girls back." He turns and crosses the room to the bed, one hand cupping my chin, his thumb stroking my cheekbone. The grim lines of his face soften momentarily, but not the dark shadows in his eyes. "I can't sleep, Darya. I can barely breathe."

He cuts off abruptly, pulling his hand back and inhaling sharply as he fights for control. "I have a friend." His voice is rough with exhaustion. "Makari Tereschenko. He's a . . . colleague, on the project I told you about. He owes me a favor. He has an army, Darya."

I sit up, tucking the sheet around me, trying to make my befuddled mind work properly. "An army?" Something about the slight emphasis on the word makes me think he isn't just talking about any normal security detail.

"I don't mean *vor*." He reaches for his cuff links. "Mak runs the biggest private mercenary force in the world. He commands missiles, tanks, weaponry—enough to overturn multiple countries. I contacted his people several days ago. I just received a message that he's available for a meeting. I'm heading to the lab so we can talk on a secure line."

My nausea flees, replaced by a cold, stark wash of terror.

"Didn't you hear me yesterday? You can't go in there with guns blazing, Roman."

He clips a cuff link into place and frowns at me. "Actually, I fucking can. More guns than Vilnus Orlov has any hope of fighting back against."

"No." I swing my legs over the side of the bed, swaying as I try to gather myself. "You don't know him like I do, Roman. He'll be expecting this." I rub my eyes.

"Darya, please." He sits down on the bed, his hands gentle on my shoulders. "I need you to rest, and I want you to trust me. I heard you yesterday. Now you need to listen to me. I'd never do anything to endanger the girls, and that includes launching a war before I have all the facts. But I have to get the pieces in place, get ready for the moment when we *are* ready."

"What about the vault?" I press my cheek against his hand. "Vilnus will contact you about that, and soon. What are you going to tell him? We need to speak to my father, to find out what he knows—"

Roman's face tightens. "I think it's better that we leave your father out of this."

The hard, measured tone and suddenly glacial expression tell me more than his words need to.

I cover the hand holding mine with my other one. "Please, Roman, listen to me. I know you have every reason to hate my father. I'm not happy with him myself right now."

His brow creases at that, a flash of surprise in his dark eyes.

"Do you think my father has told me all his secrets?" I shake my head wearily. "Sergei Petrovsky isn't one for confidences, Roman. And he's traditional. I'm his daughter, not his son. It might have been me running with him all these years, but even now, it seems Alexei knows more than I do." It's hard to keep the bitterness from my tone. "Alexei booked a ticket for me using the name on my new passport. That name, and the passport, was a secret known only to Papa, me, and a contact of

Papa's whose name not even I know. Alexei has clearly been talking to Papa."

The fact that my father and brother have been making plans behind my back doesn't just hurt.

It fucking pisses me off.

I've grown up in a world where men are the protectors. In the normal course of events, Roman wouldn't even be having this conversation with me. He'd be acting, while I sat here and wrung my hands.

But I've had six years of being forced into decisions, of facing danger.

I'm not about to be put back on the sidelines again.

"It isn't a question of trusting you." I hold his hand, meeting his eyes directly. "It's a question of you trusting *me*. I know you're more than a match for Vilnus Orlov, Roman. But you need to stop seeing me as someone you have to protect and start seeing me as a resource, someone who has knowledge that can help you."

I'm fighting to keep my voice steady and even. So much rides on this discussion, on Roman's ability to be a different man than those among whom he was raised.

"We come from a world where women stay in the background. Do as they're told, accept that men will take care of business." I hold his eyes. "But how did that work for my mother? For yours? Would things have been different if our fathers had listened to them? I'm not asking you to put me in danger, Roman, or to make me part of your business. But I spent years locked up in that compound with the Orlovs. Any plan you make will be better if you include me in it."

I see the emotions warring in his eyes, and I understand them. Roman is a warrior. Even admitting he might have a vulnerability is difficult. Accepting help from a woman he believes is his job to protect is entirely counterintuitive.

But I'm long past diplomacy or playing the victim. I've seen too much.

I squeeze his hand, holding his eyes. "I don't want to say things that will cause you pain." He frowns, and I go on in the same low, steady tone. "But you need to know that Vilnus Orlov plays games, Roman. He played them with my mother, until he killed her. He played them with me until I almost lost my mind. He plays games with women—and girls—that he hides from others, even from his own men."

I see the horrified flash of understanding in Roman's eyes, the panic he can't quite hide.

I nod. "The only reason Vilnus spared me from actual rape was because he was afraid of losing his chance at the vault. But he doesn't need to protect Ofelia in the same way. He knows you're going to come for her, but there's no chance he's going to allow you to take his only leverage, no matter how hard you come at him. He will do everything in his power to hide them from you. And believe me, Roman—it is Ofelia who will pay for any mistakes you make. She will pay in ways no man ever has to, and she will pay over and over, until Vilnus gets exactly what he wants."

Roman is staring over my shoulder, his eyes blazing, mouth set in a thin line. "I'll kill the bastard."

"I know you will." My immediate answer, and the fierce rage I can't hide, breaks through Roman's internal fury. "I know," I say when he meets my eyes. "But killing Vilnus won't mean a damned thing if Ofelia returns to us broken. I want him dead just as much as you do. More, perhaps." His eyes narrow at the dark edge in my voice. "But more than that, I want Ofelia returned to us unharmed. And the best way to ensure that happens is to let Vilnus think he's winning. Keep him happy until we have every fact at our disposal. Can you do that, Roman?"

His hands are stiff in mine, his eyes turbulent with barely suppressed fury, but after a time, he gives a curt nod.

"I can do that." He leans forward and kisses me, his lips lingering for a long time. "I suppose," he says slowly when finally he pulls back, "that we had better have a conversation with your father."

I nod. "I think that would be wise."

"Fine." He stands up and moves to the door. "Set it up. I'll go to the lab, and we'll meet with him when I get back."

14

ROMAN

I ride the MTT to the lab. Luis is taking Mickey and will meet us there. There's no chance I'm leaving him out of this after our discussion yesterday.

But I need the freedom of the road to digest the past twenty-four hours. To make space for the planning that is coming.

I also know there's no chance in hell I can trust myself to hold a civilized conversation after what Darya has just told me.

What the fuck did he do to her?

I kick the engine into gear with savage force, roaring onto the highway at enough speed to make an oncoming car swerve in alarm.

The scars on Darya's back, carefully inked over, were already evidence enough that she'd suffered. Somehow, though, probably because the alternative was too dark to consider, I'd let myself believe they were a one-off incident, a warning of some kind.

The realization that Vilnus Orlov treated Darya as his own personal plaything, that he laid his hands on her body and threatened her in the most primal way a man can a woman, hardens the fury inside me to a lethal edge.

The thought of him doing the same, or even worse, to Ofelia, makes me want to wield that lethal edge with murderous insanity.

I'm going to tear that bastard to pieces with my bare hands.

Men like me take care of business. We keep our women safe. Even the thought of Darya being anywhere near the attack on the Orlovs makes me feel sick and ashamed.

And yet . . . she's already in it. She's already been not just near the situation, but further inside it than anyone else I know. She's absolutely right about having knowledge that can help. And oddly, I *want* her input. I even want her to know about Mercura and what is at stake. I want to tell her how Mickey has, in barely a matter of weeks, become an integral part of my operation. Tell her that I can see him rising to take it over one day.

I roar out of the city and onto the mountain curves, leaning into every one, pushing my body and the bike to their limits.

After the devastation of the past days I can't bear the thought of doing anything that will endanger the fragile connection between Darya and me. Despite the power of our connection, the bliss of losing myself inside her again, there's still some odd tension I can't quite put my finger on. There's something self-contained in the way she holds herself, as if her attention is focused inward on something I can't quite see. It frightens me, makes me wary. I pushed her away more savagely than most women would ever come back from. I can't help but wonder if I've lost part of her forever, if my words that night at the ball did more damage than she's prepared to admit.

I push the bike just a bit harder, wind whipping at my body. I know I'm racing from the thought of Ofelia and Masha in the hands of Vilnus Orlov. I know I'm racing from even more than that.

I haven't had time to process the DNA bombshell. Not really.

There'll be time to do that later, when the girls are safe.

That is true enough. It's certainly rational. But I'm honest enough to know it's also bullshit.

The fact that Ofelia is my daughter terrifies me. It shatters my being in a way I can't allow to happen, not when I need to focus. It raises a thousand feelings of guilt and shame that I can't face, not now, not when so much rides on my ability to remain strong.

Even if I manage to get her back safely, I can't help but wonder if Ofelia will even want to speak to me, let alone build any kind of relationship with me. God knows I've let her down in every way a father can. Worse, I have no idea if I am even capable of becoming the father she needs. The one she deserves.

Fuck. If the MTT goes any faster, it will fly off the edge of the mountain.

That doesn't stop me from trying.

I ARRIVE at the lab to intense activity and Mickey frowning at me over his screen.

"Darya should be here."

"Next time." I force a smile. "She's exhausted. She needs to rest." He subsides, but the look in his eyes tells me it's a temporary reprieve. The days of Mickey taking orders without question are definitely gone.

"Pavel has set the call up in the secure room." Dimitry nods at a door leading off the main floor. "Five minutes."

I make a coffee and head in, closing the door behind me. I don't want any witnesses to this call. Not yet.

The line lights up right on time, and I answer immediately.

"You rang?" Mak's upper-crust British drawl might be responding to an invitation to lawn bowls. Fucker always sounds like he's just stepped out of Buckingham Palace.

"I need that favor." I launch in without preamble. "Vilnus Orlov has kidnapped my daughters. He's holding them in a compound in Miami, the same one that used to belong to the Petrovskys."

"Ah." In the brief pause that follows, I can hear wind roaring and a strangled yowl that sounds like Chewbacca from Star Wars.

"Jesus, Mak. Where the fuck are you?"

"Somewhere I'm not supposed to be," he says cheerfully. "Atop a sand dune, using a camel to shelter from a wind storm. Been a little occupied, or I'd have gotten back to you earlier. On the upside, I can safely assure you there's nobody in earshot."

"Sounds like fun."

"It's been a riot. But the cocktail choices are limited, and I do like a good martini. Tomorrow too late for me to get to you?"

"Yesterday was too late. But I'll take what I can get."

"Done." Mak pauses, but doesn't hang up. "If you'll allow me to give you some unwanted advice?"

I grunt assent.

"Hold off on throwing anything at that compound until we've had a chance to talk. I've learned a thing or two about Orlov over the years. Wouldn't like to see your girls caught up in anything more unpleasant than they already are."

"Be here tomorrow, and I won't have to."

"I'll see you then." He ends the call. I sit in silence for a few moments, aware that I've just taken a step into very murky territory. Mak might talk about owing me a favor, but the truth is that after this I will be in his debt. Deploying his mercenaries to fight North African coups is one thing. Using them to launch an attack in downtown Miami is quite another. Closely as he might work with the CIA and MI6, my favor will put Mak on the radar of domestic authorities, something I know he's diligent about avoiding.

Then again, I have handed Mak a slice of Mercura, and that is no inconsiderable gift.

Beyond all that, I'll pawn my own soul and count it a bargain if it means I get my girls back.

My phone lights up with a message from Dimitry: *Get out here as soon as you finish that call.*

He's right outside the door when I open it. "You're not going to fucking guess who I just spoke to."

I brace myself. "Who?"

"Nikolai." He nods slowly, wry-mouthed at my expression. "He wouldn't pass on a message, said he wants to talk to you."

My fists clench involuntarily. "And did he say where this conversation might take place? Because as far as I'm aware, the little *mudak* hasn't been seen since the night of the explosion. Which I assume means he's still carrying Inger's fucking handbag. Which in turn means that he's working with the goddamn Orlovs."

My hands are shaking by the time I've finished speaking. Nikolai is the one part of this I haven't given a second's thought to. Family or not, Nikolai is already a dead man.

The only question is when and how he dies.

Dimitry shakes his head. "Apparently he's at Pillars. Abby found him, bound and gagged and dumped in the alleyway outside. She said he's pretty banged up."

I snort. "Doesn't mean he didn't help them."

"No, it doesn't." Dimitry looks as pissed off as I feel.

"Take two cars and some good men to Pillars and pick the bastard up. He can recover from his injuries in that warehouse we used to get shipments in. Unless he's got something useful to say, I'll get to him when I'm good and fucking ready."

"Copy that." He turns away then halts, turning slowly back.

"Um. Abby," he says, color stealing up his neck. "She wants to know—"

"Darya's fine. She's at home, resting. She doesn't have a phone yet."

And I'm not sure I want her having visitors yet, at least not ones who actively helped her escape.

"Sure." Reading the warning in my eyes, Dimitry beats a hasty retreat. I get the feeling he's having a less than peaceful time of it on the domestic front, not that I give a fuck.

Abby's fortunate she has Dimitry protecting her. I might not have been quite so forgiving otherwise, no matter how many times he assures me that she was "only trying to help." Abby, in my opinion, is altogether too smart for her own good. She also seems to be strangely unconcerned about criminals, be they Russian or Colombian. Most civilians, in my experience, either run at the first sight of our business or have an unhealthy fascination with it that is equally dangerous. Abby doesn't appear to fall into either category, which is unusual at best and suspicious at worst. But she's also Dimitry's woman—and therefore his problem.

"Pavel." I come back into the main operations room, and the tech kids cast me nervous glances, all except Pavel, who is white-faced and hunched over his screen. "Where are we with the camera feed in the compound?"

"Mickey." Pavel keeps scrolling as he points three seats down, to where an equally intent Mickey is staring at another screen.

"Okay, then. Mickey." I keep a lid on my frustration with no small effort. "You want to tell me where you're at?" I know Pavel is going as hard as he can, and I know he cares about finding the girls as much as I do. Unfortunately, I also know this entire mess is my fault. Pavel and the entire team have been pulled off Mercura right when the project needs them most. To their credit, not one of them has complained. Or at least not to me.

Then again, complaining would not be a safe decision right now, something they all undoubtedly know well enough.

"See for yourself." Mickey moves slightly aside so I can look over his shoulder.

"Holy shit!" I stare at the crystal clear color feed, my spirits lifting marginally. "You're in?"

"It looks like it, doesn't it." He doesn't sound remotely triumphant. "It's a proper live feed, according to all the data. There's only one problem: there's no sign at all of the girls." He flicks through the feeds, all of which show various angles throughout the compound. The rooms are vast and opulent enough to host the haughtiest of Europe's royal families.

Christ, no wonder Darya knew how to handle the matrons at the ball. Despite my loathing of Sergei Petrovsky, it's hard not to be impressed. The compound is as lavish as any imperial Russian palace and decorated with superb taste.

But no matter how many bedroom suites Mickey zooms in on, there isn't a single trace of the girls. And while there is a clear and present security detail, it's only about half of what I'd have in Orlov's place if I were expecting an attack.

I can't help but think of Darya's warning: *"He will already have removed the girls from the compound, or he'll have hidden them someplace you don't know about."*

"What about the basement?" I lean in, scrutinizing the screens. "There's an entire underground chamber, where the vault is. Is there a feed showing that part of the compound?"

Mickey glances sideways at me, then hits another key. My gut lurches as the ornate wall of my father's vault comes into view. He zooms in, showing the intricate iron entwined over the door.

I notice a cleverly designed hatch that I immediately recognize as the hiding place for the bio sensor pad, amid a deceptive tangle of design that makes my fingers itch to explore. As devastating as our current predicament is, I can't help but admire the genius structural plan and artistry on the vast door. There's no way the Orlovs could blow that vault open, not without collapsing the entire underground structure. And not even the most sophisticated safe cracker would be able to untangle the mass of false leads my father has built into the door. The vault might contain a fortune, but the door itself is a work of art to rival anything behind it.

I clear my throat, uncomfortably aware that I've been silent for long enough to be remarkable. "Show me the rest of the feed."

Mickey tilts his head. "Not a lot to see." He flicks through the cameras, showing one bare room after another. The doors hang open. The basement rooms appear to have been unused for years. "This feed was bloody tough to get into," he adds. "They've wired it outside the main system, and it took ages to hack. They're clearly not keen on anyone seeing what's down there."

I frown, staring at the screen. "But no sign of the girls?"

Mickey shakes his head in frustration. "No," he says shortly. "Unless there are rooms hidden from view." He glances at me. "Is this all there is of the underground bunker?"

I shake my head slowly. "I don't know, Mickey. I was just a kid when my father took me there, and it was years ago. I don't know what's down there these days."

I already know what he's going to say before he opens his mouth: "Darya would know."

Yes, Darya would know.

But bringing her here means bringing her into Mercura, into the entirety of my operation. My men won't like it.

Tough.

The truth is that this is long overdue.

I look around to find most of the team casting me surreptitious glances. "Pavel," I snap.

"Boss?" His head spins around so fast it almost comes off his shoulders.

"I'm going to bring Darya here later today. Set up a private room. I don't want her in the middle of the operations center."

"Boss." He nods. "Um—are you going to tell her about—"

"That's not really any of your business, Pavel, now is it?" I glare at him until he gulps and shakes his head.

My curt tone is unfair. Pavel's question is entirely valid. So close to the hard launch, security around Mercura has never been tighter, and Pavel is responsible for maintaining the high levels of secrecy.

But the truth is, I don't like the answer any more than he does.

I need Darya's input around the compound and the Orlovs. To do that I need her to see what I am seeing, so she can explain it to me, and that means bringing her here.

The problem is that even if I want her input, I don't want her anywhere near business. I want her home, and safe. Even the thought of placing her in danger, after all we've lost, makes me feel physically sick.

"Well, I think that the sooner she's here, the better." Mickey speaks without looking at either of us. "She's the only one who's actually been inside this place." He gives me a sideways look. "Unless I count Sergei, but it doesn't seem like you're keen on involving him. And like you said, you were too young to remember."

I nod wordlessly, trying not to think of that long-ago night, of my father rolling me in a blanket and thrusting me in the back of the car when Mama was asleep.

"We've got something to do, you and I," he whispered in my ear. *"A job only you can do, Roman."* That is about all I recall of that night, apart from the odd, rubbery feel of the stuff Papa used to take an impression of my fingertips. But even that memory is

enough to throw me back there, to the clapboard house where my parents raised me.

Why were we living there, I wonder, while Sergei Petrovsky was living in a goddamn palace?

Why did my father care so much about guarding Sergei's treasures?

Even to the point where it meant losing his wife—and endangering me?

I swallow hard on the bitterness of old hurt. It has no place in the midst of this crisis. I won't allow old wounds to interfere with whatever help Sergei may be able to offer. When it comes to the compound, to getting my girls back, I'll kiss the old bastard's ring and genuflect a thousand times if it will help.

Even if all I want to do is thrust a knife through Sergei Petrovsky's lying, cowardly heart.

What pisses me off the most is that part of me had begun to actually like the prick. Had even, if I'm honest, found a certain peace in his company, an almost familial comfort.

Well, that's fucking gone.

Sergei Petrovsky is a source of information now, nothing more. And once I have that information?

I can't kill him. It would upset Darya, and I won't ever do anything that might hurt her again. But if that bastard thought he was closely guarded before, he'd better get used to cavity searches and bars on the window now. He'll live out his days with my men watching his every goddamn bowel movement, and my children nowhere near him.

15

DARYA

"*Da*."

Papa answers my call on the first ring.

"Papa." I close my eyes in relief. Some part of me I don't like to acknowledge was afraid of what Roman might have done to my father.

God knows he has good reason.

"Darya!"

I flinch at the exhausted rasp of his voice, wondering if he's slept at all since the last time we spoke.

"Don't hang up," he says hastily. "I need to speak with you—"

"I'm home, Papa." I cut him off. "With Roman."

"Oh, thank God." His relief is palpable. "When can we talk?"

"Roman has asked me to set up a meeting with you." I twist the bed sheet around my hand. "Today, if possible."

"As soon as you can." He's switched to Russian, something he rarely does on the phone and an indication of how agitated he is. "Darya, the children—the guards won't tell me anything—"

"They're gone, Papa." I wrap my hand more tightly in the sheet, watching dispassionately as my fingers turn white with blood loss. "The Orlovs took Masha and Ofelia."

"*Ya yego ub'yu.*" *I will kill him.*

He says the words in a cold, detached tone I've never heard him use, not even after he discovered that Mama was dead. He doesn't swear or rage. Just that one sentence in hard, flat Russian: *I will kill him.*

"Yes, well." As much as I share his sentiment, I'm not entirely at peace with Papa, not after reading Roman's letter. "I doubt Roman will offer you that chance."

And to be quite frank, it's a wonder it isn't you that Roman is coming after, given all you've taken from him.

Papa, for once, is silent.

"Roman is with his men now. I imagine he will return some time this afternoon. We will come to see you then." I speak in English. It's a subtle expression of my own anger. Russian is for family, for my childhood, for poetry and stories and safety.

English creates a slight degree of separation that I need just now.

My father has kept secrets. Dangerous secrets that destroyed Roman's childhood and are directly responsible for endangering Masha and Ofelia. Love him though I do, I'm not certain I'm quite ready to forgive him.

And if I feel that way, how must Roman feel?

I shudder at the iron control he will need to tolerate any kind of interaction with my father.

"Come as soon as you can." Papa delivers the words in curt Russian, hanging up before I can answer. There have been many times in my life when I've felt angry at my father's aversion to emotional expression, at the hard rein he keeps on his own emotions. Right now I'm grateful for it. I'm in no mood to pretend an affection that I don't currently feel.

My stomach lurches, and I throw off the bedsheets, making it to the bathroom just in time. I sag limply against the porcelain, my heart fluttering. I'm not certain if the morning sickness is linked to my emotions or not, but it's exhausting. I retch again, not hearing the bedroom door open.

"Ah—excuse me—I didn't know you were here." Maria, Roman's maid, hovers in the bathroom door, looking at me with concern. "You're unwell. I will call for a doctor."

"No, Maria." I hold up a palm and lift myself off the floor, shaking off her hand. "There's no need. It's just a stomach bug, nothing more." The last thing I need is for her to call a doctor and alert Roman to my condition. We all have far too much on our collective plate right now to add anything more to it.

"You need to see a doctor." Maria gives me a rather owlish look.

"I'm fine." I let go of the sink and give her as convincing a smile as I can muster. "I just need a shower. I'll be out in a moment."

"Hmm." She stares at me through narrowed eyes, as if weighing what to say. It's the first time we've met since my return, and I can sense her internal conflict. Maria has been loyal to Roman and the children for a long time, and it took time for her to trust me when I first arrived. I suspect my unannounced departure has damaged our earlier alliance. "I'm glad you are home," she says finally.

I notice she doesn't shut the door the whole way when she leaves. I suspect she wants to keep half an eye on me.

I head into the shower, wondering rather tiredly if I'm going to face the same wariness from all of Roman's people. It feels exhausting, especially when I can't tell anyone the entire truth.

When I emerge from the bedroom, Maria is gone, but she's left a fresh pot of ginger tea on the kitchen counter, beside a plate with some plain crackers. Perfect for my shaken stomach. I take grateful mouthfuls of both, hoping her gesture constitutes the first thawing of relations.

The new phone Roman left beside the bed for me lights up with his number.I punch the answer button immediately. He launches in without waiting for me to speak. "Have you spoken to your father?"

"Yes. I told him we'd come to see him this afternoon."

"We're going to see him now. Luis will take you; I'll meet you there." He pauses. "Darya, if you don't mind—will you wait in the car until I arrive?"

It's my heart, rather than my stomach, that clenches now, despite the courtesy of his tone.

He still doesn't trust me.

It hurts. Even if I understand why. "You have my word that I won't speak to my father until you are with me."

My efforts to keep resentment out of my tone mustn't be too effective, because Roman actually laughs. It's a choked sound that never really makes it to full laughter, but I hear the intent nonetheless. "It isn't that I don't trust you, Darya. It's him I have a problem with."

I frown. "My father would never endanger me, Roman."

"Your father has been endangering you for years." His answer is sharp and immediate.

It's also painfully undeniable.

"I need to know you're safe, Darya. Okay? I can't lose—I need you safe."

I nod slowly into the receiver. I understand what he means. I might not like it, but I understand. After thinking Roman was lost to me over these past days, it makes me nervous when he is not in touching distance. If he feels even half of what I do, then I guess I know why he wants me safe. I look at Maria's pot of tea, remembering her wary face, and think that it's going to be a while before the status quo is restored.

"I promise I will stay in the car." This time I give my word quietly, injecting the promise with as much reassurance as I can. "I'll wait outside the villa until you arrive, Roman."

"Thank you." His response takes a beat longer than normal, and the words have a rough edge that betrays the emotion behind them.

He hangs up.

I sip my tea in silence until Luis knocks on the door and it's time to go.

"Thank you for waiting." They're Roman's first words upon opening the car door for me. He presses my hand gently, giving emphasis to all he isn't saying.

"I understand." I smile, hoping to take some of the shadow from his eyes but knowing the same darkness clouds my own.

There'll be no light, for any of us, until this is over.

"I know your father has things he wants to say." Roman holds both of my hands in his own as we stand just beyond the wall of the villa. "But there are questions I need him to answer as soon as possible in order to find the girls. I'm not sure how much of his story I'll be able to hear before I interrupt."

"That's fine." I return his grip with my own fingers, wanting to reassure him of my support. "I'll let you take the lead, ask what you need to. The only thing that matters is getting the girls back." He nods, but his face remains grim and unsmiling. I want to ask a thousand questions of my own, but I can't force Roman to bring me into his confidence. It's going to take time.

Time we don't have.

The security detail at the villa isn't the subtle presence it was before the bomb. Now armed men stand at every window, eyes scanning the surroundings with incessant scrutiny.

Roman isn't leaving anything to chance.

Papa is sitting on the terrace with his back to us. Smoke curls up from the cigarette he usually tries to hide from me, and the ashtray at his side is evidence that this is far from being his first today. He doesn't turn when Roman opens the door.

"Please, sit." He speaks in Russian with his back still to us, gesturing at two chairs arrayed in front of him. A coffee table bearing a Russian samovar of tea and three glasses rests on the small coffee table between him and our chairs. He clearly saw me arrive and knows I sat out front in the car until Roman got here.

Roman pulls a chair out for me, then takes his own. He unbuttons his suit jacket and slings one leg over the other, his hands resting on the wicker sides with every appearance of relaxation. The truth is that he's coiled tight as a leopard, every muscle taut. His eyes are black and unreadable, mouth a grim slash as he eyes my father.

"I need to know the layout of the underground chamber in Miami." He doesn't bother greeting Papa. His words are an order rather than a request, delivered in a tone no less dangerous for being calm and detached.

"I asked one of your guards to sketch the layout for me," Papa says. He seems entirely unsurprised by Roman's abrupt opening. He nods at a piece of paper on the table. "The dimensions are in exact proportion, exactly as it was built. Unless Orlov tore up part of the compound, he cannot have made any meaningful changes." His Russian is clipped and direct, his speech unusually clear. Piercing blue eyes meet Roman's without wavering. There's a fierce light behind them, a savagery my father has always kept carefully hidden from me, even during the years Orlov held us both. "What else do you need?"

He's speaking to Roman as he would one of his *vor*. I can see it in the lethal stillness of his shoulders, the harsh set of his mouth.

"Anything that will help us when we attack." Roman's

response is equally curt. "Hidden traps, obstacles our men will encounter. Anything you can tell us that will help us gain access."

"I've noted them all. And there are tunnels." Papa shifts the top paper to reveal more drawings beneath. "Each has a door with a digital code. I've written the codes beside each one."

Roman's eyes narrow suspiciously. "And you're sure the Orlovs don't know about these?"

Papa nods briefly. "Alexei has been using them for years. The Orlovs have never caught him."

Alexei has been using them? For what? I conceal my surprise with an effort.

I stare at the drawings, mentally recalling the places Papa has marked. Some of the tunnels I know about, but there are many others, carefully concealed in the architecture, that I never suspected existed.

"Why didn't I know about these?" I ask carefully, reluctant to meet my father's eyes in case he sees the anger simmering in mine. "Some of these tunnels come out onto the street. If I'd known about them, we might have escaped the first time we tried, instead of running into the woods and getting caught. We could have been gone, and the Orlovs never would have known."

"Because your father wanted to keep them safe for the moment he was ready to return." Roman's lip curls in contempt. "Because the vault is all that has ever mattered to him. Isn't that right, Sergei?" His hands don't move, but his eyes glitter with a fierce, dangerous light as he holds Papa's gaze. Despite my love for my father, I share his anger.

Why did he never tell me about all of the other tunnels?

"You are right in part. I did keep that secret safe, or at least I did for a long time, but not for the reasons you think." My father's tone remains even. He doesn't react to Roman's hostility. "At first I had no choice. Initially, after my stroke and the

Orlov coup, I was unable to either speak or move. I wasn't able to tell my children about all of the tunnels even if I wanted to. I was also not permitted access to my wife or either of my children, except to see them through soundproof glass when Vilnus tortured them."

I look at him in surprise. Papa has never told me that.

Vilnus did the same thing to Alexei and me, made us look at Papa's prostrate body through a large glass window that faced onto the clinical room in which Papa was kept. He told us Papa was dying, that he would never regain consciousness. But the room in which Vilnus tortured us was in the underground chamber, far from Papa's clinical bed. That room had a wall of darkened glass through which I assumed Vilnus's men were watching us suffer. I figured Vilnus just got off on having an audience.

Never did I suspect that my father might be the audience to which Vilnus was playing.

To me, my father was unconscious in his bed, far from where we were screaming under Vilnus's knife. It was one of my only comforts in the time Vilnus tortured me, that Papa couldn't actually see it. The thought that all of Vilnus's depredations were, in fact, carried out in full view of my father makes me sick and ashamed to the core.

Papa watched, I think, twisting inside with horror. *He saw the way Vilnus touched me, how he violated me.*

Another thought, even more terrible, strikes me: *Papa must have watched them rape Mama. Watched them tear her apart.*

Roman's expression of contempt has remained unaltered throughout Papa's words, as has his posture. Now he takes a slow, deliberate sip of tea, his eyes not leaving Papa's face. "Before you start trying to justify your betrayal of my parents, and the greed that you placed over the lives of your own family, I suggest you disclose anything else that might actually fucking help."

In another time, I might have leaped to Papa's defense.

I don't.

Roman's loss is mine, too. No matter my love for my father, Roman's family is mine now. I resist the urge to place a hand on my stomach. Roman is my family now. The father of my child. Father to the children I have come to see as mine.

As he said, nothing else matters. Not until the children are safe.

"You were right when you said I wanted to keep the tunnels safe." Papa inclines his head in Roman's direction. "I argued with Alexei about the one we did use, in his room. I was worried they would find it and search for others. But Alexei was careful, just as we planned, and they never did."

He leans forward. "But you're wrong in thinking that decision was mine, Roman. After I woke, my first thought was to take my children and run. I'd have used those tunnels without hesitation and never cared about whether Orlov found the others or not. But someone asked me not to. They reminded me of an old promise, and they held me to it."

Roman's eyes narrow. "I suppose this is the point in the conversation where you reveal all those deep dark secrets of yours."

Papa's expression is as fierce as Roman's contemptuous sneer. "There is only one secret that matters, and had you given me the chance to talk, Roman, it would not have remained a secret after the first day I realized who you are." He stubs out his cigarette and folds his hands in front of him. Sitting back in his chair, he eyes Roman directly. "The person who asked me to keep the tunnels a secret was your mother. She's alive, Roman. Rosa is alive."

16

———

ROMAN

Rosa is alive. My mother is alive.

My vision blurs, the world swirling around me as his words sink in.

"*Yerunda.*" The Russian word rasping from my throat sounds like someone else is speaking.

Sergei shakes his head slowly. "It isn't bullshit, Roman. It's the truth. Your mother left the United States years before the Orlovs attacked my family, before we even knew they were a threat. She was running from the Cardeñas cartel. Rosa's father was their boss. She escaped his home in Colombia when she was a teenager, after he arranged a marriage for her she didn't want. Her father had discovered she was in Miami. Aleksander, your father, asked me to get her to safety."

Suddenly I'm eight years old, sitting on the landing in my parents' house, hearing my father's words to Sergei Petrovsky: "*Get Rosa out of the country. Give her a new identity. Hide her tracks well, and don't tell me how you've done it, until and unless we know it is safe."*

I know what Sergei is saying is the truth. I know it because I heard my father say it himself. But knowing it logically and understanding it emotionally are two entirely different things. The person making sense of Sergei's words isn't a thirty-two-year-old man running a billion-dollar empire. He's an eight-year-old child who came home to find his mother gone and then watched his father die.

My limbs feel like stone, cold and locked in place. "You expect me to believe that my mother simply abandoned my father and me?"

"Of course she didn't abandon you." A flash of anger lights the old man's eyes.

Good, I think savagely. I want him angry. I want him hurt. I want Sergei goddamn Petrovsky to feel even an ounce of the agony I do, at the thought that for all of those long, lonely years, the thousands of nights spent shivering in back alleys, my mother was out there, alive. Keeping my face studiedly neutral, I stare the old bastard down as I try to master my inner turmoil.

"Rosa loved you more than anything, Roman. You and Aleksander were her world. Her love for you both was the only reason she ran in the first place. Against my own—" Sergei cuts off abruptly, turning away and wiping a hand over his face.

Against my own advice.

I know what he isn't saying. I remember how Sergei argued with my parents, tried to talk them out of their plan. And no matter how much I wish I didn't, I clearly remember my father's response: *"I'm asking this of you now, for your children, as well as my own: get my wife to safety. Allow her to carry out my wishes. Let me do this for you, that all our children might live the life we dream for them."*

I don't feel comforted by my memories. And I sure as hell

don't forgive Sergei Petrovsky. I remember all of that conversation, the promises he made to my parents.

Promises he utterly failed to keep.

I hear my father's voice in my mind: *"The Cardeñases have a Russian connection. Rosa's contact told her that is how they found her."*

"She wasn't just running from her father." I stare him down. "She was running from someone else, too. A Russian."

Sergei nods. "Your father knew it was a Russian who had betrayed her whereabouts to the Colombians. But we didn't know who or why. I didn't know it was the Orlovs until after the coup."

"My father had been dead for seven years by then." I barely manage the words. "What were you doing during that time?"

"Waging war against the Cardeñas cartel." Sergei's face is suddenly hard as a winter sky, his eyes cold and deadly. "They claimed responsibility for killing your father. They said it was punishment for having married Rosa. Half of the Russian families in Miami went to war with me to avenge your father." He meets my eyes starkly. "Vilnus Orlov included."

I control my revulsion with no small effort. It makes me sick to think of Vilnus Orlov "going to war" alongside Sergei.

My father's blood was still wet on his hands.

I'm not sure what makes me more furious: Vilnus's appalling hypocrisy or the fact that Sergei fell for it.

"And in the middle of this war, you never bothered to come looking for me?" I throw the words at him, my voice hard as Sergei's face.

He meets my eyes without flinching. "Your house was burned to the ground. We searched every ash. We found the remains of two bodies. Dental records confirmed they were you and your father. Orlov must have switched the records, of course, and planted the second body, but I didn't suspect that until many years later."

I shudder despite myself. I've read the newspaper reports, of course. Knew some boy had been killed in my place.

"They came for me, you know." I take a dark satisfaction in seeing Sergei recoil. "The Orlovs. Men with sparrow tattoos on their hands combed every street for me, for years. But I wouldn't leave Miami. I couldn't. I thought my mother would come back."

Sergei's eyes swirl with some emotion I can't quite read.

Suddenly, I'm impatient. There's no time to visit the past.

"Where did she go?" My voice rasps painfully. "No. Don't answer that. My father gave her some kind of key. What did she do with it?"

Sergei lights another cigarette, draws on it deeply. "It takes more than just fingerprints to open the vault." His eyes flicker to Darya, who is watching him as closely as I am. "There are also two keys. Your father gave one of them to Rosa. After I got her out of the country, she followed Aleksander's orders to the letter. She went to Switzerland and placed the key to the vault in a safety deposit box. Then she ran, just as your father ordered her to."

Switzerland.

The word thrusts me back to the horrible day when I stood in front of the safety deposit box, staring at the Fabergé egg inside it. Expecting to find my mother. Finding that meaningless piece of goddamn history instead.

"Bullshit," I say, again in Russian. "I went to Switzerland. She wasn't there. I opened the safety deposit box—"

"That was the first time I truly believed you might still be alive." Sergei's mouth twists painfully. "Your mother always believed it," he says softly. "She never gave up, Roman. Not for a moment. And she never stopped looking for you. But it wasn't until she told me that box had been opened that I began to think she might actually be right, that by some miracle, you really might have survived."

I can't meet his eyes. I can barely breathe, let alone speak.

It's too much.

I don't know what to believe. I'm torn between wanting to tear Sergei limb from limb and bombarding him with the million questions torturing my brain. It's a relief when Darya interrupts us.

"And the other key?" Her voice is almost as hard as my own. "Where is the other key, Papa?"

He meets her eyes, and for the first time, his composure cracks slightly. "Your brother has it."

The hurt and anger in her face fires my own.

"You have to be kidding." I stand up restlessly, unable to sit still. "The same brother who's been working with the Orlovs for fuck only knows how long has the other key?"

"Alexei isn't working with the Orlovs." Sergei's answer comes hard and fast. I rather suspect that if he had a gun, I'd be staring at it right now.

Not that I give a fuck.

"Then why did he stay?" The heartbreak in Darya's voice kills me. "If you thought Roman was dead, then you knew there was no way to open that safe. Why would you make him stay?"

Sergei stares at Darya for a long time, as if warring with himself. When he finally answers, his voice is rough and uneven.

"Not me." He speaks as if the words are being wrenched from somewhere deep inside him against his will. "I pleaded with Alexei to come with us. But he said that Rosa had visited him. She . . . came through the tunnels when I was still uncon-scious. She told Alexei that the Orlovs were scouring the city for Roman." His eyes flicker to me. "That's why she was so certain you were still alive."

"And neither of you told me this." Darya's voice is hard as glass. "Not in all these years."

Sergei reaches a hand out to her, but she jerks away from it.

"Orlov was torturing you!" His voice breaks. "Alexei wasn't going to give that bastard anything to use—"

He swallows, gaining control of himself before he goes on.

"I promised Rosa long ago that I would protect her son. When I was unconscious, she reminded Alexei of that promise. Alexei promised her he would stay close to the Orlovs, find out if Roman was still alive." He looks at me, then back at his daughter, his face white with grief. "You must not blame Rosa. She'd suffered so much. If there was a chance—even the smallest one —that you were alive, I owed it to her to find you. Owed it to Aleksander."

He meets my eye without flinching. "Even so, I'm ashamed to say that I still begged Alexei to run with us. I was furious when I discovered that Rosa had risked her life by coming back to Miami and breaking into the compound. I was even more furious when she told Alexei that he couldn't run, that someone needed to stay, in case you ever came back. I argued with him. I said that if you were alive, Roman, there must be another way to find you, one that didn't involve him staying in that house." His lips harden into a grim line. "But Alexei . . . he refused to go back on his word to your mother. And that promise aside, he was determined to stay and one day fight to regain what we'd lost." Sergei's face is gaunt. "I didn't agree with him. But I respected his decision."

Darya makes a low noise of frustration. She stands up and moves away, turning her back on both of us. Sergei's eyes follow her, but he doesn't speak.

I fold my arms and stare the bastard down. "Tell me where my mother is now."

"At this moment," he says quietly, "I believe Rosa is in Switzerland."

"Then why didn't she find me when I opened that safety deposit box?"

"Rosa wasn't in Switzerland when you went to the bank." Sergei is still watching his daughter's stiff back.

I can't stand the sadness in his eyes; I don't want to feel sympathy for him.

"Until recently," he continues, "Rosa hadn't been back to Zurich since the day she closed that safety deposit box. It was months before she got the news that someone had come to open it, and even after the bank notified her, she wasn't sure that person was you. We were both worried it might be a trap. You must remember, Roman: I'd seen what I thought was your body with my own eyes. I truly believed you were dead. Despite what Rosa said about the Orlovs hunting for you, I thought your mother's faith was just grief, wishful thinking." He shakes his head tiredly. "She went to Switzerland anyway, of course." He drags his eyes back to mine. "I had no chance of stopping her. Rosa never was one for being told what to do."

There's a reluctant admiration in his voice that I don't want to hear.

Sergei's reminiscences only further remind me of what I've had to live without all these years. The fact that he, and not I, could see my mother, touch her, talk to her . . .

I clench my fists to stop myself from beating him senseless and swallow hard to bury the lump of hurt and loss blocking my throat.

"After she told you the box had been opened, what did you do?" I wince at the pain I can hear in my voice. I don't want the bastard to know the effect his words have had on me. I don't want to give him a single fucking thing.

He's taken enough from me already.

"The bank wouldn't show Rosa footage of whoever had opened the vault. But there was no doubt it *had* been opened, and the key was still inside it, as was the egg. There was no trap, nobody waiting to capture her. I truly began to think she might be right." He half smiles. "Oddly enough, that was when Rosa became the skeptic. I think she was afraid to start believing again, after so long. Either way, neither of us had the faintest idea where you might be." He looks at me, his eyes painfully gentle. "Right up until the day I saw you with your father's earrings.

"Even then, it seemed impossible. An unimaginable coincidence." He shakes his head. "I thought I was seeing things. Imagining what I wanted to."

I can't do this.

Not now. No matter how fucking much I want the truth.

Right now, what I want to do most is run as hard and fast as I can, a million miles from here.

Away from the sympathy in Darya's eyes and the pain in Sergei's. I neither want to understand his pain nor hear his fucking explanations.

I've lived without answers for two decades and more. I can live without them until I have my girls back and Vilnus Orlov is dead.

And just like that, my world snaps back into focus.

"None of this matters." I brutally cut off whatever Sergei was about to say. "We don't have time for any of this. We've got the codes to the tunnels and a map of the underground chamber. Everything else can wait." I stand abruptly. "We need to go, Darya."

For a horrible moment I think she will stay with her father. I'm almost afraid of how furious that makes me feel, how utterly alone.

When she slowly stands beside me, it takes all of my self-discipline to hide my relief.

"Wait." Sergei presses against his chair, grimacing with the effort to stand. "There's so much more you both need to understand. I haven't begun to explain—"

"Will any of it help me get into that compound and get my

children back?" I stare down at him, daring the old bastard to waste one moment more of my fucking time.

He stares at me for a long time. Then he nods in reluctant acquiescence, slumping back in his chair, his face pale and tired. "You know the key is in the Fabergé egg?"

My mouth twists in contempt. "I figured. Is there any other trick I should know about?"

"No." Sergei shakes his head. "Your father designed the vault to be opened by three sets of fingerprints and two keys. He hid one inside the egg your mother took with her." He meets my eyes. "And like I said, Alexei has the other one."

"Oh, and he's just going to hand that over, is he?" Fury churns inside me.

"Yes." He meets my eyes steadily. "Yes, Roman. He will."

I stare at him for a long moment, anger and pain like poison inside me. "Well," I say finally, "I guess we're about to fucking find out, aren't we, Sergei?"

I'm about to walk away when Darya speaks up. "Wait." She's staring at her father, her eyes narrowed. "If Rosa wasn't in Switzerland all that time, then where was she? And how was she talking to you about going back to Switzerland when we were on the run?"

When Sergei meets his daughter's eyes, it's the first time I see his composure truly begin to slip. "Dayushka," he says hoarsely. "There's so much you don't know—"

"Argentina." She says the word flatly, a statement of fact rather than a question. "That's who we traveled all that way to find, Papa, wasn't it? Rosa is your contact in Argentina. All this time, both you and Alexei have been communicating with her. And neither of you ever told me."

"We had to protect you—" Sergei stretches a hand out toward her. Darya jerks back as if she's been stung.

"Protect me?" Her voice is low and furious. "While I was looking over my shoulder and working every job I could to keep food on the table, you and Alexei tried to *protect* me?" Her strangled laugh is painful to hear.

"Please, Dayushka." Sergei's voice cracks. "Just let me explain—"

"No." Darya cuts him short. "No, Papa. Not this time."

She slips her hand into mine. "Take me home," she whispers.

We turn around and walk away, leaving the old man sitting in his chair, alone in the growing chill.

ROMAN

Darya is quiet in the car as I drive us up to the lab. The rocky mountain landscape is lit gold in the dying afternoon sun. She stares at it through the window, her face turned away from me. The light turns her skin to a glowing, buttery sheen. With her hair in a loose knot on her head, a few strands drifting about her face, she has an incandescent beauty that makes my heart twist. Her hands rest on her belly, one thumb stroking mindlessly back and forth over the thin fabric of her sundress. She seems entirely turned inward.

I need her.

It isn't only the sexual desire, although that is always there between us. I need her smile, her touch. After Sergei's revelations, I need to know that Darya and I are connected, that we're both safe.

That we are here, together.

On a broad curve there is a scenic lookout point, bordered

by granite boulders. I pull the car into the gravel, facing it out over the valley below, and step out, walking around to open her door. I give Darya my hand and she takes it, moving straight into my embrace. I wrap my arms around her body, shivering as hers go about me. One hand cradles her head against my chest, the other at the base of her spine, pressing her body flush against my own. She smells of vanilla and coconut, feels warm and vital against me. When my thumb touches her jaw, I can feel the rigid tension beneath her velvet skin. I stroke her face softly, feeling the tension slowly melt from her body and my own heartbeat gradually settle against hers. We stand like that for a long time, the shadows slowly growing around us, just breathing.

When Darya pulls back, her face is wet with tears. "I'm sorry." Her voice hitches, her eyes on mine wide and dark with hurt.

"For what?" I hold her face, using my hands to collect her tears.

She shakes her head, her eyes fluttering closed then opening again. "That your mother has been alive all this time. For the secrets my father kept from you. For . . . all of this." She drops her forehead against my chest, her head still shaking, as if she can somehow push away the revelations of the past hour.

I kiss the top of her head, inhaling her essence like a tonic. "None of this is your fault. None of it, Darya. Neither of us are responsible for the sins of our parents."

"You have nothing to be responsible for. Your parents did nothing to deserve any of this."

"That's not entirely true." She looks up, frowning. "The conversation I told your father about, the one I overheard between him and my parents? I need to tell you what was said." I lead her over to one of the boulders looking out over the valley. Drawing her down to sit opposite me, I take her hands and tell her everything I recall of what was said between Sergei and my parents.

"Sergei didn't want my mother to run," I say at the end. "He wanted to protect my parents and me. It was Rosa who insisted she had to leave, and my father who forced Sergei to let her go. Whatever Sergei's faults, and whatever else I might lay at his door, I can't blame your father for my parents' decisions." I tip her face up so she meets my eyes. "And you shouldn't either."

She shakes her head again, that wordless gesture of rebuttal, as if trying to push away all she's learned. "How can you defend him?" Her voice isn't quite steady, tears brimming again. She swipes her eyes angrily. "God, I wish I could stop crying."

I touch her cheek. "You have reason enough." It occurs to me that I've seen Darya close to tears more in the past day than ever before. She's not given to fits of crying, normally holds her emotions tightly within. I guess the trials of the past week would test anyone's resilience. "I'm not defending Sergei." I pause, searching for the right words. "But perhaps I understand him."

"You're joking." She frowns at me. "Are you saying he did the right thing, concealing Rosa's identity from me as well as from you? I still can't believe he did that." She goes on without waiting for an answer. "You have no idea how difficult it was, getting to Argentina. An entire sea of immigrants was coming the other way, and none of them understood why we were going south. Nobody wanted to help us. Papa was sick, and I'd never gone further than the walls of our compound without security. I might as well have been an infant, for all I knew about the world. I trusted Papa implicitly. Everything he told me to do, I did. So when we got to Argentina, and he told me his contact was too dangerous for me to meet, I believed him."

Her face hardens. It hurts me to see her pain, the effect of those years.

"I took Papa to meet this contact in an apartment building

in a run-down part of Buenos Aires. He made me leave him in the foyer. I remember the floor was pockmarked, paint peeling off the walls. I wanted to stay and try to catch a glimpse of this person we'd battled mud, hunger, and exhaustion to find. But I'd been raised in a household where men took care of business and women took care of the kitchen. Papa's word was law. When he told me to leave, I obeyed his orders. Never once did he tell me it was a woman he was meeting, or anything about who she was, why she was important. Why didn't he tell me?" The palpable hurt in her voice breaks my heart. "Why couldn't he just trust me? And what is so damned important about the Naryshkin treasure that it needs all this secrecy? It's just . . . stuff, no matter how valuable. How can it truly matter to them all so much that they'd tear all of our lives apart, just to keep the contents of that vault safe?"

She's crying again, and I wrap her in my arms, rocking her until the sobs subside, stroking her gently as my shirt turns damp.

"I don't understand it either." My lips rub against the silken mass of hair. "I guess there's more to the story. Maybe we'll find out, after all this is over. I just couldn't listen to any more today."

"Me either." Her voice is muffled against my chest. "I was too angry, and your face when he told you about Rosa . . ." She lifts her head and without warning kisses me, her mouth fierce on mine.

I understand it. I understand *this*, the primal need for connection in place of words.

I take her passion and return it, my hands twined in her hair, my body suddenly raging with need. I want her with a blind, mindless urgency.

"Oh God, Roman." Her moan against my mouth rips through my body, sending my dick into overdrive. Her hands delve into my shirt, and the soft cry she gives when she touches my chest has my body pounding for hard, fast release.

I'm also horribly aware that since her return, our only time together was exactly that.

I can feel her devastation and hurt. Darya already knows how desperately I want her.

She also needs to know how fiercely I love her.

I stand and move us both to the Maybach. Hitching Darya onto the hood, I spread her legs and stand between them, her musky scent hot and intoxicating. I tug the sundress down to her waist, releasing the clasp of her bra. Her breasts surge into sight, somehow even more lush and rich than I remember, tawny in the afternoon light. The swollen buds atop them thrust toward me as she arches her back, moaning, and my good intentions are almost shot to hell right there.

Forcing my lust under control, I bend my head to her, taking first one creamy mound then the other, and she cries out, her hands in my hair pulling my face against her. I lathe her with my tongue, her body twisting under me as she pushes herself into my mouth. She seems to swell under my tongue, her whole body bucking under my touch.

I'm achingly hard, and reveling in it.

"Roman," she gasps, arching toward me, the thin material of her sundress and my suit pants doing nothing to mask the heat of her against my cock. "That feels so good."

I grunt in answer, rolling one of her nipples between my finger and thumb, devouring the other. I'm obsessed with the sight of her arched naked on the hood, glowing and golden like some kind of ancient goddess. I love this, the way her body comes immediately to life, racing toward orgasm the moment my hands are on her. It's a heady rush, more powerful than any high-speed engine could ever be. My dick is rock-hard and desperate for release, but despite the fact that we're bared to the sight of anyone who might come around the corner, and the fact that an entire team is waiting for us at the lab, I don't want to rush.

I press her breasts close together and bend my head to them as her soft, panting moans become louder, music to my ears.

"Oh." Her head goes back. "Oh, Roman. Don't stop. Don't stop . . ."

I lift my head just before she tips over the edge, capturing her mouth, my hands in her hair. Her breasts are completely bared, the sundress bunched around her waist but still covering her thighs. I stand slightly back from her and she gasps, her eyes flying open.

"Look at me," I growl.

Her molten eyes stare into mine, her lips swollen and parted from my mouth. Slowly, deliberately, I inch the sundress up her legs, my thumbs inching closer to the heat at her center. A slight breeze stirs her hair, brushing tendrils over my face. She quivers as I massage her inner thighs with my thumbs, spreading her legs wide for me.

"I think you need this as much as I do."

Her sharp intake of breath as I speak travels straight through me. I edge my hands up her thighs, feeling the tension in them. I pull my shirt off, and she gasps at the contact as her nipples, swollen and wet from my mouth, come up against my naked chest. Her cry makes my cock leap.

"Did you think about my hands on you when we were apart?" My hands clench around her thighs, just hard enough to make her gasp.

She nods.

"Say it."

"I thought—*oh*—I thought about your hands on me."

"Nobody else but me will ever touch you like this. Say it." I circle my thumbs on her upper thighs, one maddening inch away from a pair of rose-colored silk panties that are dark with her arousal.

"Nobody else will ever—*ah*—touch me like this." She gasps the words, quivering in anticipation.

I touch her lower lip with my tongue, and she makes a soft, breathy noise that makes my cock jerk in anticipation. I hook my fingers through her underwear and pull them off, pushing her sundress up to join the top half at her waist, spreading her legs wide so she's exposed completely, not taking my eyes from hers.

"You know what I thought about? What I couldn't stop thinking about?"

She shakes her head slowly, her eyes on mine as dark as if she's drugged, wet lips parted, breath hitching in her throat.

"I thought about how you moan when I touch you here." I draw one finger down the crease between thigh and heat, and she quivers, then goes utterly still, her eyes locked on mine. "How delicious it is to feel you swell under my hand." My thumbs gently manipulate her folds, rolling the swelling bud beneath them, and she moans. I put my mouth close to her ear. "How fucking hot it feels when I finally touch you."

My thumb slides over her clit, and she grips my shoulders, her cry cutting the air.

"Christ, Darya." She's slick and needy, her clit a throbbing pulse under my thumb as I slip a finger inside her. I let her rock on it with increasing urgency, her hands clutching my shoulders.

"Most of all," I growl, finally releasing my cock, "I thought about being inside you."

The glazed light in her eyes as she looks down between us sends me into overdrive. She wraps her hand around my throbbing shaft, and I leap at her touch. I slip another finger inside her, groaning at the wet heat of the ribbed walls inside. I dip my head to her breasts again, and she bucks wildly against me, her hand curled around my cock, stroking me with increasing urgency. Her lips touch the shell of my ear.

"I don't want to wait," she whispers, and I throb fiercely in her hand. "I want your cock, Roman. I need you inside me."

My hands slip under her ass, cupping and spreading her so she's laid out before me in a swollen, glistening feast. I stare at her slick folds, my mouth watering. "I have to eat you," I say roughly.

"No—I'll come—"

"I don't give a fuck." I lower my face to her, and she screams at the first long stroke of my tongue, her heels scrabbling for purchase, hands in my hair as she thrusts herself into my mouth. I leave my fingers inside the hot tunnel, covering her clit with my mouth. I bathe her with my tongue, groaning at the sweet taste, working her impossibly swollen core until she's bucking against me.

"Roman!"

Her orgasm hits with savage immediacy. She clenches around my fingers, pulsing into my mouth, and I ride the long, intense waves with her, my cock so fucking hard it's painful. When I lift my head her eyes are closed, her body still rippling around my hand. Spread and wet on the black surface, she's never looked fucking hotter.

"Stay there, *milaia*," I say against her ear, my body surging as I ready my cock. "Stay with me."

I enter her with a driving intensity, and her scream echoes around the valley.

Deep inside her, the ripples milk me like a thousand tiny fronds. My hands under her ass pull her down to meet me, and when I angle myself up and find the magic fit, she bucks again.

"Oh." The moan rips from deep inside her. "Roman, that's it. I'm still coming . . ."

"I know, *milaia*. I can feel you all over my cock." It's all I can do to retain control, but I don't want this to end. Her fierce, pulsing contractions around my shaft are a paradise I want to lose myself in, an island of mindless sensation amid the darkness all around us. I thrust deeply and deliberately, gasping at every tightening of her body, reveling in her small cries. The savage ripples fade, but she keeps rocking with me, a slow, deep rhythm that has me groaning her name and muttering an endless stream of mindless words into her ear.

"You're so fucking hot, *milaia*. So wet and tight."

She moans, jerking against me.

"Christ, Darya, the way you feel . . ." I hold out as long as I can, riding the crest of the storm with every stroke. But then she grips my arms and her movements begin to speed up.

"I'm going to come again." She says it breathlessly, and I lose my shit.

I drive into her with a roar and with the hard, fierce strokes that tip us both over the edge. Her walls convulse around me, and I erupt in a hot, pulsing torrent that pours from the base of my spine, almost blinding in intensity.

We cling to one another until the last of the waves finally abates.

Darya peeks up at me, my cock still inside her. "Lucky this is a quiet road."

We laugh softly, our bodies still joined, arms around each other, because sometimes when the intensity is too much, laughing is the only thing left to do.

18

DARYA

Roman doesn't let go of my hand for the rest of the drive to the lab. I think we both need the physical reassurance. After my father's bombshell, and with the gaping hole left by the girls' absence, I want only to be as close to Roman as I can be. Going by the way his large hand covers my own, he feels the same way.

The lab comes into view as we crest a hill. It's a gleaming white building of stone and glass, sleek and low against the mountain before us. I recognize it by the word *HALE* written in large silver letters across the wall.

"Wow." I'm accustomed to the impressive Hale Property office building in central Malaga, but this is something different again.

Roman's mouth curls in a smile I can't quite read. "That's just the icing on the cake. Wait until you see what lies underneath it."

"Underground, you mean?"

When he nods I shake my head, repressing a wicked urge to laugh. He glances at me. "What?"

"I was just thinking that building bunkers underground must be in the Borovsky genes."

Roman gives a surprised snort of laughter. "We're joking about this now?"

"You just discovered your mother is alive. I just found out my father's been lying to me my entire life. Our children are missing, and"—*I'm pregnant with your baby*—"we just had sex on the hood of your car in broad daylight. I think we're both badly in need of as much humor as we can manage, don't you?" I meet his eyes, grateful he doesn't seem to have noticed the slight halt in the middle of my sentence.

"*Our children.*" He squeezes my hand gently. "It's nice to hear you call them that."

"I know I'm not their mother, Roman. I'm not trying to replace anyone."

"You're more of a mother to the children than their own has ever been." His eyes burn fiercely, mouth tightening. "I just wish —" He clamps his mouth shut. His hand grips mine tightly enough to cut off the blood supply.

"This isn't your fault, Roman," I say quietly. "It isn't anyone's fault except Vilnus Orlov's. He's the one who started all of this. He betrayed my father and killed yours, all because he wants whatever is inside that vault."

He frowns as he glances at me. "What do you mean, *whatever is inside* it? Haven't you ever seen what's inside?"

"No." I shake my head, and he huffs in surprise. "I never needed to. I knew there was a fortune in there. People talked about it all the time—or rather, whispered—even when I was in hearing distance. I know there are some Fabergé pieces in the vault, and jewelry that came out of imperial Russia. My earrings, for example. And once, when I was very young, my father showed us a Fabergé egg that his father left him. He explained that there is always a trick mechanism built inside the eggs. That one had a jeweled cocoon. When Papa pushed a button, the cocoon opened and a filigree gold butterfly emerged."

Those days seem so long ago now. Another life. I glance at Roman. "From what you said, your father hid your key to the vault inside one of those eggs. Which reminds me," I say as he turns up the long driveway leading to the Hale building. "How did you know how to get into the safety deposit box?"

"My father tattooed the code for it on the sole of my foot, over a year after my mother left. He made me memorize the name and address of the bank. I guess my mother must have told him where she hid it, despite his instructions. I know my father was getting increasingly paranoid. I think he knew his life was in danger." Roman shakes his head. "He said that if anything should happen to him, I should go to the bank and that my mother would find me. He also warned me not to go there unless I was absolutely certain I wasn't being followed." He glances at me. "I had no way of getting there at first. Later, I wanted to be sure nobody was following me. I didn't go until long after I'd left Miami, when I had a passport with the name Roman Stevanovsky. I hoped . . . I thought that perhaps my mother would magically appear when I opened the box. She didn't, of course."

His lips tighten. I squeeze his hand, and he forces a smile as he pulls into the underground garage. "Anyway. I used the Fabergé egg inside the box as collateral for a loan. Mikhail and I used some of the loan to build Hale. But more importantly, I used it to build what you're about to see." He gets out of the car and comes around to my door, helping me out. Expecting him to keep moving, I'm surprised when he stands still, holding both of my hands in his.

"The place I'm about to take you is what you've heard

Mickey and I call 'the lab.' It's not the software development center in the building above. That's just for show, something to justify what lies below it, if anyone starts taking too much interest in us."

I look at him curiously. "What *does* lie below it?"

He holds my eyes, his face entirely serious. "A project so secretive only a few dozen people know about it, including an elite board made up entirely of Russian businessmen—bratva, like us. A project I've killed to protect and paid countless millions to develop." He takes a deep breath. "Under normal circumstances I would never involve you in this. But I don't know how to bring you into the search for the children without bringing you here. And after hearing your father today . . ." He pauses as my hands grip his convulsively. "I guess I understand how painful it's been to discover your father didn't trust you," he says quietly. "I saw your surprise earlier when I told you that I understood Sergei. What I meant is that I understand his desire to protect you, to shield you from anything that might possibly place you in danger."

I tense instinctively, and Roman half smiles.

"Then I realized how damaging that secrecy has been. You were right in what you said to him. After all those years of hardship, all you endured to keep both of you alive, you deserve much better than being lied to."

He interlinks his fingers with mine, drawing me against his body. "I don't like the idea of involving you in business," he says roughly. "In fact, I fucking hate it." His mouth twitches at the corners, although the dark humor doesn't reach his eyes. "But this is about the children. I want you here, beside me. I *need* you here, Darya. And whether it kills me to admit it or not, we need your help." He gives me a wry smile. "Don't ever fucking remind me I said that."

I stand on tiptoes and touch my lips to his. "Show me this project of yours."

"This is incredible." I stare around at the vast expanse of the Mercura server center from the fishbowl window of the operations room, trying to take it all in.

When we first got here, Roman tried to steer me straight into a private room, but after I saw Mickey inside this one, there was no chance that was happening. "And you're just about to launch this cryptocurrency? Mac—Mer—"

"Mercura. We were." Roman might be six and a half feet of solid criminal muscle, but he seems strangely at home here. For all that he snaps at the motley crew of employees he refers to as tech heads, it's clear how much they admire him. Hearing my fierce man spout digital terms I don't even begin to understand, rapping out orders and moving from one screen to another, is a revelation. The scope of his vision is breathtaking, so far beyond anything I could have imagined as to verge on the genius. I'm awestruck by what he's attempting and by what he's already achieved. I feel like I knew only a fraction of him before now.

If I'm honest, it's seriously hot.

"Now everything is on hold, obviously." Roman's voice drags me back from the gutter, though when he sees the flush on my cheeks, his lips curl in a knowing smile.

"I see." I spin around, avoiding his scrutiny and focusing on Mickey. "And you!" I point an accusing finger at him, and he grins back at me. It's the first time I've seen him even remotely lighthearted since we met in Granada. "*This* is what you've been working on all these months?"

"Yup." Mickey tilts his head at Roman. "It's his fault. He's a really bad influence, Darya. You should probably take him in hand."

Oh, I already have.

What is *wrong* with me today? I swallow. I need to get a grip on myself and stop thinking about what just happened on the hood of Roman's Maybach, or the fact that he still has my panties balled up in the pocket of his suit pants.

"Fuck off." Roman throws one of Pavel's stress balls at Mickey's head, then shoots me an apologetic glance. "Sorry." He's clearly not used to moderating his language in here.

I bite back a smile. "I think I'll cope." My gaze shifts to the screens in front of Mickey, and my insides shift uncomfortably, all thought of lighthearted banter or car sex driven instantly from my mind.

A bank of square video windows shows my family's Coconut Grove compound from different perspectives.

It's the first time I've seen the inside of my childhood home since I ran. The images hit me in a bittersweet rush of emotion.

The best memories of my childhood took place running through those marble corridors.

The worst stuff of my nightmares happened in the rooms below them.

"Mickey." I fight for an even tone. "Can I look through the camera feeds?"

"Of course." He moves to make room for me, and Roman rolls a chair into place so I can sit beside him. The other tech kids gather around, shooting me surreptitious glances. Since Roman explained that most of them have been staring nonstop at my photograph for the past few days, I guess I can understand the fascination of seeing me in the flesh.

Roman clearly doesn't appreciate their interest, however. He narrows his eyes at one of the more avid starers, and the poor kid scurries back to his desk like the demons from hell are behind him, burying his head in his laptop. Roman glares at his red neck hard enough to bore holes in it, then eyeballs the rest of the room with a death stare savage enough to make his meaning perfectly clear. The tech kids, clearly utterly terrified, all turn hurriedly back to their screens. I suppress an extremely inappropriate urge to laugh.

I move the mouse, scrolling through the camera feeds from the different rooms, breathing deeply to calm the sudden rush of emotion that accompanies certain images.

There's my bedroom, untouched since the day I left it. I zoom in to the door. The camera feed is crystal sharp, clear enough to see every mark in the wood.

"What's that?" Mickey points to a dark hole in the door.

"It's where the door handle was. Vilnus removed it right after the coup. He . . . didn't like it when Alexei or I closed our doors."

"That was your bedroom?" Roman's voice is chilling.

I nod. When I glance sideways, his hands are clenched into hard fists. The tech kids exchange nervous glances. I scroll on hastily, slightly surprised at how little the compound has changed, even down to the places the guards are stationed. Looking at it through the video feed is like taking a museum tour, peering in at a place frozen in time. It's unsettling.

I realize, with a faint sense of surprise, that I don't want to go back there. Somehow I always thought that when we finally defeated the Orlovs—something I never allowed myself to doubt would happen—I would go back to the compound, pick up the reins of my old life. I never thought much past that, it's true. But looking at the lush gardens and vast marble spaces now, empty but for the familiar guards stationed at every corner, I suddenly realize I don't ever want to live that life again. The girl who once tried to slam her bedroom door in Vilnus's face, who changed her clothes beneath the bed covers to avoid the camera's ever-present eye, who obediently wore the dresses he laid out for her when he decided to parade her for the paparazzi—that girl died somewhere on the long trek to Argentina. I don't want to be her again. I've come too far, survived too much.

When I think of home now, I think of Roman's penthouse. Of the children's apartment. Of the finca in the mountains, which I suddenly miss with a fierce ache.

I don't miss Miami. Whatever happens after this, that life is over for me.

None of the cameras show any faces I know. Not Alexei's or Orlov's or Inger's. There's no sign of the girls anywhere.

Then again, I think, *there wouldn't be.* Vilnus would never keep them in the upper rooms, where they might be easily taken in an attack.

Even so, the compound seems remarkably lightly guarded. Even before my family went to war, we had more security watching us than this.

"How do I switch to the underground feed?"

"There's nothing there." Mickey is clearly unimpressed by this development. He hits a key. "The rooms are bare, except for when the guards do a security pass every half hour."

"We think Orlov is holding the girls somewhere else, or hiding them, just as you said he would." Roman's voice is tense. "But we have no idea where."

I flick through the different cameras again, this time more slowly. I halt the camera on one point and zoom in, my heart sticking in my chest.

"What is it?" Mickey's watching me.

"This isn't right." I point at what used to be Vilnus's torture room. I remember every dip in the concrete floor, every old mark on the walls. I spent so many hours face down in that room I can remember the cold, musty stench of it even now. "The darkened glass on the far wall. See that crack in it?" I zoom in further, tracing my finger down the hairline fracture, right at the edge of the glass. It's barely visible, only clear on a tight zoom. "That happened when Vilnus lost his temper one day. He threw a knife at the window."

"Tell me how to get into the vault, and all this will stop, Darya . . ."

I suppress a shudder at the echo of memory. "That crack was fixed a few months later. This is an old feed."

I turn to find Roman staring at the screen, his face hard. "You're certain?"

I nod. "I . . . spent a lot of time looking at that window."

His knuckles tighten on my chair back, hard enough to bend the plastic. The room is silent, every eye warily watching Roman.

Only Mickey seems unperturbed. He hits a few keys, frowning. "If there was another feed, I would have found it. This is it."

"Ha." The collective eyes in the room all swing to me. "Can I have a go?"

He raises a skeptical brow. "Do you have some inner tech genius you've been keeping under wraps?"

"Not me." I smile faintly. "But my brother does. His best friend, to be exact."

"Lars Andersson." Mickey breathes the name with an almost religious reverence, and a ripple of interest travels through the room.

I glance around curiously. "You guys know him?"

"*Everyone* knows him." He throws Roman a rather challenging look. "We've been playing a bit of online hide-and-seek with him these past few weeks."

By the way Roman is glaring at Mickey, I suspect this is one part of the story he'd rather have kept to himself. "We think Lars might be working with your brother," he says tersely. "But we're not sure how."

"Well, I'm not sure either, but if you've found a connection between them, then I can almost guarantee they're working together. Lars and Alexei have been best friends from the day they met at some gaming convention when Alexei was eight. Alexei pestered our father to let him go to boarding school in London just so they could room together."

I half smile, remembering the two boys at the dining table,

spouting digital terms until my father roared at them both to *get outside and kick a ball, for God's sake.*

"The summer before . . . everything happened, Lars and Alexei were trying to build some computer game together. My parents were worried about how much screen time the two were having, so they put a limit on the amount of hours the boys were allowed to work in Alexei's room."

The mutinous muttering from the tech kids gives me a fair idea of their collective opinion on that particular ruling.

"Well, obviously they didn't like being told what to do. So Lars rigged up a kill switch on the camera feed for the underground bunker and replaced it with a looped video." I grin around at the captive faces. "Alexei and Lars spent the rest of that summer hunkered down in one of the underground rooms, geeking out to their heart's content. Sorry," I say, realizing that the term *geek* is probably a bit undiplomatic in present company. But going by the avid expressions of the tech kids, any comparison to their hero is clearly a good thing. "Anyway, my father discovered their secret at the end of the summer. He told the boys that if they were so clever, they could damned well use their skills for something useful. He got them to hack all the security camera feeds so he knew where the weaknesses were. Then he got them to design a new system and set up kill switches and alternate feeds on all of them. It was a good idea. After the Orlovs' coup, Alexei and I took advantage of it to have conversations in private. Until Vilnus caught us trying to escape with Papa." I can't help an involuntary shiver. "Papa was still unable to move or talk then. Alexei rigged the cameras, and we managed to get Papa out of his hospital bed. We took one of the hidden tunnels out beyond the walls to the clearing behind the compound, but Vilnus caught us before we'd even made it to the tree line."

"Do you know what happens to little Russian blyats who think they can fly away? Do you?" Vilnus's scarred, brutal face is only

inches from mine. He hits my cheek, hard, with his open palm. "They have their wings cut off."

My smile fades, the scars on my shoulder tingling at the memory of his knife on my flesh.

The tech kids shift uncomfortably. I don't have to look at Roman to know how deadly his expression must be, from the way they're all avoiding looking at him.

"Anyway." I strive for a lighter tone. "After that, Vilnus made Alexei give him access to the feeds. He took away anything we could use to access the internet: phones, tablets, laptops. Fortunately, Alexei managed to steal a phone and message Lars, who then hacked the system from Sweden. He sent Alexei a code that we could use to mask the feed to all the underground rooms, including Papa's hospital bed." I lift a shoulder. "It didn't help, really. The Orlovs found our only phone, and Alexei couldn't contact Lars for updates. But going by what you've told me, Alexei and Lars are definitely back in contact. Alexei knows we'll be looking through the feeds. If he's trying to help us, his code might still work."

I pretend not to see the cynical look that passes between Roman and Pavel. I know they believe it's wishful thinking to hope Alexei actually has good intentions.

I'm not going to lie. After everything that's happened with Papa, I'm worried it's wishful thinking, too.

I pull the keyboard closer, my heart tripping like I've run a marathon as I enter the code.

For a terrible moment the screens go blank.

Oh, God. I've ruined all Mickey's hard work.

And Alexei really is working with the Orlovs.

I close my eyes.

Then Roman's hand grips my shoulder so hard it makes me wince. "Look," he says hoarsely.

I open my eyes, and there they are. Ofelia and Masha, in crystal clear, devastating real time.

The tech kids whoop and cheer, but I don't hear them. I'm frozen in my chair, staring at Ofelia and Masha's white, terrified faces.

Worse, I'm staring at a vivid, savage line marking the side of Ofelia's face. At her torn dress—and the dark purple blood stains all over it.

Roman's fingers are digging like pincers into my shoulder. The room has fallen entirely silent, but for the whirring of machinery. I don't need to look around to know that everyone is covertly watching Roman.

I reach up and cover his hand with my own. His is cold and iron hard, and terribly, frighteningly still. I try to communicate comfort, to head off the dangerous rage emanating from his every pore, but I'm struggling to contain my own.

The feed might have been old, but that fucking room is exactly the same as I remember it.

The stillness of the air, the horrible deathly fear that permeates the very walls. The light gleaming from the wall of darkened glass feels as evil and insidious as I remember it.

I'm still staring at Ofelia when Dimitry whistles behind me, finally breaking the terrible silence. "Jesus. There's a fucking army down there."

For the first time, I drag my eyes away from the girls and take in the horde of security patrolling the corridors.

"He's got every inch of the place covered, not to mention booby-trapped." Roman's voice is hoarse, barely controlled, his knuckles white on the chair back beside my face. "We'd have walked into a fucking death trap without this feed. Mickey, get the view on the door outside the girls' room."

I'm hardly breathing, my stomach churning. I know that Roman is dealing with the horrendous sight of Ofelia by focusing on logistics.

I also know he's close to losing it completely.

"Fuck." Dimitry hisses an intake of breath and shoots Roman

a look that does nothing to settle my stomach. "That room is wired to blow. There's no way we're getting in there by force without putting the girls in serious danger."

"We'll find a fucking way." Roman's voice is cold and deadly. "Mickey—give me a clear feed on the guard in that corner." His fingers touch my shoulder. "Maybe you should get a coffee, Darya."

I shake his hand off, my eyes locked to the screen. "Not a fucking chance."

I know why he wants a clear feed.

I already know what it's going to show.

And I won't look away.

Stationed directly inside the girls' door, rifle across his chest and sparrow tattoo glaringly visible on his hand, is my brother.

19

OFELIA

I'm dozing against the wall, Masha clutched to my chest, when I'm woken by the soft thud of Alexei's rifle butt against the floor.

My eyes fly open to find him watching me from beneath a lowered eyelid. He's still entirely still, his head bent as if he's dozing, but I know him well enough by now to see the tension in his body and the warning in his lone eye.

Bathroom time, he mouths.

Our breaks are strictly monitored, and we visited the bathroom across the corridor barely two hours ago.

There's a reason for this.

I subtly shake Masha, who wakes instantly, staring up at me with unblinking eyes. I hate how quickly she's become attuned to the tension we're living with, reacting to my smallest signal.

"Excuse me." I say it loudly for the cameras. "I don't feel well. I need the bathroom."

Alexei stands up threateningly. "You've already had your break," he snarls.

I glare at him. "I can't help it if I need the bathroom. Unless you want diarrhea all over this floor, I need the bathroom. Now."

He makes an annoyed sound and looks up at the camera in the corner, lifting his shoulders as if to say *what do you want me to do?*

A disembodied voice comes through the speaker. "Take them to the bathroom."

Alexei pushes off the wall and gestures impatiently to the door with his rifle. "Come on, then."

I uncoil my stiff limbs, trying not to wince at the stinging of his most recent knife cuts. Fortunately, I've learned they usually don't open again. Alexei's cuts are thin and incredibly precise. They bleed profusely—Vilnus, I've learned, likes the sight of blood, and Alexei always gives him a good show—but they are surface wounds, designed to produce the greatest show for the least pain.

I don't need a therapist to tell me how twisted it is that I feel grateful for the care Alexei takes when he cuts me.

We walk out of the room, the muzzle of his AR cold and hard at the base of my spine as he nudges me across the corridor to the bathroom. He accompanies us into the small space. The toilet has no door, and the mirror is polished metal instead of glass. The bathroom is an uncomfortable reminder that Masha and I are not the first ones to be held captive in this horrible place.

There is one advantage to the bathroom, however.

There's a place in the corner, under the camera, that is out of sight of the watching eyes, which are instead trained on the toilet itself. Best of all, Alexei told me, there's no audio feed in this room.

The bathroom is the one place we can communicate, however small those communications might be.

I push Masha toward the sink. "Wash your hands and face," I tell her, smiling. I put my mouth close to her ear as if I'm kissing her cheek. "Keep the water running."

She knows better than to nod.

I pull up my dress and sit on the toilet, my head in my hands as if I'm hiding from the cameras. In reality, I'm listening hard.

"Roman will be coming for you soon." Alexei's voice is low, and I don't have to look at him to know his mouth is barely moving, although his rifle will be trained on me. "He's hacked into the video feed, which means he and Darya are working together."

I want to ask when *soon* might be, but in full view of the camera, I can't. Alexei being out of sight is one thing—me, quite another. The one time I tried to stand in the corner myself, the door was flung open in seconds, and three guards chewed Alexei out.

"They will attack in the next few days," he goes on. He has an uncanny ability to read my mind. "Until then, no matter what Orlov does, you have to obey him. I know it's hard."

Hard?

I almost laugh.

Hard is a small word for what these days are like.

For the daily visits from Vilnus, when he asks Alexei to use his knife and watches me with eyes that touch every inch of my flesh.

Hard doesn't begin to cover the humiliation and rage I feel every time Vilnus makes his guards watch or the shame I feel when they openly stare at my most intimate parts.

"Orlov will tell you lies."

Alexei's voice is so low I have to strain to hear him.

"He will likely bring your mother back and use her to manipulate you. Vilnus wants you scared and disoriented when Roman comes for you. He wants you so scared that you will obey him, or me, instead of Roman. But when Roman comes, you *must* do as he says. If he attacks me, you let him, do you understand me? Nothing matters more than you and Masha getting out of here. Don't hesitate, no matter what you see. And between now and then, no matter what Orlov does to you, don't lose your sanity. Remember who you are. The end is close, Ofelia. It's coming. You just have to hold on."

No matter what Orlov does to you.

There's something odd in his voice that sets my nerves on edge.

"Masha," he says. "Don't look at me. Just listen."

Masha keeps her head down and keeps washing her hands.

"No matter what happens to your sister, you have to stay calm, okay? Vilnus will hurt you if you try to fight. I'm going to make sure you go home safely, *myshka*. But until then, I need you to do exactly what he says."

"'Kay." Masha's one-syllable response is low, and her lips hardly move.

I hate how fast she's learned the rules here.

My only comfort is that so far nobody has touched her.

A guard bangs on the door. "Hurry up, Petrovsky."

I stand up and flush the toilet, keeping my head down. Alexei prods my back with his rifle. "That's long enough," he says, in full view of the camera.

We exit the bathroom, and the two guards standing there grin knowingly at Alexei. "You're starting to like babysitting that tasty little piece a bit too much, Petrovsky," one of them says. "Maybe it's about time I took over. Wouldn't mind taking a knife to her myself." His eyes roam over me in a way that makes me pull the torn remains of my dress closer around my body. "Orlov is going to break her in, you know," he goes on conversationally. "He might let you cut the bitch, but there's no way he'll let you pop her cherry."

"Vilnus can fuck her bloody for all I care." Alexei's face doesn't change at all. His eye remains dull, distant.

The guard's lip curls. "You're a twisted fuck, Petrovsky, you know that? I bet you'd slice her open from ass to pussy if he told you to."

"You think I enjoy babysitting two spoiled fucking cunts?" Alexei's face is flat and unemotional, and he uses the expletive as casually as if he's ordering tea. "But you're right about one thing: my knife belongs to Vilnus." He stares at the guard with a blank, dead eye. "It has ever since he gave me this." He holds up his fist, showing the men the sparrow tattooed there.

The guard shakes his head contemptuously. "If you think Orlov will ever trust you, you're a fool. The day he opens that vault is the day you die. That sparrow won't save you."

Alexei shrugs. "That's his choice. It's not my place to question what he does." His eye flashes suddenly, and he takes a step closer to the guard. "But it's not your place either. I suggest you don't joke about touching the Stevanovsky girls. We both know what Vilnus does to anyone who lays a hand on what is his."

"You're fucking pathetic, Petrovsky. A mad dog on a leash." The guard twirls his finger close to his temple to indicate insanity, but I can't help but notice he takes a step backward. "Maybe I should put you back on the table and give you a few more cuts, just for old time's sake. Maybe make you fuck that pussy you seem to like cutting so much. Can you even get it up without a knife in your hand? I doubt it—"

In a sudden, terrifying movement, Alexei is up close to the guard, his knife at the man's throat. "Vilnus commanded me to guard them," he says in a low, chilling voice. "And like I said, my knife belongs to him. So if you come for those girls, Carlos, you better make sure I'm dead first. Because if you don't, I'll strip every last bit of flesh from your body." His lips part in a smile so disturbing it makes me shiver. "You know what I can do with my knife. You've seen it yourself. I suggest you don't test me."

The two men back away, holding their hands up in a gesture of surrender, and even I can see the fear in their eyes.

What, exactly, have they seen Alexei do?

I shut my mind to that. I don't want to know.

"Don't you have patrols to make?" Alexei stares at them with a cold, dead expression.

The men cast a wary look at the cameras overhead and step aside.

We shuffle back to the room, and I sink to the floor in the corner, my heart still thudding, careful not to look at Alexei.

That's another rule I've learned.

The delicate balance of our strange existence here depends, I've concluded, on him remaining our guard. By the contemptuous way the rest of the men treat him, it's clear they consider Alexei almost subhuman, but they also fear him. Even Vilnus, for all his bluster, listens when Alexei talks. He compensates for that by humiliating Alexei every chance he gets. He has made him our guard as some kind of punishment. So long as he believes Alexei hates his duty, and that we're terrified of him, Alexei will remain our watchdog.

I shudder to think of what will happen if he is taken away and I'm left in the hands of someone like the guards we just encountered. I've seen the way they look at me.

I've learned to obey Alexei's commands, to hang on to the lifeline of his quietly breathed instructions, the strange comfort of his lone eye staring fiercely into my own. That way the torture Vilnus forces him to inflict shrinks to a private space where there is only Alexei, me, and the cold blade pressed against my flesh. It becomes a strange, intensely intimate dance between just him and me, a place where we are entirely alone, the only two who truly understand what is happening.

I've never been more intimate with a man than a couple of kisses with schoolboys, both times at private parties in the homes of girlfriends. They were brief, fumbling encounters that left me with more questions than answers. I guess if I ever imagined having a real boyfriend, it might have been Matvei, who I danced with the night of the ball. He, at least, understands some of my world, if not the entirety of it. And he seemed genuinely nice, if a little bit naive.

Alexei isn't anything like the boys from my school or the cultural center. He's much older than me, to start with. I know Darya is twenty-seven, so he must be close to that, or in his early twenties at least, which makes him older than me by six to ten years.

And the fact that you're even thinking about this is completely twisted.

The fact is that my lack of any real sexual experience hasn't stopped me from thinking about it, even before I came here.

I think about sex more, I've always been convinced, than other girls my age.

Not that I'd know. I've never had friends I could talk to about that kind of thing. Girls my own age always seem impossibly young to me, like they live in a different world. I don't remember a time when I wasn't aware of the adult emotions in the room, the undercurrents other people my age seem to simply not notice.

The idea of having a boyfriend, someone like Matvei perhaps, seems to belong to that other world, the one of teenage sleepovers and dating. If I'm being honest, I can't even imagine myself in that world.

My life isn't like that. It never will be.

Any boyfriend I ever have will be carefully vetted by Roman, and my every move with him watched. If I had to take a guess, I'd say that if it is left up to Roman, my virginity is likely to be guarded, quite literally, at gunpoint until there's a ring on my finger.

Maybe that's why I'm having such a sick reaction to Alexei Petrovsky.

Because there's nothing normal about the way I feel when he puts his hands on my body. Even if it is to cause me pain. And the more he does it, the more my body wants him to.

I know what Stockholm syndrome is. I did a project on it for media studies. The teacher showed us a photograph of the bank robber, Jan-Erik Olsson, who held up a Stockholm bank in 1973 and was so charismatic that his hostages wound up taking his side against the police. I've always thought the entire concept was crazy; how could you possibly like someone who has a gun to your head?

Only now that I've spent days with Alexei Petrovsky's gun trained on me, and his knife slicing my flesh, I understand it far better than I ever could have imagined.

I JOLT awake in the middle of the night, startled by a noise I can't place. I know it's night because the harsh fluorescent lights in our room are dimmed some time after the dinner tray is removed and we've visited the bathroom. I hate not knowing what time it is exactly. The only way I can measure it is by how much I feel like I've slept. I also know that Alexei usually leaves us at some point during the night, replaced by Dima, the same man who drove the limousine the day we arrived, whom Alexei clearly trusts. It's usually only for a short time, when Alexei showers and changes, and, I assume, tries to sleep for an hour or so. At first, I think that is what I'm hearing, just the change of guards.

Then I realize that Alexei and Dima are talking.

It's a low, hushed whisper, barely audible, and they clearly think I'm asleep.

"How many?" Alexei asks.

"All of Dom's crew. And Krasky's. Your own crew, of course. At least sixty, all told."

"It will go down sometime in the next few days. Tell them all to be ready, Dima. This place needs to be disarmed the minute Borovsky breaches it, or they'll all be blown sky-high."

"We know. We'll be ready, Lex."

"I don't like the way Orlov is looking at Ofelia," Alexei mutters. "He might come for her before it goes down."

Oh, God. That's what he meant about "whatever Orlov does before then."

I shiver inside.

"Surely he wouldn't be that stupid?" Dima makes a disgusted sound. "Borovsky will fucking slaughter him."

"Borovsky will slaughter him regardless." Alexei's voice is cold and dispassionate. "Either way, it makes little difference to Orlov. If Borovsky's dead, he can't hurt Orlov anyway. If he lives, he might murder Orlov with his bare hands, but he will still be too late to undo the damage Orlov has done to his girls. I know Orlov. I know how the sick fuck thinks."

"Jesus." Dima sounds appalled. "What are you going to do?"

"There's nothing I can do. We have to ride this to the end, or we're dead men and it's all been for nothing." In the dim light, I see Alexei's grim expression. "I'm likely dead either way. I can't see Borovsky forgiving the man who took a knife to his only child."

Dima clicks his tongue. "If it wasn't for you, she'd have been raped on day one, and you know it. The only reason Orlov's kept his hands off that girl is because he gets even more of a thrill out of making you cut her."

"Well, I can't hold him off much longer. Even his men are starting to eyeball her." Alexei shakes his head abruptly. "Look, Dima. If this goes down and I take a bullet—"

"You won't."

"I fucking might. You know it as well as I do." Even as a whisper, I can hear the hard note of realism in his voice. "If I do, I need to know you'll get those girls to safety. Promise me."

"You know I will, Alexei. You have my word." The man's answer comes immediately.

There's a pause. I barely dare breathe for fear they realize I'm listening. Finally Dima breaks the silence.

"About Ofelia. What will you do if Orlov orders you to . . ." He leaves the sentence hanging, but I don't need him to finish it.

"I don't know." Alexei's head drops into his hands, the butt of his rifle rubbing tiredly over his head. "I have no goddamn idea, Dima. I just hope he doesn't."

"But that's the problem, isn't it?" Dima rubs a hand over his face. "That bastard has been playing his games with you for so long, he knows exactly what buttons to push. Be careful, Alexei. If he gets even the smallest idea how much the thought of raping that girl sickens you, it will be the best fucking game he's ever played."

Alexei stands up abruptly. "Don't you think I know that?" he hisses. "Don't you think I fucking *know?*"

A long, tense silence ensues. It's broken in the end when Dima touches Alexei's shoulder briefly. "We'll be ready, brother. You have my word."

He leaves the room, and I lie on the floor, my heart thudding, listening to Alexei's uncharacteristically harsh breathing.

It's all I can do to stop myself from crossing the room to offer him what little comfort I can.

The utter irony in feeling the urge to comfort my possible future rapist is not lost on me at all.

Nor is the fact that instead of feeling horror at the thought of Alexei taking my body, I feel a strange, uneasy excitement.

I shiver beneath the thin blanket and wonder what the hell is wrong with me.

2 0

ROMAN

By the time we leave the lab, shock has solidified into an ice-cold killing fury that consumes every cell of my body.

I sent Dimitry to the warehouse to speak to Nikolai. At this stage, I'll take any information I can get, even if it comes from that little fuck. I need some space.

From Dimitry. From the tech kids. From Mickey's devastated eyes.

I don't need anyone telling me just how bad this is.

Darya is silent in the passenger seat. The dark horror in her eyes only makes it worse. I'm not sure what broke her more: seeing the girls in that place, the fact that it's her brother who is standing guard over them, or the brightly colored Orlov tattoo on Alexei's hand.

I know she wanted to believe that Alexei is an ally. That he used that code knowing she would crack it.

Maybe part of her still wants to believe that.

I don't share her faith.

Alexei's sparrow isn't the broken-winged mark of a runaway. It's a full-blooded sparrow, eyes bright and beak closed.

A sparrow that has drunk blood. One that sees everything, but says nothing.

The Orlovs only give that tattoo to their closest, most trusted *vor*. To men who've killed for them.

Whatever Alexei Petrovsky once was, he's an Orlov now.

And he's holding my daughters inside a locked room that is wired to explode the minute anyone breaks into it.

Alexei Petrovsky is a fucking dead man. Whether he gives me the key to the vault or not.

For all I care, the vault can blow sky fucking high.

Let's be honest. Darya's brother or not, I've known since before the ball that it was only a matter of time before I put a bullet through that prick's head.

Watching Darya relive the years she spent as the Orlovs' prisoner in that fucking compound almost drove me mad. It's bad enough knowing how she got the scars on her shoulder. Seeing the place where it happened—not to mention seeing my own girls in that same goddamn room—ripped my heart out.

That missing doorknob in her bedroom, the realization that Orlov had access to her at any time of the day or night, sends me into a cold-blooded ocean of rage I can barely contain. The mere thought of that first escape attempt, of her wheeling Sergei's unconscious body out of the compound and trying to run with Orlov's men following her, is worse than any nightmare. I thought she'd been tattooed with the broken-winged sparrow as a warning. That was bad enough. Knowing it was carved as a punishment is even worse.

How the fuck did she survive that?

The endless years of constant fear, of never knowing when they were going to invade her bedroom, come for her?

I can't prevent the shudder of icy fear that goes through me even imagining it. My years on the streets were hard, the nights lonely and full of fear.

But whatever I endured pales in comparison to what Darya lived through.

No death can ever avenge what those fuckers did to her. What they're doing to my girls now.

I grip the steering wheel hard enough to break the fucking thing. I wish I was on my MTT. Right now I crave the mindless escape of speed and wind.

I need to plan.

I'm not a man who likes waiting. We've got the layout of the compound now, got the codes to the tunnels, and I know where the girls are. Waiting until Makari arrives tomorrow is going to be the longest fucking night of my life.

I'm almost relieved when the phone rings. I hit the answer button. "You're on speaker in the car," I snap at Dimitry. "Darya's with me."

I don't want to risk him saying anything that will upset her any more than she already is.

"I was hoping you might have time to meet me at the warehouse." The careful way he words his request puts my teeth on edge.

Fucking Nikolai. I forgot all about the prick. I feel a flash of irritation.

"I thought I told you to handle it."

"This is me doing that." Dimitry's flat tone is its own message.

"Fine. I'll take Darya home, then come." There's a small sound from Darya beside me. I turn to her, trying to soften my face.

"Abby," she whispers, and that one word is so full of quiet desolation it needs no other explanation.

I lean toward the phone. "Your girlfriend needs to come to

the penthouse." I give it to him in a clipped tone that should communicate that I'm not fucking about. "Tell her to pack a bag so she can stay a few days."

"I can keep Abby safe—"

"I don't give a fuck about Abby's safety." I hear the savagery in my voice, but right now I just don't care. "Darya needs her, so tell her to come."

Dimitry pauses just long enough to let me know I've trodden very close to a dangerous line. I can't blame him. I also can't fucking help it, not at the moment. "Boss," he says eventually. He hangs up without waiting for me to end the call.

Fuck. I grind my teeth. I'll need to fix that straight away. Dimitry deserves better from me.

They all do.

Darya touches my shoulder softly. "We'll get the girls back, Roman. I know we will."

I cover her hand with my own, try and fail to smile. "Of course we will."

But even if we manage to get Ofelia and Masha back in one piece—which, given the fucking arsenal Vilnus has guarding that basement, is no certainty—in what condition will we find them?

With how many bloody knife cuts scarring their bodies? With how much emotional damage that can't be undone?

Every minute we wait, Vilnus could be sharpening his knives. And why is there still no ransom demand? What the fuck is he waiting for?

We remain silent for the entire drive back to the penthouse, our interlinked hands at least some form of comfort. It hurts me to leave Darya at the penthouse. Right now I don't want her out of my sight, not even when she's safely in my fortress. I don't like not being able to see her, to touch her.

I ride the elevator to the penthouse, checking it myself before I allow her through the door. I wrap my arms around her, trying not to let my tension show. "I'll be home as soon as I can, okay?"

She nods against my chest, clinging to me in a way that makes me curse Nikolai, Dimitry, and even Abby to the lowest hell.

The elevator dings, and I spin around, my hand going straight to the holster under my jacket. Then Abby steps out, her face pale and drawn. With an inarticulate cry, Darya runs to her friend, and Abby holds on to her like she's a buoy on a stormy sea.

I leave the two friends wrapped in each other's arms and go to find out what the fuck Nikolai has to say.

———

THE WAREHOUSE IS right at the end of the industrial port, with the sea on one side and a vacant block on the other. It's stacked high with rusted old shipping containers that do a good job of concealing it from view. The warehouse is isolated enough that it doesn't matter how loud anyone screams, and is easy to escape by boat if the authorities get too curious.

Dimitry is waiting outside it, and by his stiff stance and grim face, I'm lucky I'm still walking after what I said about Abby.

Men like us don't joke about the safety of our women. It was wrong, and I know it.

"Abby's safe." I greet him with my hand out.

After a brief pause, he takes it.

I grip his shoulder, hard enough to leave marks.

He nods.

Thank fuck for that.

At least one thing in my life is uncomplicated.

We turn toward the warehouse. "Nikolai?" I make the name a question.

"I ripped the fucker up as much as I could without making

him lose consciousness." Dimitry shakes his head. "He said he's only allowed to deliver his message to you. Someone obviously scared him enough to make him actually hold out until I agreed."

"He'd better make it quick. I have a bullet with his name on it just itching to be fired." I rip back the sliding wooden door on the warehouse with enough force to almost take it off the rollers.

Nikolai is sitting in the middle of the vast concrete floor, although *sitting* might not be the correct term. His naked body hangs from chains suspended from an overhead steel strut, his wrists dripping blood where the steel has cut through the flesh. His torso is a sea of red, evidence that Dimitry has indeed ripped him with fist and knife to the point where he's barely able to lift his head.

Dimitry is more of a blunt-punch kind of man, and this kind of torture isn't usually his style. Not that I'm complaining. I couldn't give a single fuck.

Nikolai is a dead man regardless of what he has to say. And the more he suffers before that bullet comes, the better.

"Put some pants on him," I snap at one of my men. I have no desire to interrogate Nikolai while his dick is hanging out. Even the thought of it being inside Inger makes me physically sick. The two of them disgust me to the core.

Nikolai's head rises slightly as he's forced back into the bloodstained suit pants he must have been wearing ever since the night of the ball. I take a closer look at the marks on his body. Not all of the wounds are fresh. I remember that Abby found him beaten almost senseless outside Pillars. Close up, I can see she wasn't exaggerating. Dimitry might have opened a few of the cuts with his fists, but most of the knife wounds are crusted over, days old, and the rainbow bruises on every part of his body have clearly been building up for some time.

"Cut him loose and sit him down." I kick a chair across the

floor, and Nikolai slumps into it, rubbing his lacerated wrists. I throw him a plastic bottle of water, and he gulps it greedily.

I wait until he's had a few good mouthfuls, then knock the bottle out of his hands.

"This is as good as the next few hours are going to get, Nikolai, so make the fucking most of it."

His bloodshot, exhausted eyes are full of resentment when he raises them to me. "I didn't know about the bomb, Roman. Neither did Inger. We just wanted to run away together, with Masha. I thought she was my daughter." He scowls. "Inger told me she was."

I look at the men standing around the edges of the warehouse. I don't want witnesses to the rest of this conversation.

"Everyone out," I order curtly. The men file out without a second look, except for Dimitry. He knows the order didn't apply to him.

I wait until the door has closed before turning back to Nikolai. "You thought Masha was your daughter, so you decided to fucking *kidnap* her?" I only just resist the urge to add to his bruises. "Way to start your journey into fatherhood, Nikolai. Risk Masha's life, not to mention Mickey's and Ofelia's, by blowing up the ballroom, then hand two innocent children over to the most sadistic bastard in Miami. What the fuck were you thinking?"

He's shaking his head. "It was supposed to be just Masha, but Ofelia was with her when the bomb went off. We didn't know about the bomb, Roman, I swear it. Inger and I planned to take Masha and get straight on the *Guapa*. Orlov told us he'd bought it for us as a present. He said he'd help us get it to Miami, but after the explosion, he said there had been a change of plans."

"And you believed this shit?" I'm so dumbstruck I'm almost speechless. "Why the fuck would Orlov help you and Inger?"

"Because he's an old friend of our family." Nikolai scowls at me. "And because, like a lot of Papa's old friends, he doesn't like what happened to the Stevanovsky clan after you took over."

A friend of the family?

Dimitry and I exchange a silent look. This is fucking news to me. I've never spoken about the Orlovs to Yuri, but I know most of his contacts. If that name had ever come up, I'd have fucking remembered it.

"Since when are the Orlovs old family friends?" My eyes narrow on Nikolai like a laser.

"I don't know." He tries to shrug, winces. "Always, I guess, not that we had Christmas together or anything. I don't think Inger was lying about Masha," he adds, like I could give a single fuck. "She believed Orlov's promises too."

I actually laugh out loud at that. "You're an idiot if you believe that, Nikolai. Inger has been fucking Orlov for years." He flinches as if he's been hit, and I go on, taking a perverse pleasure in twisting the emotional dagger. "She's probably fucking him right now and laughing at how stupid you were to help her."

Nikolai shakes his head. "No, Roman. You're wrong." He tilts his head toward the torn, bloody suit jacket lying on the floor nearby. "Look in the pocket."

I nod at Dimitry, who picks the jacket up and shakes it out. A small bundle falls out, tumbling to the concrete floor with an audible thud. He picks it up and begins to unravel it, but we both already know what we're about to see.

Inger's red-nailed finger falls onto a nearby table, still wearing the enormous diamond ring Mikhail gave her on their engagement.

"He made us watch." Nikolai's voice cracks. "The girls and me. Inger was crying, screaming for him to stop."

He made them watch their mother scream in pain.

I might loathe and despise Inger, but that doesn't lessen my horror at the girls being subjected to her suffering.

"Whatever attack you're planning, Roman, don't." His voice is hoarse and broken. "Orlov is expecting you. He's got an army guarding that underground bunker. And the whole thing is wired to blow."

"Tell me something I don't already know." I resist the urge to add to Nikolai's scars. I don't have time for this shit. "Just tell me what the fucker wants. You said you would only talk to me. So talk."

"Orlov gave me a message for you." He spits out a glob of blood and mucus, eyeing me sullenly. "He wants the vault open. He said to come to Miami with your key and Darya Petrovsky, or he'll kill the girls." Nikolai swallows painfully. "If you try anything, anything at all, he will kill them. Starting with Ofelia." He squints up at me. "He said you know why he's going to kill Ofelia first."

The instant flash of rage I feel is so lethal I almost kill Nikolai then and there, just to murder something. Someone.

He has my daughters. I don't give a fuck what the DNA test says. They are both my girls. The fact that Orlov thinks it matters to me which of them he threatens tells me exactly how lacking in conscience he is.

His demands are nothing less than what I expected. And yet hearing them affects me more than I thought it would.

He will kill the girls.

I don't have the luxury of believing Orlov might be bluffing. I *know* what he's capable of. And he's been waiting for this a long time.

Rage and a sickening fear churn like acid inside me.

Nikolai's face swims back into focus.

"Where was Orlov holding you?" I snarl. None of the camera feeds, underground or above, showed any sign of Nikolai or Inger. "Where does he have Inger hidden?" I rap the questions out hard and fast.

I need to know everything Nikolai can tell me before I put a bullet in his head.

He eyes me resentfully. "At first they took us all to the compound. Vilnus made me take a good look at it, showed me how he'd wired it up to blow. That's where they did . . . that." He nods at Inger's finger on the floor without looking at it, his face pasty. "It was that psychotic fucker Alexei Petrovsky who did it." Nikolai's mouth tightens. "He's a sadistic bastard. The other guards call him Vilnus's rabid dog. The mad *mudak* beat me unconscious."

For the first time, I almost feel kindly disposed toward Darya's brother.

"You said *at first*. What happened after the compound?"

"Vilnus took Inger and me away, to some house out by the Everglades. He left the girls in the underground bunker, guarded by Alexei Petrovsky and an entire fucking army."

"What house out by the Everglades? Who owns it?"

His face screws up in confusion. "How should I fucking know? It was big, that's all I remember, at the end of a long driveway." He scowls at me. "We weren't exactly making small talk while I was getting beaten half to death. You need to get me to a doctor, Roman."

Dimitry and I exchange an incredulous look.

Does Nikolai actually think he's getting out of here alive?

It beggars belief.

I fold my arms. "Then why don't you tell us what you *do* know, Nikolai?"

"Orlov knows Ofelia is your daughter. There was some DNA test that got flagged."

"I'm aware." I fold my arms, glaring at him.

He spits again and gives me a spiteful look. "Did my brother know he wasn't Ofelia's father?"

Oh, I'm going to enjoy killing you, Nikolai.

"Of course he didn't fucking know. None of us did until Mickey ran those damned tests."

His mouth twists. "Not that Mikhail would have cared anyway. He always loved you more than he did Inger. No wonder she ran to me." A spasm of something contorts his face. "I thought Masha was my daughter, right up until they showed me that test. Inger . . . told me she was."

"Bullshit." I stare him down. "Mickey told me that you and Inger argued about her being at parties with Orlov. And you've been taking photos of Masha for months. You clearly suspected she wasn't yours."

"Inger promised me she was." He looks as pathetic as he sounds. "And she wouldn't get a paternity test. She said it would only cause problems if people knew. It was only after . . . what happened at the compound that she told me the truth."

"I don't give a fuck about your love life, Nikolai." I'm getting impatient.

But he seems intent on finishing his sorry tale. The only reason I don't stop him is because there might be something helpful amid the bullshit.

"Orlov raped her."

I roll my eyes. "Sure, he did, Nikolai. Jesus." I shake my head. "Even you can't be stupid enough to believe that."

"It's true." He shoots me a resentful look. "She was flirting with Orlov that summer, true enough, and we did argue about it. But you know what Inger is like. She flirts with everyone. Apparently one night Orlov wouldn't take no for an answer. She told me that he slipped something in her drink. When she woke up the next morning, she was too embarrassed to make a fuss, so she never told anyone, even when she found out she was pregnant with Masha."

Sadly, I can actually believe that. Inger has never known when to back off. And I vaguely recall her being extra hysterical that year. I put it down to her trying to screw a bigger settlement out of Mikhail.

Fuck it. I don't want to feel sorry for Inger.

"Even if that story is true, then why the fuck would Inger ever trust him? Why would she think he'd buy her a yacht?"

Nikolai's swollen eyes meet mine. "That's exactly why she believed him. Orlov claimed he'd always felt bad about what happened, that he'd always regretted that night. He said that buying the *Guapa*, helping Inger and me run away together with Masha, was his way of making good. He even offered me a place in his organization." The hint of defiance in his voice almost makes me laugh.

Almost.

"And you actually believed all this?" I'm incredulous. "You honestly thought you were such a fucking prize that Vilnus *Orlov* would offer you a job? More to the point, was that all it took for you to betray your entire family? To betray Mikhail's legacy and everything your father built?"

"You kept secrets from me!" The words explode from Nikolai, and for the first time, I catch a glimpse of real anger. "Lance Ryder told me all about you. About how your father was the one who built the Petrovsky vault. I didn't believe him at first. I even asked you outright, that day at the parade. You could have told me the truth then, but you didn't. Orlov believed it, though. I met him with Miguel when I was in Miami with Cádiz FC. He does business with the Colombians that invested in Cádiz. That was when he offered to help Inger and me." His face turns petulant. "Orlov said that if Ryder's stories were true, you'd used our name to hide, to build a legacy for yourself, while all this time, you've been plotting to open that vault and take what's inside it. He said you betrayed our family, used our resources to start whatever the fuck it is you're doing up in that research facility." Nicky gives me a look I imagine he thinks is cunning. "Orlov plans to steal whatever you've got going on up there as well, you know. I heard him talking to Inger about it."

Dimitry makes a hard noise, takes his gun out, but I shake my head. Let Nicky talk. The more the dumb fuck says, the better, as far as I'm concerned.

"He said you and Darya Petrovsky are working together." Nikolai throws the words at me as if I'm going to actually explain myself to him. "What I want to know is if that's why my brother died, too. Did Mikhail work out what your game was, Roman? Was it you who planted that bomb in his car? Was that bullet you took for Mikhail even real? Or did you set that up too, just so you could win my father's favor and steal from us?"

I'm too fucking flabbergasted to do anything other than stare at him in silence. Nikolai's chest is heaving, his eyes flashing with pain and rage.

"You caused all of this," he says. He spits again, his eyes not leaving mine. "Ofelia and Masha were kidnapped because Orlov wants you and Darya to open that vault. I was beaten almost to death just to send you a message, and the woman I love is probably being raped at this minute, all because of your greed. You stand there and accuse me of endangering the children as if you're some kind of hero, like you follow some fucking code of honor that makes you better than everyone else. But the truth is that if you want someone to blame for what's happened, Roman, you should look in the fucking mirror."

His rasping breath is the only audible sound in the silence that follows his diatribe. His face is a picture of disconsolate anger, like a toddler after a tantrum.

A huge part of me wants to simply kill him and be done with it.

But another part of me knows Nikolai is right.

Not about everything, obviously. His accusations about Mikhail are next-level fantasy. But the part about this being my fault?

Yeah.

Yeah, that's fair.

Not that it's going to stop me from killing him.

I slow clap. "Looks like you've got it all figured out, Nikolai."

He scowls and spits on the floor.

"So I guess you want in on the vault, huh, Nicky? And the research facility?"

He eyes me suspiciously. "I think I deserve that much, after everything that's happened."

"Sure." I nod like I'm actually agreeing, then hold up a finger. "Just one last question. You're doing good, Nicky."

Dumb fuck actually looks relieved, as if he genuinely believes he's going to walk out of here alive.

"Did Orlov ask you about the research facility? Did Alexei?"

"Seriously?" He looks at me incredulously. "Even now, *that's* the shit you care about? Of course Orlov asked about it. He asked on that first day, when we were in the compound. But it's not like I had anything to tell him. It's not like you've ever taken me up there, is it?"

There's no faking the indignation in his face. Nikolai truly has no idea about Mercura, it's obvious.

"And there isn't anything else you've left out of this story? Nothing more you can tell me about the compound that might help us get the girls back?"

"No." His face sinks back into sullen petulance. "I've told you everything I know." It's the whiny voice again, Nicky the victim, and it does my head in. "I want to talk to my father. I'm not your lackey, Roman. I'm Yuri Stevanovsky's son, his true heir. I bled in that room. I nearly fucking died. And then you bring me in here and beat me all over again. My father is going to finish you when he finds out what you've done."

That's it.

Whatever final hesitation was holding me back, whatever

faint sense of guilt or family allegiance I might have felt, slips away.

I cross the floor in three paces. Squatting down, I use my gun to tilt Nikolai's chin up so he's facing me. "Tell me, Nicky," I say in a conversational tone. "When did you first fuck your brother's wife?"

His eyes shift left and right, searching for an escape that's never going to happen. He licks his lips nervously. "I was fifteen," he says finally.

"Fifteen!" I tilt my head in mock respect. "How did a fifteen-year-old pimply little fuck get Inger's legs open?"

He visibly squirms. "I caught her," he mutters eventually. "Sleeping with the pool boy. I promised her I wouldn't tell Mikhail about it—"

"If she fucked you as well," I finish for him. I shake my head slowly. "Jesus, Nicky. You really are a piece of shit, aren't you?" I get my face right up into his, close enough that I can smell the blood and rancid sweat coming off him, the rottenness at the core of the little *mudak*.

"Mikhail Stevanovsky was a brother to me," I say softly, staring right into Nikolai's bloodshot eyes. "I took a bullet for him, not just once, but many times during the war. I never once counted the scars. I'd willingly take a thousand more bullets if it would give Mikhail one more day on this fucking earth. I'd do it not because of your father, and not because of anything he could offer me, but because I fucking loved Mikhail, and always will.

"It was Mikhail, not me, who made the decision to keep you out of Hale. Because despite the fact that you were his brother, he didn't trust you at all. Even so, he gave you Pillars and a chance to prove yourself. But that wasn't enough for you, Nicky, was it? Nothing this world can give you will ever be enough.

"Not Inger, not even the *pakhan*'s chair you think you

deserve—nothing will ever satisfy you. Do you know why that is?"

He doesn't answer, just watches me. His eyes have grown increasingly wide and more fearful as I've spoken. He's starting to understand what's going to happen.

"Because you're a cockroach, Nikolai. You creep around in dark places and feed on anything you can find. You don't build anything. You don't create anything. You just sit inside houses other people build for you and eat until there's nothing left. Then when you fall down, you lie on your back with your legs waving in the air, because you're too useless to pick yourself up and too fucking stupid to learn from your mistakes.

"I don't mind cockroaches, Nicky. I've always held the opinion that there's room in this world for all kinds of creatures."

I stand up and nod at Dimitry.

"But that doesn't mean I don't step on the fuckers when they're living in my goddamn kitchen."

We put more bullets in Nikolai than is strictly necessary to end his life.

I don't regret a single one of them.

21

DARYA

"I really am sorry I blackmailed you into helping me." I squeeze Abby's hand.

"If you apologize one more time, I'm not giving you any more of this wine. Oh, wait." She looks at the lone wineglass on the table. "I haven't given you any of the wine anyway. Which means I drank that whole bottle. Which means . . ." She makes a conclusive circle with her index fingers and holds them up with dramatic flair. "That you're either someone impersonating my friend—or pregnant."

"Abby!" I almost choke on my peppermint tea.

"Well, which is it?" She opens another bottle and fills up her glass. "I mean, I already have to learn to call you Darya, so I guess you are a different person. But if memory serves, you were supposed to be taking a test last time I saw you. Which leads me to conclude that option B is still on the table." She closes her eyes briefly as she swallows a mouthful of wine.

When she opens them to look at me, her wineglass pauses in midair and her eyes widen.

"Wait. You're not really fucking pregnant, are you?"

I grimace. My right shoulder moves a hesitant inch upward, and I give her a tentative smile.

"Shut the front door!" Abby's mouth is open, her wine threatening to spill onto the couch. I hastily take it from her hand and put it on the coaster. "I mean . . . wait." Her eyes snap back into focus, and she pins me with a hard glare. "Tell me you didn't know this when you ran."

"There wasn't much I could do about it—"

"Oh, dear lord." She is shaking her head slowly, still staring at me. "No wonder CEO Man was ready to rip the entire town apart."

"No." I look around nervously. "He doesn't know. Abs, you can't tell him. He has enough going on with the children missing."

"He doesn't fucking *know?*" She snatches up her wine and downs most of it. "Are you insane? However much he might piss me off, even I know Roman Stevanovsky isn't the kind of guy you keep secrets from, Luce—Darya. Fuck." Her face screws up impatiently. "It's going to take me some time to get used to that. Anyway. You can't keep that from him. It's not fair."

"I know, Abby, alright?" I stand up restlessly, making myself more tea to keep my hands busy. "But I really don't want him to deal with it now. *I* don't want to deal with it now. He needs to focus on getting the girls back." The familiar horror presses against my chest. "We both do."

The gleaming steel surface blurs with the memory of Ofelia and Masha's terrified faces. They haunt my every minute, whether my eyes are open or closed. It's hard to sit still. Hard to think, let alone speak, even to Abby, when I can so easily picture them in Orlov's hands.

"You don't know what Vilnus Orlov does to girls." I start to pour tea but stop because my hands are shaking. "You can't begin to imagine how sadistic he is."

Abby looks at me for a long moment, her expression unusually opaque. Then she stands up abruptly. "Right. I've had a horrible day dealing with Nikolai crying about how unfair life is. You've had a horrible day dealing with . . . well, everything. We're both going to take long, hot showers, then I'm going to make us a proper meal. And then"—she points a firm finger at me—"you and I are going to sit down and do something we should have done a long time ago."

"What's that?"

She fixes me with a stern eye. "You're going to tell me the truth. Abby and Darya, two point oh. The reboot. This time with the life story. The *real* one. Deal?"

I meet her eyes and smile faintly. "Deal."

It's AFTER MIDNIGHT, and Roman and Dimitri still aren't home. Abby's amazing spaghetti marinara is long finished, as well as a panna cotta I found in the fridge and most of two bottles of very good red wine, neither of which I've touched. We're ensconced on the couch, my third pot of peppermint tea almost finished and Abby eyeing the rapidly dwindling contents of her glass.

"So all this time," she says, staring at me in fascination, "I was living with a bratva princess? Heiress to some great fortune from imperial fucking *Russia?*"

"Well, not heiress, strictly speaking." It's incredibly cathartic to actually talk about it, or at least the parts I know. "We're Russian, and *very* traditional. My brother is my father's heir. Daughters are there to look beautiful, take care of their papas, and marry into profitable alliances."

"Well, in that case, I'd say you've smashed it out of the park." Abby holds up one hand. "*Beautiful:* tick. A hundred ticks. *Take care of your papa:* fucking target hit, above and beyond. *Marry profitable alliance:* Oh, let me check. Does billionaire bosshole tick that particular box?"

I'm laughing despite myself, despite everything. "I'm not really sure my father will see it that way. For that matter, Roman has never mentioned marrying me."

She rolls her eyes. "That's coming, Darya. That's been coming from the day you came down from his coffee delivery with your shorts undone and that glassy-eyed look. The man is obsessed with you, anyone with eyes can see that."

There's no time for either of us to be obsessed with anything at the moment.

Guilt and exhaustion wash over me again, as they do every time I momentarily forget the agonizing terror of Masha and Ofelia being in that compound.

Abby covers my hand comfortingly. "There's nothing we can do but wait," she says, for the fiftieth time tonight. I nod. There isn't much else to be said.

"But I want to know more about this Naryshkin fortune," she says. "What's the actual story? Did your father really escape with it?"

I know she's trying to distract me. But I don't particularly mind. I'm exhausted from worrying at the thought of the girls in that damned room.

I turn my teacup in my hands. "There are parts of Papa's story I know," I say slowly, "and parts I don't. Some that I'm just starting to piece together now. I'll tell you what I do know, the part of the story my father impressed upon us as children.

"Papa's father, my grandfather, was a prince who was imprisoned during the revolution. Papa never told me that my grandfather's name was Naryshkin; that part I've pieced together myself over the years, and it's only speculation. What I do know is that my grandfather and his best friend risked their lives helping many Russian aristocrats escape—including Peter

Carl Fabergé, the jeweler. They remained loyal to the imperial family to the very end and were thrown into a gulag with one of the royal sons as a result. They risked their lives again to help him escape and got him safely to exile in Finland. They and their families were imprisoned in a gulag for the rest of their lives as punishment. Both my father and his best friend were born in the gulag."

"Your father was *born* in prison?" Abby is openly shocked.

"And raised there." I smile. "He never spoke about it like it was a hardship, though. When he spoke about it at all, which was rare, he told us about being taught by the imprisoned aristocrats in the gulag. Literature, music, languages, art . . . Papa said once that he and the other sons were schooled as rigorously as any student in an elite college. He used to describe sitting around a lone candle during freezing nights while someone read from a book they'd hidden." I smile, remembering Papa's reverence for the written word. "Our home was filled with books in Russian, French, Latin, Italian—room after room of rare books. I think if Papa could own every book in the world, he would, just to make sure they were safe.

"The older men also taught their sons useful things. How to hunt and fight. But most of all, they taught them their own skills. Everything from watchmaking to leather work, any skills they had were passed on to the sons born into captivity, as best they could be." I cast Abby a sideways glance. "Including safe making—and breaking."

"So that was Roman's grandfather? A safe maker? What did you say his name was?"

"Borovsky. He was *my* grandfather's best friend, although Papa never told us his name when we were growing up. He never used names in general. Everyone he knew in the gulag was explained to us using nicknames: Papa's father, for example, was nicknamed *Graf,* or the Count; Roman's grandfather, Borovsky, was *Glaza,* the Eyes. My father never mentioned his own nickname, but he did say that his best friend, Borovsky's son, was known as *Ruki*—the Hands."

"And you think this Ruki was Roman's father?"

I shrug. "I don't know. You have to understand how secretive Russians are, particularly those who were raised in gulags. My father will never stop looking over his shoulder until the day he dies. They trust no one but one another. My father might have told Alexei his stories, because Alexei is his son, the rightful heir to our tradition. But not me." It's difficult to keep the bitterness out of my voice. Especially after all we've been through together, all I've done to keep Papa safe, it's hard to accept that he still sees me as his daughter, someone to protect and shelter, rather than trust as he does Alexei.

If Roman and I do make this work, I vow, *it's going to be different between us, traditional or not.*

"Anyway," I go on. "When Papa was around thirty years old, long after their parents had passed, the gulags were closed, and he and Ruki were released." I shoot Abby a wicked grin. "And this is the part of the story Papa would reluctantly tell, but only to us, his children, and only after too much vodka, when he was in a very good mood.

"During those long nights spent telling stories in the gulag, Ruki had been taught by his father how to make—and crack—safes. Papa had been taught how to fight and hunt. When they were released from the gulag, they broke into Papa's family home, which by then had communist officials living in it. Papa never told us exactly what they stole. All he ever did was give us a wink and a wicked grin and tell us that he and Ruki 'took back what belonged to Russia.' Then they fled the country."

I can't help the note of pride that comes into my voice in this part of the story.

"They walked the entire way to Switzerland, just the two of them, in the dead of winter. Those were the stories my father would tell, about the rabbits they caught, the berries they ate.

It's why I remember the name Ruki so well. Papa always told us that his father had taught him that only one thing mattered: *keep Ruki safe*. Keep his best friend's hands safe. Papa told us his father even had a saying for it, that Alexei and I learned when we were children: *Glaza boyatsya, a ruki delayut*. In English it means *the eyes are afraid, but the hands do*. It's a bit like 'feel the fear, and do it anyway.' Papa always said that until he and Ruki were safely far away from Russia, his job was to make sure that Ruki's hands were kept safe, no matter what happened to them both."

"But what did they steal? Or—take?" Abby is fascinated.

I shake my head, smiling. "I don't actually know. No," I laugh, when she starts to protest, "truly, I don't. I don't know much before Papa came to America. I do know that he lived in France before that. Mama told me he was even married there and had children. I don't know what happened there, only that his wife and children died. He never spoke of those years, just like he never opened the vault in our home and showed me what was inside. When I'd ask, he'd always say, 'that is a story for another day, myshka.' Then he would take me to the library and give me a book and say that the only true treasure lives in our heads and hearts."

My heart twists at the memory. I can almost smell my mother's cooking stealing through the compound, feel the rich paper of Papa's old books beneath my fingers.

There's something incredibly cathartic about telling someone about my past. I've never told my story to anyone. Our family was a tight circle of trust, our stories told in our kitchen, and only ever to us. I don't know when I first knew that our secrets weren't ever to be shared, but I do remember the heavy feeling that came with keeping them. The shadows of the past lingered in every corner of our room, in the books my father reverently took down from the shelves, in the priceless art on the walls. We were surrounded by the past, but it was also a world my brother and I were never allowed to fully understand. The past was a mystery that haunted my father's eyes when he thought we weren't looking, that lived in the thousand brutal scars on his body. When I got older, I understood that the stories he'd told us of the gulags were rose-colored memories fit for children. His own father died when Papa was still a teenager, and yet he lived in the gulag for years after that. The gulag raised him. It created Sergei Petrovsky, the man who built and then lost a family in circumstances he'd never speak of. The gulag created the fierce *pakhan* he then became, the warlord who created an empire that inspired both respect and fear.

Papa might have told my mother the full story of that past, but he never told us. Not ever.

"Wow." Abby's eyes shine, her wine forgotten. "That's the most incredible story." She shakes her head. "How did it end? I mean . . . how did your home get taken from you?"

My smile fades. "Papa had been at war with a Colombian cartel ever since I was a child. He'd made allies of the biggest Russian families in Miami, formed a coalition to fight the Colombians. I don't know if anyone told me Papa was the head of that coalition; I just knew, from the way the other men who visited us deferred to him. But then Papa had a stroke."

I will remember that day as long as I live: my mother's shriek, the shrill of ambulance sirens.

"The doctors said he probably wouldn't survive. Mama, Alexei, and I slept at the hospital, too scared to go home in case he died while we weren't there. While we were sitting at his bedside, one of Papa's allies, a man named Vilnus Orlov, launched a coup."

I wrap my hands around the teacup, trying to warm myself on the inside. But there isn't anything that can melt the frozen memory of that night, and what came after it.

"We had no idea," I tell Abby softly. "When Vilnus came to the hospital and offered to drive us home, told Mama she needed to take a break, we thought he was being kind. It was only when we got inside our home that we first saw the bodies and the blood." I grimace. "Vilnus hadn't even bothered cleaning up before he brought us home. He was too anxious to get us locked up, I guess. That first night, I slept in a bloodstained room, beside a dead body." My mouth tightens. "It didn't get any better after that. Vilnus had launched the coup because of what was rumored to be in the vault. He wasn't happy when none of us could tell him how to open it.

"We were kept alive because Vilnus worked out that our fingerprints were needed to open the vault. Unfortunately for him, our fingerprints alone weren't enough."

"Roman." Abby nods. "Dimitry kind of told me this part."

"Yes. Roman's fingerprints are needed, too." I don't mention the key. That is Roman's secret, not mine to tell. "Vilnus was convinced that we knew more about how to open the vault than we were telling him. We didn't, or at least not back then. When my father didn't die, Vilnus thought Papa might have the answers he wanted. But Papa was unconscious for months, then a complete invalid for years after that, and Vilnus got impatient.

"He targeted my mother, because he knew it killed Alexei and me to watch her suffer. Then, after she died, he and his men used their fists, and knives, on Alexei and me. It was like a sport to them. They did anything they liked to us, except to the parts of us the rest of the world could see. And they didn't rape me. At first, because it would have lessened my value. Later, because they were scared I'd cut my own fingerprints off."

Abby blanches.

I hear the brittle note in my voice and shake it off, thrusting the memories away. I don't want to think about what Vilnus did to me, not while he still has Masha and Ofelia. And besides, I forced myself to deal with those memories long ago.

Vilnus Orlov stole years of my life. I wasn't going to allow him to make me a victim for the rest of it.

"Finally I managed to escape with Papa," I say. "You know most of the rest, or at least the parts that matter."

Abby pours the last of the bottle into her glass, her face pale. "How old were you?" She glances up briefly. "The night of the coup?"

I stare at the wall behind her, seeing the bloodstained walls, the head blown clean off the guard who had watched me every day since childhood. "I was just seventeen," I say softly. Her face swims back into focus. "One year older than Ofelia is now."

She grips my hand. "They'll get her back, Darya. You know they will."

I clutch her hand silently, unable to echo her reassurance. We sit in silence until the night is deep and my eyes are drooping.

Finally I give up and see Abby into the guest room. Then I crawl into Roman's enormous bed and fall into oblivion as soon as my head is on the pillow.

<hr>

I come half awake to the vague rumble of voices, which seem to be getting louder. Through a fog of exhaustion I feel the mattress shift as Roman kneels against it, his lips on my cheek. He smells like blood and gunpowder, and my stomach lurches with fear.

"What happened?" I ask, almost dreading the answer.

"Nothing that matters. Go back to sleep," he whispers against my hair.

"The girls?"

"Not yet. I promise I'll wake you if anything happens."

"Mickey?"

"Safe in bed." He pulls the covers up over me. "Dimitry and Abby are on the floor below us in your old apartment. I'm going to take a shower. Go to sleep, *milaia*." His lips graze my cheek again, and I turn toward him, but he's already stripping off his clothes, heading for the bathroom. I watch through eyes that keep closing, seeing the old scars on his flesh as if they're new, the war wounds from the years he's spent fighting. No amount of scars can dent the breathtaking power of him, the solid wall of muscle that is his back, the hard-corded thighs. In the dim light of the bathroom I watch him shower, marveling that he's mine, that even amid this chaos, we've somehow still got one another.

I'm dozing when he makes it to bed, only semi-waking when he rolls me into his arms, murmuring soothing words into my ear. I fall back to sleep with his hard body cradling mine, his hand cupped around my breast and his breath warm and sweet on my neck.

When I wake again, Roman is already gone, and I discover with a shock that it's almost midday. There's a message on my phone: *I'll call as soon as there's news. Abby is in the kitchen.*

I shower and come out into the kitchen to find her perched on a stool, eating watermelon with her coffee.

"There's no news," she says by way of greeting.

I nod silently and try to sip the peppermint tea she's made me, fighting the ever-present morning nausea. For once I seem to be winning, but that might just be because there's not much left to throw up.

"Did they tell you anything?" I ask, already knowing the answer.

Abby lifts a shoulder. "Nikolai is dead."

I nod slowly. It should mean more to me, but somehow I'm not surprised. Maybe I knew already, by the stench on Roman's clothing when he came in, the way he held me close when he came to bed.

I can't feel sad. I didn't like Nikolai, and he helped kidnap the girls. I can't forgive that, and I know Roman couldn't either.

But it's also a reminder that war is here again, that there will likely be more scars on Roman's body soon.

And what if this time he doesn't walk away?

My hand covers my belly. *What happens to you then, little Borovsky? What happens to all of us if Roman loses this battle?*

"Don't think about it." I look up to find Abby watching me. She shakes her head slowly. "Whatever you're thinking, don't. It hasn't happened yet, and it probably won't. You and your baby are going to be fine, even if I have to drive away with you myself." She looks so fierce I almost smile.

"Did they tell you where they were going?" I ask.

"Roman has a meeting with some guy up at the lab, that's all I know. Dimitry said it's someone who can help, so that's good, isn't it?"

"I guess." I stir my tea without seeing it.

What kind of help? What's he planning? God, I hate this. I know he's left me to sleep, and I trust him to tell me what I need to know, but knowing nothing at all is killing me.

"Fuck it," I say aloud and pull out my phone.

Abby grins. "You go, girl."

I hit Roman's number, and he answers on the first ring.

"Are you alright? Is everything okay?" His voice is taut with an undercurrent of fear.

This is horrible for him, too.

"I'm fine. I just woke up. Are you okay? Abby said you're meeting someone today."

"I'm with him now. I'll tell you about it as soon as we're done, I promise."

"Okay." I clutch the phone, unwilling to hang up.

"But actually, since you've called, there is something I wanted to ask you." His voice is studiedly casual, which makes me nervous. "When you were in Miami, did you know anyone who lived out on the edge of the Everglades? A friend of your father, or of Vilnus Orlov? It would have been a big house, with a long driveway."

I frown, trying to remember. "I think the only time I went to the Everglades was with Papa, and then it was only to go on a boat. I don't remember any house that fits that description. Why?"

There's a slight pause, and I can tell Roman is trying to work out how much to tell me. "Just say it, Roman." I hear the tension in my tone, but I'm not going to hide it either.

"Nikolai told me he and Inger were held in a house out there. That's why we didn't see them on the cameras. We've got satellite pictures of all the houses in the area, but it would help if we could narrow it down."

"Inger?" I can't keep the anger out of my voice. "Do we actually care what happens to Inger?"

Roman chuckles, a warm sound that travels all through my body. "You really are a savage at heart, *milaia*, aren't you?" He doesn't sound too sad about that, if I'm being honest. He lowers his tone. "From what we can put together, Inger might not be entirely guilty. Either way, I'll deal with her myself. I don't want the children wondering where she is or what happened to her."

I guess I can understand that. I don't like it, though. And I'm not sure how long I would be able to hold myself back if someone put me in a room with Inger and left a gun on the table.

Scrap that. *I don't think I'd even need a gun.*

"Darya." Roman's voice is tense again. "There's something I should tell you."

"I know Nikolai is dead." I cut him off. "It's fine, Roman. I'm fine. I'm . . . glad, I guess."

There's a short pause. "Okay." His voice is low, warming, and I want him here, beside me. "I'll call as soon as I can, Darya." But he doesn't hang up immediately. I cling to the receiver, holding on to the connection. Finally, he says roughly, "I love you."

The raw honesty takes my breath away.

His words aren't said when we're alone, in bed, with him wrapped around me.

This is Roman in his office, surrounded by his men.

He needs me as much as I need him.

"I love you, too." My voice isn't quite steady. I close my eyes, picturing him on the other end. We hang on in silence for a moment, then he ends the call.

I look up from the phone to find Abby with a forkful of watermelon halfway to her mouth, staring at me. "Wow," she says. "First a baby, and now the L word over the phone, in broad daylight? You better watch out, Petrovsky. Shit's getting *waaaayyyy* real, girlfriend."

22

ROMAN

I turn to face the team in the secure room at the lab, my expression daring any man there to comment on my conversation with Darya.

They don't.

Smart.

I hated leaving her this morning, before we'd even had a chance to talk, let alone anything else. And I need the *anything else* like air right now.

But she's exhausted, bone weary from the way she's been sleeping, and I can't afford to lose a minute, even if that means leaving her naked body sprawled across my bed like a goddamn fantasy.

I pull my mind back to the room with an effort. I'm sitting in the secure room with Mak, Dimitry, Pavel, and Mickey.

Mickey was sitting outside the penthouse door when I opened it this morning, already at work on his laptop. No chance he was letting me drive away from the house without him, just like I never had a hope of coming into this meeting without him sitting in.

"Darya doesn't know anything about the house in the Everglades," I tell them.

Mickey scowls. "Who gives a fuck about the house in the Everglades? My sisters aren't there. They're in the compound." He turns his laptop around accusingly. I wish I could rip it out of his hands. I'm pretty sure he spent all night in bed staring at the camera feeds, just so he could watch over his sisters. His eyes are bloodshot, his face pale and drawn. I feel like every day that passes adds a year to the boy he was only months ago.

"An operation is only as good as the intelligence behind it." Mak addresses Mickey directly. Despite his courtesy, there's a quiet reprimand in his voice that makes Mickey color slightly. Mak has only been in the room for a matter of minutes, but already it seems he might be the only person beside Pavel, Dimitry, and me to whom Mickey might actually listen.

It isn't just Mak's tall, rangy frame and clear military skill that lends him such an instant air of authority, but the calm, measured way he analyzes every piece of information and the speed with which he is able to assimilate it.

"The fact that we can't locate that house is a concern," he says now, "but I do have an idea." He turns to Pavel. "See what you and Mickey can find on a Miami business called Fedorov Industries."

Pavel, getting the hint, stands up and nods to Mickey, who of course looks at me.

"I'll tell you everything we talk about, I promise." I don't know how many times he's made me say it, the little prick.

Mickey gives me a hard glare to make sure I get the message, then leaves.

Mak raises a sardonic eyebrow. "You sure the two of you aren't related?"

Dimitry almost chokes on his coffee.

"Fuck off." I lean on the table. "What is Fedorov Industries?"

"It's not so much what," Mak says, "but rather who. I told you on the phone that there are things about Orlov you should know."

I nod. Another thing I like about Mak is that he doesn't fuck around when he has something to say.

"The Fedorovs were one of the early bratva clans in Europe. Came straight out of the Russian gulags, back in the fifties. Brutal fuckers. They set up camp in Paris and for decades ran everything there from girls to gambling. Even the local criminals didn't mess with them, not after the bosses of three Paris families were found without their heads in one of their own bars."

"Nice." Dimitry refills his coffee and casually bites into an éclair.

Mak shakes his head. "You lot are just as twisted as any of my army boys. Anyway." He turns back to me. "The Fedorovs weren't just interested in owning the game. They were also dedicated to reclaiming all the treasures that had been smuggled out of imperial Russia by the aristocratic exiles during the revolution. Most of the pieces had been traded years ago. In the years after the revolution, Europe was awash with what is now seen as priceless art: Fabergé eggs, elaborate jewelry. Back in the early years, there was so much of it on the black market that the pieces were virtually worthless. People were trading Fabergé necklaces just for enough food to feed their families."

I nod impatiently. "We don't need a Russian history lesson, Mak. My father was a jeweler and a safe maker. I know all this."

"It matters," he says calmly. "Trust me. The Fedorovs didn't give a fuck about history or the Russian aristocrats clinging to a faded past. They were a new generation, with no respect for the old traditions. By the time they ran Paris, it was forty years after the revolution. The imperial treasures hadn't just regained their value—they'd become prizes sought by every collector in the world. The Fedorovs were ruthless in tracking them down, and they weren't shy about the tactics they used to acquire what they wanted. They burned jewelry shops, robbed houses, and tortured families for information. Eventually their search led them to two old friends, one a jeweler and the other an art dealer. The two men were rumored to have escaped Russia with a stolen fortune: the Naryshkin treasure."

Dimitry and I exchange a look. "Okay," I say. "You've got my attention now."

"The Fedorovs went in with their usual brutality. When they didn't get the results they wanted, they tortured the men's families. Killed them, in the end. Wives, children—all of them, brutally tortured to death. Then the Fedorovs locked the bodies inside the men's businesses and set the buildings on fire. There was nothing left of their families but ash.

"It wasn't the first time they'd pulled this trick. It was an effective deterrent for anyone else who might feel inclined to hold out on them.

"Only this time, the Fedorovs had picked on the wrong two men.

"Why the men escaped death that night, nobody knows. But the hell they unleashed after the death of their families is still whispered about in some circles today. These men didn't just go to war, Roman. They went on a rampage that was nothing short of a bloodbath.

"They didn't just take revenge on the Fedorovs.

"They annihilated them.

"And they didn't just take back what had been stolen from their own shops. They also reclaimed every last valuable piece the Fedorovs had acquired from impoverished Russians. A literal fortune. And they did it all without anyone knowing their real names. They were like ghosts, whispered about but never named. People were either too scared or too admiring to risk pissing them off. They were known simply in Russian as *Golova*, the Head, and *Ruki*, the Hands. People said the Head did the killing and the Hands did the stealing.

"By the time the war was done, the Fedorov clan was destroyed. The Head and the Hands didn't try to take over the Fedorov organization. They simply annihilated it, then vanished, seemingly into thin air.

"Along with a reputed fortune, of course.

"One of the Fedorov clan killed during that war, along with two of his sons, was a man named Victor Orlov."

Oh, shit.

"And let me guess," I say slowly. "Victor had a son who survived. Named Vilnus."

Mak nods. "Yup. There were also a few surviving Fedorovs and Orlovs. People who'd been smart enough to run when the blood began to flow. Most of them moved to the United States. Russian clans are loyal, you know that as well as I do. One of them must have paid Vilnus Orlov's fare, because some years later, he turned up in Miami."

I frown. "How the fuck did he wind up allied to Petrovsky, with that kind of past?"

His mouth twitches. "I take it you are aware that Sergei Petrovsky is indeed the legendary Head of my story?"

If there's one thing I know about Mak, it's that his intelligence is second to none. "Let's not fuck about, Mak. You know who I am. You know who Petrovsky is. You probably know the fucking brand of toilet paper Putin uses. So just get on with it, *da?*"

He tilts his head to one side, a smile lurking at the corner of his mouth. "You do take all the fun out of life, Roman. But out of courtesy for your situation, I'll answer.

"Orlov, or whoever paid his fare and was pulling his strings, had done his homework. He knew who Petrovsky really was, knew about the Naryshkin legacy. By that time, Petrovsky had built himself a fearsome reputation in Miami. He was known for being old-school: honor, tradition. The Head might have been a ruthless fuck, but he played by the rules of an earlier, more honorable time.

"So Orlov didn't lie to him or pretend to be anyone other than who he was. He came to Petrovsky with his hat in his hand, claiming the Fedorovs had disowned him back in Paris despite his father dying for them. He said that they'd left his sisters to be raped and killed, and him to starve. He claimed that he and the Orlovs were in a blood feud with the remaining members of the Fedorov clan. He asked Petrovsky for his help in avenging his family."

Dimitry rocks back in his chair and gives a low whistle. "Jesus. Smart."

"It worked." Mak shrugs. "Petrovsky helped Vilnus take his revenge, though he was careful to make sure it was Vilnus who pulled every trigger. Rumor has it that Orlov even killed Fedorov women and children, something Petrovsky never approved, but which he probably took as proof of the depth of Orlov's rage. By the time it was done, I guess Petrovsky thought that Orlov had proved his loyalty."

"Only Orlov was just biding his time," I say softly, my hands clenched on the tabletop. "The slimy fucker used Petrovsky's support to eliminate his competition for him."

Mak points a finger at me. "Exactly."

I sit for a moment, mulling this all over. "So tell me why you have Pavel and Mickey looking up Fedorovs, if they're supposedly all dead?"

"Ah." Mak's twisted smile makes another brief appearance. "Well, it seems Vilnus wasn't quite the outcast he claimed. For several years before he turned up on Petrovsky's doorstep as a poor lonely orphan, he had in fact attended an elite boarding school in New York. Under an assumed name, of course." He takes a photograph out of the manila folder on the table in front of him and slides it across to me. An adolescent Vilnus Orlov stares back at me from a school photo taken in the late sixties.

Red-hot rage seizes every cell of my body. I don't trust myself to pick the photograph up; I'm certain I'd tear it to pieces.

"His school fees were paid by one Andras Peretz, supposedly a Jewish refugee from Poland." Mak takes another photograph out of the folder. The face on it sends shivers down my spine, though I'm not sure I've ever seen it before. It's the man's eyes. I've seen eyes like that before, on men who have killed too much. Dead, entirely devoid of any kind of emotion. The man staring back at me is no refugee. He's a stone-cold killer.

"Andras Peretz disappeared about six years ago. Nothing dramatic, he just faded from sight. Around the same time, Vilnus Orlov registered a business name: Fedorov Industries." Mak looks at his watch. "And any moment now, we're about to find out what Andras Peretz is calling himself these days."

He just finishes speaking when Mickey bursts back in the door, waving his laptop excitedly. Mak sits back in his chair, lacing his hands behind his head with an air of quiet satisfaction.

Smug bastard.

"Surely you could have done this yourself," I mutter. "Since you're fucking encyclopedic about the rest of it."

"Why should I do all the work?" He arches a lazy eyebrow. "It's your shit show."

Dimitry explodes again, sending éclair across the table. I glare at them both, but neither look in the least repentant.

I suppress the urge to smile. Despite the shit storm circumstances, it's good to work with Mak again.

"Fedorov Industries." Mickey is stammering in his haste to get his words out. "The registered CEO is a man named Ilyan Fedorov. I had to trawl the dark web to get a picture, but this is his company ID." The same dead eyes of the man who recently called himself Andras Peretz stare back at me from the plastic card on the screen. "And Ilyan doesn't just own a house in the Everglades. He owns an entire fucking compound—or rather, his company does." He clicks, and another image appears, an enormous house with a long driveway set just back from the swamp.

"Ah. Ilyan." Mak reaches into the manila folder and withdraws an old newspaper cutting, yellow and faded. "I did suspect as much."

The cutting he hands me is a French article about two cases of suspected arson: fires in a Paris jewelry shop and at an adjoining art dealership, which claimed the lives of two Russian men and their entire families, women and children included.

Ilyan Fedorov is named as the prime suspect.

The photo of him is grainy and indistinct, but even though it's a much younger man, there's no mistaking the brutal, dead eyes are the same as those of Andras Peretz, and of the man on the Fedorov ID card.

I stare at the photograph for a long time.

This man is the reason my father and Sergei parted ways when they reached America. He's the reason for the secrets my father kept his whole life. Ilyan Fedorov is why Darya's parents and mine didn't have Sunday lunch together, tell stories about Russia like my friends' parents used to do.

Ilyan Fedorov is the reason Sergei and my father wouldn't risk anyone knowing they were connected.

They wouldn't risk losing their families a second time. They knew that Fedorov would take revenge the first chance he got.

I hear my father's voice, that long-ago night when I sat on the landing: *"We both know what happens to those who wait to long to act, Sergei. I will not make that mistake again."*

It was Ilyan Fedorov who told the Colombians where to find my mother. I'm as sure of it as I am that he was responsible for my father's death—even if it was Orlov who wielded the knife. My father's house, too, had been burned to the ground after they killed him. It's too macabrely similar to what happened in France to be a fucking coincidence.

When I look back up, the entire table is watching me expectantly. I stab the Everglades compound on Mickey's screen with one finger.

"Fedorov is pulling Orlov's strings. Get rid of him, and we weaken Orlov. We take that house first. We take Fedorov. Then we come for the rest of the fuckers."

Mak inclines his head. His smile is almost as cold as Fedorov's. "That, my friend, will be a pleasure."

23

ROMAN

I head back to the penthouse for siesta. Plans are in place now, or at least in the process of being made, and I need to see Darya.

The penthouse is dark and quiet. Dimitry picked Abby up earlier, so I know she's gone, but I thought Darya would still be here. I pick up my phone to text her, wondering if I'll ever stop feeling a lurch of fear when I find her gone.

"She's asleep." I look up to find Maria, the maid, watching me from the corridor. "She is very tired."

"Thank you, Maria." I smile at her, throwing my jacket over the chair, my mind already debating the various ways I intend to wake Darya up.

"Um, Señor Stevanovsky." Maria doesn't move as I approach, her hands twisting nervously. "I know it's not my place, but I think Luc—I mean Darya. That is, Señorita Petrovsky . . ." She reddens, her voice trailing off as she stumbles over the names.

"Calling her Darya is fine, Maria. What is it?" I'm still smiling, but it's an effort. My mind and body are already in bed with Darya.

"She needs to see a doctor." She looks at me worriedly. "It isn't right for her to be so sick and so tired. She's barely keeping anything down at all. Even in these first months it isn't normal to be so ill."

"In the first months of what?" I frown. I know Darya has been exhausted, and I've noticed she's not eating much, but I didn't realize she's been sick.

"Oh!" Maria reddens, her hand coming up to cover her mouth. "I thought—I didn't realize—I should go." She backs hastily toward the elevator, eyes darting nervously away from mine.

"Wait." I don't grab her arm, but the command in my voice is clear enough, because she stops dead in front of the elevator, turning reluctantly to face me.

"In the first months of what, Maria?" I step closer to her, my heart thudding hard in my chest, my voice low. "Why is Darya so unwell?"

She bites her lip. "I found this when I cleaned her apartment just after she . . . left." She reaches into the pocket of her apron and comes out holding something that looks like a pen. "I held on to it because I thought she might like to keep it, for sentimental reasons, you know? But she didn't say anything, and I didn't want to intrude . . ." Maria shifts from one foot to the other, looking desperately uncomfortable. "I'm sorry," she says, her eyes downcast. "I thought you knew."

The dim light of the penthouse darkens around me, the only light in the room emanating from the white stick in her hand. I can hear the slow pulse of blood through my body, a dull roar in my ears. I watch my hand reach out and pluck the stick from her hand, feeling as if I'm watching somebody else move. The stick feels cold and oddly impersonal.

"Thank you, Maria." I know it's me speaking, but my voice seems to come from a long way off. "I'm glad you kept it for us." However I might feel, I must be managing a good act, because her face brightens with relief.

"I'm so happy for you both." She smiles at me mistily, her voice catching. "With . . . everything that is happening, I am glad there is some good. But you must get her to a doctor, Señor Stevanovsky." She gives me a rather stern look. "A woman in her condition must be cared for, especially in these early stages."

"Noted." I usher her into the elevator, the same fixed smile on my face as she babbles on about morning sickness. When the doors close on her mid-sentence, I stand in front of them for a solid ten minutes, just staring at the pink plus sign on the white stick.

I walk down the corridor with the stick gripped so tightly in my hand my nails dig into my palm. I'm strangely terrified of dropping it.

When I push open the bedroom door, Darya is curled in a tight ball at the edge of the bed, her arms wrapped around her belly. I sit on the mattress beside her, just watching her body rise and fall as she sleeps. Even in the half-light I can see the hollows in her cheeks, the dark shadows under her eyes. I wonder how I didn't notice before.

I place the white stick gently down on the bedside table. My other hand cups Darya's face, my thumb smoothing a loose tendril of hair back from where it's fallen across her eyes. She stirs in her sleep, moaning softly against my hand in a way that does dangerous things to my body. She turns her lips into my palm, her eyelids cracking slightly open. "Roman." She mouths my name sleepily, her lips curving into a smile against my hand.

My thumb travels over the bee-stung lips I adore, tracing their fullness as if I'm feeling it for the first time. "Darya. Go back to sleep, *milaia*. You should rest."

My mind is jumping about disjointedly, trying to work out

what to do first: get the doctor here and wake her before she's rested, pluck her from the bed and take her directly to the hospital myself, or get my entire staff working on converting one of the lower floors to a medical suite. It's while I'm busy wondering just how disruptive the noise of that conversion might be to Darya's sleep that I realize she's watching me.

"What is it?" She pushes herself up on one elbow, eyeing me worriedly. "What's happened? Is it the girls?"

"No." I cover her hand with my own, shaking my head in reassurance. "No, Darya, we have plans to get the girls back."

"Tell me." She sits up, her eyes fixed on my face, but all I can see are the way her collarbones stick out, the pallor beneath the tawny skin.

"The plans can wait." I reach for the glass of water by her bed and hold it out to her. "Drink some of this, and then you're going to see a doctor."

She eyes the water uneasily. "A doctor? I'm fine, Roman. The girls—"

"I have an entire army working on getting the girls back." My voice is more curt than I intend it to be. She frowns, and I make an effort to soften my tone when I speak again. "I will get the girls back, Darya, I promise. Right now, I'm more worried about getting you to a doctor."

Her eyes narrow slightly. The opaque mask drops over them at the same time her hand steals to her belly.

"I've seen you do that with your hand a dozen times since I found you in Granada." I nod at the glass. "Drink, Darya."

She sips the water gingerly, eyeing me cautiously.

"I've seen you disappear into yourself, somewhere I can't follow. Turn in on yourself like you're hugging a secret." I cup her head again, my thumb smoothing the hair back from her temple. "I thought it was the weight of the past, of fears about the Orlovs."

She sits up properly, drawing her knees to her chest and

wrapping her arms around them, hand gripping the water, face unreadable as it has been so often lately.

"I might know exactly when to pull a gun, Darya, but when it comes to reading emotions, I'm not the most perceptive man. Maybe if I was, I wouldn't have needed the maid to show me this."

Darya follows the direction of my gaze to the white stick on the nightstand. She freezes like a deer caught in the headlights. When her eyes finally move back to mine, they are a deep, haunted world of topaz emotion, the glass of water forgotten and tipping dangerously toward the bed cover. I take it from her hand and rest it back down beside the white stick.

"I understand why you didn't tell me before you ran." The hand that isn't holding her face clenches the bed covers convulsively, hopefully out of her eyesight. "I'm not saying I agree with it. But I understand it." I force the tension from my voice with an effort. "And perhaps, given all that has happened with the girls, I can even understand why you might have hesitated to tell me since you've been back."

That sounds less convincing. My ability to shield my emotions goes only so far.

"What I cannot understand is how you could endanger your own health like this." My hand stills on her face. "Maria tells me you haven't been eating. That you've been sick for days. More sick than is . . . normal."

"For pregnant women." Darya's voice rasps like old metal, her arms clutching her knees to her chest, her eyes wide and hurt. "Say it aloud, Roman. I'm more sick than is normal for someone who is *having a baby*."

I frown. "We can pick over words later, Darya. Right now you need to see a doctor."

"No, I don't!" Swinging her legs over the bed in a sudden gesture, she faces away from me, her shoulders rising and falling rapidly. I want to touch her, but I'm not at all sure she wouldn't jerk away from me, and I'm not sure I'd be able to restrain myself from throwing her down on the bed if she did.

Not that I would throw her anywhere, because she's fucking *pregnant*, and . . .

Oh, Jesus.

I don't realize I've said the last two words aloud until I hear Darya's harsh laugh.

"Yep." Her voice is muffled by her hands covering her face. "And that right there is exactly why I didn't say anything. It's fine, Roman." She stands up and walks stiffly away from the bed toward the bathroom. "There'll be time for us to talk about this when the girls are home safe. For now, you don't need to worry about me. About . . . us. I can see a doctor, if it makes you feel better. But I'm fine. *We're* fine." The way she touches her stomach again makes it very clear who the *we* in her sentence relates to.

I leap from the bed and cross the room, blocking the entrance to the bathroom. Her head is down, her arms folded across her body in that protective way that makes my teeth go on edge, as if she's the only thing standing between the world and our baby.

Our baby.

And despite the war I'm about to walk into and the dark nightmares that haunt the edge of my every waking thought, those two words shine so brightly they're almost blinding.

Our baby.

A child made by Darya and me. A future I never imagined I could have, never dared even to dream of.

Darya, dancing in the kitchen with her belly ripe and swollen.

Darya, swimming in the sunlight at the finca, holding a giggling baby in the air.

"Darya." I tilt her face up. "Darya, please look at me." When she raises her eyes, they gleam with unshed tears, a hard brilliance that breaks my heart.

"I didn't do this right," I say roughly. "I'm probably not going to do any of this right. I'm better at bullets than babies, like I said. I always thought my life would be the former, with no place for the latter. I never thought . . . In a lifetime, I never imagined I'd be given this kind of chance. And I'm terrified I'm going to fuck it up."

Her brow crinkles. I brush the hair back from her face, trying to let my smile show the wonder that I feel but am doing an epically bad job of expressing.

"I want you to see a doctor because I want to take care of you and our baby." Even saying the words aloud feels impossibly beautiful. But the joy of speaking them is nothing compared to seeing the dawning hope in her eyes, which both touches me and breaks my heart at the same time. "I'm sorry that I didn't get this right, and I'm sorry in advance for all the things I'll likely fuck up in the future. But never for one moment think that this isn't the best goddamn thing that's ever happened to me in my life, Darya, because it is." I pull her against me and wrap my arms around her, almost scared of holding her in case I crush the tiny life between us. "Our baby is a fucking miracle. And I swear to you that I'll take care of you both, now and forever. Do you hear me, Darya?" I pull back from her, holding her face in my hands, my thumbs wiping the moisture away from the corners of her eyes. "Do you believe me?"

"Yes." She nods in my grasp, her eyes melting into mine. "Yes, Roman. I believe you. But—" She flinches, her eyes closing.

My hands drop, tension gripping my chest. "But what?"

"But I think I'm going to be sick." She pushes past me, hand over her mouth, and makes it to the bathroom just in time.

I stand at the doorway grinning like a maniac, wondering how it's possible to feel so happy and so fucking terrified at the same time.

24

DARYA

In the end Roman and I compromise by me seeing an obstetrician that afternoon. Dr. Ballasteros is a female doctor of my choosing, rather than Roman's normal *sew 'em up and take the bullets out* male option. She reassures both Roman and me that my morning sickness isn't grave enough to require hospitalization and gives me some medication to ease the symptoms.

"Apart from the sickness, everything looks in perfect shape. It is important that you get enough rest and remain stress free." She gives Roman a rather old-fashioned look. I'm guessing the strings he pulled to get an appointment on such short notice haven't gone unnoticed. "But other than that, Mrs. Stevanovsky, I think you can look forward to feeling much better very soon." She nods at the changing rooms adjoining her suite. "You can change here, if you like, while I talk with your husband."

I open my mouth to correct her, then see Roman's frown

and close it again. He made the appointment. And I'd be lying if I said I didn't like how the words *Mrs. Stevanovsky* sound.

I'd be lying if I said I felt anything other than absurdly touched by everything that has happened since I woke to see that white stick by my bedside.

I wipe off the gel from the appointment and change back into my clothes, still stunned that Roman seems to be actually happy about this, about having a baby he never planned for, especially given the chaos we are in the middle of.

In the limo, his hand closes over mine. "I have to go back up to the lab this evening, work with Mak and Dimitry to iron out our plans. And tomorrow, I have to fly to Switzerland."

I nod. "To see your mother?"

His mouth tightens into a grim line. "Whether we use it or not, I need to get the key to the vault. I'm not sure whether I'll have time to see my mother. I'm going straight from Switzerland to Miami."

He's going to war.

My heart skips a beat. I know it has to happen to get the girls back. That doesn't mean the idea of Roman bursting into the Miami compound with a gun in hand doesn't terrify the fuck out of me.

I fix on his comment about his mother; it is the easier part for me to focus on right now.

"But we have to see your mother, at least." I turn his hand over in mine. He lets me hold it, but his eyes remain firmly fixed on something out the window. The traffic is heavy, barely moving. It would be faster to walk home, not that I imagine Roman will be letting me walk far anytime soon. His overprotectiveness is sweet. It's also annoying.

"Not 'we.' Me. You're not going to Switzerland." He says it with the kind of finality I normally wouldn't argue with.

"You can't open the Miami vault without me." I try to make my voice calm, but I can't quite disguise my agitation. "I have to be there, Roman, whether either of us want that or not. I may as well be in Switzerland too."

"No chance you're coming to Miami." He shakes his head once, sharply. "And we're not opening that vault, not yet anyway. We just need the Orlovs to believe that we will, which is why I'm getting a gel imprint of your fingerprints done tonight. They won't know that gel imprints don't work, or even if they suspect, they won't be sure. The technology was new then." He glances at me, his face set in implacable lines. "Vilnus Orlov already has our daughters, Darya. There's no way I'm giving him a chance to take you and our baby. I don't have a fortress in Miami, but I do here, one that will be locked down more closely than Alcatraz. I need to know you're here, and safe, or I won't be able to do what I need to."

I nod slowly. "I understand that. Can we compromise by allowing me to come with you to Switzerland? I can fly back here after we've got the key."

And after we've met your mother. There's no chance we're going to Switzerland without meeting Rosa Borovsky, urgency or not.

"Women aren't supposed to fly during the first trimester. Especially with bad morning sickness." He glances sideways at me, his mouth curling slightly at my surprise. "I looked it up while Dr. Ballasteros was examining you."

"I'm over ten weeks, and she also said the morning sickness should begin to recede almost immediately. To be honest, I already feel better." It's true; I suspect that half of my symptoms were stress related, because ever since I realized that Roman actually wants this baby, my entire body has felt more settled. "Please, Roman." I squeeze his hand. "I can't just sit here, waiting. At least let me come for that first part."

"I'll call the doctor and ask her." Roman shifts across the seat and pulls me back against his body, his arms wrapping over my front. "I don't want to leave you." His lips move against my hair, and I hold his arms, relishing the reassurance of them around me. "Even the thought of leaving you alone . . ." His voice roughens, and he pulls me closer.

"I'll be fine." I turn in his arms, my hands coming up to his face. "But take me to Switzerland." I kiss him.

He kisses me back hungrily. But as fast as the fire between us flares, he slows his kiss, lessens his grip on my body. His mouth moves beneath mine gently, with none of his customary fierce desire. I press against him, my hand sliding up his denim-clad thigh, edging toward the hard bulge threatening to thrust above his leather belt. My other hand slides beneath the navy linen beach shirt, touching just enough tanned, hard chest to set my insides churning.

He groans into my mouth, but one of his hands halts mine on his thigh, and despite the fierce tension I can feel in his body, he pulls back from me. "You need to rest, Darya." He tries to smile, but nothing can diminish the dark lust in his eyes, the way they linger on the new fullness of my breasts, swelling over my sundress.

"Am I going to rest for the next seven months?" I trail my mouth up his neck, my whole body shivering with the desire to touch him.

"Darya—" But even as he's protesting, his hands are roaming up the backs of my legs, teasing the lace at the edge of my panties. I feel a stab of triumph as his tongue swipes my mouth and his hands cup my ass. He rolls me against the rigid outline of his shaft. "Fuck."

He hits the button that darkens the glass between the driver and us, and I smile against his mouth.

"*Vedma,*" he murmurs against my lips.

"*Pakhan,*" I murmur back, and the rumble of his laughter soothes every piece of my shaken soul. In a single movement he flips me over and lays me down on the back seat, tugging my panties over my legs and opening me to his mouth.

My eyes roll back in my head. "*Oh . . .*"

He licks me with a slow, sensual delicacy that is a world away from the leather seats and tinted windows of the limo. He holds my hips and tracks every crease and fold until I'm moaning and squirming beneath his hands, craving the hard length of him inside me. He chuckles when I writhe, the vibration of his laughter tripping me closer to the edge. He doesn't even have fingers inside me and his mouth is driving me insane, my hips bucking off the seat as his tongue hits my center, curling and pounding me with such certainty I have no hope of holding out.

My hands twine in his hair, and one of his comes up to stifle my scream as I thrash against him. His mouth holds me in an endless moment of spasm after spasm, the world around me disappearing. I'm just coming back to earth, my eyes still closed, when he lifts me from the seat and steps out of the limo, growling an order at the driver.

I didn't even notice that we came into the garage.

He doesn't put me down inside the elevator, cradling me against him until we reach the penthouse, where he walks us straight down the corridor to the bedroom, slipping my dress off as we go and leaving it in a pool of cotton on the floor. He lays me down, unbuttoning his shirt as he stares down at me. "I can see it now," he says roughly, one hand stroking the curve of my breast, the faint swell of my belly, as the other tears his clothes off. "I don't know how I didn't see it before. Your body is so beautiful, *milaia . . .*"

When he joins me on the bed he slides gently inside me, moving slowly, his body rigid with tension.

"You won't hurt me," I whisper.

"You don't know that," he growls.

"You won't hurt me, Roman." I thrust upward to meet him, and he groans, his arms quivering with the effort of holding himself back. "You won't hurt the baby. I promise."

"I don't want to jolt you around—"

I put my mouth close to his ear. "Let yourself go." I wrap my legs around him, urging him onward. "It's what I want, Roman. And it's what you need." I grasp his ass, pulling him deep inside me. "Just let go."

He scoops me up and folds me around him, sinking into me with a savage sigh that sends me spiraling into bliss, thrusting with sure, deep strokes that hit every part of me.

"Fuck, Darya." He lifts my ass high and drives home in a final, heady surge. "Fuck, I love you."

———————

"ILYAN FEDOROV." I repeat the name as Roman rubs the towel through his hair and reaches for his clothes. The sun is golden and brilliant beyond the window, the last burst of daylight over the water before night falls. "So you think this man is behind Vilnus Orlov, controlling him?"

I watch with unabashed pleasure as Roman drops the towel from around his waist and pulls on black leathers, his eyes running over my naked body on the bed as he does. I'm not going to lie—I still get a thrill from seeing how immediately his body reacts to what he's seeing.

"I'll never focus if you lie around looking like that." He pulls the sheet up and tucks it around me with the twisted smile I love. "Yes, it looks like this Fedorov bastard is the one who started it all, back in Paris."

"Paris." I repeat the word slowly. It's strange how one word can evoke so many emotions that I never truly realized I felt until now, after Roman explained what he has learned about our fathers' shared past. "Papa would never take us there. Even when I was at finishing school in Switzerland, he'd holiday with us in Italy or at Lake Geneva—but he'd never take us to Paris. And my mother never went there either. I remember once there was a school trip to France; Papa refused to sign the form. He took Alexei and me to Barcelona instead. He never explained why he hated France. I just knew that he did."

I sit up, clutching the sheet around me, my chin resting on Roman's shoulder as he pulls on his boots. "It's like all the other shadows that were never spoken about in our house, this darkness that sat around us, all the secrets I could sense were there but never understood. When I think of France even now, I feel this uneasy sensation of fear and danger. I never knew why I was afraid of Paris. I just knew it was a dangerous place for some reason."

Roman tilts his head toward mine, his cheek touching my head in a brief but incredibly comforting gesture. "I don't remember my father ever mentioning it at all." He presses a kiss to the top of my head and stands up. He's in his bike leathers, a white T-shirt molding his chest, the jacket slung over a nearby chair. The last rays of the afternoon sun turn his muscled biceps a tawny gold and highlight the warm depths in those midnight eyes. He's so damned beautiful I want to tear all his clothes off again, and at the same time, I want him up at the lab, working to bring our girls home.

"But I do know what you mean about the atmosphere of secrecy," he says. "The first thing I thought, after Mak explained what had happened, is that Paris is the reason our fathers never met up for drinks or dinner. They lost what must have been a lifetime of friendship, all because they wouldn't risk a public relationship that might expose their families to Ilyan Fedorov." He pulls the jacket from the back of the chair with savage force, his jaw hard. "Not that it helped. They lost everything anyway. We all did."

I touch his hand, feeling the tension coursing through him. "We can't blame them for that, Roman," I say softly.

"Can't we?" He shakes his head, his mouth a tight line. "It seems to me there's a lot they could both have done and didn't.

It all comes back to that damn vault." He shakes his head, breathing deeply to calm himself. "Anyway. None of that matters now. We'll finalize everything tonight at the lab, and then I'll fly to Switzerland first thing tomorrow." He pauses, looking down at our joined hands. "I'll call Dr. Ballasteros." His voice is careful and measured. "If she agrees that it's safe, then you can come too. But, Darya." He fixes me with a stern look that is meant to quell my excitement, but absolutely does not succeed in doing so. "If she says it isn't safe—"

"I know, I know." I stand up and wrap my arms around his neck, kissing the hard corded muscle there. "Only if she says it's okay. I get it, Roman." I kiss him until he groans and wraps his arms around me, hauling me hard against him. "Thank you," I whisper in his ear.

His kiss is long and sweet, and I never want it to end. I want him to know it isn't just Switzerland I'm thanking him for, or even his willingness to include me in every step of this. It's for all he has said since the moment he placed that white stick by my bedside. For making me feel safe and loved. For reassuring me that I won't ever have to be out in the cold again, running alone in the darkness with a small life to protect. I realize that right up until today, until I saw the fierce wonder in Roman's eyes, part of me still feared it would come to that. Feared he would resent me or reject this baby, and all that it means to be a family.

But he called it a miracle.

I cling to him, wanting to hold on to those words forever. They feel like a miracle in themselves. A small explosion of rich, pure joy amid the horrific darkness we will live until Roman has the girls back safely.

"Go," I whisper against the shell of his ear. "Go, and do what you must so our girls can come home."

OFELIA

"I'm starting to think your daddy doesn't care what I do with you, *kotya*." Vilnus lounges against the door of our cell, smoking, flanked by a small party of his guards.

I swear the watch party gets bigger every day.

"We sent Roman a message days ago. He still hasn't answered us." Vilnus drags heavily on his cigarette and casts Alexei a calculating glance. "Probably too busy fucking the Petrovsky whore."

His men all laugh obediently.

Alexei doesn't move. Not by so much as a flicker does his face betray the fact that Vilnus is talking about his sister.

"I'm beginning to think we might need to give Roman a little push. I thought that sending him your mother's finger might serve as a warning, but it doesn't seem to have made an impression. Perhaps a video might be better." He steps into the room, licking his lips in a way that turns my stomach. "Something creative. His sweet little teenage daughter getting broken in with a knife at her throat, for example."

His men laugh again, though this time, I can hear the faint note of unease behind their laughter. After the conversation I overheard between Alexei and Dima the other night, I've realized that not all Vilnus's men are loyal to him. I've begun to notice those who vie for his attention, and the others who stand slightly back, keeping their expressions carefully neutral.

"I could do it myself." Vilnus's eyes flicker to Masha. "Like I will with this one, when the time comes. No daughter of mine goes to their wedding bed without feeling my cock inside them first."

None of his men laugh at that. Several of them look away, clearly uncomfortable.

It seems that even in the home of the most brutal of bratva criminals, some things are still despised by most men.

Unfortunately, their disgust only seems to spur Vilnus on even more.

"You don't like that, do you?" He looks around at his men contemptuously. "You don't understand. I don't fuck them because I like it. I don't. They're my children, my blood. I fuck them so the men they marry know who owns them. Know what I'm capable of. A man who can fuck his own daughter? That's not a man you fuck with. My sons-in-law are loyal to the bone *because* they know what I'm capable of."

He stares around the room until he gets a reluctant mumble of assent. He nods as if he's satisfied. I wonder if he sees the contempt in their downcast eyes. But then again, from what I've seen, Vilnus Orlov isn't the kind of man who cares much for what others think of him.

His eyes scan the room, then settle on Alexei.

"What about you, Petrovsky?" He kicks the seated figure with one booted foot. "You've always had a soft spot for little girls. Took me years to teach you to take a knife to them, didn't it? Had to almost cut you to shreds before you'd lift the blade yourself. I still remember the first time you did it, cut into that Colombian bitch whose father screwed us on a deal. Thirteen, I think she was. You threw up all over the floor after the first cut, if I remember correctly."

His men laugh aloud at that one. I keep my head down, not game to let Vilnus see the fury in my eyes.

"Thought you'd actually hit me when I made you fuck her." Vilnus is staring at Alexei, waiting for a reaction, but the other man just stares at him blankly out of his lone eye and doesn't move at all. "But you got used to it after that, didn't you, Petrovsky? Even got a bit of a taste for it. Used to be our favorite afternoon sport, didn't it, boys? Locking Petrovsky in here and waiting for him to whip out that big cock of his and fuck whatever little virgin we threw in front of him?"

This time the laughter comes more readily, with a dark, dangerous edge that strings my nerves tighter than a piano. Somehow I just know that's exactly what Orlov did to Alexei, used him for entertainment, over and over, until he believed he had him cowed.

But he doesn't.

I hold on to that truth, to the man who whispered to Dima in the darkness, like the spark of hope it is.

"You're mean." Masha's voice pipes up so unexpectedly I don't have time to stop it. She's staring at Vilnus accusingly, and with a terrifying lack of fear. From the corner of my eye I notice Alexei tense.

"Masha," I hiss, covering her mouth with my hand. "She's sorry," I say hurriedly to Vilnus. "She's young—she doesn't understand what she's saying."

"Oh, I think she does." He is smiling, a broad, fat-lipped, sickening grin. "She's an Orlov, that one." He crosses the room and kneels down in front of us. Close up, he's utterly repulsive. "Tough as her papa, aren't you, princess?"

Masha shakes her head violently, dislodging my hand. "My papa dead."

Vilnus's smile widens. "Oh, no, he isn't, my little hellcat." He prods himself in his chest. "*I'm* your papa, Masha."

She frowns. "No!" She shakes her head decisively.

His hand whips out, faster than a snake, smacking her across the face hard enough for the crack to echo around the room. "Who's your papa, Masha?"

I bite my lip with the effort of restraining myself.

Masha doesn't answer, just stares at him, open-mouthed with shock, her eyes wide.

His hand whips out again.

Crack.

Her head is knocked sideways under the weight of his blow.

"No!" The word escapes me before I can stop it. Once it's out, I can't stop. "Don't touch her again." My voice is low and trembling. "I don't care what you do to me. Just leave her alone."

"Ah." Vilnus leans forward. One pudgy hand comes out and strokes my cheek, slowly, insidiously. "I knew you'd beg for it eventually. You've got that look about you, Ofelia. I can always tell when a girl is coming into heat. I bet you've been thinking about it, haven't you? Did you like it when Petrovsky's knife touched your fresh pussy? I think you did. I think he liked it, too. I can tell, you see. I've practically raised that boy."

I'm pressed hard against the wall, but there's no escaping his roaming hands or his insidious words. Masha seems to have realized her mistake, because she's closed her mouth and is now simply staring at Orlov, her bright blue eyes entirely blank, like she's gone somewhere else.

It takes a minute for me to realize that she isn't looking at Orlov at all, but over his shoulder, to where Alexei is watching us. His eye isn't blank anymore. It burns like arctic fire, holding Masha's eyes as if he holds her heart and soul in his hands.

I hear his whisper in my mind: *No matter what Orlov does to you, don't lose yourself . . .*

"I think you want to fuck this one, Petrovsky." Vilnus says it without turning around. His hand rests on my breast, squeezing it uncomfortably hard, his eyes watching me keenly. I force myself not to react. "But it must be a quandary, no? What will Roman Borovsky do to you when he discovers you broke in his only daughter? What will your sister say when she realizes the kind of animal you've become? After all she did to protect you back in the day?"

He turns abruptly to look at Alexei. But the dull mask is firmly back in place, his lone eye the dull, disinterested opaque it always is in Orlov's presence.

"My *sister*," Alexei says flatly, with just enough contempt on the second word to send a ripple of real fear through me, "left me here without a second thought. She and that greedy bastard she calls father are dead to me. They have been from the day they ran."

Vilnus's lip curls. "So you always say," he says silkily. "Even when I cut you to ribbons, you insisted you had no part in their escape. But I wonder how true that really is, Petrovsky. What if I make you fuck this one now and send the video to your sister? Something tells me that there'll be no coming back for you after that."

Alexei lifts a disinterested shoulder. "It would be an effort. She's got barely enough meat on her bones to get a cock rise out of me."

The ripple of laughter that goes through the watching men clearly gets under Orlov's skin, because his smile fades, replaced by a sour, mean expression.

His hand tightens convulsively on my breast, and I wince. "Then you won't care if I fuck her myself."

Alexei yawns. "I don't give a shit who you fuck, Vilnus. At

least I can get some sleep while you do it, since you've kept me on nonstop babysitting duty for the past week."

Vilnus's eyes narrow. But whatever response he's about to make is cut abruptly short by a commotion in the hall.

"I am sorry to interrupt your games, Vilnus." The newcomer speaks in Russian. He's an old man, dressed impeccably in a black tailored suit and crisp tie. His voice is calm and measured. His eyes barely skim over me, but even that brief touch is enough to send a cold shiver through my body.

They're the darkest, coldest eyes I've ever seen. Not dark like Roman's, which always have a hint of warmth lingering beneath them. Not an inscrutable mask, like Alexei's.

These eyes are completely dead—and they terrify me more than even Vilnus's hand on my breast.

I'm not the only one intimidated by the newcomer.

Vilnus swings around. "Ilyan." He's clearly unsettled by the visitor's arrival. "I didn't know I was expecting you."

"Let's just say I grew impatient." The man called Ilyan stares flatly at him. "I'm changing the plan."

"I thought we agreed—"

"*We* didn't agree anything, Vilnus. I gave you a plan, and you followed it. That's how this relationship works." The man's contempt is scathing. He glances at the gathered guards. "You can leave us." They clearly know who gives the orders, because they all scatter without a moment's protest.

All except Alexei.

"Borovsky is taking too long." Ilyan speaks without preamble. He looks at some point over Vilnus's head, as if he can't be bothered to actually meet the other man's eyes. "Something is up, and I don't like it."

"He's got no chance of taking this place," Vilnus says defensively. "It's too well protected."

"Maybe. But I'm taking precautions nonetheless." He steps aside. "Come here, my dear."

As the tall, slender figure enters the room, Masha tenses against me, and I suck in my breath. "Mama," I breathe, relief washing over me in a hot tide.

"Ofelia." Inger says my name hollowly, like she's somewhere else. She's dressed as impeccably as ever in a designer dress. Her hair is carefully coiffed, and she's dripping with expensive jewelry. I feel a savage rush of anger.

How can she look like that while we are here, in the same blood-stained rags we've worn for days, enduring Vilnus's daily torture?

"Your mother and I are taking a little trip." Ilyan doesn't try to smile at me. He doesn't even look at me. "I brought her here to say goodbye—and to remind her of what happens if she disobeys my orders." He puts his face close to Inger's ear. "Do exactly as I say, or your daughters will die, my dear."

What?

The blood drains from my face, the room spinning around me.

The room is suddenly silent. I can actually hear the beating of my own heart. Masha is stiff and silent beside me, her eyes glued on Mama.

"There's nothing you can do to save them from Orlov, of course." Ilyan's voice continues, cold, flat, and utterly impersonal. He might as well be delivering a shopping list. "It's too late for that. I don't get between Orlov and his little games. But it's not too late for you and Nikolai. That's why I brought you here. If you follow my orders like a good girl, you will see him again. You can have the future you dreamed of, together, with enough money to live out the rest of your lives in luxury. Maybe, if you lie well enough, you can even convince Nikolai that the story you told him was true. He never needs to know that you kidnapped your own daughters in cold blood for nothing more than money."

Inger sways, her face white. Ilyan is still gripping her arm.

The hand from which her ring finger was cut hangs just beneath his grasp, the stump covered in a neat bandage.

Even the dressing looks like it comes from a designer label. My thoughts are wild, disjointed. I can't make sense of anything.

I stare at Inger blindly, feeling as if the earth itself has shifted beneath my feet. "Mama." My voice is little more than a croak. "That's not true, is it?"

But somehow, I already know it is.

"It wasn't supposed to be like this." Her voice is low, despairing, and she finally looks at me directly. But there's no humility in her face, no apology, only defiance. "I just wanted enough money to start a new life." Tears spring into her eyes. "Roman took you all away from me, turned you against me."

"I'm Roman's *daughter*." The anger catches me by surprise, comes without any warning, but once I start speaking, it's like a torrent that can't be held back. "And Roman didn't take us. You gave us away, Inger. A long time ago, even before Papa died. Masha doesn't even know you well enough to call you Mama. I had to *teach* her to call you that."

My breath hurts in my chest, and the anger I can't control feels as if it's been sitting inside me forever. "Did you ever love us?" I stare at her furiously, refusing to give her the satisfaction of crying. "Did you ever care about us at all?"

"Of course I did!" Inger wipes a lone tear from her face angrily. "But I was *sixteen*, Ofelia. I was a child when I got pregnant with you. The same age you are now. What was I supposed to do, just stop living my life? I didn't want a second child, did you know that? I'd been offered a modeling contract back in Miami, a whole career. But Mikhail couldn't have that, oh no." Her face falls into the familiar, resentful lines that have made me feel guilty my whole life. "He wanted the perfect bratva wife. Stay home, fuck him when he deigned to visit, and get fat with baby after baby. What did it matter what I wanted?"

I shake my head, barely even aware of the others in the room through my anger. "What about Mickey, then? Is he even Papa's son, or did you sleep with someone else again?"

"How dare you!" Inger spits the words furiously. "Of course he's Mikhail's son! Like I had a chance to meet anyone back then. I barely even managed to see Nik—" She breaks off abruptly, twisting her head away.

"Nikolai." I finish the sentence for her. "That's why he was always at our house, isn't it? I used to wonder why he spent so much time there, when he didn't even like us. You were sleeping with him all that time."

"Nicky loves me." She flings the words at me defiantly. "He's the only one who has always been there for me. He helped me get a modeling contract and brought Yuri's yacht over so I could have a proper holiday."

I'm dimly aware of Vilnus and Ilyan both standing back, watching our exchange with something like amusement, but I almost don't care. Maybe it's the horrific week of pain and fear, or maybe it's a lifetime of being the only adult in our tiny family of three, the one person to whom Mickey and Masha looked for reassurance, for something like maternal care.

Whatever the cause, I'm so blindingly angry that I can barely breathe.

"I didn't sleep for years after Masha was born. Did you know that?" My voice shakes unsteadily, the words coming from a place of pain inside me that I didn't even know existed. "You left for a modeling job when she was barely three months old, not that you'd been there much before that. You were too busy trying to get your body back in time for the contract you had coming up. Papa was always working, and none of the nannies could make Masha settle. It was me who got her to take the bottle. Me who woke up when she cried. I was the only mother she knew, and then, when Papa died, you tried to take her away from me." My tears break through in a rasping pain that hurts my chest.

"'Felia." Masha's little arms reach up around my neck, and I hug her fiercely, holding her against my body like a talisman. "Don't cry, 'Felia."

"I'm okay, *myshka*. Don't worry." I pat her back mindlessly, burying my head in hers, trying to gain control of myself.

"I can't fight you, Ofelia." Inger's voice is thin and plaintive. "You're too strong for me. You always have been, ever since the day you were born. You're just like Roman. So cruel and selfish. I remember standing over your crib when you were a baby and seeing him look up at me through your eyes. I knew you were his. And I knew even then that I didn't like you. I knew you'd be exactly like him, and I was right—you're cold and unfeeling, like Roman is. You've never cared about me at all, and now you've poisoned your brother and sister against me." Her lower lip quivers, and she starts to cry in earnest, fat, pathetic tears that roll down her face and drip onto the floor. "That's why I have to look after myself now. If you want to know who's to blame for all of this, Ofelia, it's you. You and Roman caused all of this."

I stare at her over Masha's shoulder, utterly incredulous.

"You're trying to blame this on *me?*"

Inger sniffs dismally. "It's not my fault, Ofelia. None of this is my fault. It's Roman—if he'd just been kind to me—but he just shut me out. You all did, like I was nothing. What was I supposed to do?"

I look between her and Ilyan. "So you're going to just leave us here, to these men? Don't you care what happens to us at all?"

She gives a helpless sob. "I can't help you now, Ofelia. It's too late. But you'll be okay, whatever happens. You've always been so much stronger than me." Her face twists into a petulant scowl. "And anyway, Roman will come for you. He won't be able to help himself. He always has to be the hero." A flash of spite crosses her face. "Although I doubt he'll survive this time."

Which means that neither will we.

I stare at her in complete disbelief.

Part of me wants to keep arguing with her. But another part, the piece of me who just spoke up for myself for what feels like the first time in my life, instinctively knows there's no point. Not just because my words will have no impact on Inger—but because I don't want to waste them on her anymore.

Inger has never been a mother. Not to me. Not to Mickey. And certainly not to Masha.

She's brought all of us nothing but pain, confusion, and turbulence for as long as I can remember.

"Say goodbye to your mother, girls." Ilyan looks bored. "It's the last time you're going to see her."

I stare at Inger. At the tight, discontented lines of her face, the way she can't quite meet my eyes, the pathetic way she clings to Ilyan, as if she truly thinks he's going to somehow save her. I think of the years I've spent twisting myself inside out, trying to get the smallest hint of real affection from her, when all that time she resented my very existence.

I think of the nights I've woken to Masha's screams. Of how many times I've reassured her that she's done nothing wrong, that she's not the reason her mama is never home.

I remember the times I've seen Mickey's face crumble when Inger has made fun of his computer skills or ridiculed his previously thin frame.

And I think of all the times I've defended Inger. To Papa. To Roman. To the old Russian grandmas, the teachers at my schools . . . to anyone who has tried to criticize her.

Because she is my mother.

Because I believed Papa when he told us that we stand by family, no matter what they do.

And most of all, I defended Inger because, somewhere deep inside myself, I've always believed it was my fault that she didn't love me. That there was something wrong with me, something inherently unlovable about who I am.

But now, listening to her complain about how unfair her life has been, while casually abandoning Masha and me to rape and possible death, I know, with a deep, comforting certainty, that the problem was never me.

Sitting here in a torn, bloodstained dress, with my baby sister terrified and shaking in my arms because of Inger's betrayal, I know I'm done with our so-called mother forever.

"Goodbye, Inger." I stare at her, even though her eyes can't meet mine. "I hope you and Nikolai are very happy together. Because I can promise you this: even if by some miracle Masha and I survive, you won't ever see us, or Mickey, again. We're done."

She doesn't react at all, just looks at the floor, as if all she wants is to get out of here.

"Come now, Inger." Ilyan has watched the entire scene with complete disinterest. "I only brought you here to remind you of what will happen if you double-cross me. Your daughters are lost to you, but you can still have Nikolai." He cuts his eyes to Vilnus, and for the first time, his lips almost curl, though the flicker of humor doesn't meet his eyes. "I know you're disappointed, Orlov. All those years and money you wasted on Inger, only to discover it is Nikolai she wants. But that's women, I'm afraid."

"What do I care?" Vilnus shrugs, but his attempt at nonchalance isn't fooling anyone. "I'll enjoy the daughter more anyway."

I shudder, pulling Masha closer. Inger doesn't even look at me.

"Well." Ilyan looks at his watch. "This has certainly been entertaining, but Inger and I have a plane to catch. Stay by the phone, Orlov." He gives Vilnus a hard stare. "When this is done, you can do whatever you wish to Roman's daughters. But for now, we need those girls in good enough shape to bring Borovsky here. That means that no matter how hard your cock is, you need to keep it in your pants until this is over. And make sure you keep that lying Petrovsky dog on a tight leash." His eyes, black and dead, rest on Alexei, and the evil in them is the most terrifying thing I've ever seen. "When this is done, Sergei Petrovsky's devil-spawned son belongs to me."

If I'd thought Ilyan sinister before, I find him utterly chilling now.

He glances at Masha and me.

"A pleasure, my dears. Though sadly, I doubt we'll meet again."

His eyes fix on Alexei again, and when he speaks, his voice is as dead and flat as his eyes. "My people are watching your every fucking move, Petrovsky. You so much as twitch in the wrong direction, and I'll take your other eye. Then I'll take your cock and feed it to your cunt of a father, while I torture his daughter until she's mad with it."

Alexei stares straight ahead, his face the opaque mask I've come to dread.

It's like he's not even inside his body.

Then again, if I had to endure the kind of sadism Alexei has clearly lived with since he was a teenager, I'd have probably found a way to escape as well.

Ilyan glances at Vilnus. "Get Petrovsky out of this room, and keep him under lock and key until this is over. I don't want him anywhere near these two girls again, do you understand me?"

Vilnus gives a sullen nod.

A moment later, the door closes, and all of them are gone.

Masha and I hold each other on the floor, but my tears have all dried.

Somehow, I doubt I'll cry again anytime soon.

Not that it matters.

We'll be dead soon anyway.

I look over Masha's shoulder, but the corner is empty.

Alexei is gone, and we are all alone.

26

ROMAN

The bike and I are one, hitting speeds higher than any bike has a right to go. I lean into a corner, striking sparks off the tarmac, riding the mountain roads like a meteor shot across the sky.

I feel both a thousand feet tall and the smallest I ever have.

I've gone from being a man without name or family to having all of it, rich and sweet, laid before me like a banquet I barely dare to taste. And now, someone has walked in and stolen part of it from me.

I can't relax until I have Ofelia and Masha back.

Even after I get the girls back, I have so much to lose. So much that Ilyan Fedorov, or men like him, can try to take away. The merest thought of someone laying hands on Darya, on the faint bump in her belly that I still can't quite believe is real, ratchets up my internal tension to the kind of torque no engine can hope to match.

And I can't come down from this crazy edge of joy either. A joy that feels indecent while the girls are still in Vilnus Orlov's fucking hands.

My fear lends a savage edge to the ride, and to the joy.

I flick open the visor on my helmet, reveling in the cut of the wind against my face.

"Fuck!" I roar the word into the wind, roar the pain, rage, and joy out together, the bike leaping beneath me.

I storm into the lab with the wind still in my hair and the wildness like an electrical current in every cell. I stalk through the ops center, not trusting myself to speak just yet. Dimitry and Mak are in the secure room, poring over a schematic of the Coconut Grove compound. Dimitry looks up as I open the door.

"Jesus." He raises his eyebrows. "What the fuck happened to you?"

I feel the shit-eating grin spread across my face before I can stop it. "Darya's pregnant."

For once, Dimitry is stunned into silence. He and Mak look at each other, then back at me. A slow smile dawns on Dimitry's face. He crosses the floor in two strides and pulls me into a wordless bear hug that almost crushes me, thumping my back with a closed fist. When he finally pulls back he puts his hands on my shoulders, shaking me until my teeth rattle.

"Fucking brilliant," he says roughly. Then he says it again. "Fucking brilliant."

The severity of his grip and depth of emotion in his eyes say more than words ever could. Dimitry, more than anyone, knows what this means to me.

Mak, standing behind him, thrusts out his hand and smiles wryly. "I think he means to say congratulations," he says in that cut-glass fucking Eton accent. The faint rebuke doesn't take anything from the genuine warmth in his eyes. "Allow me to add mine, Roman. This is wonderful news."

"Damn right it is." I still can't wipe the stupid smile off my face. I take the glass of cognac Mak has magically produced. Fucker probably keeps a decanter with him when he's on camels in some third-world shithole.

Not that I'm complaining.

"Have you told Mickey yet?" Dimitry asks after we've clinked glasses.

I shake my head, my smile fading. "He's got enough on his mind right now."

"If you'll excuse me," Mak says, exchanging a look with Dimitry, "I would suggest that is bullshit. Mickey has a very big mind. The only thing there isn't space for in that head of his is lies, Roman. The kid can sniff them out from across a crowded room. In his current mood, I wouldn't go hiding anything from him."

Dimitry nods vigorously. "Get him in here. As a matter of fact, let's wait until he's here to drink to this."

I frown. "I don't think it's appropriate to be celebrating anything until the girls are back, especially in front of Mickey."

"I doubt he'll give you the chance anyway." Dimitry grins at me. "One look at your face was probably enough to make him suspicious. Your poker game is shot on this one, brother, let me tell you."

He's barely finished speaking when there's a knock on the door.

"Roman!" Mickey's voice is tense and demanding. "What's going on?"

Dimitry's grin widens. "Told you."

I take a deep breath.

The truth is, the thought of facing Mickey with this scares me a whole lot more than I'm willing to let on, even to Dimitry. News like this, when his sisters are still missing? So soon after the DNA test results, and after getting Darya back? There's every chance Mickey will throw Mak's cognac right in my face.

And I wouldn't blame him. Not at all.

Oh, well. It's got to be faced eventually. And after this thing is done, I might not be in any shape to take the fist he's probably about to plant in my face.

I open the door.

A white-faced Mickey stares at me, clearly dreading the worst. My levity disappears immediately, along with my hesitation.

"It's okay, Mickey," I say calmly. "It isn't anything to do with the girls. Our plans are still in place. We'll get them back. I promised, remember?"

He frowns, his eyes dropping to the glass in my hand. "Then what's that all about? Some kind of Dutch courage ritual thing?"

"Not exactly." I put the glass down on the table and face him squarely. "I wish this news was coming at a different time, Mickey." I hold his eyes, steadying myself. "I just found out that Darya is pregnant."

I'm not sure what I was expecting, but his stark, horrified face definitely isn't it.

"Hey." I grip his shoulders, holding his eyes. "You can hit me if you want. I'd understand. I'm sorry, I shouldn't have told you—"

"She was going to run while she was *pregnant?*" The terror in his eyes cuts me off. "With the *Orlovs* coming after her?"

I close my eyes reflexively.

I've done my best not to think about that from the moment I saw the white stick. I don't want to be angry at Darya. And I wasn't lying to her earlier. Logically, I *do* understand why she didn't tell me before she ran.

But that doesn't mean that the thought of her on the run, alone, pregnant, and hunted, doesn't strike my heart with the same stark terror I can see in Mickey's face. The same hideous, sickening horror I felt when I knew the girls had been taken.

It isn't until I open my eyes that I realize I've been gripping

Mickey's shoulders hard enough to leave marks. He hasn't moved. But perhaps my touch communicated more than words could, because his eyes have softened slightly when I meet them again.

"At least she's home now," he says quietly.

I nod, my hands still on his shoulders. "Thanks to you, Mickey. And when we get Ofelia and Masha back, that will be thanks to you, too."

Dimitry pushes past me, thrusting a glass of cognac into Mickey's hand. "We waited for you until we raised a glass to the latest Stevanovsky to enter the world."

Mickey takes the glass and turns it slowly in his hand, staring at it. When he looks up again it's with the crooked smile that I find all the more precious for being so rarely seen. "Not a Stevanovsky." He raises his glass to me. "To the latest Borovsky. One I will be proud to call family, as will my sisters."

Dimitry grips Mickey's shoulder with a bear-sized hand. Mak nods approvingly. We clink glasses, and I swallow, not least to hide the lump in my throat.

Then Mickey coughs, his eyes streaming, which makes us all laugh.

He frowns at us all in bemusement. "What kind of psycho actually *chooses* to drink this stuff?"

<hr>

It's past ten p.m., and apart from the brief cognac pause at the beginning, we've been refining plans all evening. Bryce, Luis, and Pavel have joined us in the secure room.

"The jet is fueled and waiting." Pavel glances briefly at me then back at the large screen in the secure room. "Zurich is two and a half hours away. The flight logs will be hidden from public view. Nobody will track you."

"Good." I look around the faces at the table. Bryce, Luis, Dimitry, Pavel, and Mickey are all tense and alert.

Mak, on the other hand, could be on holiday at the fucking Ritz, the way he lounges against the wall.

Fortunately, I've seen him in action enough times to know the lethal capability his insouciance disguises.

"Once our business in Zurich is done, I'll fly to Miami with Mak's people, as discussed." I nod at Bryce. "You and the rest of my personal security detail will remain with Darya."

Mak tilts his head at Dimitry. "Except for him, obviously."

Dimitry tilts his head with a rather hard grin. "Glad we got that straight."

"Dimitry stays with me." There was never a chance he wasn't coming to Miami. "Luis will coordinate with Pavel and hold point on the ground back here in Malaga."

"So Darya is definitely flying to Zurich." Mickey says it flatly, his eyes on me.

I nod. "The doctor cleared it."

Dimitry snorts. "You mean you have as much chance of keeping her away as you do Mickey."

Pavel smirks, then, seeing my face, hastily composes himself and buries his head in a screen.

"Everyone is fully briefed on Darya's condition." I glare around the table. "I have obstetricians on speed dial in three different countries, and you all have their numbers. Even the faintest sign of something going wrong . . ." I don't need to finish my sentence. Bryce, Pavel, and Luis are already nodding vigorously.

"As for you." I fix Mickey with a hard eye. "I know that we agreed you could be in Miami. But I won't change my mind about where you stay while this is going down. Mak has a secure location already set up on the ground. That's where you'll be throughout this whole thing."

"For the hundredth time, I copy that, loud and clear." He

shakes his head and taps away at his laptop, not bothering to look up.

"Make sure you bloody well do." I eye the top of his head skeptically. "Mak, Mickey is flying direct from here to Miami with you, as agreed."

I don't add that Mickey's well-being rests in Mak's hands.

I don't need to.

I look around the room. "As I said, from Zurich, I'll travel with Mak's team. Bryce, you're heading up the security detail that will bring Darya back here to Malaga in my jet." I turn to Pavel. "I want you watching every fucking mile of her flight. Anything so much as smells off, you coordinate with Bryce and Luis to mobilize everything we have. I've got people on standby in every major city from Zurich to Spain. If you need to emergency land, if you need anything, you have the contacts."

They all nod. It isn't like I haven't said it all a hundred times.

I glance at Mak. "Over to you."

"From Zurich you're invisible." Mak clicks, and the screen changes to a split screen showing both the Everglades house and the Coconut Grove compound. "We'll land at a private airstrip outside of Miami and meet the rest of my team in a secure location for a final briefing."

"But you're not sharing this location with us." Pavel, for once, speaks up without being asked. His dissatisfaction with this particular part of the plan is patently obvious, as it has been all night.

"Nope." Mak grins at him. "Like I said, my team will take it from Zurich."

Pavel scowls at me. I suppress a grin of my own. "We've got Lars Andersson somewhere in the mix, Pavel. We have to assume he's watching everything we do. So far, Mak's presence here is entirely off radar. I'd like to keep it that way. If we assume Andersson will manage to track our flight log to Zurich, all he will see is Darya and me arriving and then leaving the same day. That's what I'd like him to see."

"I told you the flight logs are hidden!" Pavel doesn't attempt to hide his indignation.

"And we've both seen firsthand what Lars Andersson is capable of." Mickey doesn't look up from his screen, but I notice that Pavel takes more notice of him than he does of me. That should piss me off, but it doesn't. It never ceases to astonish me just how quickly Mickey has earned the respect of the entire ops center. "I'm still trying to crack these fucking trojans he came at Mercura with. Sorry," he mutters, glancing up at me.

I frown. "You're working on those *now?*"

He lifts a shoulder, his fingers still flying as he meets my eyes. "It relaxes me."

"Jesus," mutters Dimitry, shaking his head as the other men in the room shake with silent laughter.

"Of course it does," I say dryly, seeing my own amusement mirrored in Mak's eyes. "Well, Einstein, you might need to give the keyboard a rest and get some sleep. Wheels go up at oh six hundred tomorrow." I glance around the table. "We all good?"

I don't need their nods. We've been good for hours, but that doesn't mean I haven't hammered home every goddamn point.

There's too much at stake not to.

"Einstein?" Mickey rolls his eyes as he closes his laptop. "What about Gummo? Or Mitnick? Einstein was just a physicist. Gummo is the crypto king, and he's so damned good nobody even knows his real *name.*"

27

DARYA

"Thank you for this." I hold Roman's hand as the jet roars down the runway for take off. "I know it wasn't easy for you to agree to take me with you, but I'm glad you did."

"I'm glad you're with me." His fingers tighten around mine, and he shoots me a half smile that makes my stomach turn to mush. "Not that I'll take a decent breath until I know you're safely back in the penthouse, mind you. But still." He raises my hand and brushes his lips over my knuckles, sending fire through my veins. "It's good to know you'll be with me in Switzerland."

The jet takes off, and I watch the glittering morning sea fade beneath us as we circle over the rugged mountain coastline and head north. I lean back in the leather seat and sip the ginger tea the stewardess brought. Roman, I note, is strictly on water only, as is the very large security detail traveling with us. I have no idea how he managed to convince Swiss immigration to clear a private force of extremely heavily armed men to land.

Then again, I stopped asking questions like that a long time ago.

Even compared to my own father, who was in his time the most feared *pakhan* in Miami, Roman lives in a different world of wealth. It's a world that exists beyond governments and the rules they make. Beyond even the megacorporations that conspiracy theorists love to talk about.

Roman's world is the one that truly makes the rules. Men like him just do it from the shadows and let others pretend to be in control.

"I still think we should have spoken to Papa before we left." I turn away from the window and look at Roman. His face is set and hard, as it always is when my father is mentioned. I understand it, but it hasn't ceased to make me sad. I'm angry at Papa too, for all the secrets he kept from me, for never trusting me the way he did Alexei. But learning about Ilyan Fedorov, and the horrific way he murdered both Papa's and Aleksander Borovsky's wives and children in Paris, has helped me to forgive him. At least to understand where his almost pathological obsession with secrecy stems from.

The knowledge doesn't seem to have had the same effect on Roman, however. He still tenses at any mention of Papa's name, and he wouldn't even consider talking to him about our plans before we left this morning. More concerning, at least to me, is his avoidance of any discussion about his mother. I still don't know if he intends to contact her when we reach Zurich. I know he wants to stay focused on rescuing the girls. But the fact that we are going to Switzerland with no plans to even meet with Rosa is something I find deeply disturbing.

"There's nothing to be gained by talking to your father about Ilyan Fedorov." His voice is tight, his mouth a grim line. "He clearly couldn't find him all those years ago, or I think we can safely assume the man would already be dead. Telling Sergei we've found him now would only pose a security risk to our operation."

He doesn't need to explain what he means by *security risk*. And I can't really argue with him. Papa has been in touch with Alexei all this time, and despite all that my brother has done, Papa still seems convinced of his innocence. Certain that Alexei remains loyal to him, and to the legacy Papa and Aleksander protected all those years ago.

I know that Roman doesn't share Papa's faith, and I don't blame him.

I'm not at all sure I share it either.

Has Alexei remained loyal to Papa's legacy? To the Petrovsky fortune?

Yes, I believe he probably has.

But loyal to me? To the principles of honor and integrity I've always believed he possessed?

I'm not so sure about that. Not anymore.

Alexei's actions have made clear how determined he is to maintain control over that vault. He undoubtedly feels he's earned his inheritance, after all these years bowing to the Orlovs.

I want to believe that the use of that old security code is a sign that my brother is trying to help us. But I've had to face a lot of hard facts since that bomb went off.

It's still difficult to accept, given the pain that Alexei and I endured at the hands of the Orlovs, that my brother could ever be complicit in kidnapping Roman's children. But there's no way around the facts. And the facts are that Alexei knew that the children were in danger the night of the ball.

Which means he knew about the bomb—and that he waylaid me as a decoy to draw Roman's men off the dance floor.

I can't forgive that, family legacy or not.

That thought process reminds me of something else. "I've

been meaning to ask you." I turn to Roman. "In your letter, the one you put in my purse the night of the ball, you mentioned that you believe Alexei is planning to use your project as leverage with the Orlovs." I don't mention Mercura by name, not even here, among Roman's security team, and I speak in a voice low enough to go undetected. I'm more than aware of how confidential the launch is. "Do you still believe that?"

He nods slowly. "Remember when I told you, the day you came up to the lab, that Lars Andersson has been working with your brother?"

"I remember."

"Well, Andersson has been hacking into my project for months now. That's what Mickey has been working on—trying to unravel the trojan viruses Andersson is using to break through our security. More importantly, he's trying to work out what the trojans are for."

"Wow." Despite the depressing nature of his answer, I can't help but be impressed that Mickey's skills are considered so highly by Roman and his team. I remember how brilliant Lars Andersson was, even as a teenager. The thought that Mickey, who is at least a decade younger than Lars, might be able to match him, is extraordinary. "And has he worked it out?"

"That's why I'm so concerned about your brother's motives." Roman casts me a rather grim sideways look. "From what Mickey can tell, the sole purpose of Andersson's trojans is to test the resilience of our project. To point out the flaws, so to speak. So far, rather than sabotage us, all he's actually done is make the entire platform more secure."

"And you think that means he's planning to steal it?"

I can see the regret in Roman's eyes when he nods, the concerned way he's watching me.

I know why he hasn't spelled this out for me before.

And part of me wishes I never brought it up.

Because I don't need to ask what this means if it's true.

Alexei endangered our children's lives. Then he helped them be kidnapped by sadistic monsters. On top of that, he's planning to steal Roman's flagship multibillion-dollar project.

We're long past questions of loyalty or honor.

We're also past asking if my brother will die.

He will. Roman will make sure he does.

The only question is when.

I look down to where my fingers are still entwined with Roman's, at the scarred knuckles and muscular length of the hands that have brought so much pleasure to my body and solace to my heart.

I try not to imagine those hands pulling the trigger on a gun aimed at my brother's head.

OFELIA

I wake from an uneasy sleep to find our new guard gone and Vilnus standing over me.

I can smell the alcohol and cigarettes on his breath. He's swaying, and even in the dim light, I can see how unfocused his eyes are.

I ease myself carefully away from Masha's sleeping body, tucking her safely behind me.

"Roman Borovsky's daughter." His fat lips curl into a sneer. "Do you know how long we searched Miami for that little fuck?" He rips open his shirt to expose his enormous belly and points to a thick, gnarled scar that crosses his torso from shoulder to the opposite hip. "That's what Ilyan Fedorov did to me when I told him we'd killed Roman's father, Borovsky, the old safe maker. How was I supposed to know that Borovsky senior used his own son's fingerprints to lock the Petrovsky vault? Or that he'd hidden the key?" He steps closer, his clearly excited groin barely inches from my face. I swallow my revulsion.

Keep him talking.

"What's inside the vault?" I ask. "Why is it so important to everyone?"

"Ha!" Vilnus's laugh is without humor. "That depends on who you ask. A fortune in Fabergé jewelry, if the rumors are true." His hand darts out and tugs one of the earrings I'm still wearing, hard enough to hurt. "Speaking of fortunes, I'm surprised little Darya didn't pawn these long ago. She and that old bastard Sergei could have been living rich all this time, on the price they'd have fetched."

He fondles the earring. I try not to flinch.

"Little Darya." The way he says her name makes my stomach turn. "She got used to the knife, eventually. At the start she'd scream when I used it on her. But by the end, I think she actually liked it. She'd lie there, all quiet, just waiting for me to get to work."

I can't suppress a shudder at that.

"That's where Alexei learned his skills with the knife, you know. From me. From watching me work on his sister. And afterward, when I had to use it on him."

He actually sounds like he's boasting. As if he did Alexei some kind of favor by cutting into his flesh.

"Alexei said you've been like a father to him." It's a lie, of course it is. But it seems to work.

A self-satisfied smile stretches the fat lips. "Old Sergei made a big mistake when he left that one behind. Alexei won't ever forgive his father and sister for abandoning him. Why should he? Sergei must have known I'd blame Alexei for his escape, but he ran anyway." Orlov smirks. "I kept Alexei in this room for a whole year after they left. There's no inch of his body my blade hasn't touched. Of course he hated me at first, but he came around. He learned to respect me more than he ever did that old cripple of a father of his."

I nod obediently, as if I'm believing every word of this garbage.

"I tried to defend Alexei, you know. When Fedorov insisted he was lying."

God, is he actually trying to justify himself?

"I told Fedorov the boy didn't know where Sergei had gone. No man—especially no teenager—could withstand having his own damned eye carved out of his head and not start talking. But Fedorov has never believed him." He shrugs, his hand dropping away from my earring, to my relief. "That's why Alexei is so determined to steal your daddy's pet project now. He and I take that, and it doesn't matter what's in that vault. Fedorov can have the fucking thing. Alexei and I will be rich enough to buy the entire contents of it, and for once Fedorov will be the last to know." He leers at me. "Everybody gets what they want. We'll have Darya and Sergei back here soon enough, along with that prick Borovsky." His face spasms with old anger. "Do you know how many stinking homeless camps I trawled, looking for that little fuck? Fedorov might want the Petrovskys, but it's Roman I'm looking forward to spending some time with."

His eyes glaze over, and his hand comes around to grip the bulge at his crotch.

"I'm going to enjoy fucking you while he watches." His voice is hoarse, his breath coming in short pants.

I try not to tremble with fear. *Is he going to rape me?*

I desperately want to run, but there's nowhere to go, and Masha is still asleep on the floor behind me.

"You look like your mother, do you know that?" He unbuckles his belt, his eyes locked onto my breasts. "I bet you like it rough like she does, too."

Fear and revulsion choke my throat, along with a sickening sense of inevitability.

I have to do something. I can't just sit here and wait like some useless victim.

"I thought your boss, Fedorov, said you couldn't touch us." My voice sounds like it's coming from someone else.

I'm surprised it still works at all.

"Ha." Orlov unzips his pants and reaches inside them. "Fedorov isn't my boss. Not anymore. Not now that Petrovsky and I are working together. And besides, Fedorov isn't here, is he?" He pulls out his cock, shaking the limp mass in front of my face. "Look at it," he grunts.

I'm frozen, barely able to breathe, let alone move. I've never felt more sick or terrified in my life. I know there's nowhere to run and no way to fight him off. He's more than twice my size and clearly drunk out of his mind.

If I was on my own, I could at least try to dodge him.

But not while Masha is tucked behind me. I'm not leaving her, not even for a moment. There's no way I'm going to risk Orlov getting his hands on my little sister.

If Darya survived years under his knife, then I can survive this.

It's almost as if I can feel her here, with me, sense her quiet strength.

Darya never gave up.

Orlov never broke her, no matter what he did. He didn't break Alexei, even after he cut his eye out.

He won't break me either.

"Open your eyes!" Orlov's command is hoarse, the sound of his hand slapping his own flesh sickening. I force myself to look up.

"Yes!" His fat tongue pokes between his teeth, his hand moving faster, but his member is still limp and lifeless. I might never have seen a naked man in the flesh before, but even I know what an erection should look like. "Gonna fuck that pretty little mouth," he grunts, pushing his groin closer to my face. "Gonna make you suck me like the fucking whore you are—"

I'm bracing myself, trying not to gag, when suddenly Orlov goes still. His mouth opens, and his eyes go blank with shock and confusion. A moment later they close, his body sagging limply against the tall, unsmiling figure behind him. Alexei lowers Orlov's bulk to the floor, his lone eye icily furious, his mouth a thin line.

"Dima," he says in a low, quiet voice. The door to our cell opens, and the guard pokes his head in, his face grim and wary. "Get him upstairs." Alexei nods at Orlov's prone figure. "Tell them he fell on the stairs. I'll wait ten minutes before I switch the code on the camera feed."

"What about the guard who was in here?"

"Dead." Alexei says it dispassionately. "His body is hidden in that end tunnel. We'll need to get rid of it before dawn."

Dima nods, as if there's nothing at all strange about what Alexei has just said. He lifts Orlov's body as easily as if it's a sack of potatoes and closes the door behind him.

"Th-thank you." My voice is barely audible. I'm suddenly freezing cold, trembling so badly my teeth actually chatter.

Alexei kneels down a few feet away, but doesn't try to touch me. "Did he hurt you?"

I shake my head, biting my lip in an effort to gain control of myself.

"'Felia." Masha's head pokes up under my arm, her face white and frightened. "Is the bad man gone?"

Oh, God. She was awake.

I pull her close to me. "He's gone, *myshka*. It's alright. I'm fine. We're fine." I stroke her head, murmuring to her quietly, trying to steady my voice. Masha clings to me, her head buried in my side. Her thumb creeps up to her mouth, and I close my eyes briefly in an effort to stop a hot rush of tears.

It's taken me most of the past year to train her out of sucking her thumb, a habit that started the day Papa died. Seeing her do it again is somehow devastating proof of our horrible reality.

"Dima will stay with you tonight. Make sure nobody else comes in here." Alexei is watching me closely.

"What about you?" My voice is barely a whisper. "Won't you get in trouble?"

"He won't remember any of it tomorrow." His mouth twists contemptuously. "As far as he knows, I'm locked in a room down the corridor. That's where I'll be when he wakes up. We'll work out a story to explain the missing guard." His eye drops to Masha. He says her name gently.

Her head lifts a fraction, her eyes peeking at Alexei then dropping again.

"Your sister is very brave, *myshka*. And so are you."

Masha turns her head, looking at Alexei directly. Her thumb slips just below her mouth. "I don' like it here."

"I know you don't. But soon your papa is going to come to take you home. I need you to be a brave girl until then. Can you do that?"

"Papa?" She frowns. "My papa dead."

I swallow hard, barely able to breathe through the painful lump in my throat. "He means Roman." I kiss the top of her head. "He means that Roman is coming for us."

Masha nods slowly. "Roman is papa now? Roman an' Luce?"

"Yes, Mash. Roman is our papa." The tears slip from my eyes, tracking down my face and into her curls.

"Papa Roman." She nods as if this makes perfect sense, still staring at Alexei. "You made the bad man go away."

"For now." He doesn't smile. His eye shifts to me. "I'm trying to get a message to Roman. My friend Lars has been using a code I thought Roman would understand, but so far, no luck. Is there any word I could use that would convince him the message comes from you?"

"Just give me your phone. I'll call him right now." My heart leaps at even the thought.

Alexei shakes his head slowly. "I wish it was that simple. Orlov has taken our phones. We're all confined to the grounds and under close watch, especially after what went down at the airport. Lars, my friend, is on the outside, but we have very limited contact. He's been hacking into the Hale computers to try to get a message through."

"Hacking?" I feel a surge of hope. "Then it's my brother, Mickey, you need to get to. He's like a computer genius. Seriously," I say when he looks skeptical. "Mickey actually works with Roman. If your friend can get to him, he'll tell Roman."

"Okay." Alexei still looks unconvinced. "Do you have a code word Lars can use? Something that will make Mickey believe it's coming from you?"

"I do." I smile shakily, tears hovering on the edge of my lashes. "Poppins. Tell him to use Mary Poppins."

"Poppins!" Masha beams, her thumb slipping out of her mouth. "Luce is Poppins!"

"Yes, sweetheart." I kiss her cheek. "Luce is Poppins. She and Papa Roman are coming to rescue us, soon. Alexei is helping them."

Masha slides away from me. Standing up, she walks hesitantly over to where Alexei is still kneeling. Reaching out one small hand, she tentatively touches his eye patch. He flinches slightly.

"Where is your eye?"

Alexei gently removes her hand to stop her lifting the patch. "The bad man took it," he says quietly.

"Does it hurt?"

His mouth twists. It's almost a smile. "Not anymore."

There's a noise from the corridor, and Alexei glances toward the door. When he turns back, his mouth is a grim line once more. "If anyone asks," he says curtly, "the guard left while you were sleeping, and you don't know where he went. I'll try to get the code word to Lars, but I'm not sure when I'll get a chance."

He stands up, and so do I, pulling the torn remains of my dress around me. Given how much of me he's seen already, it's probably stupid to feel self-conscious now, but I do. "Thank you," I say quietly.

His eye drops to the purple bloodstains on my gown, and his mouth hardens. The life in his eye dies, replaced by his customary flat, opaque detachment. "Don't ever thank me," he says curtly. "Not after what I've done to you."

He leaves the room with the silent, lethal swiftness with which he arrived, there one moment, gone the next.

It feels empty without him.

I shiver, wrapping my arms around myself.

Masha looks up at me. "Lexi our friend," she says solemnly.

"Yes, *myshka*." I tousle her hair, trying to still the odd, uneven thudding of my heart. "Lexi is our friend."

29

DARYA

Zurich is a picture-perfect postcard of pristine blue skies and white peaks, the last shreds of snow clinging to the mountains around the city.

I haven't been here since my year of finishing school, right before the Orlov coup. It feels odd to be back here again, like visiting another life, one where my greatest concern was what clothes to choose for dinner with my parents in the city.

Some things are the same. The private airport, the limo waiting for us on the tarmac, the heavy security detail guarding our every move.

The biggest thing that has changed is me—and that means the entire world has.

We glide through the city streets toward the downtown bank that holds Roman's safety deposit box. He is tense on the seat opposite me, his face as remote as carved marble. We still haven't discussed Rosa. I have to respect his wishes, even if I disagree with them.

There's still time to change his mind.

After we've opened the box. After he's got the key.

We drive past the grand arches and enormous stone facades of the more famous banks and turn down a smooth cobblestoned road in a quieter part of the city. The door we arrive at is plain black, set into an unremarkable dull stone building. There's no gold plaque or garish sign announcing the name of the institution. Just a plain intercom that admits us to a formal entry, where Roman has a brief conversation with a cool blonde woman behind a counter. He punches in a code, we both walk through a biometric scanner that records our details, and the woman hands him a small key.

Another door, another conversation, followed by an elevator ride, and we're met by a man in a very expensive suit. We decline his courteous offer of coffee or champagne, and he leads us to a small room.

The room is empty but for a gleaming steel table, atop which is a large square metal box with several dials and two locks on the front. The man waits outside while Roman turns the dials to enter his code, then comes in with a gold key, which he uses on one of the locks, then leaves again. Roman waits until the man has closed the door behind him before turning his own key.

The lock releases with an audible click.

Roman lifts the lid.

I gasp.

It isn't like I haven't seen a Fabergé egg before. I have, more than once. In my own home. At auctions. In catalogs and online.

But I've never seen one like this.

The eggs I've seen before were a handspan tall.

This one stands at least a foot—and it's magnificent.

Made of varicolored gold, decorated in crisscrossed threads of rose-cut diamonds and pearl, and encased in translucent sapphire enamel, the jeweled egg surpasses the most opulent imperial examples I've ever seen—and I'm familiar with most of them. It gleams up at us from a velvet casing, the carved golden display stand nestled at its base.

"It's something, huh?" Roman smiles at me as he lifts it out. "Wait until you see what's inside." He handles the delicate piece with the same exquisite care he does my body. Watching his fingers delicately probe for the hidden spring that opens the egg is surprisingly intimate, bordering on the erotic.

He glances at me and raises his eyebrows, his lips curving in the secret smile that always sets my skin aflame. "Now what," he murmurs close to my ear, "has put that particular look in your eye, *vedma?*"

He presses the button with his eyes still on me. "It always fascinates me," he says as the lock clicks open, "to discover new ways to make that delicious blush appear. You do realize that if we were playing our old game, Miss Lopez, I would definitely have won the day."

Now his grin is unmistakable. In the middle of a Swiss bank secure room, handling a black-market masterpiece worth untold millions.

"You're incorrigible, Mr. Stevanovsky, did you know that?"

He kisses the tip of my nose. "I think Mr. Borovsky is more appropriate in this moment, Miss Petrovsky." He turns back to the egg and gently allows it to fall open in his hands. The egg parts like an orange cut into four segments, revealing an exquisitely carved double-headed eagle wrought in gold, wearing a brilliant diamond and sapphire crown. The outstretched wings of the eagle are traced in thin strands of seed pearls, the eyes gleaming fierce ruby red.

"The double-headed eagle." I stare at the interior in wonder. "The symbol of the House of Romanov. This is one of the original eggs created by Fabergé for Empress Maria Feodorovna. It's . . . this is priceless, Roman."

He nods, his mouth quirked in a peculiar smile. "It's one of the nine missing imperial eggs, and possibly the most valuable of them all. The question is—where inside it did my father hide the key to the Petrovsky vault?"

He turns the egg around carefully, his fingers tracing the whorls and jewels. He closes his eyes, and for a long moment we stand in the perfect silence of the locked room, surrounded by the magic and mystery of a past that died long before either of us were born.

"Ah." Roman's eyes open, the dark depths gleaming. "I should have known." He twists the crown atop the double-headed eagle, and the whole piece lifts off, revealing a small disk of flat gold. He presses the seed pearls on either side of it. The disk splits neatly in two, and the head of a slender, finely wrought key rises from a narrow cylinder running the length of the eagle's body. It's one of the most delicate, ingenious mechanisms I've ever seen.

"You know," Roman says, frowning as he plucks the key out and pockets it, "my father was a gifted jeweler. But his specialty was safe making. Even if he could have brought himself to corrupt such an incredible piece of art, I honestly doubt he could have done this kind of work. I think this is part of the original piece, made by Fabergé himself."

"Really?" I stare at the opened egg. "I wonder what that means?"

"Your father said there were two keys." He slowly reassembles the egg, carefully locking each piece back into place. "I'd say the chances are pretty strong that the second one will be located in an egg exactly like this one. Fabergé was renowned for his love of symmetry and clever mechanisms. This is a prime example of his finest work." He glances at me, his expression darkening when he sees my face. "We'll find it, Darya."

"I know you will." I bite my lip.

"But?" Roman's eyes narrow.

I force myself to meet them anyway. "But I know you'll have to kill Alexei as soon as you do."

He doesn't try to argue with me. He doesn't say anything.

He just slips the key into the breast pocket of his shirt and wraps me in his arms. We stand there for a long time in the silence, my heart beating quietly against his, the golden key to our lethal legacy lying between us.

30

ROMAN

Part of me can't help but look around the bank as we make our way to the exit.

If Sergei was telling the truth, and in this, at least, I believe he was, then Rosa—*my mother*—has some way of being alerted when I access the safety deposit box.

I hate myself for wanting to find her here.

You've already done this.

The last time I stood here, I was in my early twenties. The scars on my hands were fresh then, still raw from the blood they seemed permanently drenched in back in those days. I was deep in Yuri's wars, unaware that they'd only just really begun. I hadn't even been sure I was going to come here at all.

I was in Zurich with Mikhail. We'd met with several bankers, searching for financial backing, ostensibly for Hale, but really for Mercura. Yuri wanted nothing to do with our ideas.

284

He was entrenched in the old way of doing business. Mikhail and I dreamed of a different way, a cleaner way.

Nobody was interested, of course, not back then. We were two young upstart criminals, bearing a family name that was suspicious at best. Mikhail and I had been turned away with scorn from every door. We'd headed to one of the seedier bars in the edgy Langstrasse district to drown our sorrows.

When Mikhail slipped upstairs with two very expensive hookers, I'd slipped out and come here.

Maybe it was the alcohol. Maybe I felt like I had nothing to lose. Or maybe I was just sick of running from the past.

What I remember most is standing here, in the marble foyer, staring around in vain for a mother who never came.

I didn't expect it to hit me like this again.

To feel this heart-wrenching disappointment a second time.

I thought myself immune to it, or at least so occupied with bigger things that I wouldn't get sidetracked by emotions.

Yet here I am, my gut churning like the engine of my goddamn MTT and my nerves more knotted than one of Fabergé's fucking locks.

"Is she here?" Darya's hand slips into mine, and I grip it like it's a lifeline. I'll never know how she does that, how she seems to know just when I need the silken warmth of her touch. For all my objections to her accompanying me on this little excursion, I'm suddenly passionately grateful she's with me.

"No." I shake my head curtly. "No, she's not."

"Okay." She squeezes my hand, resting her head briefly against my shoulder. "Then we're done here."

I stride out of the stale air and gulp the fresh day gratefully. Darya's presence at my side is both strength and comfort. Dimitry is standing by the limo, eyes scanning the street.

"Let's get the fuck out of here," I growl as we approach him. "I never want to see this goddamn place again."

"Then it's fortunate I made it in time."

The voice coming from behind us jerks me to a halt faster than a bullet to the head.

My breath chokes in my throat, my heartbeat slowing to a dull, sick thud.

It can't be.

Dimitry stiffens, reaching for his gun. I'm trying to find my voice, but it's gone.

In the sudden strange fog that surrounds me, I'm dimly aware that bullets are about to disrupt the peaceful Zurich morning.

Thankfully, Darya finds her voice when I can't. "Wait, Dimitry."

He must hear the urgency in her voice, because he actually does as she says.

Darya turns around, and I follow her hand like it's a lodestone, both hoping and dreading what I'm going to see.

"Roman."

The woman standing in front of us is smaller than I remember, but then I was only eight the last time I saw her. Her black hair has been dyed blond, a short bob in place of the smooth chignon I remember. Large dark sunglasses hide her eyes. But even after more than twenty years, her face is as familiar to me as if I saw it yesterday.

"We can't talk here." Some long-standing instinct kicks into place inside me, cutting through the mental shock. "It isn't safe." I wrench open the limo door, and Darya, taking one look at my face, hurries inside without any argument.

I nod at the woman on the pavement, her face unreadable behind the glasses. "Get in." I close the door behind her.

Dimitry's hand is still on his gun, but he's watching me, eyes narrow. "Friend of yours?"

"Something like that." I meet his eyes, my heart suddenly racing in my chest. "She's my mother, Rosa."

"R OMAN."

It's the second time Rosa has said my name since we met on the street, but my ability to answer her hasn't improved. Nor can I think of her as *Mama*. I find it hard to look at her. She's sitting beside Darya, and I'm on the seat opposite. I stare blankly at a point on the black leather seat between them, taking in my mother's figure in my peripheral vision.

Rosa may well be smaller than my child's eyes remembered, but she matches Darya's five foot ten. She's wearing brown low-heeled boots and dark suede pants with a cream knit sweater and subtle diamond studs in her ears. Carrying a suede Hermès bag and with an elegant French manicure, she looks like any upper-middle-class wife out for a day's shopping in downtown Zurich.

"I've been staying in a room just off Oberdorfstrasse for weeks, hoping you would come." Rosa's voice is low and slightly unsteady. "My contact called when you collected the key to the safety deposit box. I came straight away."

"That's a risk." I still can't look at her, but in a weird instinct, my logical brain continues to run with detached efficiency. "Are you certain you weren't seen?"

Darya's foot slides between mine, both warning and reassurance. I know my voice sounds hard, but it's an effort to speak at all, let alone to moderate my tone.

"I've managed to evade sight for over twenty years, Roman. No, I wasn't followed." There's no boast in her words, only quiet resignation. "I don't believe there is anyone watching the bank. Or at least there wasn't, before today."

"Why would that change today?" I seize on her final comment.

"You're in a limousine, Roman. Traveling in your own plane,

I imagine, since we are en route to the private airport. These things are easy to track."

When I don't immediately answer, she shifts in her seat, turning sideways. "You must be Darya." I hear the slight catch in her voice, note the effort she takes to breathe in and steady herself. "I am so very happy to finally meet you."

"And you are Rosa Borovsky." Darya takes the proffered hand, smiling.

My mother's mouth twists at the corners. "It's been a long time since anyone called me that."

"Would you prefer us to use a different name?" Darya's smile is understanding. "I know how . . . hard it can be, living two lives."

"I know you do." Rosa presses her hand, then releases it and turns back to me. "I know you both do. Rosa is fine. It's probably best that you don't know the name I'm using now."

I give a rather hard laugh. "I take it this is just a fleeting visit, then. Not planning to stick around?"

Darya frowns at me. "Roman—"

"It's fine." Rosa interrupts her. She folds her hands in her lap and watches me across the limo. "You have every right to be angry, Roman."

"Good to know." My fingers itch for the Scotch bottle, but today alcohol is not an option. I meet her eyes briefly, but my own slide away. Even that fleeting glimpse is enough to jolt me to the core.

For so long, I've seen her eyes only in my dreams.

It's been years since I allowed myself the luxury of actually remembering them.

Those memories are too painful.

Liquid brown eyes, laughing into my own as she held my hands and danced with me.

Eyes soft with love as she read me to sleep.

Memories like that undo a man. Break the walls I needed to build in order to survive.

And today, of all days, isn't the time to take that fortress down.

My anger makes no sense, after so many years of longing to see my mother again. But it's there, as uncontrollable as it is savage. I'm not proud of it, but nor am I capable of processing it.

Not today.

"Look, Rosa."

She flinches when I use her first name, but it's the best I can do. I force myself to meet her eyes, taming the sudden rush of adrenaline with the discipline of long practice. "This isn't the day for a family reunion." I take a card from my shirt pocket and hold it out to her. "This is my number. Feel free to call it the next time you're in Spain." I knock on the window, and Dimitry lowers it. "Tell Bryce to pull in at the next truck stop. Our passenger won't be traveling with us."

He wisely doesn't argue, just nods and raises the window again.

"Roman!" Darya is glaring at me. "We can make time—"

"No." Rosa cuts her off in a subdued tone. "After what has happened, our conversation can wait."

My inner tension ratchets up even further. The limo turns into a service road, but I'm no longer paying attention. "What do you mean, 'after what has happened'?" I fix on my mother's face, any hesitation I previously felt about looking at her dropping away. "What do you know?"

"I know that Vilnus Orlov has kidnapped your goddaughters." She meets my eyes steadily. "That he's holding them in Miami."

"And how, exactly, do you know this, Rosa? Who are you talking to?" I clasp my hands between my knees, pinning her to the seat with my eyes. "Or should I say—who is talking to you?"

Darya is very still. Her smile has faded, and her eyes on Rosa are narrow and wary. It hurts me to see her like this, and that does nothing to alleviate the churning anger inside me, anger I neither understand nor, at the present moment, have any wish to examine.

"Sergei sent me a message. But I knew before that. Alexei, he—"

"Alexei is talking to you. Of course he is." Darya's voice is hard. Her eyes shift to mine as the limo glides to a halt. "I agree with your son, Rosa. I think this is a good place for us to part ways."

"Not a chance," I interrupt her. "Not if she's talking to Alexei."

Darya frowns, but she doesn't argue with me.

"I'm sorry, Rosa, but for now, I'd prefer it if you remained under my protection. Darya is flying back to Spain today. You will travel with her."

Rosa stares between us both, her bewilderment apparent. "That isn't wise, Roman. Darya will need to be in Zurich anyway, when—"

"When what, Rosa?" I cut her off, my rage rising faster than I think I'm going to be able to control. "When you call her brother, so he can betray her again? Or her father, so Sergei can lie to her again? No." I shake my head, my fists balling tightly as I stare her down. "I won't allow anything to put my family at risk, Rosa. Not even you."

Her face pales. "I *am* your family, Roman. I would never do anything to put you at risk."

"Really." I almost spit the word. "You'll have to forgive me if I find that rather difficult to believe." Leaving Darya inside the limo, I open the door without waiting for an answer, pulling Rosa out with me. Dimitry and Bryce step out of the limo, eyeing me warily.

"Pat her down. I want her phone and any other device." Holding her elbow tightly, I take the bag from her shoulder.

"This isn't necessary, Roman." Her voice is quiet, almost defeated, as Dimitry starts patting her down. "You have this wrong. My phone is in my bag," she adds. I find it, a basic model Nokia, and hand it to her.

"Unlock it."

"The code is 0627."

The twenty-seventh of June.

The date she left Papa and me.

I don't react, just unlock it. The messages are empty, as is the call log.

"Is anyone expecting your call?" I snap.

"No."

"Will anyone call, expecting you to answer?"

"I don't know. I don't make calls, I only answer them." She stands unmoving as Dimitry searches her thoroughly.

"Tell me what they know," I say as he pats her down.

She frowns, shaking her head. "What who knows?"

I click my tongue impatiently. "Are the Orlovs expecting an attack? What has Alexei told you?"

"Nothing." Rosa looks genuinely bewildered. "He never said anything about an attack. I only know that he was expecting Darya in Zurich days ago."

"Yes, well, Darya isn't following her brother's orders anymore. Wait." It's my turn to frown. "If it was Darya who he was expecting, why were you waiting near the bank?"

"Hoping." For the first time since I pulled her out of the limo, Rosa's eyes cloud over with unshed tears, her voice trembling. "I hoped that when Darya came, you might come after her. Alexei said you . . . might."

I ignore that. "Why would you know if Darya had arrived in Zurich?"

"I only knew I would be contacted as soon as she reached Alexei's safe house in Zurich."

Khuy. Cold horror washes through my body in a sickening wave. *That's how close we came. To Darya, pregnant and alone, being back in the hands of Vilnus Orlov.*

I can't look at my mother anymore. I can barely see for my fury.

"She rides in the front seat with you." I push Rosa toward Dimitry, waiting until he has hold of her arm before I let go. "Get us to the fucking airport. If she so much as moves between now and then, do whatever you have to." I slam the door behind her. "Bryce—in the back."

I take a series of deep breaths before I open the door and climb back in next to Darya. She grips my hand wordlessly, and my fingers close over hers like they're a goddamn lifeline.

"Change of plan." My voice is still hard with tension. "My mother—*Rosa*—will travel with Darya. But to London, not to Malaga."

Bryce frowns. "Our security team is waiting in Spain."

"Rosa has been talking to Alexei. We need to assume the Orlovs know we're in Zurich and are expecting Darya to fly back to Malaga."

Bryce blanches.

"Change the flight plan to London. Contact Vera, Yuri's wife. Her London house is just as safe as my penthouse. I did the security myself when the children stayed there. Contact our London people, have them clear the house immediately, then get our own team out there. Once in London, Rosa gets her own dedicated guard. And she doesn't speak to a single fucking soul I don't personally clear from this moment on."

"Copy that, boss." Bryce is already on his phone.

Darya squeezes my hand reassuringly as I punch out Pavel's number. He answers on the first ring. "Boss."

I explain the situation briefly. "I don't want their arrival in

London to make the slightest fucking blip on anyone's radar. That means customs, air control—any damn thing. I don't give a fuck who you have to hack, bribe, or kill to make that happen. From Zurich, Darya's jet is invisible. You got it?"

"Got it, boss."

"Let me know when it's done." I press end on the call, adrenaline coursing through my body. Bryce is on the phone in the other corner of the limo.

I turn to Darya. Her eyes are wide and pained, her body stiff with tension, and her tremulous smile breaks my fucking heart. I touch her cheek. "I'm sorry."

"No." She shakes her head. "You did the right thing, Roman. Even if Rosa means well, Alexei . . ." Her voice breaks off, and she shakes her head. "You did the right thing."

I raise her hand and press my lips to it, holding them there for a long time, just inhaling the sweet scent of her, the silk comfort of her skin against mine. Right now I need her nearness like a dying man needs water.

"Vera isn't the best company," I say as we enter the airport gates, "but I'll make sure she stays out of your way. I don't need to warn you not to speak about any of this to her."

Darya nods, her eyes not leaving mine. "Roman—I want to talk to your mother. She might know something that can help us. Help you."

When I don't answer, she leans into me, her lips grazing my cheek. "I know you don't trust her. Neither do I, not until this is over. But if there's anything at all that she knows and we don't— surely we should find out?"

I don't like the idea of Darya anywhere near Rosa. I'm still haunted by how close she came to being in Alexei's hands in Zurich. "Do you remember when you told me about your brother's letter? You said he gave you an address in Zurich."

She nods.

"My mother was the contact you were meant to meet."

Her hand flies to her mouth, her eyes widening as the implication settles in. "Oh, God."

I nod grimly. "Talk to her if you like. I won't stop you. But you need to be fucking careful, Darya. There'll be time after all this is over to work out who is and isn't innocent, who knew what. But for now, until we have the girls back, I don't trust anyone. Not even when they're under lock and key in my own house."

She's already nodding. "I'll be careful, I promise." Her brow crinkles. "What about Fedorov? Do you think I should ask her about him?"

"No." I answer immediately. "I don't want anyone outside our immediate circle so much as hearing that fucker's name, let alone that we're coming for him."

"I understand."

The limo slows to a halt beside the plane. Bryce exits, diplomatically leaving us alone. Darya looks up at me, her eyes wide and luminous. "This is it, isn't it," she says quietly. "The last time I see you before you do this."

"Yes." I pull her onto my lap, desperate to feel her close. I've been dreading this, the moment before we part. Dreading the questions I don't want to answer and the emotions I can't handle.

But instead of questions or emotions, Darya just takes my face in her hands and kisses me.

Fire.

Her mouth is hot and fierce and says more than any words ever could. She puts into that kiss every night we've spent together, all the love and pain and life we've somehow found in these past months. Her kiss is comfort and savage force, a surge of energy through my body that I know is meant to carry me into war.

And I take it. I take every moment of it, thrusting the sweet heat of her into my every cell.

When she finally pulls away, the knotted tension in my body has been transformed, changed to steady, sure purpose, honed and fierce as any ancient blade.

"Go, *pakhan*," she whispers, her eyes holding mine as her hands hold my face. "Go and get our babies back."

31

DARYA

Roman stands on the tarmac as our plane takes off. I stare at him out the window as we roar down the runway, drinking in his tall, wide-legged figure, his arms folded across his chest. Clad in black, face grim and set, the sun gleaming off his aviator sunglasses, every muscled inch of him spells darkness and danger.

I've never loved him more.

I put my hand on the window, not knowing if he can see me or not. He raises his own in a final salute. I watch until his figure fades to a speck far below and the plane turns west.

I turn back to find Rosa watching me. Her sunglasses are gone. Her eyes are a soft brown, shadowed with old pain. I can see Roman in her face, in the determined set of her jaw, the high forehead and sculptured lips. They curve now in a half smile so similar to her son's it makes my heart twist.

"You love him." It isn't a question.

I nod. "I do."

Her eyebrows arch curiously. "How did that happen?" Then, as if recalling the circumstances of our meeting, her smile falters, the light in her eyes fading. "If you don't mind me asking."

"I don't." I take the ginger tea the stewardess offers and sip it gingerly, though my sickness is notably absent, probably scared away by the drama of today. "I was working in a café across the road from Roman's business. He came in every morning for coffee."

I realize I'm smiling. Those days seem so far away now, like another life.

"Ah!" Rosa's eyes sparkle. "So it was love at first sight?" Her voice has a faint lilt, a singsong accent that is a reminder of her Colombian heritage. It reminds me painfully of my own mother.

"Not exactly." I actually laugh softly. "We used to try to outsmart one another. I would do the crossword in his favorite paper. He would try to . . . make me uncomfortable. Every day was like a little battle of wills, I guess."

Rosa's smile widens, and when it does, her entire face lights up. "But this is exactly how love begins, I think, no?"

I lift a shoulder. "Maybe, yes."

"But he didn't know who you truly were? Or you him?" Her forehead wrinkles when I shake my head, her eyes searching my face. "How can such a coincidence happen?"

"I don't know." My smile fades. "It wasn't . . . easy, for either of us, when we found out the truth. I was working as Roman's au pair by then, living in his house."

"Yes." She sips her glass of champagne. "Your father told me this, but I could hardly believe it. I thought that he must be losing his mind at first." She smiles at me apologetically.

"Did *you* know who he was by then?" It's something I've wondered ever since Papa told me about Roman opening the vault. "Roman, I mean. Did you know he had changed his name to Stevanovsky? Where he was?"

"No." Her face falls, and she seems to shrink into herself. It's awful, like watching the sun disappear behind the clouds. Worse than that, because I know intuitively that I'm watching Rosa slip back behind the running mask. I know that mask. I wore it for six years.

I can't help but wonder how it would feel to have worn it for over two decades.

"The alert system from the bank was set up more than twenty years ago, when technology was much different than it is now. And it was set up carefully, to avoid any kind of trap. It took months for news to reach me that someone had accessed the safety deposit box. When I finally came to Switzerland I was cautious. You must realize." Her eyes meet mine, opaque with old pain. "At that time, Roman had been thought dead for nearly a decade."

"My father said you never believed that."

"No." Her mouth almost smiles, then falls still again. "No, I never did. But what mother wants to believe her child dead? It was all I had, the only reason—" She cuts off abruptly, but she doesn't need to finish the sentence.

The only reason I had to stay alive.

I understand that better than she could ever know.

She takes a deep breath. "I still didn't know much. The biometrics Roman used to enter the bank showed his finger-prints, but there wasn't an optical scan when I first closed the box, so that didn't help, and I know better than anyone that fingerprint casts can be made. The bank wouldn't show me the footage of the person who opened the box. And then there was the fact that the egg was still inside it—along with the key. Afterward, when I told him, Sergei and I argued about that, about what it might mean." She smiles at me sadly. "We argued about everything. It was when you were still in Argentina.

Sometimes we could manage to meet, when you were working."

I tense, and she touches my leg, a gentle gesture of apology. "You must not judge your father for keeping my secrets. I had been running a long time by then. I was . . . hardened. Fearful. And, I confess, I was angry, too. Sergei still had two children. I had lost everyone, everything, that mattered to me. He didn't want me to go to Switzerland at all, but I insisted." Her mouth twists. "After Switzerland, we swapped sides in our argument. I was convinced that whoever had opened that box was impersonating my son, trying to draw us all out. Sergei argued that anyone other than my son would have taken the egg and run.

"In the end, it was Alexei who initially made the connection. Or rather, a journalist whose articles he was following."

"A journalist?" I frown. "Not Lance Ryder?"

Rosa nods. "He did a piece on your family that concerned Alexei deeply, since it used your photo."

I nod. "I saw it, in a doctor's office in Spain."

"Yes. Well, Alexei has a Swedish friend—"

"Lars Andersson," I supply.

"Yes, yes. This is his name. Well, the Swede paid Lance Ryder to stop writing about your family and offered instead to pay a high price for any information Ryder discovered about the Naryshkin treasure. He lied to Ryder, told him that Alexei knew very little about his own history. Andersson told Ryder that if he discovered information that helped him and Alexei open the vault, they would pay Ryder a generous cut of the contents."

So Ryder really was working with Alexei.

I think of the man Papa saw with a camera outside our old apartment. Of the day our lockbox was stolen. Of Ryder thrusting a camera in my face outside the café.

"It would have been nice," I say tightly, "if my brother had mentioned that the journalist was working for him. But then, it isn't as if any of you told me anything."

Rosa leans forward and puts a hand on my knee, her face sympathetic. "Don't be angry at your brother. Or your father. Any contact between the three of us has been very minimal. Months, sometimes years, passed without any communication at all. I never knew where you and Sergei were. Neither did Alexei. And he never told me about Lars Andersson or Lance Ryder." The sadness in her face is palpable. "We have all had to hide, Darya. Your brother perhaps most of all."

Perhaps. But all I really see is Alexei's determination to open that vault. Even if it meant exposing Papa and me. I can't forgive that, let alone him endangering the children.

"It was Lance Ryder who first made the link between Hale Property and Roman Borovsky." She sits back, pouring herself some water. Her hand isn't quite steady. I'm not the only one who is finding this conversation difficult.

"Ryder tracked the anonymous buyer of Borovsky pieces at auction back to a Roman Stevanovsky. Then he discovered that a Swiss bank had given Roman extensive financial backing to start Hale Property, without any obvious security.

"That was the first time Alexei contacted me with the news that he thought Roman was really alive and living under the Stevanovsky name." Her hands clasp and unclasp in her lap. "I was still in Argentina then. And the message was brief, with less than half the information I have told you now. I still barely dared to hope."

I know that feeling. Hope is almost the worst kind of torture. It's easier to sit with grief than it is with the tremulous promise of hope, something that can disappear at any moment, leaving you lower than if you'd never had it at all.

"It was only when Sergei contacted me independently with the same news that I finally accepted it might be true. We were afraid that if I came to Spain, I would risk exposing you both. I had to wait until Alexei contacted me again." Her face tightens. "Those weeks were . . . long."

"When finally I managed to speak with Alexei, things began to happen very quickly. He put me in touch with his friend, this Lars Andersson, who helped me get into Switzerland unseen a couple of weeks ago. He told me that you would arrive soon and said I would be contacted when you made it to the safe house in Zurich. He said there was a chance that Roman might be with you. Or follow you. That was why I went to the bank every day. Just in case, you understand?"

Her voice cracks, and she turns away quickly, but not before I see the sudden sheen of tears in her eyes. "I thought it would be different." She swallows, trying to regain control of herself, but her voice is low and strained. "I didn't expect Roman to welcome me with open arms, of course not." Her voice breaks again, and it's some time before she gains control of herself. "But I didn't expect him to be so angry. I should have, I suppose." Her voice fades tiredly. She still doesn't look at me.

I don't want to feel sorry for her. I am still angry, no matter my sympathy for her struggles.

Roman and I have both lived in darkness for most of our lives because of the secrets kept by our parents. Despite the compassion I have for the years she spent running, another part of me feels frustrated that all of this has been about that damned vault.

And nothing she says will ever remove the horror of that blast.

I swallow my anger, knowing it won't help. But in the silence that follows her story, I know I need to say something to help her understand.

"Our children were taken." They may not be the right words, but they're all I can manage. "And Alexei knew about it. That is too much for Roman and me to forgive."

Rosa's head snaps around, her eyes wide with shock. "You cannot think that Alexei knew about that bomb!"

"You said it yourself." I'm unable to hide the anger in my voice. "Alexei told you it was going to happen."

"No!" Her face is white, her lips quivering with emotion. "No, I don't believe that. Alexei would never endanger you like that, let alone children. Never."

I close my lips on all the things I want to say, knowing they won't help.

Rosa stares at me, clearly trying to work out how to argue the point, but I don't have the energy for it.

"Excuse me." I stand up, my stomach churning.

I head to the bathroom and throw up, again and again.

When I come out, I choose another seat, as far away from Rosa as the private jet will allow. I close my eyes, trying not to think about where Roman is right now, or about all the things that can go wrong.

32

ROMAN

Makari's meeting point is a warehouse by an old air base near the Miami waterfront, lit by bare globes hanging from the ceiling. There are half a dozen armored vehicles at the far end and two choppers in the hangar next door. Mak's team is standing around the wide, flat ops table on which the schematics are laid out. A bank of laptop screens are set up on a trestle table behind them. I strip off my traveling clothes, replacing them with the same formal black business suit the team is wearing, handmade specially with bulletproof lining.

Mickey is sitting on a crate opposite me, his face pale and set. For once, his laptop screen is closed.

"You'll stay here with the backup team." I eye him sternly. "No fuckery, Mickey."

"I know." He gives me a rictus smile that doesn't get anywhere near his eyes. "I'll be watching, though." There's a live feed from our lapel cameras to the coordinating team here in the warehouse.

"Just make sure that's all you do." I sit down on a crate and reach for my shoes.

He leans forward, his eyes narrowing. "What's that tattoo on your foot?"

"This?" I grin, holding the sole of my foot out to show him. "Funny you should ask. I would normally have avoided that question. But since it's largely irrelevant now, the tattoo is a set of numbers. It's the code to access the safe deposit box where my mother hid the key to the vault." I pull out the small golden key and show him.

"You're taking that with you tonight?" Mickey's still staring at my foot as I pull my boots on, his face oddly still, as it often is when he's thinking something through. "Does that mean you're planning to actually open the vault?"

"It means I need the Orlovs to believe I *can* open it." I lace the boots and look at him curiously. "You know that, Mickey. You've been involved in all the planning. You know that's how we plan to distract Orlov while we hit the Fedorov place."

He nods, but his eyes are still far away. Knowing Mickey, he's thinking of every angle of our plan, still trying to find holes in it. I reach forward and touch his leg. "The best minds in the business have gone over this a hundred times," I say quietly. "You need to trust me on this, Mickey. And if you find that hard, then trust Mak." I give him a half smile. "Even I defer to him when it comes to the operational part of this. When it comes to stealth missions, he and his men are unparalleled. I'm a big believer in hiring the best of the best, as you know from working with Mercura. Mak is the very best at what we're about to do."

"I know that." He gives me a strained smile.

I nod at the table. "Want to listen in to the final briefing?"

He shakes his head, already reaching for his laptop. "You don't need me. And there's some things I want to check."

I grip his shoulder. I know how he feels. This close to going in, time slows down, tension turning every second into an hour. He's been running on adrenaline for days, and this operation isn't some existential cyber challenge with an anonymous opponent. It's a deadly race to save his sisters. Mickey has been remarkably collected during the planning phases, but it doesn't surprise me at all that so close to the bullets actually flying, he's searching for a distraction.

"Mickey." His eyes flicker up to me. "When I take the call from Orlov—"

"I know, I know. I can't be there." He nods. "You have to take the call in the hangar, where he can't see anything, and you don't want them to know I'm here. I get it."

"I'm sorry."

He gives a curt shake of his head. "Just get my sisters back."

I head over to the table. The men leaning over it might look like any ordinary security detail, but then they are accustomed to becoming whatever the job requires. I don't need Mak to give me their résumés to know they're drawn from the top echelons of special ops around the world. They nod at me courteously, and I take my place beside them as Mak takes point at the head of the table. Like I said to Mickey, Mak is the best at what he does. Ego doesn't play a part in moments like these. He wouldn't tell me how to run Mercura; I don't tell him how to run his team. I made the original plan. The execution of it I trust to Mak's expertise.

"Orlov is expecting our video call at nineteen hundred hours." He points to the schematic of the Miami compound. "Roman told him in the initial call from Spain that he wants proof of life on that call, to speak to the girls in person, before he agrees to come to the compound and open the vault. Bravo Team is already in place around the Everglades house. The moment we set the meet time at the Petrovsky compound into motion, they will be watching. Fedorov will have to travel by chopper if he's going to make the meet—it's too far by car. The team will get the go-ahead to take him as soon as he moves, ensuring that both Inger and Fedorov are taken alive. That operation will be done on the black. No choppers, no gunfire, no noise or lights. Fedorov's men will be dead before they even know there's an attack in progress.

"Timing is everything, which we all know. Fedorov's chopper, flown by our people, must take off from the Everglades without any trouble. Orlov has to believe Fedorov is on his way. Then we need to arrive at the Petrovsky compound in Coconut Grove before our team in Fedorov's chopper does."

"We're certain Fedorov is still in the Everglades house?" One of the operatives asks the question.

"Pavel has had trouble hacking the feed inside the house there, so we have limited eyes inside, but his chopper is still there. Bravo Team has been covertly watching the Everglades property for days and believes they have identified Fedorov. It's the best we can do on short notice."

"What have we got from Charlie Team outside the Coconut Grove compound?" It's another of the operatives.

"They've had the place under surveillance for three days, but they couldn't get in tight without raising the alarm. They'll move into their close positions as soon as we start traveling to the meet. They're coordinating with Pavel to shut down the feed inside the compound while they get weapons in place for us by the time we enter, but they'll wait for my direct signal before they go in themselves. Alpha Team, once inside the compound, you're on Roman's signal, not mine."

The questions continue, incisive and direct, examining every loose end, checking numbers, resources, movements, and intelligence. I let Mak take them all. We've already been through this ourselves. Even with my eyes closed, I know every inch of the layout of both the Everglades house and the Petrovsky compound. I can see the entire operation in my mind as if it has already happened, the weak points, the possible changes.

"Roman." Mak turns to me. "Is there anything you want to add?"

The faces at the table look at me.

"You all know what's at stake here." I meet each man's eyes long enough for us to gain the measure of the other. "Orlov has no need to keep my daughters alive. He won't hesitate to kill them if he gets even the faintest hint of what's going down. He's going to be suspicious, which is also why he has Alexei Petrovsky guarding the girls' door. He'll want to see that vault open before he hands the girls over, and he has to believe that is what's happening. He won't summon Alexei to the vault until the last minute."

I tap the vault on the schematic of the Petrovsky compound. "That's the tricky point, as Mak has already explained to you. Alexei Petrovsky is the wild card. He hasn't come this far just to open the vault for Orlov, and we don't know what fucking trick he has up his sleeve. Until we do, and until I give the signal, nobody makes a move, or I'll shoot you myself."

It's cold, but it's also necessary.

It's a measure of the caliber of those at the table that none of the men so much as flinch. They all know what will happen if Orlov gets even the faintest suspicion that there's any agenda other than his own on the table.

"I know you're the best at what you do. Stick to the plan, do your job, and in a few hours my girls will be back and you boys will have good Scotch in your hands and much bigger bank accounts for your trouble."

They nod, but apart from a few small smiles, the atmosphere is quiet and controlled.

Focused.

Exactly as it needs to be.

In the last minutes before we get going, I call Darya. "You made it to London."

It isn't a question. I was informed the moment they landed and at every point since.

Doesn't stop me hating the fucking fact that she isn't here.

"How are you feeling?"

"I'm okay." But her voice is thin, and I know from Bryce that she spent most of the flight to London in the bathroom. I also know she's not spending a great deal of time in Rosa's company, but I don't blame her for that at all. If I had a convenient alternative, I'd have put my mother in an entirely different building.

"You need to be resting." I stare out the hangar door at the swamp stretching into the distance, glad she is miles away from what's about to go down and simultaneously wishing she would magically appear.

"I'll rest when you call to say the girls are safe." Darya lowers her voice. "Vera's an interesting character, by the way."

I snort. "I'm still surprised she didn't leap at my offer of an all-expenses-paid holiday instead of staying while we take over her house. But if she's upsetting you, I can certainly make her leave."

"No, no. This is her home, and you have enough on your plate." She pauses. "Let's just say that I now understand why the children aren't overly keen to spend time with their babushka."

I grin. "When Mikhail and I were younger, we'd literally shoot one another in the leg to avoid a Sunday dinner with Yuri and Vera. Believe me, if I'd had a convenient alternative to her home in London, I'd have used it. But my team knows that place inside out, and they're used to guarding the children there. It was the best I could do on short notice. I'll have you out of there tomorrow, I promise."

"It's fine, really." I hear her moving, then the sound of a door closing. "I love you," she says quietly. "I wish I could show you how much."

Maybe it's the adrenaline, or maybe it's just been too long since I've had her body beneath me, because I'm suddenly iron-bar hard and gripping the phone tight enough to break it.

"Tell me what you're wearing."

"Right now, not a lot." I can hear the smile in her voice. Darya knows this isn't really about titillation. It's about connection, about some primal need to feel her here, with me, as I go to do what has to be done. "That rose silk cami set you like to take off."

"That really isn't much." I close my eyes, picturing her in the Knightsbridge mansion, standing by one of the tall mullioned windows. If I concentrate hard enough, I can feel the silk of her skin beneath my hands, inhale her vanilla scent. "You should put on a robe. You'll distract my security team."

"I was wearing a robe. Then you called, and suddenly I felt too hot." Her voice is seductively playful. She knows the game we're playing, knows exactly what I need and why I need to hear it.

"Roman!" Dimitry calls my name, and I hold up a finger without turning around.

"I have to go."

"I know," she says quietly.

For a moment I hold on to the phone, just listening to her breathe. I remember feeling the soft swell of her belly under my hand, rich with our child.

"God, I love you," I say roughly. "I need you to take care of yourself and our baby, Darya. Will you promise me you'll do that?"

"I promise."

"And when I get home, I'm going to take that body apart, piece by fucking piece."

The audible hitch in her breath fires every last nerve I possess.

"Come back to me," she says, her voice a husky comfort and

the only motivation I will ever need. "And when you do, I'm going to hold you to that promise."

I end the call and turn around, every cell in my body more ready for this fight than for any other I've faced in my entire life.

"Let's fucking do this."

33

DARYA

"Then it's begun?"

I turn around to face Rosa, my heart still tripping wildly. Contrary to what I told Roman, I'm wearing soft wool trousers and a V-cut knit sweater. Even in summer, London isn't exactly cami weather, especially close to midnight.

But Roman didn't call to hear about my wardrobe. He called because he's going to war, and he needed to know that I am going in with him.

"Yes." I meet her eyes. "It's begun."

She sits down heavily on a chair and runs a shaking hand over her face. "I forgot what this feels like."

More to distract myself than anything else, I say, "Did Roman's father go to war like this too, then?" Perhaps because of the delicate beauty of his jewelry, and maybe because of the stories my father used to tell about his friend Ruki, I don't have an impression of Aleksander Borovsky being warlike.

"Not Aleksander, no." Rosa's lips curve in a soft smile of reminiscence. "It was always Sergei who did the fighting. Aleksander was Ruki, the Hands. He told me that even back in the Paris days, Sergei had kept him from the worst of the killing. By the time he met me, Aleksander was no longer involved in Sergei's business. In fact, since they'd arrived in Miami, they'd gone to great lengths to ensure there was no connection between them at all. We even used hidden tunnels in the compound when we visited one another, so nobody saw us. Sergei and Aleksander were closer than brothers. But they were also pathological about keeping their relationship hidden."

She gives me a half smile.

"That didn't stop them from seeing one another, often. And although Sergei would never discuss business, we would always know when things were bad, because he would call Aleksander and me to sit with Maria, so she wouldn't worry. Roman was just a baby then, yes? He would crawl all over the kitchen floor while Maria and I baked. We used to bake to distract ourselves," she says wistfully. "Aleksander would sit at the kitchen table, tinkering with jewelry. He would give Roman small locks to play with." Her eyes are misty with recollection. "It is so strange, these things that I remember. At the time, I hated the waiting. We were all so afraid that Sergei wouldn't return. No matter what Aleksander said, I knew he was just as afraid as Maria and me. But now, when I am thinking back, those days feel like the happiest time of my life."

I'm curious despite myself. "How did you and my mother meet?"

"On the way from Colombia to the United States." Rosa answers immediately, and her face alters, the years momentarily falling away. "We were both nineteen, and neither of us spoke any English. Maria was an orphan from a small village. She had no future that didn't involve poverty and, eventually, some kind of forced marriage, so she had nothing to lose by leaving. My family had already made a marriage for me." She tilts her head to one side. "Not a marriage I wanted. I felt that I, too, had nothing to lose." Her smile fades. "I was wrong about that, as it turned out."

She glances back at me apologetically. "But you asked how Maria and I met. We were in the back of the same truck, right at the beginning of our journey. The driver took a liking to Maria —rather too much of a liking, if you know what I mean. One day he stopped the truck in a remote place and tried to pull her out of the back. Maria was kicking and fighting him, but he was too strong for her. We all knew what he planned to do. None of the other passengers wanted to intervene, in case they were denied the ride they had paid for. But I had grown up with men like him—and I was running from one who was far worse. So I hit the driver over the head with a rock."

I give a startled cough of laughter. "What happened after that?"

"We took his gun. It was the only one on board, and we were on a remote back road, as I said." The look Rosa shoots me is almost mischievous, and despite everything, I find myself liking her. "We gave all the passengers a choice—they could come with us or stay on the ground with the unconscious driver." She shrugs. "They chose to come with us, of course. Your mother and I drove that truck until it fell apart beyond repair." Her smile fades. "Then we walked."

I sit back in my chair, digesting her words. "My mother never talked about that journey," I say slowly. "She never really talked about you at all."

"No," Rosa says quietly. "No, I imagine she wouldn't have. It was many years before I could say her name without crying. Leaving Aleksander and Roman was the most difficult thing I have ever done, or ever will do. But leaving Maria . . . it was like leaving part of my own body. We had been together for so long, through so much. I think that was why we were all so drawn to one another, your papa, Aleksander, Maria, and me. We all knew what it was to fight for our survival against impossible odds, to feel utterly alone in the world but for that one friend. We became one another's family. And for the precious years we were together, that felt like an almost unimaginable blessing. One none of us ever took for granted—and one we were all prepared to lay down our lives to protect."

The sadness in her voice is so palpable I don't want to interrupt her. Outside the window a soft rain begins to fall, the yellow garden lights turning the droplets a gleaming gold as they run down the window. The night outside seems almost uncannily quiet for so deep in the city. The five-story mansion is set behind a tall stone wall and surrounded by a thick garden and stone facade that effectively mask it from the street. We could be in the middle of a forest for all it feels like London.

"It was my family who came for us, in the end." Rosa's voice is quiet. She's curled into the large armchair, her face shadowed in the dim light of the lamp on the coffee table. "By then, we'd stopped spending so much time together. The rumors had begun to spread. People were talking about the vault beneath your father's house, whispering about what it might contain. Aleksander and Sergei didn't want to draw attention to their relationship." Her mouth curls sadly. "Alexander and I had to use the tunnels Sergei had built into the compound to visit him. Our visits were rare by then, so perhaps that is why I remember so clearly the way Sergei's face lit up whenever he saw you and Alexei. I had never seen him so truly joyful as when he was with you both. You must remember," she says, her eyes cutting to me, "all that Sergei and Aleksander had been through. Neither of them had come to America expecting to have another chance at family life. I sometimes think that Sergei could never quite believe it had happened. I still believe that is why he built that fortress. He was always preparing for the day when he would lose it all again." She shakes her head. "I have wondered, sometimes, if it was our combined fears, the way we chose to deal with them, that created our own downfall."

It's like hearing the story of someone else's life. I'm both greedy for every detail and dreading the tragedy I know is coming in her tale.

"I know some of this story," I say quietly. "My father spoke a little of it, but never of his past, before Miami."

Rosa's mouth twists. "Aleksander told me once that both he and Sergei learned early on that the only way to deal with death or loss was to cut all memory of it out of their lives. He said that in the gulag where he and Sergei were both born that was the only way a man survived. He learned to leave grief behind, to never speak of it again. To cut the pain out of his heart and mind, or else he went insane." She meets my eyes. "I know it must seem unfair to you, even cruel. But when life is full of death, we survive as we must. And some wounds are too painful to ever reopen, *mija*."

My heart clenches at the old endearment. Nobody has called me *my daughter* that way since my mother died. Hearing it now is a bittersweet echo of the past, a reminder of all I've lost, and of all I still have to lose.

"I think I can understand what you mean," I say quietly.

"Yes." Rosa nods slowly, her face sad. "I guess you can."

"Your family." I return to the story, unwilling to allow myself to think too long on those things I might still lose if tonight does not go well. "The Cardeñas cartel."

"Ah. I see Sergei told you that much, at least." Her mouth tightens. "They'd never stopped looking for me. I was my father's only child. He had promised me as wife to the head of a rival cartel. Traded me like livestock. When I ran, I shamed my father and caused a war. Families like mine don't forget insults like that. And there's always someone willing to hand over information when the price is right."

"I understand why you left Roman and ran." It's true; I do. "I know you were afraid that your family would hurt your husband and son. But I'm not sure I will ever understand why that vault was so important to you all, no matter what is inside it. Why would you risk losing your own son, just to protect his inheritance? It makes no sense to me." I frown, staring at her. "There is nothing—*nothing*—I wouldn't do to protect my children. I can't imagine thinking a vault was so important that I would leave my child in danger."

Rosa flinches slightly at the last line. "We thought that linking all three of you to the vault might *save* you from danger." Her voice is subdued. "It wasn't what was inside the vault that we were trying to protect, but the opposite," she says quietly. "We thought that one day that vault might be the thing that protected you. A bargaining chip to trade for your lives, if you had to."

I swallow a sudden, bizarre urge to laugh.

Or throw up.

"It didn't quite work out that way."

"No, it did not." Rosa doesn't try to defend herself, for which I'm grateful. "What I can say is that I never thought the Cardeñas cartel would come at us with the power they did, nor that the war would rage on so long. They didn't have that kind of power when I left Bogotá." Her face darkens. "If we'd known Vilnus Orlov was bankrolling them behind the scenes, not to mention selling Sergei out the entire time, it might have made more sense."

It wasn't the Orlovs bankrolling them. It was Fedorov. For a moment I consider telling Rosa about Ilyan Fedorov. I have so many questions, things she might be able to answer. But then I remember Roman's warning not to mention even the name to his mother.

Following his directions has never been more important than now.

Are they fighting now? Is Roman standing in front of a hail of bullets while I sit here?

I shiver.

I'm almost grateful for the interruption when the door opens and Vera enters the room.

My gratitude lasts about as long as it takes to absorb the scowl on her face. A scowl which, after even the few hours I've spent in her company, I've begun to think is a permanent fixture.

"You're both up late." She glares pointedly at first Rosa, then me. "Is anyone ever going to actually explain to me what is going on?"

She speaks English with a heavy Russian accent. Perversely, I haven't actually told her I speak Russian, not least because Rosa doesn't, and I don't have the energy to deal with Vera's seemingly permanent state of bitter discontent alone.

"Your guards have taken my phone," Vera continues in a strident tone, "and the landline is dead. I've been given no explanation for why my home has been invaded. The only contact I've had from Roman in weeks was the call to inform me that you were coming to stay, but what you're doing here without the children, when you are *supposed* to be their au pair, I'm sure I don't know!"

She pauses to inhale. Her nonexistent bosom heaves up and down on a chest so thin it's hard to believe a morsel of food ever passes her lips. Her penciled eyebrows arch so high they almost disappear inside her enormous blue-rinsed coiffure, over black eyes that watch us as beadily as any crow's.

"I haven't heard a word from Inger," she snaps, fingering a diamond necklace so heavy it's a wonder it doesn't crack her skinny neck. "And I don't understand why I'm not allowed to call darling Nicky."

Darling Nicky?

Oh, God. Nobody has told her about Nikolai being dead.

I suppose I shouldn't be surprised, given the tension we've been living with. But still.

Nikolai was her son.

She's lost both of her children now.

I want to feel the horror of that.

But the truth is that from the moment we walked through her door, Vera Stevanovsky has been so damned nasty to us both that it's difficult for me to feel anything for her other than distinct dislike.

From being openly insulting about Roman to never allowing me to forget that I'm the hired help, she's made it perfectly clear at every possible opportunity that our presence in her house is an enormous imposition.

"I will be having words with Roman when he returns from wherever he is, you can depend on that. What are we coming to, if I must entertain his staff as if they are royalty?" Vera stabs a wooden side table with one sharp fingernail. "Two strangers in my house," she mutters, glaring at us. "Yuri should never have handed that bastard boy the *pakhan*'s chair."

"Mrs. Stevanovsky." Rosa stands up, her normally soft brown eyes flashing with a rather dangerous light. "Roman placed us under your roof because he wants to keep us safe. I doubt he would appreciate his . . . *Lucia* being treated with disrespect."

According to Roman's instructions, we're in Vera's house under our cover names. Lucia, in my case, and Sofia, in Rosa's.

I didn't realize quite how grating it would be to disappear back into the shadows of Lucia Lopez, nor how accustomed I've become to being seen, if not as Roman's wife, at least as his partner.

Roman warned us that, for security reasons, neither Vera nor Yuri know the children are missing.

He neglected to mention that they don't know their only remaining son is dead.

Then again, given that it was Roman who killed him, I guess that omission might have been on purpose.

Fuck.

I can't tell her. Not now, not while Roman is risking his life to get the children back. I remember what Ofelia told me about the way Vera reacted when she received word of Mikhail's death, locking herself in her room and screaming for hours on end.

Something tells me she's likely to take the news about Nikolai even more badly.

It's past midnight, and my morning sickness has returned with a vengeance amid all the stress.

I'm not telling her the truth. It isn't my call to make, and I won't endanger Roman, no matter how indirectly.

All of this passes through my mind rapidly. I blink back to the present to find Vera staring at Rosa in open-mouthed astonishment, clearly still astounded that a stranger had the temerity to confront her in her own home.

"Well," she mouths furiously. "Of all the ungrateful, rude—"

"We're so sorry, Mrs. Stevanovsky." I interrupt her, placing a calming hand over Rosa's and forcing myself to smile. "We have had a very worrying few days. There was a security scare with the children, and Mr. Stevanovsky wanted to make sure they were safe. I know he deeply regrets disturbing your peace, but he told me that you are the only person he trusts to keep us safe in his absence. We're both so grateful for his care, and for your patience."

The black eyes drop to me, and Vera's thin lips curl in contempt. It's my turn to feel the anger rise. I'm grateful for Rosa's warning squeeze of my hand.

"Hmph." Vera's eyes flash spitefully, and she stalks out of the room, leaving an overwhelming cloud of Lancôme Climat perfume in her wake. The scent of violets almost makes me heave again.

"*Dios mio*," Rosa mutters as the door slams closed behind Vera. "Please tell me Roman does not call that woman mother."

I snort into my hand. She catches my eye and gives a soft chortle of her own. A moment later, we are both doubled over, hands stuffed in our mouths to try to stifle our laughter. Perhaps it's the tension, or perhaps it's just the layers of insanity we've both been living for so long, but we both laugh until tears run down our cheeks.

When we're finally done, Rosa takes my hand, and I let her.

Roman will be on the call to Orlov right now.

34

ROMAN

"Roman Borovsky."

Vilnus Orlov's bloated face stares out of the screen in front of me.

The years have not been kind to him.

He's fatter than I remember, his eyes narrow slits, and smoke from a cigarette coils up from a hand that is out of sight of the camera.

"Put the girls on." I don't bother acknowledging his greeting. The fucker knows why we're here.

Orlov's fat lips curl in an unpleasant smile. "Your daughter is safe, as is mine."

I ignore that. Masha might be his blood, but she's my family, now and always.

"That white screen behind you won't help, you know." His voice is conversational. "There isn't an inch of this city where I don't have eyes."

321

"Show me the girls, Orlov, or this call is done."

He takes a drag of his cigarette, the red sparrow on his hand vivid on-screen, and blows the smoke toward the camera. His smile doesn't reach his eyes. They're the same cold blue I remember from the night he murdered my father.

He nods at someone off-screen, and the camera flickers as it changes view.

"Roman!" Ofelia's pale face and wide, stark eyes come into view. Her arm is tightly around Masha, who looks defiant and tearstained as she clings to her sister.

It takes everything I have not to put my fist through the screen.

"*Umnyashka.*" I force myself to smile at Ofelia. "*Myshka,*" I say, shifting my smile to Masha. "Are you okay?"

"I don't like it here." Masha sniffs, glaring at someone off camera.

My fingers clench beneath the table. "I know, sweetheart. I'm sorry."

"We're okay." Ofelia stares directly at the camera with a hard wariness that breaks my heart. She turns to Masha, revealing a vivid red mark down one side of her face.

"What happened to your face?" There's nothing I can do to disguise the fury in my voice.

"It happened when the bomb went off." Her eyes flicker up to whoever is standing behind the camera. "I'm okay. It doesn't hurt anymore."

But you'll have that scar for the rest of your life. As if the scars inside weren't enough.

Inhale. Exhale.

"This will be over soon, I promise."

Ofelia nods her head slightly. "I know." Her tremulous smile breaks my fucking heart.

Thank God I made sure Mickey isn't watching this.

"That's enough." The camera moves again, back to Orlov's

sneering face. "They're alive, as you can see. Open the vault for me, and you can take them home."

"We will be at the compound in an hour." My voice is calm and measured, and nothing like the vicious killing rage racing through my body.

"Only one car. No weapons. And don't even think about trying anything, Borovsky. You know what will happen if you do."

The camera switches back to Ofelia's pale, set face and Masha's defiant glare. I stare directly into Ofelia's midnight eyes, wondering how I never saw myself in them. "I'll be there soon, okay?"

Be ready.

Ofelia gives the barest nod of her head, her lips pressed hard together. Masha hiccups.

Orlov's face fills the camera again.

You will be dead soon, you fat fuck.

"One hour, Borovsky."

The screen goes black.

"Mother*fucker!*" I push the chair back so hard it flies across the floor. I grip the edge of the table in front of me, battling for control. Nobody speaks. They know there's nothing they can say that will make this better.

"It's go time," I say tightly, staring at the schematics in front of me.

Mak nods. "Bravo Team, we're on the clock," he says into his headpiece. He nods at me. "I'll keep you posted."

I stalk out to the armored limo flanked by Dimitry and four members of Alpha Team, but all I can see are the two small, terrified faces of my daughters.

Mickey glances up from his position by the door as I pass. His eyes narrow when he sees my face.

"They're okay," I snarl, wrenching the limo door open.

He stands up and walks over, putting his hand out. I ignore it and pull him into a brief, hard embrace.

"I'll bring them home, Mickey."

He meets my eyes steadily. "I know."

He watches us enter the limo, but he turns away before the car even starts moving, opening his laptop again, his face a mask of concentration.

I know he'd only be a liability on the ground, but that doesn't stop me from wishing I could take him. If anyone has earned the right to be there when the girls are found, it's Mickey.

The freeway glides by. Nobody speaks. We're all counting minutes.

Almost thirty of them have gone by when my earpiece crackles to life.

"Everglades secure."

Mak delivers the news without embellishment. My initial rush of relief fades when he continues, "No sign of either target anywhere on the premises."

"What the fuck?" I stare at Dimitry across the limo. "We've had men watching the place for days. What do they mean, there's no sign of Inger or Fedorov?"

"They knew we were watching." Mak's voice is tight and controlled, but I can hear the tension beneath it. "The guard outside was heavy enough, but inside the place was deserted. Barely so much as a skeleton crew—and one man who is clearly a stand-in for Fedorov himself. Dressed the same, similar height, age, features."

"Jesus." I pass a hand over my face. "He was expecting us."

"That, or he deliberately runs a dupe system in case anyone is watching."

"No." Unease trickles down my spine. "He's up to something."

"We still going ahead?" Dimitry eyes me across the vehicle. We're ten miles from the Coconut Grove compound.

"I think we have to." I focus on the earpiece. "Mak?"

"I don't like it at all, but I agree. If we hesitate now, we risk losing our only chance. But we need to assume we're walking into an ambush. If Fedorov wasn't at the Everglades, then he's either in the Coconut Grove compound or somewhere close. I've got people on the water now, and covering every angle, but there's no sign of him yet."

"Goddammit." I pinch the bridge of my nose. Every instinct is screaming at me that something is wrong.

I pull out my phone and dial London. "Bryce. We've lost Fedorov. Is the house secure?"

"Yes." His answer comes immediately. "There's no problem there. We're watching every corner."

"Good. I want every man we have on it, and I don't want Darya and Rosa out of your sight for a moment. Any sign of trouble, get them both into the safe room. Where's Vera?"

"Right now, she's in the kitchen. Boss." Bryce pauses, just long enough to make my unease ratchet up a notch.

"What is it?"

"Vera. She's not at all happy about me taking her phone or monitoring the line here. And—well, she's asking about Nikolai. She wants to talk to him."

Fuck.

Amid everything else that's going on, I've neglected to mention to Vera that her remaining son is no longer with us. Or that I was the one who put the bullet through his head. I'm not saying I forgot to tell her; I just didn't.

"Head her off for the next hour or so. I'll call as soon as this is done and deal with her."

"Copy that." Bryce hesitates. "She's being particularly unpleasant. With Darya."

"*Khuy.*" Christ, Vera is a fucking nightmare. "Tell Darya and

Rosa to be ready. We'll get them out of there as soon as I can. And stay fucking vigilant, Bryce. Nobody, and I do mean nobody, goes in or out of that house until I give you the go-ahead. Shit's about to go down."

"Copy that."

I end the call with my gut churning, and not just because Fedorov is missing. "I never should have put Darya in that fucking house."

"It isn't like you had a whole lot of options." Dimitry looks as tense as I feel. "And at least we know it's secure."

"Vera's being a cunt."

He snorts. "What else is new?"

"I should have moved her out."

"No." Dimitry shakes his head. "Not worth the risk. Good thing you got Bryce to take her phone, too. She'd already be complaining in Yuri's ear, and that's the last thing we need, on top of everything else."

I know he's right, but I hate the thought of Darya anywhere near Vera. The woman was always toxic, even before Yuri went to jail. She never approved of Yuri adopting me, not that I cared. Mikhail and I lived in our own place, and if we showed up for Sunday lunch, it was usually with crippling hangovers and dark sunglasses. I've always been astonished that Vera's bitter anger and Yuri's boastfulness could have produced a son as warm and generous as Mikhail. I never particularly liked the children spending time with Vera, but Inger and she were always close, and it seemed a small act of kindness given all Vera has lost.

Still, I'll breathe easier when Darya is out of that house, secure though it might be.

I glance at my phone, mentally doing the math. *It's one a.m. in London.*

I know Darya won't be sleeping, will be staring at her phone, waiting for my call.

My fingers tap my leg impatiently. I know Mak's men will be

waiting with weapons inside the hidden tunnels as we speak. But I've never itched to feel steel in my hand more than right now.

I feel naked without it.

The miles inch by, my tension ratcheting up with every one.

WE PULL up at the tall iron gates, and our driver hits the intercom. The gates open, and we head down the wide approach to the circular driveway around a fountain at the entrance. Orlov isn't trying to be subtle about the force he has guarding the place. There are combat suits and dark glasses hidden behind every fucking shrub on the way to the front door.

Our lone vehicle, with barely half a dozen men, looks pitiful by comparison. Then again, we are supposedly here to trade, not to fight.

The open vault in exchange for my daughters.

We step out, gravel crunching beneath our shoes, and submit to being patted down by Orlov's men. Loathing crawls down my spine as I watch hands tattooed with red sparrows touch my body.

I remember hands just like those around my father's neck. Torturing people across Miami in their search for me.

Hands like those carved lines into Darya's flesh.

The killing fury simmers just under the surface, white-hot but carefully restrained. There'll be time for killing, soon enough. Until then, I have to play the game.

We are led through the wide marble corridors toward what I know, from studying the schematic, was once Sergei's study. Darya told us that is where Orlov would make the meet.

"It's where Papa always met his men," she said. *"Vilnus loves that room. Sitting in my father's chair makes him feel powerful."*

Sure enough, heavy doors open to a bookshelf-lined room with rich leather couches set around low coffee tables. A wide, heavy wooden desk stands at one end, beneath an exquisite painting I recognize as a Natalia Goncharova, a pre-revolutionary Russian artist. It's a family portrait, set in the Russian countryside. There's something poignant in it, a sense of nostalgia edged with darkness, as if the artist painted a world she already knew was about to disappear.

It's an odd thing to fix on, given why I am here. But for some reason it gives me strength.

I can imagine Sergei there, in that painting. My father.

The world they were born to was stolen from us all, and a lethal legacy has been left in its place.

Or perhaps I just don't want to look at the motherfucker in the chair beneath that painting.

"Roman Stevanovsky." Vilnus Orlov doesn't stand up. He sprawls in the leather armchair, cigarette in hand, watching me approach. The bloated fat of his face is even more obvious in person, the narrow blue eyes gleaming maliciously.

"Orlov." I nod coldly. The last time I saw him he was in his prime, a barrel-chested wall of muscle, if an unattractive one.

Now the barrel chest is more fat than muscle, his jowls thick with drink and good food, face red veined. His fingers are stained with nicotine, and his eyes dart furtively around the room, as if to reassure himself of his own guard. By the way his nose is running, and his constant licking of lips, I'd say he's been sampling way too much of the product produced by his Colombian allies.

After so many years of living with my hatred and fear, standing in front of him now, Vilnus seems strangely inconsequential. I've squashed better men than him with my bare hands. It's like seeing a childhood nightmare in the daylight, reduced to nothing more than flesh and bone.

Flesh that I'm only minutes away from destroying.

"Your cell phones, if you don't mind." Vilnus gives us a shit-eating grin. He's clearly enjoying his moment of power.

We hand them over. I notice my screen is showing a missed call from Spain. Odd, given how late it is there. But Darya is in London, so there's nothing in Spain that can't wait.

"I expected Darya Petrovsky." Vilnus sucks on his cigarette, still smiling. "I was looking forward to seeing her again. It's been too long since we spent time together."

I smile coldly. "You won't ever see Darya again, Orlov." I throw the gel imprint down on the table. "Her fingerprints are the only part of her you will ever lay eyes on in this life."

"Strange time to make threats, Borovsky." His smile has faded. "Gel imprints of the fingerprints haven't worked in the past."

"And you know as well as I do that is because you need three sets, not two, or you wouldn't be holding my children. The imprints will work." I give him a hard smile. "Or do you think I don't know how to open my father's vault?"

His eyes narrow even further. "They'd better work, Borovsky. Because if this is some kind of trick, you're a dead man."

"Are we going to do this?" I look around the room. "I don't see Alexei Petrovsky's face among your goons."

Vilnus's lips curl. "You don't need to worry about Petrovsky. I brought him to heel long ago." His smirk becomes unpleasant. "He's been enjoying getting to know your daughter. I let him practice his knife skills on her. She has more in common with Darya than you might imagine. I think Ofelia enjoys the touch of a blade almost as much as Darya used to."

The blood pulses slowly through my brain. I almost relish the spread of red fury through my body.

Vilnus Orlov is going to die. Very soon.

Followed by Alexei Petrovsky.

But not until I have everything I came for.

"If you're done playing games, I have a plane to catch."

Vilnus's expression grows sour. He clearly expected me to take his bait.

He thinks he can anger me, throw me off-balance. If I wasn't so coldly furious, I'd find it insulting.

He nods to the men behind us, and I feel the cold muzzle of a machine gun in the base of my spine. "Walk," he barks. "And don't even think about trying anything."

"Really, Vilnus?" I give him a contemptuous smile. "We're in your house, with your guns all over us, and you're still worried?" I shake my head in mock disappointment. "Then again, you always have liked to stack the odds. How many men were there the night you came for my father? Half a dozen, wasn't it—against one old man and a little boy?"

Vilnus stares at me. "You were there," he says flatly.

"I was there." I almost enjoy his shock. "Watching through the kitchen window. And afterward, I was in Miami the whole time. Did you know that, Vilnus? All the years you searched for me, I was right under your nose. What was it you said—that there isn't an inch of the city you don't have eyes on? Forgive me if I find that difficult to believe."

The first flicker of unease crosses his face. Maybe I shouldn't taunt him. But now that I'm here, standing in front of him, any trace of trepidation is gone. He can't hurt the girls, not anymore. I have too many men here, too many guns trained on every corner of this property. All we're doing now is playing the game, just long enough to smoke Fedorov out.

"Walk," he says again, but this time there's a slight tremor in his voice, and the way he looks around warily doesn't escape me.

If Fedorov is here, I'm guessing Vilnus is starting to wish he'd show himself.

He's not the only one.

We walk through the long corridors and pass through

several heavy coded doors. There are too many of us for the elevator, so we take the stairs down to the basement.

It smells dank, the air close and unpleasant. Low light glares from stone walls, and our footsteps echo against them. It sickens me to think of the girls down here.

To think of *Darya* down here.

We round a corner into the most heavily guarded corridor we've been in yet. The men are clustered around a closed door, beside which is a darkened window. Vilnus halts in front of it, grinning evilly. "Feast your eyes, Borovsky."

It takes all my restraint not to smash through the window the moment I see Ofelia and Masha. They are huddled against the back wall, their faces white with fear. Ofelia has her arms around Masha, hugging her sister close to her chest. She's still wearing the ball gown she was in the night she was taken, but now it's torn and dirty, hanging in bare rags from her body.

The guard with his back to us has his machine gun pointing directly into their faces.

"Dima!" Vilnus bangs on the door, and the guard turns around. I'm oddly relieved to see it isn't Alexei Petrovsky. "Get Petrovsky," Vilnus orders. The man slips through the door, closing it behind him before I have a chance to get inside the room.

"Alexei spent several days getting to know your daughter before I took him off guard duty." Vilnus is clearly enjoying himself. "He took a great deal of pleasure in cutting that dress away, piece by piece."

"Keep him talking." Mak's voice crackles in my ear. "We still don't have Fedorov."

"Fatherhood doesn't suit you, Vilnus." My voice is as cold and hard as the concrete walls. Not a chance I'm showing this fucker the barest twitch of emotion. "Does Inger know you're trading your own daughter for the vault?"

"I should think so. It was her idea." His smile stretches wider.

"And I have plenty of daughters, Borovsky. You're welcome to that little hellcat. But until that vault is open, both of them stay exactly where they are."

"That's not going to work, Orlov. The vault isn't opening until the girls are safely out of here."

"No." Vilnus wags his finger in front of my face. "You can go inside and check the girls yourself, but only briefly. In a moment, my man will bring Petrovsky here. He can look at this imprint of yours. If he agrees it will open the vault, you will be permitted to station one of your own men inside the room with the girls until we open the vault together. When the door is open, and only then, you can leave."

"Fine." My mind is racing, but my voice is calm and even. "Open the fucking door."

He punches in a code, and the door to the girls' cell clicks as it unlocks.

I step inside.

35

DARYA

It's just past one in the morning when Bryce knocks on the door.

"Come in!" Rosa and I leap out of our seats as he enters the room. "Is there news?"

He shakes his head. "Not yet, I'm sorry. They've made it to the compound and gone inside. That's all I know. It's something else."

"What?" We both sink back into our chairs. My heart is thudding.

"It's Inger. She's at the front gate."

I stare at him in surprise. It's the last thing I expected.

"She's not in a good state." Bryce's face is hard. "She's barely conscious. She's been badly beaten."

"Then she needs a hospital." I fold my arms across my belly. I don't care about Inger right now.

"I agree." He looks uncomfortable. "But she's insisting on

talking to you. She said the girls' lives depend on it. I'd call Roman, but—"

"No, no. They're in the middle of it all. We can handle this." I tap the chair arm. "Get her on the phone. But she doesn't come through that gate, Bryce. And when she goes to the hospital, she stays under guard at all times."

He punches a number into his phone, and someone answers at the other end. "Put her on the phone," he snaps, then hands his phone to me.

"Inger," I say coldly.

"Darya!" Her voice is quavery and weak. "I need to talk to you."

"Not a fucking chance." I'm gripping the phone so hard it's a wonder the screen doesn't crack. "Say whatever it is you came to say."

"It's about Ilyan. Ilyan Fedorov. He's a friend of Vilnus Orlov."

"I know who he is." I cut her off. "I also know you've been staying in his house."

"They took us there. Nikolai and me. I didn't know . . . . Vilnus said . . ." Her voice trails off pathetically.

"I don't care, Inger." I feel so furious I want to throw something. "Talk."

"Ilyan Fedorov has your father."

The world lurches to a slow, sickening halt. I lean forward in my chair.

"*What?*" I say blankly.

"Tell Bryce to call Spain. They'll confirm it." Inger is sobbing weakly. "Ilyan flew me here two days ago. He's been keeping me isolated. Then an hour ago a man came and put me in a taxi and told me to come here and deliver his message. He gave me a cell phone I have to give you, and something else that he said is proof. He told me I have to give it to you, and nobody else. He said"—she starts crying in earnest—"he said they will kill me, and your father, if you don't follow their instructions. Please, Darya."

"Give the phone back to the man who gave it to you." I cut her off when she begins to protest. "*Now*, Inger." I wait until the phone has changed hands. "Keep her outside until we call you back."

I end the call and throw the phone to Bryce. "Call the security at my father's villa in Spain. Inger said they've taken him."

"*Mierda*." Rosa stands abruptly, her hand going to her mouth. Bryce's face is white as he punches out the number. All three of us wait, the long continental beeps audible in the quiet room.

"There's no answer." Bryce stares at me. "Let me try Pillars."

We wait again.

"Fucking answering machine," he mutters.

I call Abby's number.

No answer.

Oh, Jesus.

"We need to call Mak." I nod at the door, and Bryce follows me out. I close it so Rosa can't hear. "It's Fedorov. He's got Papa, which means Miami is nothing more than a distraction. He's going to come here, Bryce." I know it, in the pit of my gut. "They need to know they're walking into a trap in Miami, if it isn't already too late."

He nods, dialing the number. "What do you want us to do with Inger?"

I frown. "Wait for Mak's instructions."

Bryce switches the phone to speaker as it answers.

"*Da*." Mak's voice comes hard down the line.

"You're walking into a trap." Bryce doesn't waste time. "Fedorov is in Spain. He's got Sergei, and he's taken Pillars. Inger is at the gate. She says she has instructions she has to give Darya in person, or they'll kill Sergei. What do you want us to do?"

"Sit tight." Mak's voice is cool and collected. "I'll send a team straight to you. Don't let Inger through that gate, and keep it locked down until my people get there. Is Darya with you?"

"Yes," I say.

"Darya, you and Rosa get inside the safe room. Bryce, put your best men on the door and two inside the room with them. I'll call when my team is close to you. Any questions?"

"No," we both say.

He hangs up without waiting for a response.

"Rosa." I put my head around the door, where a white-faced Rosa is waiting, tense and alert. "Come with me."

We follow Bryce downstairs. "What about Vera?" I ask him as we go.

"I've got someone on her door," he says curtly. "She'll be fine where she is."

The safe room is off the kitchen, behind a temperature-controlled wine cabinet. Bryce punches in the code, and the wall of wine swings open. A set of stairs leads down to a small but comfortable room, with a bathroom off on one side. There's a fridge and a couch in the center by a coffee table.

It still makes me shiver. I'm never going to like being under-ground, or locked in.

Anton and Karel, two of Bryce's men, come in with us. "I'm going back upstairs," Bryce says. "Is your phone working?"

I nod, holding it up. "I've got the charger."

"Good. I'm leaving you with the code in case of emergencies, but please, don't open that door unless it's to me or someone you trust." He glances at the two guards, who nod. "Understand?"

"Yes."

He gives me a tight smile. "I don't know many women who would have handled this situation so well. You're one cool lady, Darya Petrovsky."

I try to smile back. "I've had a bit of practice."

He gives a low cough of laughter. "Yes, I guess you have.

Okay." He eyes the two guards with me, both men I know well. "You're directly responsible for Roman's woman, his child, and his mother. Don't fuck it up."

They both nod.

"I'll be back as soon as I can."

The door closes behind him with a solid thud, and we're alone.

Rosa turns to me, tears threatening to fall from her eyes. "His child?" she whispers. Her eyes drop to my belly. "You're pregnant?"

I half smile. "Not exactly the way we'd planned to tell you the news. But yes, I am."

"Oh!" Her hand flutters toward me, the tears spilling down her cheeks. "Oh, Darya."

She grips my hand, smiling tremulously. Then her eyes fall on the men with guns standing at a discreet distance. "Is it Vilnus? Did he find us?"

I shake my head. "It's not the Orlovs." I debate with myself for a minute, but there seems little reason to keep Fedorov's name out of it now. "It's a man called Ilyan Fedorov. He's taken Papa."

The color leaves Rosa's face. Her hand tightens convulsively on mine. "*Fedorov?*"

The amount of fear in her voice tells me everything I need to know.

"Yes. It was him who was behind the Orlov coup in the first place. It seems that he's been behind . . . everything."

"Oh, God." Rosa collapses onto the couch, biting her lip. "Aleksander and Sergei were right all along. They knew. They were both certain it was Fedorov who'd sold my whereabouts to the Colombians. Maria and I always thought they were just paranoid." She raises a shaking hand to her face, rubbing her forehead slowly. "Sergei had been hunting him," she says hoarsely. "For years. Following every lead, leaving no stone

337

unturned. He and Aleksander always said Ilyan Fedorov was still out there. Maria and I both resented their obsession with him. It felt like being held hostage to old ghosts."

I know how that feels. I feel, increasingly, as if old ghosts are pulling the strings on every part of my life. I hate the power the past has over us all.

Rosa is plucking nervously at the sofa, her brow furrowed. "I've been so wrong," she whispers.

I glance at my phone. *Nothing.*

"Wrong about what?" I ask, more to distract us both from what might be going on upstairs than because I actually want answers.

"When I found out it was Vilnus Orlov who'd killed Aleksander, I blame Sergei." Rosa's accent is more pronounced under pressure. "I think I lose my husband *and* my son, because of a *fantasma.*" *Because of a ghost.* Her face is white and strained. "I was so angry that I had run from this Fedorov, when the real enemy had been hiding among us all the time." She shakes her head slowly in disbelief. "Sergei never wanted me to leave Miami at all, but still I blamed him. For trusting Orlov. For the coup. And, when I found out about it, for Maria's death. *Dios mío.*" She buries her head in her hands. "I never truly believe this Fedorov could still be alive."

"Wait." I lean forward, confused. "Why were you angry at Papa? Why did it make any difference if it was Fedorov or the Orlovs chasing you?"

She pauses, closing her eyes and taking a deep breath. When she faces me again her expression is resigned, the emotion fading or carefully controlled—it's hard to tell which.

"Because I never would have run if it was just my family or Russian enemies. Fedorov was . . . different. We knew what he had done, what he was capable of." She frowns. "But I should not speak of this. It is not my story to tell."

"I know about Paris," I say quietly. "I know he killed Papa's first wife."

"And his children." Rosa nods. "Two sons and a young daughter. Aleksander lost his wife and young son. Fedorov tortured them until they told him where every last piece of Sergei and Aleksander's wealth was hidden, and then he killed them and stole everything." She shakes her head. "I would never have left Alexander, or my son, if I hadn't truly believed that doing so would put an end to the history we had all been living in the shadow of. Aleksander and I believed that Fedorov had made a deal with the Cardeñas cartel, my family. We thought my family wanted me, and Fedorov wanted the vault. We thought that by running, I would draw them both out into the open, enabling Sergei to deal with Fedorov, once and for all.

"I was in Costa Rica when Sergei came to tell me Aleksander and Roman were dead. It was . . ." Her voice trails off, and she shakes her head, her face ravaged with pain. "There are not the words to describe it," she says softly.

There is a silence I don't try to interrupt. I think of Roman's face when he saw Rosa, of the hurt I know he tries hard to conceal.

After a time she speaks again. "The Cardeñas cartel had claimed responsibility, but Sergei was still convinced Fedorov was behind it. He wanted me to stay hidden. We fought about it for years. Bitterly." She stares at the floor. "I wanted to come back to Miami, to be with Maria, to mourn my family. Sergei said it was too dangerous, that Fedorov would have a target on my back. At first I was too devastated to argue. After a while, when it became clear that Sergei's war with my family was going to drag on, I didn't want to endanger Maria or her children. I figured it was better for everyone if I disappeared.

"So I ran again, but this time, I didn't just run from my family. I disappeared entirely, and I stayed gone.

"It was years before I heard about the coup and tried to contact Sergei again. At first, when I discovered it was the Orlovs who had murdered my family, and by then, Maria too, I was furious." Her face spasms, a memory of old anger. "There had been no Fedorov, no murderous shadow in the wings. Just greedy men who had seen the name on that damned vault and seized an opportunity. I lost my husband, my son, and my best friend, all because, as I thought, Sergei had trusted Vilnus Orlov." She shakes her head tiredly. "But angry or not, I couldn't do nothing when I realized the Orlovs were holding you hostage. I came back to Miami soon afterward. I'm not sure what I planned to do. I was just . . . angry.

"I knew all the secret tunnels leading into the compound, so I broke in. I couldn't find Sergei; I wasn't even sure if he was still alive. Eventually I found Alexei. I told him who I was and tried to convince him to get you and run with me. But he wouldn't go."

"What do you mean, he wouldn't go?" I stare at her in shock. "Papa told us it was you who made Alexei promise he wouldn't leave."

"No." Rosa shakes her head slowly. "That's just what Alexei told your father. It was the only way he could convince Sergei to leave him behind, although Sergei was still furious. The truth is that Alexei had heard the Orlovs talking about Roman, discussing where he might be. He'd worked out that if the Orlovs were searching for him, then Roman must still be alive." She half smiles at me. "You can't imagine what it was like, to have that kind of hope, after so long. It was almost terrifying. But it was also devastating. To think that Roman might have been alive, all that time, alone, without any help . . ." She rubs a hand over her face. "It still kills me," she whispers. "If I'd just stayed—if I hadn't run—"

I cover her hand with my own. "If you'd stayed, then you'd be dead too. And we would still have been held hostage by the Orlovs."

"Alexei said the same thing." Rosa's face is tired and sad. "Just as Sergei once had: that if I got caught, it would all have been for nothing. We agreed that as soon as I was somewhere safe, you and Sergei would join me. Alexei gave me an email address to use as a point of contact. I found out just recently that it belonged to his Swedish friend."

I feel a faint wash of horror. Lars Andersson couldn't have been more than fifteen back then.

We were all so young.

"Your brother is a good man," she says gently. "I wish you would believe that, Darya."

"I wish I *could* believe that."

I stare at the door, willing it to open, to have some kind of news, but it remains stubbornly closed.

"So you were angry at Papa because you thought it was the Orlovs behind the coup?" I ask it more to change the subject than because I really want to know.

"I am ashamed of that anger now." Rosa winces. "To discover that Aleksander and Sergei were right all along, that it was Fedorov behind the coup, behind all of it . . . . Suddenly every decision Sergei has made over the years makes sense. To think that now I might never have the chance to tell Sergei that, to thank him for all he has done to keep me safe and to protect Roman . . . oh." She puts her hands over her face, and I realize, with a shock, that she's sobbing.

I stare at her bowed head, her shaking shoulders, and all I feel is sadness. For my parents, and Roman's, burdened with a legacy I don't truly understand, that has taken so much of their lives.

All I know is that even as we sit here, that legacy is still threatening the lives of two innocent children. Threatening the life of the father of my child.

No matter what my father or my brother have to say, I'm not sure I will ever be able to forgive that.

36

ROMAN

"**P**apa!" It takes a moment to realize it's me Masha is referring to. It's only when she hurls herself at me, her little arms reaching upward, that I understand it's me who is *Papa*.

"*Myshka*." My voice sounds like it belongs to someone else. I catch her, and she wraps her arms and legs around me, burying her face in my neck. I can feel the frantic hammering of her heart through the thin cloth covering her back. I'm aware of Dimitry and Orlov behind me. Ofelia has come to her feet, but she still hovers against the back wall. I hear a noise behind me, the low murmur of voices, and Ofelia's eyes widen as she watches someone over my shoulder.

Petrovsky.

I'm aware of his figure entering the room to my right, but I don't trust myself to look at him. Not while I still have Masha in my arms.

"It's okay, Ofelia." I try with all my self-control to keep my voice even. "You're going to be safe now. But I need you to stay in here for a few more minutes. Can you do that?"

"No." It's Masha who answers, her voice muffled against my neck. "Don't want to stay."

"I know, sweetheart." Although it breaks my heart to do it, I slowly unwrap her arms from around my neck, holding her slightly away from me so I can look her in the eye. "But you know Dimitry." Her face lifts marginally when she sees Dimitry's crooked smile. "He's going to stay with you until I come back, keep you safe. Will you stay here with him?"

"No!" Masha's face is tearstained, her lower lip already trembling. She peeks through her hair at Dimitry as she clings to me like a limpet.

"Hey, Masha." Dimitry's voice is gentle. "I'm going to keep you safe, okay, sweetheart?"

"Masha." Ofelia steps forward, her eyes still trained on the man standing slightly behind me. The opaque mask she wears breaks my heart. "Come here, to me. You know Dimitry will keep us safe. Roman has to do something before he can take us home. Remember, we told you?"

We?

So Alexei has been explaining this fucking treachery to my daughters?

Vicious savagery clenches my gut.

The bastard used his knife on Ofelia. Scared her so much she knows the vault has to be opened before she's safe.

Oh, that fucking *mudak* will pay for this, and for every other minute of pain he's inflicted on us all.

"Masha." Ofelia is still watching Alexei, who is no more than a solid shape in my peripheral vision. She puts her arms out, gently prying Masha from my grasp. "It's all going to be okay now. Papa is here, okay?" Her face flushes slightly as she says the word, her eyes touching mine then sliding away. I can't tell if she is just indulging Masha's use of the word *Papa* as reassurance or if there's more to it.

What has Orlov told them?

But now isn't the time for those questions.

Mak's voice crackles in my ear again. "Fedorov is in Spain. Stick to the plan until you get Petrovsky's key, then it's go time."

Fuck.

I'm so stunned that I almost drop Masha as I transfer her to Ofelia's arms. My eyes meet Dimitry's over their heads. He's heard the radio transmission too, as has every one of our team.

"Ofelia, Dimitry and two of his friends will stay here with you and Masha. But I'll be back very soon, okay?" She nods, glancing in the corner again, then away.

My mind is racing, but time has slowed down. The fight isn't here anymore.

This is all just a fucking decoy.

But somehow, I suspect Orlov doesn't know that. And that's to our advantage.

"Right." I glance at Orlov, not least to avoid looking at Alexei Petrovsky. "Let's do this."

"Petrovsky." Orlov is actually grinning. "Looks like it's your moment in the sun, boy."

The bulk in the corner moves, but it isn't Petrovsky I'm looking at. It's Ofelia. She's watching Alexei Petrovsky like he's the only person in the room, her eyes wide and luminous with fear. Her neck moves as she swallows convulsively, clutching Masha hard against her.

I wait as Petrovsky moves past me to the door, taking him in for the first time with a queer inner jolt. It's like looking at a younger version of Sergei, one just as formidable. Alexei's lone eye is the same hard blue as Sergei's, his face stark and angular, hair almost white blond in contrast to Darya's dark mane. He is taller than his photos suggest and almost as broad as the door. He might have been handsome, were it not for the eye patch and the extensive scarring on his face, fine lines that could only have been made by multiple knife wounds.

I brought him to heel years ago, Vilnus said of Alexei. Taking in the vicious marks on his face, I don't doubt that is true. There's only so much torture any person can withstand, and I'd say Alexei reached that threshold long ago. He's clearly turned himself into a lethal weapon in response, going by the hard muscle filling out his suit. Alexei would be a match for either Dimitry or me in the ring, that much is clear. In the brief moment he passes me, his lone eye meets mine, hard and glacial. There's not the slightest flicker of recognition, no acknowledgment of any kind.

There's no emotion in that eye at all.

The fucker is a stone-cold killer. One who used a knife on one of my daughters and terrified the life out of the other one. He has no conscience. Whatever Alexei Petrovsky was once, the man with me now is someone else entirely, forged anew in violence and savagery.

He's beyond saving.

Maybe I needed to know that before I took the life of Darya's brother, even though I've known for a long time it was going to come to this. I needed to know so I can look her in the eye when I tell her Alexei is dead.

"This door stays unlocked," I say, pausing in the doorway.

Vilnus scowls. "Not a fucking chance."

"It stays unlocked." I don't move. "One unlocked door for another, Orlov. You've got guns covering every move we make. Nobody is getting out of here without your permission, but my girls have suffered enough. That door stays open, or the fucking vault stays closed."

His mouth works, his eyes narrowed as he tries to think this through. It's like watching a snail on valium attempting to cross a road.

"I don't have all day, Orlov."

"Fine. It stays open. But they stay inside the room, and two more of my men stay with them." Orlov delivers this nonsensical response as if it's some kind of compromise.

Fuck, he's stupid. Every moment in his company diminishes him, makes it more plain that he is no more than Fedorov's puppet, has never been capable of anything more. That thought brings me back to Fedorov's current game.

What the hell is he doing in Spain?

Thank fuck I sent Darya to London.

I think briefly of Sergei, but that is one problem I can't do anything about right now.

I leave the doorway, and Dimitry takes my place, two of Alpha Team behind him in the room, standing in front of the girls. I look at Ofelia and Masha one last time, then at Dimitry. He gives me the faintest nod. He knows it's about to go down.

I follow Orlov down the corridor that leads to the vault. Petrovsky is behind me, but my remaining two men are behind him.

He's not going anywhere.

We round several corners, all of which I've memorized from the schematic, until we come to the thing we're all here for: the vault.

The door to it covers an entire wall.

Even given the tension of the moment, I can't help but admire my father's final masterpiece. The last time I saw the vault was the night Papasha brought me here so he could code my fingerprints into the lock. Back then, it was still under construction, and my vague recollection of it is only a vast wall of half-completed metalwork, with wires and bits hanging in every direction.

The finished product is a work of art in itself, a steel wall ten feet wide and almost the same height. Curlicued metalwork stands out from the original surface, intricate and ornate. It's designed to look like climbing flowers, the design concealing the actual door. I smile inwardly. This part, at least, is going to be fun.

I take the key out of my jacket pocket and get a savage rush of satisfaction at the look of part shock, part triumph on Orlov's face. He clearly never really expected things to go this smoothly.

That's right, you bastard. Think you're winning.

I turn to Alexei Petrovsky. "I believe you have the partner key?"

This time, the look on Orlov's face is truly priceless.

"Let me guess." It's my turn to give Orlov a shit-eating grin. "You never knew there were two keys. Your tame dog never mentioned that part to you."

Orlov turns to Petrovsky, his face falling in on itself like a sunken pudding, mouthing furiously.

The smile on Alexei's face is colder than the Arctic in January. "No," he says in a quiet, lethal rasp, holding Orlov's eyes. "That part the dog kept to itself."

"That was a mistake." Orlov's voice shakes with anger.

Alexei lifts a shoulder and drops it again. It's a gesture so contemptuous he might as well be shrugging off a bug. "We'll see, Orlov." Reaching out, he presses the centers of two flowers simultaneously.

My stomach lurches queerly, time shifting like smoke. For a moment I am back in my father's workshop, watching his long fingers twist those metal flowers into being.

The center of another flower slides back, revealing a tiny black circle. Alexei presses his thumb to it, and a panel slides open.

My father clearly taught Sergei more than I thought.

"You know, Vilnus," Alexei says conversationally as he withdraws the golden key inside it, "your idiotic safe hackers actually opened that flower more than once by accident. They never even noticed. Not that it would have mattered if they did." He glances at me, and for the first time, I catch a glimmer of anger. "This key is useless without the other one."

I smile coldly. "Glad you grasp the situation, Petrovsky."

I hold my hand out, certain there's no chance in hell he's going to hand over that key, no matter what Sergei said.

"No," Orlov says, looking between us. "Hand your key to Petrovsky, or this deal is off." He's nervous, despite his bravado. Somehow, Orlov can sense he's part of a game he doesn't quite understand.

I don't move, just give him another unpleasant smile. I'd be lying if I said I'm not enjoying watching the bastard sweat.

"There's no point in me giving my key to your dog," I say contemptuously. I'm aware of Alexei, tense as a coiled snake beside me. "He doesn't know how to open it. He wasn't lying about that part."

But the truth is that after watching him open that metal flower, I'm not sure what Alexei does or doesn't know.

Not that it matters.

One word from me, and the one-eyed bastard is a dead man. I'm poised to give the order.

I *want* to give the fucking order.

Then, to my utter shock, Alexei Petrovsky gives me a twisted smile and drops the key into my open palm. "It's yours," he says calmly.

Vilnus Orlov looks between us suspiciously. "If you two are finished your pissing contest, then you can open that fucking thing," he snarls.

In your fucking dreams, Orlov.

I smile at him. "Go," I say quietly.

It all happens so fast Vilnus doesn't even get a hand near his gun.

Flash bangs fill the room with smoke. The walls on either side of us burst open, and Mak's men fill the small space, taking every one of Vilnus's guards with silenced pistols before they've so much as pulled a trigger. I have Orlov headlocked and on the ground before his guards hit the floor. My two remaining guards have taken Petrovsky. To my surprise, he doesn't struggle at all, just goes to the ground with that same twisted, cold smile, submitting without any fight as they zip tie his hands behind him.

I pocket both of the keys and quickly strap on the weapons Mak's men throw me. I can hear the shouts of the fight on the floor above as more of Bravo Team pours out of the upper tunnels.

"Get those two to the dock," I snarl at the small army surrounding Petrovsky and Orlov. "And get them there alive." I'm already running down the corridor toward the room where the girls are held, two dozen men hard on my heels, when a pack of men round the corner, guns already blazing.

I take two hits that hurt like a motherfucker despite my body armor. I shoot without pausing, taking out both of the shooters. The others behind them go down just as fast under measured, precise firing from Mak's men. I move straight through the pack, punching two stragglers as I go, intent on only one thing: getting to the girls.

They keep coming, and we keep taking them down, Mak's men covering me as I run straight through every oncomer, punching those who haven't already been hit before I reach them.

I round the final corner just as Bravo Team comes from the opposite direction. In between us is a pile of bodies and Dimitry standing in front of the open door, flanked by one of the Alpha Team men. He has blood streaming down his face, and his suit is ripped to fuck, but he's grinning like the mad bastard he is.

"About time," he greets me, punching a final Orlov resistor to the ground.

He must have taken at least a dozen of them with his bare hands, and under gunfire, before we reached him.

I grip his shoulder, and he stands aside.

Ofelia and Masha are curled into the floor, their heads down. The final Alpha Team member is sprawled across them, literally covering their bodies with his own, his large hands over their two heads. Blood leaks from several holes in his body. He stands as I approach, and grins when I throw him a pistol.

"Fun times," he says. Ignoring the blood coming from his leg, he crouches down beside Ofelia and pats her shoulder, then raises Masha up gently. "You're okay, sweetheart," he says, smiling at her. "You're going to be safe now, okay? We've got you."

"Hurry." Mak's voice crackles through the earpiece. "There's a fucking army coming at the compound."

I crouch down, horribly aware both of the blood and death surrounding us and of the need for haste. "Ofelia," I say quietly, trying to reassure the rigid figure huddled into the wall. "We have to hurry, darling."

She nods, her face white and tense. Masha turns around. "You have blood on you," she says in a small voice.

"Yes, I do. But I'm fine, Masha, and so are you. We need to go now, okay? We're going on a boat."

I pick her up and hold my hand out to Ofelia, but she pauses. "Where is Alexei?"

I frown. "Don't worry about Alexei, darling. He can't hurt you anymore, I promise."

"You didn't—Is he dead?" There's something odd about the way she says it, almost an accusatory note in her voice.

"Not yet," I say grimly. "I need him to answer some questions. We have to go, now."

She nods, but her eyes are darting this way and that, as if she's still looking for her torturer. They settle instead on the Alpha Team member, a man called Luke, if I remember correctly. He smiles at her reassuringly. "I'm right behind you, sweetheart."

She nods, gulping, and starts to move. I shoot Luke a grateful look. Despite the blood leaking from several points on his body, he's smiling as calmly as if he were taking a Sunday walk.

We move upstairs amid a pack of Mak's men, Masha in my arms, Ofelia holding my hand, Dimitry in front of us and Luke behind. The sound of gunfire punches the air as we hasten through the compound, heading for the rear exit that leads down to the dock on Biscayne bay.

We've just left the building when all hell breaks loose.

"You need to get to the boat, Roman."

I don't need Mak's voice crackling in my ear to tell me what I can already fucking see.

Men clad in black militia suits are coming at us from every direction on the compound.

There's a chopper overhead, cutting down our team with precision fire.

And on the water, two rigid-hull inflatable boats are crowding in behind ours, cutting off our escape.

Fedorov might be in Spain, but something tells me he's still running the show.

"Head to the second exfil point." Mak's voice is calm and assured in my ear. "I have backup on the way."

Mak and I designated a nearby shoreline harbor as an emergency extraction point if shit went south.

And shit has, most definitely, gone fucking south.

"They'd better fucking hurry," Dimitry mutters, glancing grim faced at me.

"I need to get the girls out of here." I'm already running at full speed for the trees that separate us from the shoreline harbor.

"Copy that." Dimitry nods at Luke. "We'll cover you." They turn to face the oncoming fire, as more of Mak's men join them. I race through the trees, pulling Ofelia by the hand, Masha clinging to me tightly.

I have to get them to safety.

Nothing matters more than that. Not Orlov, or Alexei Petrovsky, or whatever shit storm is being unleashed behind me. Nothing matters but making sure the girls get out of here alive.

The shore landing is half a mile from the compound. I'm running it as hard as I can when a shout goes up behind me.

"Over there!"

I glance over my shoulder. There's a dozen men coming for us, at double our speed.

If I stop to shoot them, we won't make the shoreline in time. Far worse, I will expose the girls to their gunfire.

Ofelia has seen them too. She turns to me briefly, her already pale face bloodless, eyes wide and terrified.

"We can do it," I say under my breath, pulling her with me. "We're nearly there."

There's a quarter mile to go, and I can already see where the trees are starting to thin ahead of us.

Ofelia stumbles, and her hand slips from mine. "Roman!"

"Ofelia!" Masha's scream echoes off the trees.

I halt, tugging Ofelia to her feet. "I won't leave you. Come on."

"No!" She tries to stand, but she's clearly turned an ankle, or worse, because her leg simply crumples beneath her. "I can't," she whispers, tears falling down her face. "I can't stand, Roman."

"It's okay." I'm looking around, trying to find shelter, but the best I can do is a large banyan tree. I pull Ofelia under the root canopy.

"I have to put you down, *myshka*," I whisper in Masha's ear as I lower her down to Ofelia's waiting arms. "I need you to hide until I come for you, okay?"

Masha nods solemnly, staring at me with wide eyes that break my fucking heart. I strip off my jacket and wrap it around them. "It's bulletproof," I say to Ofelia. "Keep it over you both."

She catches my hand. "What about you?"

I squeeze her fingers. "I'm fine, baby. I'll come back for you, I promise."

But Ofelia must be able to read the lie in my eyes, because her fingers slide from mine and she turns away, drawing the jacket around her and Masha.

I want to say more. Say something she will remember. But there's no time.

There's no fucking time.

"Hold them off. We're coming." Mak's voice is reassuringly calm in my ear. I know his team will be coming as hard as they can.

I also know there's not much chance I'll still be alive when they get here.

I take cover behind a tree off to the right and start shooting.

The black-clad guys are barely three hundred yards away. I pick off three of them before their bullets start hitting the trunk beside my face.

Hold on.

I breathe deeply, making every shot count.

The closest of the attackers is almost two hundred yards out, and I can't get a shot amid the covering fire from the men behind him.

At least the fire is aimed at me and not the girls.

Fuck.

It can't end like this. Not hiding in a fucking suburban park, with my girls cowering under a tree they should be playing beneath.

No.

Fuck that.

Suddenly I am ten years old again, running through the darkened streets, entirely alone in this world.

I will not abandon my children to the darkness Darya and I were forced to live.

I won't let them watch me die here. I won't leave them alone, facing the world with no protector.

I won't let them inherit the lethal legacy we have all been forced to suffer for.

I turn on the spot, my decision made, and race back to the tree.

Ofelia stares up at me, Masha's face buried in her chest. "You came back," she breathes. "You came back for us."

"I promised," I say roughly, scooping her up before she has a chance to protest. "Masha. Can you run?"

She nods silently, her eyes wide.

"Okay, then." I nod at the tree line ahead of us. "There's a boat on the other side of those trees. That's where we have to go, *myshka*. Come on." We race for the tree line, Ofelia's arms around my neck, Masha's little legs pounding determinedly beside me. "That's it, sweetheart," I pant, catching a glimpse of the water through the trees. "The boat is right there. We're nearly safe. My brave girls. We can do it."

A bullet hits my right shoulder just as we burst free of the trees. Then another one hits my side, missing Ofelia by inches.

I stumble, but I can see the inflatable coming toward us. My arms tighten around Ofelia, and I will my grip to hold long enough to get her there.

You can make it.

"Papa!" Ofelia's face is stricken.

"It's okay, baby. We're nearly there now." I stagger down to the mangrove shoreline, my feet sinking into the mud. My arm is losing strength rapidly, blood is pumping from my side, and I can feel Ofelia slipping from my grasp.

"Put me down," she says, struggling in my grip. "You can't hold me. He's hurt!" she screams at the oncoming boat. "Help us!"

But I already know it's too late. The men are bursting through the trees behind us, bullets hitting the water as they take aim at the boat, and there's a chopper coming in hard above, machine gun pointing lethally from the open door.

"Get down." I pull Ofelia and Masha to the mud, covering them with my body.

"Papa," Masha whimpers beneath me.

"It's okay, *myshka*," I say, cradling her head with my hand, my lips in her hair, wincing at my own lie. There's nothing okay about this. About any of it. "*Ya lyublyu vas, moi krasivyye devochki*," I whisper against her head. *I love you, my beautiful girls.*

Then I hear the screams behind me, and like some kind of miracle, I realize the chopper isn't shooting at us.

"Who the *fuck* is in that chopper?" I hear Dimitry roar behind me, and I close my eyes in relief.

I turn my head to find him frowning up at the chopper, just as the inflatable boat pulls in before me. To my utter horror, it's Mickey who leaps out, white-faced and intent, machine gun in hand. He takes aim at the shoreline, and I hear a cry of pain as his bullet finds a target, then he is down in the mud beside us.

"Fucking *help* them!" he bellows at the men behind him. They leap from the boat and start shooting at the men chasing us.

I stare up at the chopper, trying to work out what the fuck is going on. "Get your sisters into the boat," I growl at Mickey. There'll be time to kick his ass later. Right now I just need to know the girls are safe.

A bullet hits the chopper, and it banks right, veering away from us.

Suddenly there are more men pouring from the trees off to our left. Dimitry's face beside me grows grim as he kneels and takes aim. I roll onto my belly and pick up my rifle, reloading with a sinking heart.

Too many. There are too many of them coming for us.

Then, to my surprise, two of the black clad militia men chasing us fall, shot by the newcomers on our left.

"Wait!"

I hold up my hand, squinting in confusion as a blood-spattered Alexei Petrovsky stumbles from the trees down toward us. His hands are still zip tied behind his back, his lone eye glittering, mouth a hard line. "Don't shoot!" he yells at me. "They're mine!"

I stare at him in astonishment. "They're fucking what now?"

"Fuck that." Dimitry's finger is already tightening on the trigger. "We only need his fingerprints, right?"

"No!" Ofelia's cry is so heartrending it makes me turn around in shock. She is struggling to climb out of the boat, her face contorted with some emotion I don't understand.

"Papa, no!" Masha is screaming, tears running down her face, fighting against Mickey's grasp. "Don't hurt Lexi!"

Alexei hits the mud near us and stumbles, falling to his knees. "Help them!" he rasps at the men on either side of him. "Get those girls out of here now!"

For once, I have no idea what to do.

What in the fucking Stockholm syndrome is going on?

One of his men cuts Alexei's ties and hands him a gun. That makes my decision a lot easier. I aim straight between the fucker's eyes.

"Don't do it, Roman." This time it's Mickey who speaks, his voice low and controlled. "He's on our side."

I struggle to my feet. Mak's team is pouring through the trees, joining the others from the left, and the last of the black-clad militia chasing us are falling or running away.

"This *mudak* almost killed your sisters." I glare at Alexei as I speak to Mickey. "He took a fucking *knife* to them. Give me one goddamn reason he doesn't die right now."

"No!" Ofelia is sobbing. "Alexei helped us. He protected us."

Masha pulls out of her brother's grip and plows through the mud, throwing herself at Alexei's knees. "You can't hurt him! Lexi is our *friend!*"

Alexei doesn't say a word, just lifts Masha up and pushes straight past me, thrusting her back into the boat. Ofelia is trying to clamber out of it. "Get in," he says roughly.

"No!" She's crying, clinging to Alexei like he's some kind of life buoy. "Not without you!"

"I'm fine." He heaves her into the boat.

I'm not.

I'm about ready to kill anything, just to cut through my confusion.

Alexei raises his gun, and for the second time, my finger tightens on the trigger. Then he takes two measured, precise shots. Two men I didn't notice fall to the ground, right on the tree line. From their position, they had a direct shot at me.

Another moment, and I'd have been dead.

"Go," Alexei orders his men on the shoreline curtly. "You know where to wait for me."

They melt back into the trees. In the distance, I can hear sirens wailing. Clearly our little encounter has drawn the attention of local law enforcement.

"I'll explain later," Mickey says to me. "Get in. We need to get out of here." He nods at Alexei. "You, too."

I glare at Mickey as I climb into the inflatable. "You better be fucking right about this."

"I am." He helps me into the boat. "Mak's team has Orlov. He'll be at the warehouse when we get there."

"Well, that's one bullet I get to use, at least." I wipe the blood from my face, my gun still trained on Alexei as we pull away from the shore.

"No." Alexei Petrovsky gives me a death stare that could freeze hot tarmac. "Vilnus Orlov is mine."

I stare at him in absolute disbelief. This bastard has held my daughters captive for the past week. He's sitting in my boat with half a dozen guns trained on him. He's leaking blood from

multiple bullet wounds, he can't have more than one bullet left
—and now he's trying to give me orders?

"You two can argue about this later," Mickey interrupts before I have a chance to argue. "Right now you have bigger things to worry about."

We both turn to him, frowning.

"It's Fedorov." Mickey meets my gaze, his face grim. "He's in London."

37

DARYA

The intercom crackles to life at half past one in the morning.

One of the guards in the room crosses the floor. "Who is it?"

"I'm one of Mak's team. We've secured the area."

Mak said he'd call to tell us when his team was close. I get a bad feeling.

The guard, Anton, glances at me, and I shake my head. *No.* I hold up my phone to show him I'm calling Bryce's number. Anton nods and depresses the intercom button. "Where's Bryce?"

"He got hit." The intercom cuts out then back in again. "I guess you can't hear anything inside there, because there's been a hell of a fight upstairs."

Bryce's number is ringing, but there's no answer. I circle my finger in the air, signaling the guard to keep the man talking.

"Nobody contacted us," he says, watching me.

"We didn't exactly have time to send a fucking memo." The man sounds impatient.

Anton's eyes narrow. "Where are the rest of our team?"

"Locking the fucking place down. Wiping the blood off. They came at us hard."

Bryce's phone rings out. Anton raises his eyebrows at me, and I shake my head. This isn't right, and we both know it. He depresses the button again. "We'll wait in here until we get word from Roman."

There's a moment's silence, then the intercom sounds again. "That might be difficult." The man's voice sounds heavy. "The news out of Miami isn't good, I'm afraid."

My heart lurches, then settles again.

It's a line. A story. He just wants you to open the door.

But despite what I tell myself, nothing can stop the icy chill stealing through my body, nor take away the visible fear in Rosa's face.

Roman, riddled with bullet holes, eyes wide open.

Ofelia and Masha, strapped to Orlov's table, knives carving into their flesh.

I shudder and press Roman's number on my phone.

"What happened in Miami?" Anton asks through the intercom. He's been joined by the other guard, Karel, who has his gun trained on the door.

The disembodied voice comes again. "Mak lost comms with Roman's team just after they went through the gate. We got here minutes later, just in time to meet an attack force trying to get in. It's all turned to hell. Mak wants to move you before the attackers send another team."

Roman's phone rings out. Then again, it would, if he's in the middle of a battle. I try to stifle my rising panic.

I look at Anton. "Call Mak."

He shakes his head. "Bryce has that number."

I should have made sure I had it too.

In hindsight, it's a massive error.

Anton presses the intercom again. "My orders are to wait. So we'll wait."

"We don't have time for this." The man's tone sharpens. "Open the door, or Mak will put a bullet through you himself."

"I don't answer to Mak," says Anton curtly. "I answer to Bryce and to Roman Stevanovsky. Until I get word from either of them, in person, this door stays closed."

"Then you'll likely fucking die in there. Bryce is leaking the red stuff everywhere, and going from what I hear, Stevanovsky has walked into a shit storm in Miami. If you want to stay alive, then I suggest you open this door right now."

We don't bother answering that one. Whoever is standing outside that door isn't a friend.

"This safe room can take a hell of a lot," Anton says to me, but his grim face doesn't reassure me at all. "It's the best place for us, at least for now."

I nod. "I agree. Let's keep trying every number we can think of."

But before I can make another call, the intercom crackles to life again.

"Miss Petrovsky."

I freeze.

I know that voice.

"You seem to have learned a little more caution since we last met. Then again, you have learned from the best, haven't you?"

I close my eyes. For a brief moment, I'm strapped to the table again, Vilnus's knife on my skin. The man with the cold, dead eyes is standing over me, talking to Vilnus. *"What we need is the man who built that vault, but you've already killed him, Vilnus, haven't you? So now we have to find someone who knows what he does . . ."*

Oh, God.

That man was Fedorov.

The realization snaps into my brain like the last piece of a missing puzzle. It was Fedorov who came to our house all those years ago. Fedorov who had the tattoo of a rose entwined in barbed wire.

Fedorov is the only person of whom Vilnus Orlov is truly afraid.

And now he's standing outside our door.

I walk over to the intercom like I'm sleepwalking and press the button.

"Ilyan Fedorov." It takes all my will to maintain a calm voice.

"I see you've done some research as well. Or has your papa been telling tales? Don't answer that." There's a light note to his voice, as if he's smiling. "Let's ask him ourselves, shall we?"

My eyes meet Rosa's, my horror mirrored in her own. There's the sound of a scuffle through the intercom, then my father's voice booms through the speaker, loud and authoritative in Russian. "Do not open that door, Darya, no matter what you hear—"

I wince at the sound of the flesh meeting flesh, my father's grunt of pain.

I press the button so hard my finger turns white. "So you torture old men now, too, Fedorov? Little girls and old men. That's some record you have." My voice shakes, but not with fear.

The thought of that bastard hitting my father takes my fear and turns it to fury.

"Oh, I've been waiting a long time to repay Sergei Petrovsky his due, believe me." Fedorov's voice is as cold and dead as I remember, any momentary lightness gone from it. "To take back what he stole from me."

"Really." *Keep him talking.* "From what I understand, it was you who did the stealing back in Paris."

"My old friend *has* been telling you some tales, then." The sound of another blow comes through the intercom. "I imagine

Sergei left out the part where he betrayed his promises to my family. Then again, that part of the story hardly reflects well on the noble Naryshkin name, now does it? The old Graf wouldn't have approved of that, Sergei, now would he? His only son betraying the guard that helped him survive the gulag? No, the noble Graf wouldn't have liked that at all."

Even through the crackling intercom, Fedorov's caustic hatred is palpable.

To my intense relief, Papa's voice is the next I hear, his anger masked beneath a carefully measured tone. "The debt to your father was repaid long before Aleksander and I reached France, Fedorov. Your father was rewarded for the help he gave mine. As you know very well."

"But *I* wasn't!" the man hisses. He puts his mouth close to the intercom, his venom almost spitting into the room. "I was his son. The son of the man who fed you out of his own pocket when you were a baby. I grew up behind the same damn bars you did, even if it was in the guardhouse. My father always told me we would be wealthy when we got to France, because the Graf would take care of us."

"And he kept that promise." Papa's voice sounds resigned. "Your father was received in Switzerland by Fabergé himself, who personally handed him one of the rarest imperial eggs as a gift. It isn't our fault you sold it for less than it's worth the moment your father was dead."

The sound of Fedorov's blow is so vicious that I wince. The intercom cuts out, and I take the chance to press the button on our side.

"If this is a question of money," I say, desperate to stop him beating Papa, "I know we have more than enough to repay your father's kindness."

It's a long time before Fedorov answers, and when he does, he's breathing heavily.

"Oh, we're long past money." His voice shakes with rage and

the effort of beating my father. "Money I have, Darya Petrovsky. More than every one of those arrogant fucking *dvoryanstvo* who looked down on us back in the gulag. They never learned, not even after their dachas had been burned and their tsar had been shot. Even decades later, in France, they looked down on us. All I wanted was to take what my father was owed, for the years he helped men like your father and grandfather survive when they might have died. A necklace here, a trinket there. But even that, the exiled nobility of Russia could not spare for those they considered so far beneath them. Where was loyalty then, when I was starving in the Paris streets and came begging at their doors? Is it any wonder I took what I was owed at the end of a knife?"

Inside our safe room, Anton is muttering into his phone. He gives me a thumbs-up, then circles his finger again.

He's found someone who can help us.

I almost slump in relief.

Keep Fedorov talking.

"They should have helped you," I say carefully. "You had every right to be angry."

"I didn't need their help." His voice is detached and cold. "I discovered your scheme myself, didn't I, Sergei?" I wince as I hear the thud of Fedorov delivering another blow. "The Russian KGB had never found the men who broke into the Naryshkin dacha. Even if it was the sons of Prince Naryshkin and Count Borovsky who opened the vault, people speculated they must have been robbed and killed soon after or sold the contents. There was no way such vast wealth could have been carried across the steppe, if that was even where they'd gone. By the time Sergei and Aleksander did finally make it to France, they were all but forgotten, the story of the missing treasure little more than myth." Another blow makes a brutal sound, and I flinch. "That was until I discovered the treasures hidden inside crates of Graf vodka."

Graf vodka?

Instantly I see my father's hand pouring the bottle, hear him saying, *"You can't buy it here in Spain . . ."*

I see Graf vodka sitting on Roman's table, the only time I've ever seen that brand since Miami.

"It was an ingenious scheme, Sergei, I will allow that." Fedorov hits Papa again, making sure the sound travels through the intercom. Papa grunts, and I feel a surge of hope.

At least he's still alive.

"Let's lean something against this to hold the button down, shall we, Sergei?" Fedorov is slightly out of breath. "If your daughter can't watch us, at least we can make sure she listens." The sound cuts on and off, then buzzes back into life. "You would have been proud of your papa, Darya," he says in a conversational tone. "He was clever, were you not, Sergei?"

I wince at the flat sound of flesh thudding into flesh, relieved when Papa grunts again.

"Sergei's hands were nowhere near it," Fedorov says. "A vodka company owned by the same gulag guards back in Russia who had known him since he was a boy. Each shipment of vodka sent to France with a treasure hidden in the bottom of the crate, all delivered to a warehouse on the Marseilles docks. Then smaller deliveries that eventually made their way to Russian households in Europe. Who would ever think to question Russian immigrants having their favorite vodka delivered? Once I discovered the system, it was like taking candy from a baby. Follow the vodka, pluck a treasure from the family who received it. I was careful, of course. I murdered the families, burned their businesses, made it look like common thievery. In most cases I did them a kindness. Not all of the Russian aristocrats adapted to life in exile, did they, Sergei? The pampered sons and daughters of the old *dvoryanstvo* didn't like getting their hands dirty."

"They had survived." Papa's voice is hoarse, but to my deep

relief, still strong. "They had rebuilt. They deserved a new life, just as you and your father did. The treasures you stole were small things, a fraction of what they'd left behind. Sentimental items they'd risked their lives to hide in my family's dacha. Pieces that might be enough, perhaps, to buy a house, to start a business. Enough for a future. But you stole that future from them all, Fedorov." His voice strengthens with each word, and although I am on the other side of the intercom with a thick wall between us, I know that tone. Know that whatever beating he has taken is not enough to bow my father's shoulders. I can picture him in my mind, still facing Fedorov down, his piercing blue eyes flashing arctic fire.

I know how formidable my father is when he steps into his full power as *pakhan*. Despite the desperation of our current circumstances, I feel a surge of pride—and of anger.

My father doesn't die like this. Neither of us do.

"Enough!" Fedorov's voice rises. "You caused this, Naryshkin. You caused all of it. All you had to do back in France was hand over a chunk of that fortune, just a few decent pieces. If you had given me what I asked for, all those lives could have been saved."

"Those pieces weren't mine to give." Papa's voice is ice-cold. "They weren't then, and they aren't now. Our fathers swore to safeguard the future of every family who entrusted their treasures to us. Aleksander and I were raised knowing our duty was to honor that promise. We dedicated our lives to restoring every piece to its rightful owner. It was never about hoarding a fortune for us, Fedorov. That is what you have never understood. What you can't possibly understand."

"Then why did you steal them all back from me, Sergei?" Fedorov lands another sickening blow. "You like to pretend you have a noble purpose. But the truth is you're a criminal, a common thief, raised behind bars amid mud and blood." His voice drops, becomes low and dangerous, with a dark, bitter edge. "Do you remember the day the guards made us fight in the yard?"

This time the sound of his fist is hard enough to send ice through my veins.

"Tell me that isn't what this has been about, all these years." Papa's speech is slightly slurred, and I hear him spit on the floor. "Tell me you didn't murder my family in Paris because of a childhood humiliation."

"You beat me half to death in that prison yard!" Fedorov's smooth composure has disappeared, his Russian accent thick and harsh. "And my own father was so afraid of yours that he let you do it."

"You raped my sister!" For the first time I hear true rage in my father's voice. "Your father was an honorable man, and you shamed him. In a just world, outside the walls of that damned gulag, you would have paid with your life. Putting you in the yard with me, a starving child three years your junior, was what little your father could offer mine by way of apology." Papa's tone is scathing.

There's a barrage of thuds and the sick sound of my father's grunts. I wince, gripping Rosa's hand.

He can't take much more of this.

"You were nothing but gulag rats, and my father was a weak fool." Fedorov intersperses his words with blows. "I killed him in the end, did you know that?"

"I guessed." Papa coughs.

"My father would have let us starve to death, when he had a Fabergé egg hidden beneath the floorboards of our room in Paris. I begged him to sell it a hundred times, but he wouldn't do it. He said we should *wait*, keep it hidden until its value increased. I'd been waiting my entire life," he says bitterly. "So I killed him. I sold the egg the same day. But even with coin in my pocket, I wasn't good enough for you and your friends."

"You were a criminal, Ilyan." Papa's voice rasps with exhaustion. "None of us wanted anything to do with that life."

"No. You tried to leave the gulag behind, didn't you? Pretend you never slept in the mud and fought for scraps. You hid your treasure and tried to disappear. But I found you, Sergei. I found you all, one by one. And I made you all remember where you came from, in the end. You should have admitted defeat, back in Paris. Crawled back into the gutter you came from. If you'd done that, this would have all been over. But you just couldn't let it go, could you? You couldn't stand to see your precious treasures in my hands, even then."

"I told you." Papa's voice is thready, his words slurring together. "They don't belong to me, any more than they belong to you. Your crimes cost hundreds of lives. Futures that can't be put back together again, families that can't be rebuilt."

"Don't talk to me about rebuilding!" I hear a clatter that sounds like Papa's wheelchair toppling onto the tiles and a heavy thud that makes my heart sink. "It took me half a lifetime to build another empire," Fedorov hisses, "and find you again. And even when I did, when I tracked you to Miami, still you and that bastard Borovsky tried to outsmart me. Because you always knew I would come for you, didn't you? I promised you that night in France that I would see the end of the Naryshkin line, if it took me until my last breath to do it. I've kept my promise, Sergei. This war is finally over, whether you accept it or not." He puts his mouth close to the intercom. "Open this door, Princess Darya Naryshkin, or your father dies, here and now."

I hear the snick of his pistol, and my heart skips.

Do not open that door, Darya. My father's voice is cold, hard steel. "Shoot me if you will, Ilyan Fedorov. I have lived my life. I have lived more lives than any man has a right to. But my daughter will not die for your greed and corruption. And so long as that vault is closed, you need her. Eventually you will die for this, whether by my hand or by that of Aleksander's son."

"Roman Borovsky?" Fedorov's voice quavers with an almost hysterical excitement. "By now he has opened the vault—and killed your son. Poetic justice, isn't it, for Aleksander's son to kill yours?" He lands another blow. "You aristocrats always did love your poetry. Do you think we didn't know Borovsky was planning an attack? I have an entire army going after him. He won't ever make it out of that fortress you built."

"And the children?" Papa's voice is hoarse. "Did you kill them too, Fedorov? More innocent lives lost for your insane treasure hunt?"

"Children have never mattered to me, Sergei." He gives a strange, high-pitched laugh. "You, of all people, should know that. What was your youngest girl's name, back in Paris? Irina? She was eight, if I remember—"

"You bastard!"

There's a flurry of indistinct sounds, then the intercom cuts out abruptly, leaving Rosa and me staring at each other, white-faced, both of us pressed against the wall on either side of the intercom.

"Don't open it," Anton says warningly. "I've got Pavel on the line." He holds up his phone. "Mak has reinforcements on the way. His first team was intercepted by Fedorov's men, who stole their radios, then impersonated them to take out Bryce and most of his team. But their replacements are only minutes away."

"By which stage my father will be dead." I stare at the locked door with clenched fists, my heartbeat slow and painful.

Nobody tries to argue with me.

One man in a wheelchair, against an army of Fedorov's killers? We all know the odds.

"Sergei wouldn't want you to go out there." Rosa grips my hand, tears rolling down her face. "He didn't come so far, endure all he has, to watch you die, Darya. You have to honor his wishes." Her eyes drop to my belly. "It isn't just you now—"

"Don't you think I know that!" I spin away from the door, passing a shaking hand over my face. I can't cry. I'm too furious and too heartbroken. "What do they say about Roman?" I stare at Anton, who shifts uncomfortably. "Don't lie to me," I say in a low voice. "Tell Pavel I want to know what is happening in Miami."

Anton and Karel exchange a look. Anton murmurs a question into the phone, then covers the receiver, his eyes dark.

"Roman missed the first extraction point," he says reluctantly. "Pavel says they're taking heavy fire."

Rosa blanches. She staggers to the sofa and slumps heavily into it.

That means it's possible nobody is coming for us.

I'm frozen by the door, straining for the slightest sound from beyond it, but there's nothing. "How do we not have a video feed down here?" My body is rigid with frustration.

"Roman didn't want one." Karel looks at me apologetically. "In case the children were watching. He didn't want them to see people get hurt."

Yes, that sounds like Roman.

But if we survive this, we're doing things differently. Our life is dangerous. That is the way it is. The only true protection is preparation and training. I put my hands over my belly, feeling the slight swell of our little Borovsky.

If we make it out of this, I swear silently, *I will raise you to know our world—and to know how to meet it, whether you're born a boy or a girl.*

There has to be a way to live with our legacy and also to live in the world.

"God, I hate this," I mutter. "Hiding behind a locked door like some kind of helpless victim."

"Don't blame Sergei, Darya." Rosa's voice is muffled behind her hands. "This isn't his fault. None of it is."

"I know that!" That's the worst of it. After all my anger at his secrecy, hearing my father's conversation with Fedorov made me realize, with heartbreaking clarity, that my father has only ever done what he thought best for everyone.

And now he is dying on the other side of that door.

I depress the button on the intercom. "Papa?" My voice breaks on the word.

For a long moment there's nothing but dead silence. My fingers itch to open the door, but I'm more than aware of Anton and Karel watching me tensely, clearly ready to leap if I so much as reach for the keypad.

Then the intercom crackles to life, and a familiar, if unexpected voice, speaks uncertainly. "Darya?"

I stare at the intercom in shock. "*Inger?*"

I frown questioningly at Anton, who still has Pavel on the line. He murmurs into the phone then shakes his head at me, shrugging to indicate he doesn't know what is happening.

"You have to open the door!" Inger's voice is high and terrified. "Ilyan has wired me to a bomb, Darya. Please!" She's sobbing. "He's gone upstairs. If you don't open the door, he'll press the button and blow it apart. Your father will die. You could be hurt. My children will be left without a mother . . ." She begins crying in earnest.

"Papa." My voice is shaking. "He's still alive?"

Rosa swings around on the sofa, hope rising in her face.

"I just told you he was!" A familiar, strident note sounds through Inger's tears. "But he won't be if you don't act soon."

And just like that, I know she's lying.

I press the button again. "What did Ilyan promise you, Inger?" Anger pulses through me, slow and thick. "What could Fedorov possibly have offered you that was worth risking your children's lives?"

For a moment, there's no answer.

When Inger's voice comes through again, there's no trace of her earlier tears. "My children are lost to me, Darya. Mikhail made sure of that when he gave them away to Roman." Her tone is sullen and angry. "Ofelia said so herself. She told me to go, so I did. All I want now is Nikolai, and one of the Fabergé eggs. Enough to start a new life." She puts her mouth close to the intercom. "Give me the code to Roman's safety deposit box in Switzerland, tell me where Nicky is, and I'll try to convince Fedorov not to kill you. But if you don't, I'll push the button on this bomb myself and take you with me. I swear I will."

"Nikolai is dead, Inger." I say it flatly.

"Dead?" To my surprise, it's Vera's shrill voice that shrieks down the intercom, talking over Inger's protests. "My son is *dead?*"

"No!" Inger gasps. "No, he can't be. You said he'd be safe—"

The intercom cuts off abruptly.

I stare at the door, utterly confused, trying to imagine what is happening on the other side. Then Anton moves, holding up his hand to get my attention.

"They're here," he says tersely. "Mak's team is here."

We stand by the door, all four of us frozen in place, just waiting.

Finally, the intercom crackles again.

"Darya." It's Papa's voice, weak but still unmistakable. "Open the door, *docha*. We're safe."

"Papa." Tears of relief stream down my cheeks, but Anton is still barring the keypad, his face wary. He snaps a question into the phone, and his face slackens in relief. He nods at me.

"Open it."

I punch in the code, my heart thudding, and the door slowly swings open.

It stops when it hits the inert body of Ilyan Fedorov. His

shocked eyes remain open in death, a single bullet hole between them.

My father, Fedorov's pistol still in his hand, lies slumped barely a foot from Fedorov's body. His eyes are closed, his face bloody with the beating he's taken, and he's clearly lapsed back into unconsciousness. Rosa rushes straight to him.

"Sergei," she whispers, tears streaming down her face, gripping his hand in hers.

His eyelids flicker, his mouth tugging painfully at one corner. "Rosa." He tries to sit up. "Darya—"

"Safe, *lyubov' moya*." Leaning over, Rosa presses a kiss to my father's forehead. "She's safe."

"A medical team is on their way," one of Mak's men says, smiling at me reassuringly. "They're coming downstairs now. Your father is strong," he adds. He gives Papa an admiring glance. "In a wheelchair, after a beating that would have taken out men half his age, and he still managed to get Fedorov's gun and take him out. He's one tough old—" He shoots me an apologetic grin. "What I mean to say is that he'll be fine, Darya."

I tear my eyes away from my father's inert body, Rosa bent over it.

I'm too scared to ask the question I need to.

"Where's Inger?" I ask instead as Anton rolls Fedorov's body away from the door.

"Dead," Mak's man says shortly. "Vera shot her. We took her outside in case her body was wired to blow."

"And the bomb?"

He shakes his head, his face contemptuous. "There was no bomb."

I should have known.

"Vera's upstairs," Anton adds. "She's hysterical."

I'm not ready to deal with Vera. Not yet.

I swallow, bracing myself.

"Roman," I whisper, clutching my throat. "The children?"

"Safe." Anton grips my shoulder, staring into my eyes so I can see the truth in his. "Safe, and about to board a plane as we speak. You can call them before they take off if you like."

"Oh, thank God." I bury my face in my hands, my legs finally giving way beneath me, and slide down the wall until I'm sitting on the floor, heedless of the blood smeared across it. "Thank God."

3 8

OFELIA

I'm lying on the floor of the hangar on a makeshift stretcher, the doctor bent over my broken leg. Masha sits on one side of me, clinging to my hand, Mickey on the other.

The tall man Roman introduced to us as Mak strides across the floor of the warehouse, holding up his phone. "She's okay. Darya's okay."

Roman slumps to the concrete floor beside Mickey, his face white. "Thank Christ for that."

Dimitry grips his shoulder in silent comfort.

Mickey puts his head in his hands.

Masha turns into me, burying her face in my neck, her breath hot and rapid against my skin. "It's okay, *myshka*," I murmur, kissing her forehead as Mak talks in a fast undertone with Roman. "It's all going to be okay."

I watch Alexei over her shoulder. He's standing at a distance to our small group, watching Roman and Mak talk, as still and unmoving as he was in the cell. His jaw is hard as glass, his lips pressed together in a hard line, but the long hours we spent locked in that cell together have taught me to read the small changes in his expression. I can see the passionate relief beneath the cold mask he wears, can feel how hard he's fighting not to show any emotion at the news. When there's a break in the conversation, he speaks for the first time since our arrival.

"Fedorov?" His rasped word is a question.

Roman glares at him. "Dead," he says curtly. "Your father shot him, apparently."

Alexei doesn't say a word. But I don't miss the way his hands spasm into fists, or the fleeting expression of savage triumph that blazes in his face before he assumes his customary deadpan expression. By the way Roman's eyes narrow, he hasn't missed it either.

He and Alexei have yet to talk. Both of them waved the doctor away when we arrived, insisting he examine me instead. They've stayed at opposite sides of the warehouse, both patching themselves up rather than submitting to medical attention. But where Roman pulled his shirt off immediately to wash out his wounds, I can't help but notice the way Alexei turned away from the others and patched himself beneath his clothes. Knowing what I do of Orlov's work, I can only imagine the scars he carries. I understand he'd rather not advertise them.

I wince as the doctor presses my leg.

"Her tibia is broken." The doctor frowns as he looks up at Roman. "She really shouldn't be flying."

An airport crew is going through last-minute plane checks. There are so many men with guns surrounding us it feels like a war zone.

We just came from a war zone.

I shiver, trying not to look at where Vilnus Orlov, bloodied and unconscious, is lying bound and gagged in the far corner, out of earshot.

The doctor is still telling Roman why I should stay in Miami.

"I'm fine." I interrupt him and meet Roman's eyes. "They can drug me, can't they? I want to come with you."

He turns to the doctor, who nods reluctantly. "Yes, I can drug her. But only to London. Then she needs to stay there until the swelling goes down and we can operate."

"Fine." Roman nods curtly. "Do it."

"Wait." I push away the doctor's needle and look at Mickey. "What about Alexei? Is he coming with us?"

"For Chrissakes," Roman answers before Mickey can even open his mouth. He looks ready to explode. "That bastard kidnapped you, kept you captive for days, and used his knife on you too, from what Orlov said. He got off two shots that saved my life, which is the only reason I didn't put a bullet through him back at the shoreline, but that doesn't make up for what he's done. Now let the doctor give you that injection."

"I'm fine." I push it away a second time, glaring at the doctor, who looks like he's about to grab me and forcibly give me a shot. "Alexei didn't kidnap us. He saved us." I force myself to speak calmly, to try to make Roman understand. "He made sure Vilnus didn't hurt Masha and me. He did everything he could to help us, even though he knew you'd probably kill him." I can't help the accusing note in my voice, even though I can see Roman's surprise and hurt. I turn to Mickey. "Alexei got a message to you, didn't he?"

"Yes." Mickey nods, wincing as the movement opens a cut on his neck. "Wait," he says warningly to Roman, who has opened his mouth to start arguing.

To my surprise, Roman actually closes his mouth again, though his expression is absolutely mutinous.

"Ofelia is right," Mickey says tersely. "Alexei is an ally. We wouldn't have got you out of there alive without him and his men."

"We'll see." Roman's voice is cold enough to freeze the Miami humidity. "He's got a hell of a lot of hard questions to answer."

"And he will, but not right now." Mickey faces Roman down with remarkable calm. "He has to go back to secure the compound. Mak's offered to send in a team to help him. I think you should let him."

"Jesus." Roman comes to his feet, looking stratospherically furious. "Now we're helping that bastard?"

Who saved our lives, I think. No matter how much my leg hurts, how much I want to fade out into a painkiller fog, I need Roman to understand the truth. I'm aware of Alexei, still and tense, on the periphery, just out of earshot. Going by the look on Roman's face, Alexei is more likely to leave here in a body bag than with armed assistance, no matter what Mickey says.

I struggle to sit upright. "Please, Papa."

That stops them both. Mickey's eyes narrow at my use of the word. Roman kneels down, blood still surging from the wound at his side, and grips my leg. "Don't try to talk, darling," he says gently. "Just rest."

"No. You need to understand what I'm saying to you." I put my hand over his. "Alexei isn't your enemy. And he's suffered more at Vilnus Orlov's hands than anyone else. You have to trust him." I point to the cut on my cheek. "One of the men who took us from the airport did this. If Alexei hadn't turned up when he did, the man would have done a whole lot worse. Alexei killed him before he got a chance to hurt us. He made sure we were safe. Then he risked his life by lying to Orlov about it."

"Petrovsky knew about that goddamn bomb," Roman says coldly, staring across the warehouse with murder in his eyes. "He could have killed you all."

"No." I shake my head. "He didn't know about the bomb, Papa, I swear it. He and Vilnus argued about it. Orlov set off the bomb because he didn't trust Alexei to help him open the vault. He and Inger kidnapped us because Orlov wanted more *leverage*, as he called it. And because Inger wanted money."

That part should hurt to say, but for some reason, it doesn't. I'm not sure it will ever hurt again to talk about Inger. When I think about her now I feel nothing, only a cold, hard anger. And looking at Mickey's face, I suspect he feels the same.

"You need to listen to your kids, Roman," Mak interrupts us, his voice quietly authoritative. "Petrovsky's not your enemy."

"I haven't thanked you, Mak." Roman reins in whatever fury he looks about to unleash with a visible effort. He puts his hand out, though he's still watching Alexei, his eyes hard. "We wouldn't have made it out of there without you."

"Or without Petrovsky." Mak grips his hand briefly. "And don't thank me." He nods at Mickey. "It was the kid who worked it out. We'd have been dead men without him. I'd advise you to hear him out—hear them both out—before you go off half-cocked."

He reaches past Roman and takes Mickey's hand. "Good job," he says. He's not talking to Mickey like he's a kid. He's talking to him like he would Roman.

Mickey turns a fierce shade of red. "I got lucky," he mutters.

"Bullshit." Mak twists his head in a negative. "You used your brain, and then you acted fast. You ever get sick of taking shit from this one"—he grins in Roman's direction—"you're welcome on my team anytime."

He turns to Roman. "Your plane is ready as soon as you want to board. My team will meet you in London." He nods toward Alexei. "I'm mobilizing a team to go back to the compound with Petrovsky, then Dimitry and I will take a different flight to Spain, work out what happened there. Okay?"

Roman doesn't answer. His eyes are moving between Alexei and Vilnus, bound and gagged in the corner.

"You need to leave Orlov here, with Petrovsky," Mak says quietly. "The man won't breathe again, I can promise you that. But you can't take him with you."

I can see Roman struggling with this. He's staring at Orlov with an expression of old, twisted pain that hurts me to see. "That fucker killed my father," he says, the words rasping from his chest. "And he hurt Darya."

I think of the scars on Alexei's face. Of the casual brutality and cold contempt with which Orlov treated him.

"He hurt Alexei more." My voice is sharper than I intend.

Roman looks at me, frowning.

"I didn't know that Orlov killed your father," I say quietly, trying to take the edge out of my tone. "I'm sorry he did. But I *do* know what Orlov did to Alexei. Terrible things, Roman. For years. He tortured him over and over, and then he made him torture other people for his amusement. Whatever revenge you think you have a right to, believe me, Alexei has more."

Mak nods. "She's right, Roman. From what I can make out, Petrovsky has spent a decade being cut to ribbons by Orlov's knives. He's earned the right to murder the bastard. And he's still got a war on his hands to get that compound under control. His men need to see him take Orlov down, or they'll never properly respect him."

But Roman isn't listening. He's staring at me, his eyes narrowed. "You said Orlov made Alexei torture *other people* for his amusement." His voice is deceptively calm, but I can hear the lethal edge beneath it. "Were you one of those people, Ofelia?"

I thought Alexei was out of hearing range. But I can see him in my peripheral vision, very still, his lone eye moving between Roman and me. His mouth tightens, and he braces himself as if he's about to speak.

Somehow I know he's about to take responsibility for what happened in that room, for what Orlov forced him to do.

No.

I won't let him take the blame for Orlov's evil.

"Alexei never hurt me." I resist the urge to cross my fingers at the lie. I can still feel the thin lines made by Alexei's knife. But they're not deep. I can fix them myself. I'm never telling anyone what Vilnus Orlov made Alexei do to me.

Not ever.

It's a promise I made myself before I ever left that cell. I won't be the reason Alexei suffers. I know what I owe him. I won't ever let anyone hurt him because of something I say.

Alexei tenses, his lone eye darkening. His mouth opens. I know he's about to speak, to tell Roman the truth.

And I know that if he does, he will die here. Probably right in front of me.

"Vilnus tried to make him hurt me." I speak before he gets a chance, forcing myself to meet Roman's eyes steadily. "But Alexei fooled him instead."

Alexei's eye bores into mine, his fists clenched at his side. I shake my head slightly, a tiny movement unnoticed by anyone else. *Don't do it*, I pray silently. *Please, please don't do it.*

Fortunately, Masha chooses that moment to pull her thumb out of her mouth. "Lexi and 'Felia secret."

"Secret what?" Roman's voice is lethally dangerous.

Masha turns to me. "Pretend," she says solemnly, watching me. "Lexi made 'Felia pretend, didn't he, 'Felia?"

"That's right, *myshka*." I force myself to smile. "It was a game, wasn't it?"

"A game?" Roman's eyes narrow. "What sort of sick game—"

"Alexei had to pretend to hurt me."

I can see Alexei from the corner of my eye, his face white as chalk, mouth a hard line, lone eye blazing with dark arctic fire.

I have to keep talking, have to make sure he doesn't speak up and sign his own death warrant.

"We had to make it convincing enough for Orlov to believe. I screamed and cried, but Alexei never touched me." I meet Alexei's eye and force myself to smile, willing him to stay silent. "He protected me." I hug Masha tight. "Us," I say quietly, holding his gaze. "He protected us."

I don't want to think about how easy it is to lie to Roman, or about why I know it's the right thing to do. I just know that if Roman ever even suspects what Orlov forced Alexei to do to me, there's no way he will survive. I might have spent my life up until now in nice boarding schools, kept away from the blood and bullets, but I know what my family is. What Roman is. I know he has to be ruthless, just as Alexei had to be to keep us alive.

I won't let Alexei die for protecting me.

Roman stares at me narrowly for a long moment. Then he glances at Mickey. "Explain why you think he's an ally," he says curtly. "The CliffsNotes version."

Mickey nods. "It was after I saw the numbers on your foot," he says. "The series of numbers I'd been seeing repeatedly in the trojan was the same kind of code. Then Andersson sent another trojan, just as you left the hangar. This one had a more obvious message. One word embedded in it, repeated over and over."

"Poppins." I interrupt him, my heart lurching. "That was it, wasn't it?"

Mickey nods, grinning.

I turn to Roman. "Alexei asked us if there was any word we knew that Mickey would recognize was from us. We told him to use *Poppins*."

Roman frowns for a moment, then comprehension dawns. "Darya," he says slowly. "That first day in the kitchen. You were singing songs from that movie."

Mickey and I nod.

"Poppins!" Masha bounces up and down excitedly.

Roman glances away briefly. It takes a moment for me to realize he's struggling to compose himself.

"Anyway." Mickey picks up the story again. "After that, I got in touch with Lars Andersson directly." He grins. "He wasn't happy about that at all. Apparently he and Alexei have gone to crazy lengths to keep their communication a secret from Orlov and his men. But then I gave the phone to Mak, who managed to communicate the . . . urgency of our situation."

The pilot is gesturing to us to board. Roman circles his finger in the air, indicating to Mickey to hurry up. He's still watching Alexei grimly.

"Turns out Lars was in Switzerland," Mickey says hastily. "He's been there all this time, waiting for Darya to come. The code he'd been sending was for a safety deposit box in the same bank as yours. Alexei had put the Fabergé egg with the key to the vault inside it, along with his fingerprints."

"Wait." Roman looks startled. "What do you mean, he put the key in there?" He glances at Mak, who lifts a shoulder, half smiling.

"I told you to hear him out."

Roman looks between Masha, Mickey, and me, then to Dimitry, who gives him a subtle nod.

He turns to Alexei. "You," he says curtly. "I need to talk to you."

Alexei moves slowly toward us, every muscle in his body tense and alert, his lone eye taking in everyone at once.

"At the vault," Roman says as Alexei nears us. He's frowning, his eyes still dangerous. "That key you gave me was a fake."

Alexei doesn't try to deny it. He just nods.

"You gambled with my daughters' lives." Roman's voice is hard. "What if I hadn't had an army waiting to break in? What if Orlov had called your bluff?"

Alexei meets his eyes evenly. "Then you would not have been

the man I believed you to be, Roman." Something fierce flashes in his eye. "And I would have died before I let Orlov lay a single finger on either of your daughters. As would every one of my men."

There's something so lethal in his voice it makes even me shiver.

Roman's eyes narrow. "How long have you known that my father's key was in Switzerland?"

"Since Rosa told me several months ago." Alexei stares back at Roman with almost as much hostility as Roman has shown him. "Papa never even mentioned the existence of a key before that. No offense, but if I'd known where it was while they were torturing my sister, I'd have sold you out without a moment's hesitation."

Roman stares at him for a long time, his eyes hard and assessing. Then, finally, and to my great relief, he puts his hand out.

After a moment, Alexei takes it.

It's a bit like watching two boxers shake hands in the ring.

"Thank Christ," Mak mutters from behind me.

"I understand you've still got a battle on your hands at that compound," Roman says as he releases his hand. "Mak will make sure you have a team of men, and anything else you need, to take it back."

Alexei inclines his head briefly. "Thank you." His eyes slide to Orlov, his face darkening.

Roman takes a hard breath. "Orlov is yours," he says harshly.

Alexei's head snaps back to Roman, his face pale. His fists clench, his lone eye narrow and glittering. "Are you sure?"

"Make sure the bastard pays." Roman's voice is rough. "For all of it."

"Oh, he'll pay." Alexei's voice is utterly lethal. His eye flickers to me, so briefly I could almost have imagined it. "You have my word."

Roman nods. "You saved my life," he says slowly. "I won't forget that. But most of all, I owe you my deepest gratitude for protecting my daughters." He puts his hand out again.

This time, however, Alexei doesn't take it. He steps back, a fleeting look of something like revulsion crossing his eyes, there and gone so fast it might have been a shadow. "Don't ever thank me for that." He grinds the words out. Again, his eye touches my face, sliding away like a shadow, but not before I register the same flash of dark emotion in it. "Not ever."

Before the moment becomes awkward, Alexei turns smoothly to Mak, his face a mask once more. "We need to hurry." He nods at Roman. "We'll talk when you're back in London?"

"London," Roman agrees. He doesn't seem to have noticed the repressed savagery in Alexei's tone. Nobody has.

Then again, they haven't spent the past few days attuned to every slight nuance in his body and voice. It's like we have a secret language that only we two know and hear.

And from the look on his face, he doesn't seem keen to ever speak that language again.

Alexei walks away, with Mak at his side. My heart twists sickeningly in my chest. I fight the urge to scream his name, to demand that he look at me, but I know that I can't.

You'll see him again, I tell myself. There'll be another time to talk.

But I have a hard time believing my own internal assurances. The intimacy of the cell is like a dream, a strange twilight that no longer seems quite real. And something tells me that by the way Alexei turned away from me, talking to me is the last thing he wants to do.

I mask my expression as Roman turns to us, smiling, and rests his hand on my head. "Ready, sweetheart?"

"Can I give her the shot now?" the doctor asks. He's been

trying to inject me for the last half hour, and he looks extremely annoyed.

Roman raises his eyebrows at me, then rolls his eyes when I shake my head. "Of course you don't want a shot," he mutters.

"I'm sorry." I take his hand. "I just want to hear the whole story from Mickey before they knock me out, if that's okay."

"Christ, you're stubborn." But his hand tightens on mine.

I smile despite the splintering pain in my leg. "I guess I get that from my father."

Roman goes very still, his eyes drilling into mine. Finally he nods slowly, his mouth stretching into a reluctant smile.

"I guess you do, *umnyashka*," he says quietly. "I guess you do."

ROMAN

My limo pulls up to Vera's door amid a watery London morning, and I come out of it at a run.

"Where is she? Where's Darya?"

"She's upstairs." Mak's man eyes the blood seeping through the bandage on my shoulder. "Sir, perhaps you should be in the hospital—"

"Doc's already patched me up." I put my hand out, forcing myself to pause. "Thank you for making it here in time."

"It was a bit too close for comfort." The man shakes his head. "I'm sorry about your man Bryce. He did a damned good job holding Fedorov's men off. Realized what was going on and communicated to us before he went down. If it hadn't been for the work he and the rest of the team did, we wouldn't have had a chance. Do you have any news on his condition?"

"Not yet." I'm already past him, heading for the house, my eyes on the upstairs floor, where I can see a silhouette moving behind the curtains. "They were operating on him when I left the hospital."

I leave the guard outside and take the stairs two at a time, calling her name as I go. Darya turns as I burst through the door, crossing the floor swiftly so we collide in the center. I wrap my good arm around her, feeling the rapid thud of her heart like a triumph against my own, inhaling the sweet scent of her like a benediction.

"I'm sorry," I murmur against her hair. "I'm so goddamn sorry, Darya."

She turns her head from side to side under my lips. "You're alive," she whispers. "The children are alive. That's all that matters." She tilts her head back. "Where are they?"

"A private hospital not far from here. I came to bring you there myself. Ofelia's leg is broken, but they can't operate until the swelling goes down a little, so we'll be staying here in London until that is done. Masha is okay, physically at least. Mickey's with her."

"Take me to them." Darya is already turning toward the stairs. "My bag is packed and waiting by the front door." She glances back and then frowns, taking in my sling properly. "You're hurt? Why didn't anyone tell me that?"

"I'm fine." I nod at the door. "Got patched up on the plane. Let's get to the hospital."

"You don't look fine."

"Then the hospital is the best place for me. Either way, let's go." I usher her down the stairs and into the waiting limo.

"There's a doctor in with Vera," Anton tells me in a low voice as I pause at the limo door. "She's asleep now, but it took a long time to calm her down."

I nod. Vera has not only lost both of her sons, but she was also forced to shoot Inger, the only member of the family she ever showed any real affection toward. I feel sympathy for her, but no guilt.

Sooner or later, I will have to tell both Vera and Yuri that it was my bullet that took Nikolai's life.

But for now, their grief is the least of my troubles.

"My mother?"

"At the hospital with Sergei."

Interesting. I put aside the question of why my mother accompanied that prick to the hospital, for now, at least.

"He's a tough old bastard." The guard smiles admiringly. "Took a hell of a beating before he managed to escape his ties. Gave Fedorov as good as he'd gotten, then killed him with his own pistol, despite having several broken bones. If Inger hadn't turned up and knocked Sergei out from behind, I reckon he'd have taken on the rest of them single-handed."

"Hmph." I pull the door closed without answering. I might have made my peace with Alexei, but I'm still on the fence when it comes to his father.

"Is there any word about Abby?" Darya looks up at me worriedly.

"Your friend is remarkably bulletproof." I pull her close against my side. "Fedorov hit Pillars hard. We lost half a dozen good men. It might have been all of them, if Abby and Gregor hadn't managed to get the rest of the staff out of there. According to Gregor, Abby took one look at the men coming through the door and started throwing Molotov cocktails."

Darya gives a choked laugh. "That sounds like Abby. Where is she now?"

"She and Gregor got the staff safely to our dockside warehouse, but they didn't have their phones with them. Some of our men found them while I was on the plane. Dimitry is on his way to Malaga now with a full crew. They'll tidy up any loose ends."

"This is all my fault." She covers her eyes with one hand. "I should have made sure Abby was kept away from all this."

"She knows what kind of life she's in, Darya." I gently pull her hand away and turn her head so she's looking at me. "This isn't your fault, any more than it's Abby's first rodeo." I shake my head. "That girl could find trouble in the middle of a church choir."

"But she's okay?" Darya presses.

"She's fine, though she might not be after Dimitry gets hold of her. His nerves are shot to hell." I pour a Scotch from the limo bar and surreptitiously swallow two pills with it, closing my eyes briefly at the satisfying burn in my throat as the spirit slips down. I caught a few hours of sleep on the plane after Ofelia had dropped off, Masha curled into a little ball against my chest. The doctor worked around her sleeping form to sew me up. He took one look at my face and knew there was no point arguing.

Mickey spent the entire flight holding Ofelia's hand, his face pale and set. He slept barely any more than I did.

"What about Inger?" Darya searches my face. "Have you told the children their mother is dead?"

I nod. "I thought it was better they knew immediately. I didn't tell them all of it, though, just that she died in the attack."

She nods. "Good."

I don't add that I didn't tell them more because I don't entirely understand it all yet myself. There's something I'm not quite seeing, like sensing a figure in a darkened room.

Darya is already pulling the limo door open before we halt outside the hospital. It's a discreet building set between Harley Street and Marylebone and feels more like a boutique hotel than a hospital. I've booked two entire floors and paid for more than just care. Bryce's bullet wounds won't be disclosed to the authorities, any more than Sergei's bruises will. Nor will there be any record of us having stayed here.

We take the elevator to the children's floor. "Ofelia has had stitches in her face," I warn Darya. "A wound that happened in the blast."

She shakes her head, her mouth tight with pain and anger. "I hate that they had to go through this."

I squeeze her hand. "Me, too."

We step out. There's more security up here than for a royal fucking birth. Until every part of this thing is sewn up, nobody is getting anywhere near my family.

I push open the door to Ofelia's suite. Masha is curled up on the bed next to her sister, Mickey sitting in the chair beside them.

"Oh!" Darya rushes forward, and Masha leaps up from the bed and into her arms, burying her face in Darya's shoulder. Ofelia opens her eyes, then closes them in relief as Darya leans over, hugging her around Masha's body. Darya turns her head to kiss Mickey's cheek, and he settles on Ofelia's other side. All four of them stay on the bed for a long time, a tangled mess of limbs and love, and while I watch them, my whole world here in one room, all my pain is gone.

IT'S SOMETIME LATER, after the doctors have done with their fussing, that I finally let the children tell Darya the entire story.

The truth is that what I really want is to take her upstairs to the suite I've reserved for our sole use and lose myself in her naked body. But I know Darya, and I know there's no chance in hell she will relax until she knows it all.

Instead I have to content myself with sipping neat Scotch, staring at Darya's cashmere-clad curves perched on the edge of Ofelia's bed, and mentally plotting how fast I can get the story-telling done and get down to what I actually need right now.

Which is Darya, naked and moaning under my hands, while I'm sunk so deep inside her that it erases the nightmare we've all just lived through.

The fine-knit dress she's wearing doesn't help. Demure and

elegant it might be, falling to just above her knees and long black boots, but nothing can disguise the length of silk stocking–clad thigh when she crosses her legs or the swell of her delectable breasts that are just asking to be freed.

I shift uncomfortably in my chair and try to focus on the conversation.

When Mickey gets to the part about *Poppins*, Darya's hands fly to her mouth. "Oh!"

I have to look away from the sheen of tears in her eyes. Even hearing it a second time still puts an awkward lump in my throat.

She was the first one they thought of. When their lives were in danger, it was Darya the girls remembered.

I touch her hand, and she grips mine tightly.

My family. This is my family.

"Anyway." Mickey picks up the story again. "Lars told us the only reason Alexei was still with the Orlovs was so he could protect Mer—Roman's project." He hastily corrects himself. "Apparently Nikolai and Inger had found out enough to be dangerous. Alexei was worried they'd take what they knew to Fedorov, who had the resources to be a real threat, so instead he undercut them by telling Orlov, who went to Inger and Nikolai himself. Then Alexei—or rather, Lars—spent the next few months sabotaging Orlov's efforts to hack the project. Alexei's been, like, a double agent for months now. Lars said Alexei didn't have enough men to overthrow Orlov *and* Fedorov. That's why he started trying to contact us via the trojans."

"He could have just picked up a phone," I mutter.

"No." Darya shakes her head. "He couldn't. Lance Ryder was watching his every move. Rosa told me that Andersson was using Lance to gain information about you. If Andersson had started reaching out to us, all of Ryder's suspicions would have been proved correct. He could easily have wound up exposing Alexei, or any of us, to Fedorov or the Orlovs. Lars is my brother's closest friend. He wouldn't risk doing anything to hurt him." She gives me a small smile. "I guess my brother is just as paranoid about safety as you."

Mickey snorts. Even Ofelia smiles.

"Tell her what was inside the box," I say to Mickey.

"This." He shows Darya a photo on his phone.

She gasps, her eyes widening. "The other key to the vault?" She frowns. "But I thought Alexei gave it to you in Miami?"

"Oh, so did I." I'm well aware of the snark in my voice. I know Petrovsky hid that key to protect his sister. I can even admire the balls it must have taken him to look Orlov right in the eye and lie, especially given what the bastard put him through.

But when I think of what might have happened to my daughters if Petrovsky had misjudged the situation, my blood runs cold.

"It's the original." Mickey ignores my aside. "Alexei had a copy made several years ago, with enough flaws to make it useless. He had Lars Andersson hide the original in the same bank where Roman's was. Alexei had been trying to tell me where to find it all this time. If I'd just worked it out earlier," he says, scowling, "we would have known he was trying to help us. We could have done the whole plan differently."

"Alexei was always on our side," Ofelia says quietly. "I *told* you he was," she adds, shooting me a rather hard look.

"Lexi our friend," Masha adds proudly.

I resist the urge to roll my eyes. "A friend who ensured I couldn't open that vault, even if my children's lives depended on it." My voice comes out harder than I intend it to, but I also don't feel inclined to hide my dislike for Alexei's reckless tactics. "He risked all our lives. Surely someone with his level of tech capability could have found a way to warn us."

Ofelia shoots me a reproachful look. "Alexei was just trying to protect Darya. And us, Roman. If that man had managed to open the vault, then they wouldn't have needed us anymore." She shudders, and the light fades from her eyes. "They were going to kill us," she says dully. "I know they were." Her hand goes up to the livid mark on her right cheek, then falls away again. Her eyes slide away from mine.

Darya takes Ofelia's hand, squeezing it, but even then she doesn't look up.

If I'm honest, it's this that makes me want to murder Alexei Petrovsky. I've seen Ofelia do this countless times since we rescued her. Avoid my gaze, withdraw into herself, when she talks about what happened in that compound. Whatever she says, whatever assurances she gives me, she suffered in that place in ways she isn't telling me about. It's a dangerous storm inside her, one that needs to break before it breaks her.

My hands clench into fists. Ally or not, Alexei Petrovsky is damn lucky he never actually used his knife on my daughter. By the way she shrinks into herself every time she speaks about the experience, the fear of it alone will give her nightmares for the rest of her life.

Not to mention that there's no doubt in my mind that Alexei is ruthless enough to use his knife, if he thought he had no choice. Even after his sister was nearly killed by Fedorov, and with his father in the hospital, he's currently fighting a war for his home, torturing Vilnus Orlov to death, or both.

The fact that in his position I would be doing exactly the same thing is a rather uncomfortable fact that I choose not to examine too closely.

I shift restlessly, avoiding Darya's far too penetrating gaze.

"Anyway," I take up Mickey's story, forcing myself to smile at her, "it seems your brother is currently in the process of eliminating the last remnants of the Fedorov/Orlov alliance. I've loaned him some of our men to help with the cleanup."

"That was kind of you." Darya's eyes are soft.

I squirm. "It's good business sense, is what it is. The last thing we need are wild cards from that clan showing up without an invitation. We'll work with Alexei until I'm damned certain the whole lot are finished. Now." I lean forward, rubbing my hands together. "Let's talk about something other than trojans, keys, and bad men with guns. Like where we're going as soon as we can leave London."

To my surprise, it's Ofelia who answers.

"I want to go to Finca de Carrascas," she says quietly. "I just want to sit in the sun there."

"Pool!" Masha jumps up and down on the bed, her eyes shining.

"It's close to the lab," Mickey adds.

"Can we?" Darya turns to me, smiling. "It's so much homier than the penthouse. I can't imagine a better place for Ofelia to recover." Her eyes soften. "And Papa loves it there."

Her anger toward Sergei has gone entirely, after nearly losing him. And from what she's explained to me, I have a better understanding of Sergei's, and my mother's, choices. There'll be time to talk properly. Right now, however, I'm far more worried about getting rid of the shadows in my eldest daughter's eyes.

"We'll have to wait a few days." I smile at Ofelia. "But yes, I think that's a good idea." Suddenly, I have an even better one. I put my mouth close to Darya's ear and whisper something that makes her turn fiery red.

Ofelia rolls her eyes with some semblance of her normal insouciance. "Oh my God. Seriously, you two?"

"Ha. It's not what you think." I take a slightly evil satisfaction at the worried look spreading across Darya's face.

"Roman," she says hesitantly, "I'm not sure now is the time—"

"I'd say it's long past time." I pull her close, pressing my lips to her temple, then turn to face all three of my children. "I just said that I think the finca would be a good place for a wedding. Especially if all the family are going to be there."

The room is suddenly completely silent. For a horrible moment I think I've completely misjudged it.

Christ, Roman. Never make big decisions on the back of jet lag, two bullet holes, and half a bottle of Scotch.

Then all three of my children erupt at once.

"Wedding!" Masha is bouncing up and down on the bed excitedly. "Papa and Darya getting married!"

"Married," Ofelia breathes, her eyes shining in a way that makes my heart twist.

"Ha," Mickey says, smirking at us both. "About time."

Darya gives him a warning look, but it's too late. Ofelia looks between us, her eyes narrowing. "What's the rush?" she asks bluntly.

"Yeah, Roman." Mickey folds his arms and cocks an eyebrow at me. "Why don't you tell my sisters what the rush is?"

I shoot him my best death stare, but his grin just gets even more smart-assed.

"Actually, shouldn't you be talking to Darya's father?" Mickey's voice starts to break with laughter. "Then again, you might want to make sure he doesn't have a gun before you have that conversation—"

I make a grab for the little prick, and he leaps off the bed, laughing. We face each other across Ofelia, Mickey clearly prepared to dodge if I make another lunge for him.

"People," Ofelia says, holding up her hands. "Broken leg here."

"Be careful," Darya says, frowning at us both from the end of the bed. She takes a deep breath, fire-engine red as she glances at me. "Um, Ofelia. The thing is . . ."

"She's pregnant." Mickey says it triumphantly, cutting her short. "Darya and Roman are going to have a baby."

There's a second moment of stunned silence, during which I wait with more trepidation than I could have imagined for Ofelia's response.

"You're going to be married." Her eyes move between Darya and me, her expression frozen. "And have a baby. We're going to have a little brother or sister."

"Yes." Darya is watching Ofelia worriedly. "But nothing will change, darling, I promise—"

Then, like the Spanish sun after London rain, the full beauty of Ofelia's smile bursts into life.

"You'll never leave." Her voice chokes. For the first time since she left that horrible room in the basement of the compound, tears start to well up in her eyes. "You're going to stay with us forever."

Darya's face crumples, and she pushes me aside, wrapping her arms around my daughter and burying Ofelia's head into her shoulder. "Of course I won't ever leave," she says, her voice muffled in Ofelia's hair. "I'll always be here, darling. No matter what. I promise you that."

I rest my hand on Ofelia's shoulder briefly, just long enough for her to know I'm there. But then Darya gives me a fierce look, and I take the hint.

I pluck Masha off the bed and nod to Mickey.

Ofelia manages to hold on until we file out of the room.

I hear her first choked sob as the door swings closed. Then, through the narrow door window, I see her slump in Darya's arms, shuddering with the force of her tears.

I sigh with relief.

The storm has finally broken.

40

DARYA

It's late that night when Roman and I finally take the elevator to our suite on the floor above the children.

"You had a chance to talk to your mother?" I say as he closes the door behind us.

"Yes." He nods, rubbing a hand over his face. "We'll be okay. It's just going to take time to get to know one another again, I guess. I spoke to your father, too." He gives me a small smile. "I'm beginning to think Sergei will outlive the damned apocalypse."

I don't miss the reluctant admiration in his voice. I'm glad; after all we've been through, the only thing that matters to me now is that everyone I love is still alive.

"I should probably have checked on him again." I frown, glancing at the clock on the desk.

"Rosa is with him. And the hospital has a direct line to the suite." Roman walks toward me, his eyes roaming over my body.

I feel the familiar thrill of his nearness. "They'll call us if anything changes. It's only one floor below us, Darya, and I have guards posted everywhere."

His arms snake around me, and I fall against him, clutching the hard wall of his body to reassure myself that it's real.

"I know we're safe." My words are muffled against his chest. "But I don't like the children being anywhere I can't see or touch them right now."

His stubble scrapes my temple as he nods. "I get it, believe me." He tilts my head up, his thumb stroking my cheek. "But right now, I'm far more concerned about seeing and touching *you*. Without clothes on, preferably."

I give a small, choked laugh. "I'm surprised you can even think of that, given how badly you've been hurt." I touch the sling holding his arm, and he moves swiftly sideways, keeping his injured shoulder and side away from me while still holding me firm with the other.

"Even half dead and with no heartbeat, I'd still be thinking about getting naked with you, *milaia*. Give me your mouth."

He takes it without waiting for an answer, and I close my eyes and lose myself in it, because I need this every bit as much as he does. I need the vital reassurance that we are both still here, that despite it all, we have survived. Given the hell we've all just lived through, that in itself seems nothing short of a miracle.

"Christ, I need you." He pulls impatiently at the buttons of his shirt with his good hand.

"Let me." I push his hand away and undo the buttons, easing the shirt over his injured shoulder. I can't help sucking in my breath when I see the state of the body I love so much. Apart from the two bullet wounds, one in his shoulder and one through his side—perilously close to a whole host of vital organs, according to the doctor—Roman's torso is a mass of blooming bruises and open cuts. His face is little better.

"I've had worse, *milaia*." He captures my hand as it roams over the expanse of his chest, his dark eyes on mine reassuring. "I'm fine."

"You nearly weren't." My hand stops just beside the wide bandage on his side. "Any of these could have taken you from us forever."

"But they didn't." He cups my face, his eyes searching mine. "You know what this life is, Darya. No matter what we do, it won't ever change. There will always be blood and bullets. We will always have enemies. Men who want what we have and who are prepared to kill to get it."

My hands roam his body, the heat of his bare flesh beneath my fingertips, the lethal force of him hard against me. He shivers faintly beneath my touch, but he doesn't move. It's like he knows I need this, to touch him, to know he's here, that he's real.

That he's survived.

"I know." My lips graze his collarbone, and I inhale the delicious woodsy scent of him hungrily. "I've always known that, Roman. I'm not afraid of what might come at us." I look up to find him staring at me, his eyes slightly narrowed. "I'm just afraid of losing *you*," I whisper.

"I know." For once, he doesn't attempt to argue with me. Instead he cradles my face in his good hand, his eyes holding my own. "I've been afraid of that too. I didn't realize how afraid I was until I was running away from Ofelia and Masha, toward a pack of men with guns."

I tremble, my stomach lurching with the thought, but I don't flinch away from him. I can tell he needs to say this.

"I've lived most of my life alone." His voice is gravelly with exhaustion and emotion. "I thought that was just the way it would always be. I never expected to live very long, and I've always assumed the end would be violent. It always seemed . . . irresponsible to allow anyone to depend on me. All I ever hoped for was that I'd build a legacy strong enough to look after Mikhail's children after my own death, which I figured would come soon enough.

"But then in Miami, when I left Masha and Ofelia under that banyan tree and ran toward the men coming at us, I realized I didn't want to die. I didn't want our children growing up like I did. Or like you had to."

He kisses my forehead, his lips lingering there for a long moment before he goes on.

"You've had to be so strong. All those years you had to run, never feeling safe. Suddenly I realized that by racing toward those bullets, I wasn't being brave or strong. Sacrificing myself was only going to condemn you to the same darkness we've already had to live through. And worse." His hand slides to rest on the swell of my belly. "I'd be condemning our child to that same life," he says roughly. "All of our children. And I couldn't do it, Darya. I won't do it."

I cover his hand with my own, feeling the safety of his broad palm covering me. "I'm glad."

"I used to think it was a weakness." He touches his lips to my face between sentences. "That if I had a family, it would make me fear the bullets. But it doesn't. The fear makes me stronger. It makes me smarter. More determined to survive, to build an empire that can hold us all, keep us safe. Our world might always be one of violence, but I'm not afraid of having a family anymore, Darya. I want it. I want it all. I want it with you. And I want to make sure nobody can ever take it from us."

He pulls back from me and cradles my face in his hand. "I know I should have done this properly, with the right ring, and not around a hospital bed with our children watching." He gives me a slightly crooked grin, and my heart skips a beat. "I'd get down on one knee, but neither one is working too well right now. I just want to make sure you know that I'm in. I'm all in.

Now and always. So I have to formally ask you: Darya Petrovsky, will you marry me?"

My world slows down to the blood pumping through my body, the sensual seduction of his skin next to mine, the mindless abandon I feel when I drown in his dark eyes.

The safety I feel when his arms are around me.

The incomparable thrill of his body inside my own.

And the overwhelming rightness I feel nowhere but when I am with him.

"Yes, I will marry you, Roman Borovsky." I put my hands on his face and draw it down to my own, my body needing his like a flower reaching for rain. "I will stand beside you forever, and help you build everything you dream of. And I will love you, with my whole heart, until the day I die."

"You're all in," he says huskily, his good arm slipping around my waist and pulling me hard against him.

"I was all in from the moment you ordered your first coffee," I whisper, feeling the delicious thrill start to uncurl in my belly.

"Is that right?" Roman chuckles, his lips drawing a trail of fire up my neck toward my mouth. "You mean that instead of trading insults with you, I could have just done this?" His mouth lands on mine, and I open beneath it with a small cry, my body already liquid heat in his embrace. His kiss is hungry and thorough, his tongue taking my mouth with a subtle power and intensity that leaves me shaking and panting, pressed hard against his naked chest. He is hot and restless under my touch, his skin like fire, his good hand roaming over the thin knit dress covering my ass in a way that makes me want to climb him like a fucking tree.

He slides the hem of my dress higher. Then he hits the bare skin at the top of my stocking, and his hand comes to a sudden halt while his mind assimilates what he's feeling.

Then his palm splays over my thigh, his thumb tracing the frilled line of my garters slowly upward.

"I like these," he murmurs in my ear. He raises my knee so my booted heel rests on a nearby chair. His thumb strokes the bared upper skin of my thigh, tantalizingly close to where I really need it. "Maybe we should spend more time in cold climates."

Then his hand roams even higher, and I gasp as his thumb presses my swollen clit through the silk.

"You know, I planned to fuck you hard and fast." Roman's thumb makes tiny movements that have me gasping, aware of every slight change in pressure. "I pictured you naked the entire flight over here, and every moment since. I thought I needed you too badly to wait. I wanted to just get my cock inside you."

Oh, God.

My hips jerk toward him, my knee opening wider, aching for more than just his thumb. I want my underwear off. I want his mouth, his cock. I want him against me.

"But now that I have you here," he goes on, swiping a slick of moisture from my inner thigh, "I don't want to rush a single moment." Suddenly his hands are gone. My eyes fly open to find him staring at me, his arousal blatant beneath his suit pants. My dress is hitched up to my waist, so I'm standing with one high-heeled boot up on a chair, exposing my soaked underwear over my garter and stockings.

"Lose the dress," he says roughly.

My skin on fire, trembling as if it were my first time, I pull the dress over my head, revealing the black silk-and-lace bra that matches the rest of my lingerie.

"You know," he says in a low voice, "this reminds me a lot of the first time I ever fucked you. Do you remember that night, Miss Petrovsky?"

Heat rushes between my legs. "I remember," I say breathlessly.

"I think we both learned a lot that night." Roman reaches for the Scotch bottle and pours himself a glass, his eyes roaming over my body. "I discovered how much you like following orders, for example."

My body rocks toward him involuntarily, summoned by even the memory of that night.

Roman seats himself in a wide sofa chair several feet away. I almost groan with frustration.

"Take your bra off."

Oh, that low, sexy, commanding voice.

It puts me in the same trance it always does, my hands unclipping my bra like they belong to someone else, every nerve in my body attuned to his commands, the center of me swelling with every caress of his eyes.

"You're so wet I can see it from here." He states it in a calm, matter-of-fact tone, but after all this time, I can hear the telltale rough edge right behind the facade, sense the fierce control he's exerting to keep his own arousal in check. It's part of our game, part of what makes the tension between us so incredibly hot. And just like him, right now I need every moment of this sweet torture.

I want to lose myself in hedonism, in the dark heat that takes us both to a mindless ocean of sensual bliss where there is only our bodies, and the slow journey toward earth-shattering release.

"Your nipples are swollen, Darya." My hands reach up to touch them, but he shakes his head. "No. I want to watch them from here." He puts down his glass of Scotch and reaches for his belt buckle, his eyes not leaving mine. "Would you like to see what your body does to me, Darya? What thinking about you does to me?"

His cock leaps free, and my body ripples with lust. My breasts feel like they're going to explode. I whimper aloud as my eyes rest on his pulsating shaft.

"Did you know you just licked your lips, Darya?"

I don't have a clue what I'm doing. All I want is him. I'm lost in the semi-hypnotic state where all I can hear is his voice. All I can do is obey.

"The first time I saw you do that, I knew I couldn't rest until I had my cock in your mouth."

"Oh!" I clench my fists to hold back from touching myself. I know better than to try to take control.

"Then I saw those gorgeous tits, and I knew your mouth would never be enough." Roman's cock twitches, and I gasp, a rush of moisture slicking my thighs.

"You know, I'm torn right now." He takes a leisurely sip from his Scotch, but I can see the dark, almost black color of his eyes, the whiteness of his knuckles around the glass. He's barely holding on right now, no matter what he says, and that knowledge, the power it gives me, is the most intoxicating aphrodisiac I've ever known.

"Do I make you touch yourself like I did that first night?" He tilts his head to one side as if he's contemplating this. "Or do I make you come over here and spread that pussy over my face, so I can lick every part of you?"

"Oh God!" I can't hold back my cry, nor the sudden, convulsive jerk of my body. I'm barely aware that I'm clutching my own breasts until I see Roman's mouth curl into a diabolical smile.

"And just because you got impatient," he says evilly, "now you have to wait."

But he doesn't tell me to take my hands away. And by the way his cock leaps, he's clearly enjoying the way I'm playing with my nipples. Which is good. Because I really couldn't take one minute more without something touching me, even if it's myself.

"Take your panties off," he growls. "Leave the boots on."

I peel the silk and lace away, almost embarrassed by how swollen and wet I am, until I see the sudden glazed look in Roman's eyes and the drop of moisture glistening on his cock.

He takes a long swallow of Scotch, his eyes not leaving my throbbing mound.

"Put your foot back up on that chair like before." His order is low and intense, and he's rock-hard as he watches me. I can only imagine the self-restraint he's exerting to refrain from touching himself. I put my heel up on the chair, rolling my knee out so my swollen lips part under his eyes. His harsh intake of breath doesn't escape me. "Open yourself for me," he growls.

I slip my hands down to my pussy and slowly spread the outer lips apart, biting my lip at the unbearable sensation of air hitting my most intimate folds.

"Slip one finger inside yourself. Show me how wet you are." Roman is grinding out the orders, his shaft leaping at every word, and by the way he's devouring the Scotch, he's nearing the limits of his control.

Which is a good thing. I don't know how much more of this I can take.

I slide a finger inside myself and groan at the inadequacy of it. I'm so fucking wet I need a lot more than what he's letting me have.

"Show me," he growls, and I hold up my glistening hand, slick with my own juices. His cock swells to an impossible width, but still he doesn't touch himself. I know he's loving the tension, forcing himself to delay pleasure as long as he can, but it's also driving me out of my fucking mind with lust.

"Come here."

Oh, thank God.

Roman has taught me how much power there is in theater, so I don't move quickly. I take my heel down, then walk slowly toward him, rolling my hips with each step, holding my breasts up toward his eyes. I halt just beyond his reach, knowing how insane it will drive him.

"Turn around."

I do, slowly, loving his sudden, harsh intake of breath. I arch my back so my ass is thrust toward him.

"Spread your legs wider."

Once I would have felt shy, knowing how I look, exposed like this. But Roman has changed all of that, made me revel in every aspect of our mutual arousal.

"Your pussy is stunning," he says in a low voice. "Swollen and dripping wet. I can't wait to get inside you."

"Oh!" I groan, rotating my hips under his eyes, knowing how much he loves to watch me move like that.

"I'm going to lick every part of you until you're screaming. And then I'm going to fuck you so hard you forget your own name."

"*Yes.*" I'm panting now, my knees bent as I thrust my ass toward him, begging for him to take me. My hands are on my breasts, gripping my nipples. It's only when I open my eyes that I realize he's staring at me in the mirror opposite, his jaw clenched fiercely, his eyes flashing hellfire.

He's close to losing it, and I love it.

"Come to me now."

I turn on shaking legs and cover the last distance to him. His legs are spread, cock pounding hard against his belly, his Scotch glass discarded on the table beside him. I stand between his thighs, waiting.

"Knees either side of me," he rasps, and I place my dripping core wide over him, knees on each of the large armrests. He stares at me for a moment, then his one good hand comes under my ass, his large, scarred palm cradling my entire body weight, and he covers me with his mouth.

"*Aaaahhhhhh!*"

I hope the suite is as soundproof as the penthouse, because I just screamed loud enough to bring the entire London police force down on our heads.

He licks me with a slow, deliberate precision that is mind-blowing, considering the clearly desperate state of his own arousal. I shake as I try not to grind onto his tongue, knowing that will only result in longer torture. My world is reduced entirely to the delicate, lazy ministrations of his tongue, my breath caught in my throat as he expertly strokes me inexorably toward release, but never quite granting me that final explosion.

"God, Roman. Please," I pant.

He doesn't answer, just licks me until I'm shuddering, my breath hitching and my hips jerking uncontrollably.

Just when I think I can't take it a moment longer, he raises me slightly, then drops me back down—directly onto his cock.

I scream again as he fills me completely.

"Don't move," he growls. For a moment we just stay there, me with my legs spread impossibly wide, him completely still inside me.

Then his hand slips between us. He thrusts up into me so deeply I feel speared and spread, and then his thumb presses my clit.

I explode around him.

My orgasm takes me by surprise, a wrenching, almost vicious release, so all-encompassing it wracks my whole body. I clench around the iron thickness of his cock, my orgasm crashing against him like waves on a lighthouse, and he holds me in place and rides it in complete stillness.

When I finally open my eyes, he's white-faced with the effort of restraint, staring at me, his lips a thin line. I'm still grinding against him when he stands up, bringing me with him.

"You can't," I gasp, struggling against his grip. "You can't lift me one-handed—"

"The fuck I can't." He throws us both down on the bed and kicks off his pants, still inside me.

"My boots—"

"Leave them on." He surges into me then, all restraint gone, his mouth on mine full of all the demand he's kept under rein this entire time. He takes me with the battle rage and fierce desperation of near death, with the wild edge lent by fear and fury.

He takes me like the warrior he is, and he claims me for the woman I am.

He pounds deep within me until the world disappears and there is only the place where we meet. He drives me into screaming submission again and again, and when he finally hits his own bone-shattering release, his primal roar seals the bond between us like a covenant.

I am his. He is mine.

We're all in.

Now and forever.

41

ROMAN

"I never want to be cold again." Darya turns her face up to the Spanish sun, sighing in deep contentment. "It's so good to be home."

"It'll be even better after the wedding." I turn on the sun lounger to face her. The soft swell of her belly is barely noticeable, but it's an exercise of will not to touch it all the time, particularly now, when she looks absolutely delicious stretching a blue-and-white polka dot bikini in all the right places. I brush my lips across her knuckles, and she blushes in a way that makes me want to pull her inside. "You're absolutely certain a small wedding is what you want?"

"It's hardly small." She casts a wry look at the field next to the finca, where a small army of men are laboring to create the garden wonderland in which we'll soon make our vows. "By the time we factor in all of your business associates, then Mak and *his* men, not to mention my brother and *his* . . ." She rolls her eyes. "Your idea of small is very different than mine."

I snort. "I never planned on having a wedding at all."

"You have to marry her," Mickey yells from the pool, grinning at me. "You knocked her up, remember?" He tosses Masha in the air, and she shrieks as she falls back into the water.

"Watch it," I hiss, casting a wary look in Sergei's direction. The old man, however, just smiles and claps as Masha surfaces, paddling frantically. Rosa's presence seems to have had a transformational effect on Sergei's health, despite the fact that the two of them bicker so much that it's amusing to watch. His mobility is getting better every day, and his speech is almost completely restored.

I didn't so much as ask the old man's permission to marry his daughter as I informed him it was going to happen, in the same conversation I informed him he was going to be a grandfather. To Sergei's credit, he took both pieces of information with remarkable equanimity.

He almost looked happy.

Not that I give a fuck.

The only happiness I care about is that of Darya and my children. And right now, they all seem in the best spirits I've seen them since Miami.

Masha has finally ditched her arm floaties and is paddling across the pool toward Mickey's waiting arms, cheered on by Sergei. Ofelia is sitting beneath an umbrella opposite us, her booted leg propped up on cushions. Wearing a wide-brimmed sun hat, dark glasses covering her eyes, she's still pale. She's also still too thin for my comfort, though Darya assures me her appetite is improving every day. Even thin and pale, and with a heavy boot on her leg, nothing can diminish her extraordinary beauty. I dread to imagine what challenges the next few years will bring. I'm grateful as hell I have Darya beside me to help navigate them. A willing father I might have become, but handling beautiful teenage daughters isn't something I'm any better prepared for than I ever was.

"You're getting lazy, brother." Dimitry collapses in a lounger beside me, grinning. "The geeks at the lab are starting to forget what you look like."

"Bullshit." I toss him a beer from the cooler beside me. "I saw Pavel this morning."

"And we're going back this afternoon," Mickey calls from the pool. "Aren't we, Roman?"

I barely stifle my groan. "I never should have agreed to that."

Dimitry snorts. "Bet you can't wait until he gets his license."

"The day cannot come fast enough, my friend." It's not entirely true. I could insist Luis drive Mickey where he wants to go. The truth is that I enjoy the time I spend in the car with him. Mickey's mind works in a hundred directions at once, most of them leading to interesting places. He's already working with Pavel to tighten up a number of processes associated with Mercura.

And he's stayed in close contact with Lars Andersson.

This last is a development I'm not entirely a fan of. Lars will be arriving with Alexei before the wedding, so at least I can finally get the measure of the man who has been side hacking my project for the past few months. I'm not sure whether I want to hit him or shake the man's hand.

I glance over at Abby, who is walking with Darya into the house to refresh the drinks. "So you've convinced her to stay, then?" I ask Dimitry.

His smile fades. "Only until the wedding. She insists she has to go home to Australia, spend some time with her family. But she won't let me go with her, and I get the feeling it's just an excuse."

"You still think there's more going on with her than what she's telling you?"

Dimitry shakes his head. "I dunno. Abby doesn't shake easy,

but what went down at Pillars would have knocked anyone sideways." He shakes his head, expression dark. "I can't stop her going. I've just got to hope she comes back."

There isn't much to say to that, so we just shoot the breeze for a while about nothing in particular, until Darya comes out in that ridiculous bikini and I find an excuse to take her upstairs.

<hr>

"ROMAN." It's the following afternoon when my mother says my name quietly, from the open room where she's set up an informal workshop. It seems that dressmaking is the one thing that has remained unchanged in her life since my childhood. I've found a strange comfort, these past weeks, in hearing the hum of her sewing machine and the snip of scissors through silk. She's been making Darya's wedding dress. From the giggles that come endlessly from this room, she's apparently outdone herself. Not that I'd know. The dress itself is safe behind a screen, which might as well be Fort Knox for all the chances I have of seeing behind it.

"Thank you for making this." I nod at the screen. "I know it means a lot to Darya."

"It's my pleasure." My mother smiles gently. I feel slightly awkward, as I always do in her presence. We've all had time to absorb one another's stories, to forgive the mistakes of the past. But forgiveness doesn't take away the pain of more than two decades of absence. I've continued calling Rosa by her given name, for example.

Mama is a person who left when I was a child. The name itself is full of pain and abandonment. *Rosa*, on the other hand, is a kind and compassionate woman, with a rather wicked sense of humor and a core of strength I can't help but admire. It's this person I'm getting to know, and who my children have taken to as easily as they once did Darya.

"There's something I would like you to have." Rosa opens a drawer on her worktable. "When I left, your father gave me both of these. So I would remember him, he said." She smiles sadly. "As if I could ever have forgotten Aleksander. He was the very best of men." She hands me a small drawstring bag. "I've had them cleaned."

I open the bag to find two white gold wedding bands, simple and elegant. On the inside, both are engraved with a lone rose. "Aleksander made them himself," she says softly. "The rose was from his family crest. It symbolizes hope and love, optimism for the future. I don't know if you have rings yet or not, but I wanted you to have them anyway."

"Thank you." I turn the rings over in my hand, and for a moment it is as if my father's hands cover my own, large and comforting. "He never forgot you," I say quietly. "Neither of us did. The house was . . . empty with you gone."

Rosa's eyes cloud over. "I never should have gone."

"If you had stayed, you would be dead now too." I take her hand and press it gently. "Instead you are here, giving me my father's rings and making Darya's wedding dress. Running was the right choice. The only choice, really."

It's taken me a while to get to this conclusion. But the hard truth is that no matter how much I might want to blame both Sergei and my mother for the decisions of the past, I can't. I know there isn't anything I wouldn't do to keep Darya safe. Nor can I avoid the fact that only a few short weeks ago, I was actively helping her run.

While she was pregnant.

I shiver. I might never get used to the horror of that thought.

"If you would allow me to suggest something else?" Rosa looks at me tentatively.

"Of course." Part of me hates the caution with which we both dance around one another. I'm also horribly aware that nothing but time can fix that hesitancy.

"Maybe talk to Sergei before you take Darya shopping for an engagement ring."

It's all I can do to keep an even tone and not roll my eyes. "More secrets?"

She smiles gently. "This one I think you will want to hear."

———

I FIND Sergei sitting in a wide wicker chair on the terrace beyond his bedroom. He stubs his cigarette out hastily when I open the doors, then relaxes when he sees who it is. I wave a bottle of Graf vodka and two glasses, and he smiles appreciatively as I put them down on the coffee table and pour. He looks remarkably cheerful, given the impressive array of bruises on his face, and still bloodied knuckles.

"*Za zdorov'ye.*" I raise my glass.

He touches it with his own. "*Za zdorov'ye.*"

"I looked up Graf vodka," I say, glancing at him. "Apparently it was started by a group of guards at the gulag in which you were born?"

Sergei nods, his eyes twinkling. "Our fathers made the original still. By the time your father and I finally left the gulag, we'd been running the business for decades, along with the guards who oversaw it." He gives me a sideways grin. "I will always take credit for the quality of the vodka. Aleksander and I refined our fathers' recipe. I like to think we improved on it."

"Did the Russians know it was you who owned the company?" I ask, curious. "You were exiles. How did you pull it off?"

"Ah." Sergei lights another cigarette and draws deeply, his pale eyes gleaming. "The gulag never dies, not really. There was always a fine line between those who ran it and those who were imprisoned in it. Especially for men like Aleksander and me, who were born and raised behind those walls." A ruthless light crosses his face, there and gone. "That's how we *pulled it off*, as you put it: power. Guards came and went. But to us, the gulag was our home. Our school. Our world. By the time we left, that world had belonged to us for many years. Men lived and died in the gulag depending on rules we made. We owned secrets and lives that extended far beyond those walls and those years."

He turns to me, holding my eyes with his own. "Unfortunately, that world followed us into this one. It never left us in peace. In the end, it took your father's life and stole too much of yours. I failed to stand between that world and you, Roman, just as I failed to protect my children from it. I will never forgive myself for that failure, and I do not expect you to forgive me for it. But I do hope you will allow me to give you this, at least."

I'm so taken aback by his unexpected apology that I'm temporarily lost for words. Sergei reaches into the pocket of his shirt and pulls out a small box. "Aleksander made this for Maria," he says quietly. "The diamond in it is from a ring that belonged to my mother, the only thing of value she carried into the gulag. She melted the gold down long before I was born, traded it for survival. But no matter how hungry or desperate she became, she never traded the diamond."

I open the box. The square-cut diamond is simple, but also of perfect quality. It is the lone feature of the elegant white gold ring.

"I understand if you both wish to have no more association with the past." He lights another cigarette, blowing a stream of smoke over the valley. "But that diamond belongs to Darya either way. And Aleksander always said that ring was some of his best work." He lifts a shoulder, his eyes softening. "Beauty never ceased to matter to your father, regardless of the savagery that surrounded us. Aleksander was . . . different." He sounds almost wistful.

I think of my peaceful father, the gentle movement of his hands on metal, the soft touch as he guided my own.

I remember the resignation on his face the day the Orlovs strangled the life from his body.

And then I think of standing in front of Mikhail and taking the bullet that was meant for him. The first of many I would take to keep him alive, right up until a bomb I didn't foresee ended his life forever. My guilt over that failure has haunted me every day since his death. It almost stopped me from being able to give his children the love they deserve.

I know how heavy it is to carry the responsibility for lives other than your own. And I know the pain of failing to protect them.

I stare out at the mountains opposite, the late-afternoon sun turning them buttery yellow. "Perhaps," I say slowly, "my father was able to be different because he had you to protect him."

Sergei makes a dismissive noise and shifts restlessly in his chair. "Aleksander was the best of men." He says it with a finality that is meant to end the conversation.

I stifle a smile. It isn't lost on me that those words are the exact ones my mother also recently used to describe Papa.

"Thank you for this." I hold up the box, very aware that I'm still holding off asking the questions I really want to. Instead I say, "I have been talking with your son these past few days."

Sergei nods, but doesn't say anything.

"Alexei will be arriving soon." I choose my words carefully. "There are matters we would both like to see settled before the wedding."

He smiles faintly. "Go ahead and ask your questions, Roman. I will answer anything you wish."

Part of me thinks I should wait until Darya is with me. But another part of me needs to hear this alone, to learn my father's story for myself.

"What happened in Paris?" It isn't the question I thought I'd ask, but it's the first one that comes. "Darya told me about the crates of Graf vodka, and returning the treasures to the families who had entrusted them to you. I know that Fedorov eventually found you. How did you survive? Why didn't you and my father die in the fire?"

"The night he came for our families, Fedorov had Aleksander and me arrested." All trace of his previous warmth disappears the moment he speaks Fedorov's name. Sergei's voice is hard, his breathing hoarse. It's unexpectedly difficult to see the sudden, fierce agony in his face. "Fedorov owned enough Parisienne police to have Aleksander and me locked up for the night on trumped-up charges. In the morning, he came to see us in our cell. He offered us a deal: he'd leave our families alone if we handed over the rest of the treasure. Your father had two children, a boy and a girl. I had three. My eldest was a girl, Irina. She was eight."

He swallows his glass of vodka, his eyes closed. Then he takes a deep breath and begins again.

"We agreed to his deal, of course. Promises to our fathers aside, we had tried to leave the gulag behind us. We both knew nothing was more important than keeping our families safe. We led Fedorov to the Graf warehouse and watched while he took all the remaining pieces, which was no inconsiderable fortune."

He pauses. I refill his glass.

"We didn't realize it was already too late." He stares through the glass to a past I can't see, his face gaunt. "Fedorov never had any intention of allowing our families to live. He'd already killed them all and burned our businesses to the ground. After the warehouse, he took Aleksander and me to look at the smoldering ashes that remained. He left us there, on our knees, staring at the rubble where our lives had been. I imagine he thought we'd never rise up off that ground, and he was almost right."

Blyat.

I've seen a lot of pain in my life, a lot I wish I could unsee. But I can't imagine standing before the burned bodies of Darya and my children. I don't want to. Even the thought makes me want to cross myself, and I was never raised a Catholic. I have a compulsive urge to make some kind of sign to ward off evil.

"Exactly." I realize Sergei is watching me, old pain etched deeply on every line of his face. "Now maybe you understand why we did not speak of this. Such evil should be buried and forgotten." He grimaces. "Along with all that followed that night." He turns the vodka glass on the table, his mouth a hard line. "I will not go into details of what we did," he says bluntly. "Other than to say that instead of dying, Aleksander and I chose revenge. Maybe it was the gulag in us, maybe the steppe, but neither of us were able to just give up. Instead we destroyed Fedorov's empire, piece by piece. We burned every business he had to the ground. We took back every single piece he had stolen, avenged every family he had tortured or ruined. Only Fedorov himself escaped us. Paris whispered he had died in one of our last attacks, but we had no evidence to support the whispers. Fedorov was elusive, and after a time, we realized that if he wasn't already dead, he was certainly gone. Aleksander and I left Paris; there was nothing left there for us. We came to Miami. We tried to start again."

His voice is hoarse, starting to slur, but he waves me away when I mention he can stop if he wants.

"Let it be said," he rasps, tossing the vodka off like it is water. "Then done. What else do you wish to know?"

I pour us both another glass. "Promises to your fathers aside, why didn't you just get rid of the treasure, after all the trouble it had caused you?"

Sergei nods. "We talked about it. Discussed donating the entirety to a museum, or selling each piece off privately and creating a fund we could invite the remaining descendants to join. But every plan had an obstacle, a downside. They all risked exposing us. Both of us were wanted men. The KGB were still searching for us. The French authorities would have killed us on sight. And if the Americans had any idea of our true identities, we'd be jailed for the rest of our lives. Whatever our crimes, we'd spent more than enough time behind bars. Neither of us wanted to risk it again.

"The few Russians in Miami back then knew nothing of our history, and of course we had new names. Aleksander wanted a simple life; he always had. He built a small but respectable business doing jewelry repairs and making safes for small businesses. I . . . It wasn't so simple for me." He shakes his head. "Paris had taught me that a simple life couldn't ever be mine, not so long as we had a fortune in lost treasure. And after all that had been lost, after the exile and name changes and all the death, those treasures seemed the only real thing, the one solid reality in a life of smoke and mirrors. I knew crime; I'd inhaled it with my first breath, lived among violent men in the gulag for as long as I could remember. And I was angry.

"So I ran a few card games, got into a lot of fights. I was running close to spending the rest of my life in prison, whether I planned it or not, and I was getting to the point where I no longer cared.

"Then one day, when I was sitting in Aleksander's shop drinking vodka, a young girl came in with a broken necklace for repair." His mouth twists in a smile of reminiscence. "Aleksander and I stared at the necklace in shock. We both recognized the piece as one we'd returned to a woman in France many years before. Aleksander asked the girl a few questions. It turned out the necklace had, quite literally, saved the girl's mother's life. She'd been alone and pregnant, with nowhere to go but the Paris gutters, which back then was death sentence enough in itself.

"Instead, she sold one of the diamonds in the necklace and bought a ticket to the US. Started a ballet school, which subsequently became one of Miami's most popular. The girl told us her mother prized that necklace more than anything in her life. That she still talked about her miraculous delivery from certain death. She was superstitious, like so many Russians. She told her daughter that Russian émigrés like her had been raised on stories of the *angely vodki*, the 'vodka angels.' She said there were countless tales of lives saved, and changed, by a crate of Graf vodka at the door."

He lifts a shoulder, smiling wryly. "She also mentioned that nobody could seem to get Graf vodka anymore."

"Do you still own Graf?" I eye him curiously.

"You will have to ask my son when he arrives." Sergei laughs softly. "He is *pakhan* now. After all the treasures had been returned to us in Paris, we'd walked away from the vodka business, but it was a simple enough matter to buy it back under a different name. And just like that, I knew what my next step was. I set up an import-export business the next day, behind a false business wall, of course. Only this time, I understood the risk I was taking. And I made sure Aleksander was nowhere near it. He'd worked hard for a simple life, and he'd earned the right to live it peacefully."

He turns the vodka glass on the table. The rasp in his voice has gone, as have the slurred edges. Sergei's eyes are a piercing, fierce blue, as if speaking of those years has brought back the life force that drove him through them. "I was smarter," he says slowly. "I knew that so long as our fortune existed, men with guns would want it. Money and riches are like that; no matter how well they are hidden, greedy men will seek them out. Perhaps Fedorov was dead, and perhaps not. Either way, I knew it was only a matter of time before I drew the attention of violent men again.

"So I didn't try to hide. I didn't try to build a simple life. Instead, I built an army. I built a fortress. I built one of the biggest, hardest criminal empires Miami had ever seen, and the

Petrovsky legend was created." His face is animated, once again the fierce *pakhan*. "I swore that no matter how long it took, I would make sure every one of those treasures was returned to a rightful heir. And this time, I would make sure Aleksander was kept far away from the process. The decision was mine, and so would be the risk." He smiles with real affection. "But we had been partners, brothers, our whole lives. Aleksander didn't like the idea of leaving the responsibility of our joint promise on my shoulders. In the end, we compromised: he would build a vault as secure as the one his father had once built for mine, back in Russia. A place to store the treasures safely until they were all distributed." He pauses, staring at the glass, his smile fading. "And he made another promise. Or rather, we made a promise to each other. We swore the Naryshkin legacy would die with us. Neither of us had either a wife or children at that time. We never imagined we would again. Aleksander and I promised one another that, on our deaths, the master lock would be set by code on the vault, and nobody would ever enter it again.

"Then Aleksander met Rosa." Sergei's mouth tightens. "Soon after they were married, you were born, Roman."

Is it just me, or does his smile seem forced?

"Shortly after that, Aleksander's business was broken into." I stare at him, surprised. This part of the story I know nothing about.

"To anyone else," Sergei continues, "the break-in might have seemed insignificant, just a crime of opportunity. But not to us. For the first time, we began to consider that Fedorov might still be alive—and hunting us.

"The night of the break-in was the evening after your christening, Roman. Aleksander and Rosa had come to celebrate at my compound and were staying the night. It was sheer luck that they were not home. Maria, Rosa's closest friend, was visiting for your christening." He stares at the table, his face inscrutable. "We'd only met once before that night, at Rosa and Aleksander's wedding. After that night, however, I was afraid for her safety. Maria never went back to Rosa's house. We were married barely weeks later."

He says this in a matter-of-fact tone, almost as if marrying Maria was just another part of taking care of business. I notice that while he always speaks about Maria with affection, there's none of the intensity that was present when he spoke about his first wife in Paris, nor even the reverence with which he spoke about Aleksander meeting Rosa. I don't doubt that Sergei loved his wife. But I can't help but feel that marrying her had more to do with keeping her safe than a dramatic love story.

Then again, I think, closing my eyes briefly as Darya's face swims across my mind, *maybe I'm just biased.* God knows I've lived my entire life, until recently, believing love was a myth. If I hadn't met Darya, I might still believe that. *Who am I to judge?*

"Back in Paris, Fedorov had come for our families before we had a chance to get them to safety. We were determined that would never happen again. The fingerprints were our solution, our fail-safe, should everything go wrong. If by some chance we were to die, or were captured, the keys and fingerprints were a bargaining chip, something our children could use to survive, if it came to it. So, to answer your question properly, Roman."

He looks up, holding my eyes. "We didn't tie your fingerprints to the vault to keep the contents of it safe. We put them there so that if you ever needed to trade something for your freedom, you could." His mouth twists. "We thought we had made you too valuable to kill," he says softly. "It never occurred to us that we had also turned you into bait."

The day is growing late, dusk falling over the terrace. A bird caws in the distance, a sad cry that echoes the tragic past my father and Darya's have lived.

"Would you object to me telling Darya this story?" I ask him.

"No." Sergei shakes his head and lights another cigarette, his hand shaking slightly. "It's probably better if you do the telling."

"I will also need to speak to Alexei." I meet his sharp look calmly. "We need to decide what to do. This is no longer your decision, Sergei. It's ours."

He draws on his cigarette, then nods reluctantly. "I accept that."

"Good." I pour us both another glass, and we clink them together, drinking a silent toast to that decision.

"You never told Vilnus Orlov that my father hid a key. Not even when they tortured your wife and your children. You never told Alexei there even was a key—and you never told him about the one that Rosa hid." I glance at Sergei curiously, but he stares straight ahead, his face as inscrutable a mask as his damn son's. "It was Rosa herself who finally told Alexei the truth, first when she came through the tunnels, and later when she told him where the key was. You never betrayed her secret, even when it could have saved you and your children."

Still he doesn't speak.

"You had no reason to protect me all those years. You didn't believe that I was alive. You thought you'd seen my ashes beside my father's."

Sergei flinches, his eyes closing briefly at the mention of my father.

"That means there was someone else you were protecting." I clip the end of a cigar and light it, watching the smoke curl into the fading day. "How long have you loved Rosa?" I ask conversationally.

Sergei's head snaps around, his eyes blazing into mine. Then he swallows hard, clasps his hands, and turns away from me. It all happens in a second. As quickly as his emotions betray him, he regains control.

I know that trick. I've done it myself a time or two.

"I see the way you and Rosa look at each other." I swallow more vodka and pour us both another glass. "Not to mention the way the two of you fight. People only fight like that with those they care for deeply." I grin. "I should know. I've fought with your daughter like that since the day we met."

He clears his throat uncomfortably. "This isn't appropriate—" he begins.

"You married Maria to keep her safe," I cut him off. "But that wasn't because you were in love with her, was it, Sergei? It was because you knew it would make my mother happy to know her friend was safe."

When he doesn't immediately answer, I glance sideways. It's hard to be certain, but I suspect the red tinge on his cheeks has nothing to do with the rose-colored sky.

"Maria and I had a good marriage," he says solidly. "She was a lovely person. We were blessed with beautiful children."

I stifle a smile. "I have no doubt you made her very happy." I glance at him again, but he stares stubbornly straight ahead, refusing to meet my eyes. "That doesn't change how you feel about my mother. Did it happen before or after my father died?"

Sergei rounds on me at that, his eyes flashing. "Don't ever suggest such a thing to me again," he says, his voice shaking with anger. "Your mother is the most honorable woman I know. She would never have betrayed Aleksander like that. Neither of us would."

I incline my head in apology and don't ask anything more. A few moments pass, then Sergei turns to me.

"I met Rosa before your father did." His voice is hoarse. I'm almost certain he has never spoken of this to anyone. "She worked at a dressmaker's near Aleksander's shop. I went in to have a suit mended, and we began talking." He looks away, clasping his hands in front of him. "We talked all night," he says slowly. "In the end she locked the shop and made tea, and we talked until the sun came up. And then I left and never went back."

I turn to him in surprise. His eyes, when they meet mine, are resigned. "The next time I met her was a year later—when your father introduced her to me as the woman he planned to marry."

I digest this in silence, the tip of my cigar glowing in the dusk. After a while, I say, "It was Paris, wasn't it? The reason you left and didn't go back."

He doesn't answer, but I know by the hard line of his mouth that I'm right. *He couldn't risk loving deeply again, not after the way it had ended the first time.* I understand that. I'm not sure I could either, if I ever lost Darya.

I suppress a shudder.

"And afterward," I say, "when you met her the second time, it was too late. You wouldn't do anything to hurt my father." I look at him curiously. "Did you and my mother ever discuss this again?"

"No," Sergei says shortly. "It would not have been . . . right."

"Well, I think that's bullshit." I draw on my cigar, ignoring the sudden, lethal stillness that betrays his tension. "More than twenty years have passed since my father died. It's been a decade or more since Maria died. Neither you or my mother are getting any younger. And I doubt either of your children wish you anything but happiness."

Sergei presses his lips together. His fingers are clasped tightly in front of him, and he stares straight ahead, his face still inscrutable.

"I know something about avoiding love." I smile wryly at him. "Up until pretty recently, I was determined to outrun it. But if the past few months have taught us all anything, Sergei, it's that love is the only thing that really matters. Even for men like us." I tilt my head. "And if you ever remind me I said that, I will be forced to shoot you."

He gives a huff of laughter.

I stand up, crushing my cigar in the ashtray by his chair. "You weren't to blame for my father's death, Sergei," I say quietly. "No more than you, or my mother, were to blame for what happened to me. I'm not a priest, and you never asked for my forgiveness." I put my hand out. "But for what it's worth, you have it."

He puts his hands on the arms of the wicker chair and pushes himself to standing. "I've been practicing," he says wryly, seeing my surprise. "I will not be so feeble that I cannot walk my own daughter down the aisle." He puts his hand out and grips mine. "I thank you, Roman Alexandervitch," he says simply. "Your father would be proud of the man you have become, just as I am grateful that my daughter is marrying such a man."

"It is I who am grateful, Sergei Naryshkin," I say formally. "I will always protect your daughter. I want you to know that."

He nods once. "I do."

I leave him there on the terrace and slip back inside.

Much later, when I am heading upstairs to find Darya, I notice my mother sitting in the chair I recently vacated, watching the night grow with Sergei.

DARYA

I watch my brother's car snake up the mountain road toward the finca and try to still my pulse rate.

I know my brother did what he thought was best, just as my father did. I'm glad that Roman has come to peace with them both.

And yet, despite my public stance, privately I'm still not entirely happy with either my father or Alexei.

Roman, knowing how much I've been dreading this reunion, has taken Rosa and the children to the penthouse for the day, giving Papa and me time to meet Alexei in private. It's a break with Russian tradition for him, as head of the house, not to greet Alexei on arrival, but one I'm grateful for. This is a meeting best done without an audience. Alexei has clearly reached the same conclusion, going by the minimal security presence following his car at a discreet distance. Lars will be here in time for the wedding.

Papa stands beside me, leaning heavily on his cane, tense and still as the car draws to a halt. He refused to make this first meeting from the comfort of his chair.

I didn't argue. On some matters, my father is not to be defied.

Alexei, to my surprise, has driven himself. He steps out, the myriad of old scars on his grim, unsmiling face gleaming smooth in the sunlight. But it isn't his face that I can't stop staring at. It's his hand on the car door.

Or rather, the tattoo on his hand.

The Orlov sparrow is still there. But now the red wings drip blood, and rising behind them are another set, these made of vivid gold. A double eagle head looms above the sparrow, talons holding the other bird like broken prey.

The symbolism is brutal—and undeniable: the Romanov crest, the symbol of the old-world treasures our family has guarded so carefully, triumphant over the broken power of the Orlovs.

"Darya." Alexei says my name quietly. He inclines his head in my direction, but makes no move to embrace me. "I am glad to see you are well."

"And I you, brother." This strange, stiff exchange is nothing like the family ease I grew up with. Even more than back at the ballroom, my brother seems like a stranger to me. "Please." I gesture at the open door in welcome. "Come in."

But Alexei isn't looking at me. His eye, still shielded behind the glasses, is locked on Papa. His jaw is clenched hard, but I can see the faint flicker of tension beneath his silver scars, sense the emotion he's fighting to keep hidden.

"*Otets.*" His voice is gravelly, and he doesn't move toward Papa, just stares at him from behind his glasses. "*Ty vyglyadish' zdorovym.*" *You look healthy.*

I remember, with a faint shock, that this is the first time Alexei has seen Papa since the night we fled Miami.

Papa nods at him, his face grave. *"Ya rad tebya videt, syn moy."* *I am happy to see you, my son.*

Neither moves to approach the other. Papa's eyes roam over Alexei. I notice the small signs of tension in his old form: the hard set to the rangy shoulders, the stiff set to his jaw. Papa is doing a good job of hiding his shock at his son's appearance, but it's there.

Part of me has wanted this, to see Papa forced to confront the impact of his decisions, just as I've also wanted to see Alexei hesitant and apologetic before me. But now that the moment of reckoning is here, the hard core of resentment I've carried for so long just washes away, overwhelmed by a salty, trembling wave of love and compassion.

Whatever pathways have led to this moment of reconciliation, my brother and I have both traveled them in darkness, forced to grow up amid danger and hostility, fearing every moment might be our last.

If there is any lesson to take from those dark years, it's that life is too short, and those we love too precious, to hold on to past grievances. The old ties no longer bind any of us. Those who sought to hold us captive to the past are dead, defeated, or both. We might be family, but that is no longer a curse we have to live under. We've all earned our freedom.

Now we must learn what it means to be a family united by love, rather than by pain.

I step forward and walk slowly down the steps toward my brother's tense figure. "Alexei," I say softly, opening my arms. "Thank you for saving our children."

His face tightens, his entire form stiffening. "Never thank me for that," he says roughly, almost recoiling from me.

"I understand." I know the guilt he must feel at being forced to hold children captive in the same way we were ourselves. In the same place that he has been held and tortured all these years.

I take the final step toward him, placing my hands on the rangy shoulders so like Papa's. "Then let me thank you for helping Papa and me escape." I reach out and take his glasses off, revealing the fierce emotion swirling in the dark blue eye. "For staying and enduring all you did under the Orlovs. And most of all, Alexei, thank you for surviving what most men never could —and for saving our family legacy."

I wrap my arms around his neck. For a long time, he doesn't move, just stands stiffly in my embrace, his body a hard board held away from mine.

Then, finally, I feel his arms tentatively circle me.

For a brief moment we stand very still, simply readjusting to the new people we both are. Then Alexei's arms fall and he steps back, his jaw clenched tightly against whatever emotion he has learned to suppress. His eye slides to Papa, and he passes me to mount the steps, saving Papa the indignity of trying to navigate them with his cane.

He halts a few steps from where Papa stands, his back to me. Papa props his cane against the stone pillar. "*Syn moy*," he says in a low voice, gripping Alexei's hand. *My son.* "I am honored to be your father." Papa speaks in Russian, not trying to hide the emotion in his eyes. "But I also regret the pain and suffering my name has caused you to witness."

I can't see Alexei's face, but when he speaks, there is a wry twist to his Russian words. "*Glaza boyatsya, a ruki delayut.*"

The eyes are afraid, but the hands do.

Tears spring to my eyes. I remember my father saying those words to my brother years ago, when Alexei was small. It was the saying he used to encourage Alexei to leap from the high diving board or ride a horse for the first time. I realize I haven't heard Papa say it since the night we ran, when he was forced to leave my brother behind.

I stay long enough to see the savage rush of emotion animate the hard lines of Papa's face, his sudden surge of strength as he draws his son into a crushing embrace.

Then I slip back inside the finca, leaving father and son on the portico, bound by love, honor, and the burden of the lethal legacy they have both endured so much to carry.

"I AM TRULY sorry we kept so much from you." Alexei almost smiles at me. It is later in the afternoon, and the three of us are sitting around the small table out on the terrace. It's littered with a half-empty bottle of vodka, a samovar of tea, and an overflowing ashtray next to Papa that I'm trying not to glare at.

Smiling once came easily to my younger brother. Now, I've realized, his smile is a deeply hidden thing, as are all his emotions. His stillness is almost disturbing at times, as if he could fade into the stonework on the terrace itself, like a human chameleon. But if I find his camouflage disturbing, I've also felt his eye on me more than once, digesting the changes I'm sure he finds equally jarring. It happens again as I speak in response to his apology.

"I understand why you felt it was safer to keep some things from me." I look between them. "I'm not saying I agree with it, but I understand you thought that your silence would keep me safer, especially if the Orlovs caught me again. But things have changed now." I feel Alexei's gaze resting on me, assessing my tone, the confidence with which I speak. I know he is seeing a different person than the fragile sister he grew up with. "We are none of us what we once were, back when Papa and I fled Miami. So I guess what I want to know is what happens now?"

Papa and Alexei exchange a glance. I feel a familiar surge of annoyance. "I think," I say stiffly, "that I've earned the right to be included in our family decisions."

Papa inclines his head. "I am no longer *pakhan* of our family, *docha*. The decisions regarding what is said, and to whom, belong with your brother now."

"Fine." I turn to Alexei. "Then maybe *you* can tell me what happens now."

His face is the inscrutable mask I am beginning to dread, but he doesn't dodge my question. "I know the Orlov operation inside and out. It's going to take time for me to cut loose the parts of their business I don't want." His mouth tightens. "The trafficking in girls and drugs, just for starters."

I wince. I should have known the Orlovs were deep into the sewers of our world.

"Lars and I have been working on a few online projects, which is where I want to steer the Petrovsky clan." He glances between Papa and me. "I also want to keep the Petrovsky name," he says quietly. "I think it is . . . wiser to keep the Naryshkin story a mystery." He smiles wryly. "Mystery has power, for one thing. And there's still no way of explaining the fortune in tsarist Russian treasures beneath our house that won't bring a horde of federal investigation down on our heads. None of us need that kind of attention."

He shoots me a sideways look. "I had a brief discussion with your husband-to-be before I came here."

I stifle a rather childish impulse to roll my eyes, but my annoyance must be plain, because a fleeting grin touches Alexei's mouth, there and gone so fast I might have imagined it. "Don't go getting all butthurt, Dar," he says. The use of my childhood nickname, and the casual way he talks, takes me back to childhood with a jolt so sweet that it chokes my protests.

"If you are in agreement," he goes on, "Roman and I would like us all to open the vault together, after the wedding. He and I . . . well, we'd both like to continue the work our fathers started." Alexei's eye settles on Papa. "I understand that all of the pieces inside the vault are clearly marked," he says quietly, "with the family name and last known descendant?"

Papa nods, his eyes a brilliant, hard blue of both pride and pain.

"Between us, Roman and I have considerable investigative powers." Alexei's lips twitch. "We also have Lance Ryder, whose skills we plan to put to good use."

I give a surprised laugh. "You're going to work with that little . . ." I catch myself just in time. "With that horrible paparazzi pond scum?"

Alexei tilts his head. "Paparazzi scum are much more useful working for us than against us. Ryder has had his fortunes restored, and we're about to give him enough juicy gossip to keep him well fed for years. Not to mention that his own suspicions have finally been proven correct, which I think he found even more satisfying than the enormous check we gave him. Now he can follow the redistribution of the Naryshkin treasures, but always treat it as some kind of mystery, as if he doesn't know where it's coming from. Write about the conspiracy, but never really confirm it."

"Smart." Papa nods. He frowns. "But still dangerous. Are you and Roman certain you want this responsibility, Alexei?"

My brother looks at me. "Roman said it was your decision, Darya." By the rather tight note in his voice, I take it my brother didn't particularly like this stipulation.

But it makes my heart seize with joy.

Roman trusts me. He understands that I need to be a part of this, to have a voice in whatever decisions we make.

The comfort that gives me is a warm, beautiful thing in my chest, yet another confirmation that the man I love understands me in a way nobody ever has.

"Roman said that he will support whatever you decide." Alexei's voice is still hard. "If you would prefer the entire treasure be donated to a museum, we can make that happen. Or if you wish the vault to remain closed, Roman said he will abide by that, too." There's no mistaking his tension on the last sentence.

"No." I shake my head. "I don't want to donate it. And I certainly don't want the vault to remain closed." I shiver involuntarily. "I don't ever want us to be held hostage by that vault again. Thank you for agreeing to abide by my wishes. Fortunately, they align with yours and Roman's." I reach across the table and briefly touch my brother's hand. I don't miss the way he flinches, then forces himself to relax.

My brother is not accustomed to being touched, or at least, not with affection.

I'm not sure that will ever stop breaking my heart.

"I want to honor our grandfathers' promises, too." I glance at Papa, who is watching us with a quiet pride that spreads warmth through my heart. "Do you think there are still descendants to be found?"

Papa nods. "I know there are. I have some names that will help. But not today. Today, I wish us to drink tea together and to speak of my daughter's wedding." Leaning forward, he gently covers one of Alexei's hands, and then one of mine, with his own. The late-afternoon sun mellows the lines on his face, highlighting the deep emotion he doesn't try to hide. "Because, my beautiful children, family is the reason we fight—and the only prize worth fighting for."

43

ROMAN

Two days before the wedding, Lars Andersson arrives.

"Jesus." Abby whistles aloud, staring in open amazement from the terrace as she watches him climb out of the car below. "He's a fucking Viking."

I'm no connoisseur of the male form, but even I can see what she means. Lars is about as far from the typical tech geek as it's possible to get.

"Hey," Dimitry says in mock protest, pulling her against him. "Leave the poor man alone. No way is he equipped to handle the likes of you."

"Oh, and you are?" Abby rolls her eyes and elbows him, but she's smiling. I see Darya watching them covertly from a distance, her eyes glowing. If I'm honest, I'm as glad as she is to see Abby and Dimitry slowly getting back to their normal banter. Oddly, given my rather difficult history with Abby, I find myself liking her a lot more these days, especially after the loyalty and bravery she showed that night at Pillars. Gregor told me privately that if it wasn't for her, they'd likely all be dead. She might, I suspect, have a far more colorful past than even Darya is aware of, but she's one tough cookie under pressure.

"You'll have to fight Mickey for Lars, Abs," I say, grinning at her. "He's been fangirling over Andersson since he was a kid. Probably got a poster on his wall somewhere—ouch." I wince as Mickey lands a hefty blow to my ribs. "Well, should we go and meet your hero?"

He shakes his head. "If you call him that while I'm around, I swear to God, Roman . . ." He leaves the threat unfinished.

"You'll what?" I tease him. "Beat me with your mainframe?"

"Please don't try to use technical terms," Mickey says in a pained voice. "I'm embarrassed *for* you." We keep up the banter as we head downstairs, where I find Lars rather surprisingly, given his recent arrival, already stripped to his waist and on a sun lounger next to Ofelia. He's sporting lurid pink shorts, a ridiculously ripped torso, and an extremely impressive tan for a Scandinavian computer geek. Alexei stands on Ofelia's other side, clad as ever entirely in black. Apart from their identical blond, blue-eyed coloring, I can't imagine two more different men. In direct contrast to Alexei's perpetually grim-faced demeanor, Lars is all easy smiles and openness. To my surprise, Ofelia is actually laughing at something Lars has said, her cheeks slightly pink beneath the broad brim of her hat.

Seeing the two of them, Alexei as silent and deadly as any of the darkest killers I've encountered, and Lars like some kind of Norse god, on either side of my eldest daughter fills me with a dread I'm nowhere near ready to deal with.

"Andersson." I put my hand out, and Lars leaps up from the lounger with athletic ease and a broad smile to take it.

"Good to put a face to the legend," he says, shaking my hand enthusiastically. Then his eyes light on Darya, and his whole face splits into an even wider smile. Dropping my hand with an

ADHD-speed attention shift, he turns to her. "Dars!" He wraps her in a massive hug, almost lifting her off the ground. "It's good to see you, girl!"

"You're enormous," she says, laughing. "When did you get so big? Put me down, you idiot." Their familiarity is obvious. If anyone else touched Darya like that, he'd likely lose an eye, but Lars is difficult to take offense to. He has a loose-limbed, casual affection that seems to put everyone instantly at ease.

Even me, and that's rare.

"Your brother kept telling me we'd have a war on our hands," he's saying to her now, "so I thought I better get in shape in case someone took a swing at me."

"Don't tempt me," Alexei says. He's almost smiling. If it wasn't obvious before how close he and Lars are, it certainly is now. I don't think I've ever seen the fucker smile, let alone crack a joke.

Aware that Mickey is hanging back, I step aside and draw him forward. "I think you already know my son, Mickey."

Lars's eyes widen, and he drops Darya with the same sudden attention shift he dropped my hand.

"Mickey!" He leaps forward, wrapping Mickey in an even bigger bear hug than he did Darya. Mickey's look of utter shock is so comical I have to bite my lips together to stop myself laughing.

This guy is literally impossible not to like.

"You, my friend, are an absolute rock star." Lars stands back, his hands still gripping Mickey's shoulders, and pins him with what I imagine he thinks is a very serious look. "We will do big things together, Mickey Stevanovsky. Very big things."

Mickey's eyes are shining like he's just been told he's flying to the fucking moon. "I have so many questions," he begins. "You know that first trojan? What did you—"

"Oh, no, you don't." I step in between them. "Before you two start geeking out, I've got a few things I need to talk to Lars and your uncle Alexei about." I tilt my head toward the house. "Got a minute?"

I'll say this for Lars: the ADHD shift works both ways. He shifts to serious mode in a New York second, pulling on a shirt and heading for the house with Alexei. I'm halfway to the door when I glance back to find Mickey staring longingly after us.

"Hey," I say nonchalantly. "What are you doing, waiting for an invitation?"

His eyes widen in shock. Then, gathering himself with remarkable alacrity, he straightens up, squares his shoulders, and strides off across the tiles, for all the world as if he never doubted I'd ask him to join us.

I glance across the pool, to where Sergei is sitting beside Rosa, a pitcher of something that looks suspiciously like a vodka cocktail on the table between them. I raise an eyebrow in silent question. He gives me a small smile and the faintest shake of his head. It's a subtle gesture, but one I find poignant nonetheless.

There's no hint of regret in the slight movement, no suggestion that he should join us in my study.

Sergei has lived long enough to see what most men dream of: his son take over his business. Now he is free to sit by the pool, laughing as he tosses the ball to Masha in the water, making her giggle.

All men should be so lucky.

I turn back toward the house, Mickey's back ahead of me. He's almost as tall as I am now and rapidly filling out. He's already been forced to take a life to protect his family.

Sergei might have passed the torch to his son and me. But soon enough, sooner than I like to think about, it will be me handing my torch on to Mickey.

I glance over at Darya, her hand resting protectively on the soft swell of her belly.

It fills me with a quiet sense of comfort to know that whatever the future holds, our child will have the protection and love of a brother like Mickey.

I CLOSE the door of the study behind us, and the noise of the day disappears. I've had it renovated recently and made entirely secure. The study here is far more comfortable than the one in my office, or even my penthouse. Darya and I are planning to make the finca our chief residence, rather than the penthouse in Malaga. It's where we're at our happiest.

I nod at Mickey, and he pours the obligatory glasses of vodka. I raise my glass. "To family," I say, in Russian.

The other men meet my eyes. "To family."

I drink, watching Mickey out of the corner of my eye. He does a good job of not wincing as he swallows the vodka. I do a good job of not laughing at him.

I wait until we're all seated on the leather armchairs around a low coffee table before sliding an envelope across to Alexei.

"I wanted to offer you a piece of Mercura," I say without preamble. "From what Mickey tells me, you not only strengthened the entire platform, but also made sure Fedorov got nowhere near it. Mercura is secure and thriving, thanks to you both." I tap the envelope. "This gives you a seat at the table and a decent cut of the profits. I know what it's like pulling an organization out of a war. Your cut of Mercura should help."

Alexei and Lars exchange a look, then Alexei takes the envelope. "Thank you," he says quietly, putting his hand out. "You won't regret this."

"I know that." I grip his hand briefly, then settle back in my armchair. "You've already met Mak. You'll meet some of the other board members at the wedding." I crack a smile. "Those are the ones I'd call friends, or at least good acquaintances. Others I prefer to keep as far away from my family as humanly possible. I'll send you a brief on them all regardless. We don't engage in board meetings on a regular basis, for reasons I'm sure you both understand."

Lars smiles at that. "You mean like giving intelligence services across six continents a serious hard-on?"

I grin. "Something like that, yes."

I turn to Alexei. "I understand that you discussed the opening of the vault with Darya and Sergei and came to agreement?"

He nods.

"Good. I propose that we set up a small team, drawn from both of our organizations, to oversee the return of the pieces inside the vault. A sort of task force, if you will."

"That's a good idea." Alexei's eyes narrow. "I don't want that fucker Lance Ryder on it, though. He can consult, but I want him on a very short leash."

"Agreed," I say readily. "Frankly, the further that prick stays away from us all, the happier I'll be."

"After what went down with Orlov," he says, "I'm still operating on very limited numbers. While we set up the next phase of business, I'm going to need my brigadiers close. Have you got anyone you'd trust to oversee this task force?"

I clip the end off a cigar and offer them both one, which they both accept and Mickey wisely declines. "I'd like to give it to Dimitry, with your agreement. He's been my right hand for years now, and I trust him as a brother. It's time he was given a piece of the business to run. This would be a good place to start."

"I'm happy with that." Alexei leans forward so I can light his cigar. "Dimitry seems like a good man." The brief flare of the flame highlights the brutal scars on his face. There seems barely an inch of skin untouched.

Not for the first time, I silently thank all the gods that my daughters made it out of that sadistic fucker Orlov's grasp.

"I assume you two have projects of your own in the works?" I glance between Lars and Alexei.

"Yep." Lars gives me that big smile. "Actually, I was going to ask if I can borrow your man here over next summer." He nods at Mickey, who does a masterful job of not turning excited somersaults. "We'll be launching a platform of our own by then. It would be good exposure for him." His grin widens. "Not to mention a hell of a lot of fun."

I don't need to look at Mickey to know just how much he wants this. I scratch my head and pretend to ponder the question for far longer than is necessary, given that my answer is a complete no-brainer.

No harm in making the kid squirm.

"I can spare Mickey from Mercura for a summer," I say casually. "Up to him how he chooses to spend his time, though."

Lars turns to him with raised eyebrows. "What do you think, kid? Want to come and see how real men work?"

Alexei snorts.

Mickey swallows hard in an effort to maintain his composure. "Yes," he manages. "I—yes. That would be—Thank you, Mr. Andersson." He puts his hand out, and Lars shakes it, grinning.

"This is gonna be fun. Speaking of which, I've got something I wanted to show you." He's already halfway to the door when he remembers that we're still sitting. "If you're finished here, that is," he says. I wave them out, unable to hide my smile. This is, without competition, the best day of Mickey's life to date.

Alexei waits until the door has closed behind them before speaking again. "There's something else I wanted to talk to you about." Something in his voice sets my nerves tingling. His face is dark and shuttered again, any trace of his former humor gone. "I made sure Vilnus Orlov took a long time to die. I wanted to be sure I'd extricated anything that might be of use from him before I sent him to hell."

The thought of Orlov writhing in agony is one of the most satisfying I've had in a very long time. And by the cold, deadly tone of Alexei's voice, it was a job he took extremely seriously. The flat darkness in his lone eye almost makes me shiver, and I'm a man who has seen a lot of death.

"Before I gave him the final cut of the knife, Orlov let something interesting slip." He hands me a piece of paper. "Vilnus Orlov wasn't the only child who was given refuge in Ilyan Fedorov's home."

I absorb the name on the paper, trying not to let my shock show.

"I thought you should know."

I nod slowly, not quite trusting myself to speak. To my relief, Alexei doesn't ask questions. He stands and touches my shoulder briefly. "We'll talk soon, brother."

He closes the door behind him, and I'm left staring at the details on the paper, slowly piecing things together in my mind.

44

ROMAN

The parking lot of the Alhaurin prison in Malaga has only a few scattered cars. I'm here outside visiting hours and during siesta.

I pass through security without difficulty and am shown to a bare concrete room. I don't have to wait long before the door opens again. The guard sits Yuri down on a chair, then leaves, closing the door behind him.

"Roman. This is an unexpected pleasure."

Yuri's smile is tinged with unease. He knows something is off.

"I thought you didn't like to draw attention to our association." He sits back in his chair and lights a cigarette, staring at me through calculating eyes as the smoke curls between us. "Isn't that what you said last time you visited me? And yet here you are, outside visiting hours and in a private room, no less. Hardly subtle, *moy syn.*"

"I'm not your son."

"No." His smile fades completely, his eyes going flat and cold. "My son is dead. Both of my sons, in fact."

"Mikhail is dead because of a war you started. Nikolai is dead because he trusted you. If you want someone to blame, Yuri, then look in the fucking mirror."

He stares at me for a long moment. His cigarette burns down in his hand, the ash eventually falling unnoticed to the floor.

I take out a bottle of Graf vodka and pour two glasses. I push his across the table. "What shall we drink to?" I tilt my head to one side. "To health? No, that doesn't feel right. To family?" I grimace and shake my head. "No. Because we've never really been family, Yuri, have we? Wait. I know." I pick up my glass. "Let's drink to truth." I touch his glass with my own. "*Za pravdu.*" I raise my glass to my lips.

Yuri doesn't move. His face is pale. He stares at me across the table, cigarette forgotten in his hand. "Drink," I snarl.

He drinks.

I pour us both another vodka and push the packet of cigarettes across the table toward him. He wants to ignore them, but despite the dead ash of his last one still in his hand, he's unable to disguise the greed in his eyes. I feel a sudden, savage twist of hard contempt.

"Go ahead," I say agreeably. "Why do we work, if not to enjoy these little luxuries, Yuri? Isn't that what you used to tell Mikhail and me?"

He winces as if he's been struck.

You were never the man I wanted you to be. The man Mikhail and I needed you to be.

"You know," I say conversationally, taking the old cigarette out of his hand and lighting the fresh one for him, "the thing I just couldn't understand was how Ilyan Fedorov knew that Darya and Rosa were in London."

Yuri's eyes are locked on mine, but even now they slide sideways, as if he's still trying to think of a way out of this.

As if there could ever be a way out of this.

"There was no digital trail of their whereabouts," I go on. "Mak and I worked through every member of our teams, interrogating each man, but our operation was watertight. Eventually, I had to let it go. But it bothered me, Yuri. You know the other thing that bothered me?" I nod at the vodka on the table in front of him. "Drink."

He drinks.

"Vera."

Yuri visibly jumps at the name, as if he's been given an electric shock.

"The man guarding Vera was shot. At first, we assumed he had been taken out by Fedorov's men, but that wasn't the case. The bullet came from Vera's gun."

Yuri draws on his cigarette, his eyes never leaving my face.

"Your wife shot her own guard, the man who had been sent to keep her safe. And then, showing a very uncharacteristic disregard for her own safety, she went downstairs to directly confront a deadly enemy who had invaded her home. Quite the show of heroism, isn't it, for a woman who, to my knowledge, had never wielded anything more deadly than a credit card?"

Yuri licks his lips, his eyes sliding sideways, then to the floor, before coming back to mine.

"As if all of that wasn't enough," I say, "Vera then proceeded to shoot her own daughter-in-law. Without question. Without hesitation of any kind. She just pointed her gun at Inger's head and blew it half off."

Yuri blanches. His eyes drop to the empty vodka glass.

"By all means." I refill his glass, and he gulps the contents before the bottle has even returned to the table, his hand shaking. I stare at him, wondering how I ever thought this man was powerful.

But did I ever truly think that? I wonder. As I have every moment since Alexei handed me a name on a piece of paper, I remember the long-ago words of Zinaida Melikov, the Russian heiress who murdered her father: *Most of all, you should ask yourself: why did Yuri take you in? What does he have to gain?*

"Vera told us she shot Inger out of grief. It sounded plausible enough. Vera is an old woman who had already lost one son. Now her other son was dead, seemingly betrayed by her own daughter-in-law. That's enough to send anyone over the edge into insanity, right?"

Yuri doesn't answer. I pour him another glass. His eyes are slightly glassy. He stares at the vodka, but doesn't touch it.

"Drink," I say calmly.

He does.

"Then I listened to the accounts of all the people who were there that day. I couldn't play the audio back because it wasn't recorded, but between Darya, Rosa, and Sergei, I got a pretty accurate account of Inger's last words. Would you like to know what they were, Yuri?"

He doesn't move, just stares at me.

"Inger said, and I quote: *You said he'd be safe.*

"Of course, everybody assumed she was talking to Fedorov. But Fedorov was already dead by then. Sergei was unconscious on the floor. The only two people alive and conscious outside that room were Inger and Vera. We all assumed Inger's last words were a result of her grief and confusion, that she was talking to a dead Fedorov in a moment of madness.

"But it bothered me, Yuri. I'm stubborn like that. Wouldn't Vera be just as angry at Fedorov as Inger? Wouldn't that make them allies, rather than enemies? It was a loose end. One which made no sense at all. Then Vera disappeared, right in the middle of our investigation. Went to a health spa in the Swiss Alps. No phone reception, no internet. Said she needed to 'heal.' Do you know what Switzerland is famous for, Yuri? Apart from banks, chocolate, and watches, of course. I'll give you a guess. No? Fine. I'll help you out."

I pour myself a glass of vodka. "Switzerland is famous for refusing to extradite its citizens. Now, I know what you're going to say, Yuri: Vera holds passports for the UK and the US. Not Switzerland. Right?" I don't wait for him to answer. "Wrong. As I'm sure you're aware, your wife's first ever passport was issued in Switzerland. That was long before you met her, of course. The passport was issued for one Vera Peretz, a Jewish refugee from Poland. She was traveling with her 'father,' a man named Andras Peretz. Only Peretz was really Ilyan Fedorov. He used the orphaned daughter of one of his own murdered captains to help with his new identity when he entered the US. After all, people have a lot more sympathy for a man with a young daughter, don't they?"

I toss off my vodka and push Yuri's toward him. "Drink," I say quietly.

He almost chokes as he swallows it. Eyes watering, he stares at me.

"Vera Peretz owed Ilyan Fedorov everything. He saved her life and gave her the best of everything—including an adoptive brother." I lean forward, clasping my hands on the table in front of me. Yuri's nostrils flare, his every muscle tense. "Do you know how Nikolai described Vilnus Orlov, right before I put a bullet through his head?"

He makes a small, impotent noise, like a trapped, wounded animal.

I smile coldly. "Nikolai described Orlov as a *friend of the family*. The words stuck in my head, Yuri. I've been part of your family for almost two decades, and I've never once heard of Vilnus Orlov being a family friend. And I would have known. If I'd ever heard so much as a whisper of that fucking name, I'd have been gone from your household before you had time to pull a gun. But you were always very careful, weren't you, to keep that little secret? Just like Vera never disclosed the reason she hated my presence at her table, in her family."

"We didn't know." He rasps the words in a pathetic protest, the panic starting to spread across his eyes. "We weren't sure—"

"But you suspected, Yuri, didn't you?" I cut him off coldly. "Or rather, Vera did. Vera might have been long gone from her adoptive father's home, but she was still in touch with him. She'd been raised knowing about the Naryshkin treasure, the great wealth that her parents had been killed for, that had been stolen from her adoptive father. And then suddenly, out of the blue, I turn up. A homeless Russian boy named Roman, in Miami. The miracle is that she told you of her suspicions, rather than Ilyan himself, or even Vilnus. That's what happened, Yuri, wasn't it? She told you the story about the vault, about the missing boy her brother had been searching for all these years, and suddenly you realized that, quite by accident, you'd stumbled across a fucking gold mine.

"I remember being surprised when you invited me out onto your yacht after Mikhail had been shot. You'd already given me a fat envelope of cash. In my experience, men like you paid your debts, then considered matters settled. You barely looked at me the first time you met me. But a few days later . . . well. Suddenly, I was a hero. A second son. A man to whom you owed everything. Your son owed me his life, you said, and so my life was now your responsibility."

I shake my head. "And I was dumb enough to believe you," I say softly. "Lonely and desperate enough to truly believe you gave a fuck about me."

"Roman—"

"Don't," I say quietly. "Just fucking don't, Yuri. It's way too late. When was it that you became certain of who I was?"

He stares at me, body stiff, lips pressed together, as if he's actually considering not answering. Then he slumps back in his seat, lighting another cigarette, the fight seeping from his old, sagging body. "Not for a long time," he says dully. "I suspected. You had no identity, no past, and it was clear you weren't telling me the truth about your background. Then, you and Mikhail miraculously got funding for Hale. I knew nobody would have given you that kind of backing without surety of some kind. But in the end, it was Nikolai and Inger who pieced it together, with the help of some journalist."

"And all that time," I say, staring at him in contempt, "you could have told Fedorov. Or Orlov. But you wanted to take it all for yourself, Yuri, didn't you? You thought that you could play us all. You even suggested I take Inger as my wife after Mikhail died. It was only when you suspected Orlov was moving in that you told Inger the truth."

His mouth twists. "Inger was smart," he mutters, looking away. "Smarter than Nikolai."

"You thought you could use her to get what you wanted," I say. I'd laugh if it wasn't so pathetic. "But in the end, it was her who played you, although not to Orlov. She hated him, did you know that? He raped her several years ago. Even for someone without a conscience like Inger, rape isn't a crime you forgive. You were right about her being smart. Inger went to the one person you all overlooked: Vera."

Yuri spits on the floor and avoids my eyes.

"Vera hasn't been happy these past few years." Yuri sits in sullen silence as I speak. "Dependent on me for her credit card usage, confined to the London house. I never tried to constrain her spending. And that house is hardly a prison. But none of it was enough for Vera. She always liked the fine things in life, always wanted more. Maybe that's why she and Inger got along so well. Vera saw a way to ensure she had endless wealth for the rest of her days, and who knows—maybe, if Fedorov had succeeded, she would have. But I doubt it, Yuri. Fedorov was a cold, ruthless fuck.

"Which brings us to Nikolai." I sit back in my chair and pour two more glasses, sliding Yuri's across the table to him. "Do you know," I say meditatively, "I think Inger actually loved Nikolai? It makes sense, when you think about it. Inger was a narcissist. She needed constant affirmation that she was beautiful, lovable. Nikolai genuinely believed those things about her, was maybe the only person who did. She might not have been certain that you would prioritize Nikolai's life—after all, she lost Mikhail as a result of your wars. But she did trust Vera. And who knows? Maybe Vera genuinely thought that Fedorov wouldn't harm her son."

I swallow the vodka, relishing the burn as it slides down my throat. I don't feel remotely inebriated. The alcohol simply clarifies every word I'm saying, each piece of the puzzle gleaming cold and hard as ice in my mind.

"Drink," I say coldly.

Yuri does.

"Your wife is safe."

His head jerks up, his eyes narrowing.

Is it really possible that he still thinks there's hope for him?

"I hope she enjoys the Swiss spa, because she won't ever leave it. I've paid them an extremely generous amount to ensure she does not. Enough to hire an extremely good security team, which a good friend of mine will be providing. Vera will be made comfortable for the rest of her life. But her passports are gone, as are her bank accounts. In fact, Vera Stevanovsky officially died yesterday. There's even a funeral being held for her in London as we speak. Unfortunately, none of her grandchildren are able to attend, since they are still grieving the deaths of their mother and uncle. Everyone understands, of course."

Yuri's face crumples into a pinched, resentful scowl. "I had nothing to do with this. It was Vera—"

"*Yerunda*." I cut him off brutally. "That is bullshit, Yuri. You've been planning this for years. You know it, and so do I. But that all ends today. Your grandchildren will never know the truth of what you did; I will spare them that. They will grow up surrounded by love and honorable men. People who won't risk their lives or trade them to sadistic fucks for gain."

"And you truly believe that bullshit?" He sneers at me across the table, all trace of surrender gone. This is Yuri the vicious *pakhan*, who built a business on the back of girls and drugs, and held it through torture and intimidation. "You truly believe you can take care of business in our world with all that touchy-feely bullshit, Roman? The truth is that your family won't ever be safe. Not that Petrovsky slut you knocked up or the bastard she's carrying. Her father will take everything you have. And her brother is a psychopath, from what I hear—"

This time, my laugh is genuine. "It's funny you should mention psychopaths, Yuri." I pour us both a shot of vodka and cover them with my hand. "Another psychopath, Zinaida Melikov, gave me a piece of advice a long time ago. She said I should ask myself why you took me in, what you had to gain. Do you want to know what else she said, Yuri?"

He stares at me, white-faced and silent.

"She said I should kill you before you got me killed. She told me that weak men die—and take others down with them."

I slide his glass across the table. "Our world is dangerous, that much is true. But it is our job to protect our children from that world for as long as we can, and then to prepare them for it. That's what good men do, Yuri. Weak men get greedy, and then they get caught. They abandon their children to wars that aren't theirs and sell them out for money.

"Our world might be dark. It might be brutal. It might demand that we are able to be both brutal and dark when those things are required. But to survive that world, we need to be better than what surrounds us. Smarter. More honorable. We need to be a light that others follow, not the darkness that kills anything good."

His mouth twists in contempt. "You sound like a fucking preacher, Roman, not a *pakhan*."

I smile coldly. "You forget, Yuri. The Bible is the most brutal book there is. *An eye for an eye*, for example." I nod at his glass. "Drink."

He makes no move to take the glass. "Here?" he says skeptically, looking around the bare concrete walls. "You think you can kill me here and just walk away from it? There's no amount of money you could pay to make an entire prison guard look the other way. Weren't you the one telling me I needed to be more careful?"

"But that was you, Yuri." I touch the metal of my pistol, feel its comforting weight at my hip. "This is me, now. And I don't have to be careful. Not here. Not anywhere. I don't just own the guards. Or the warden. I own the men who own the prison. I own the men who they answer to. Let's just say that in five minutes, I will walk out of here, and an entire prison of people will swear under oath that they've never so much as heard my name, let alone laid eyes on me."

I nod at the glass again. "*Za pososhok*," I say quietly. *One for the road.*

Yuri grabs the glass and tosses off the vodka.

"My father always taught me that it's bad manners to offer a man a drink after that toast." I raise the pistol. "So I won't."

I walk out of the prison ten minutes later, Yuri's brains still sliding down the concrete wall.

Nobody says a fucking word.

45

DARYA

"Roman still not home?"

Evening has fallen when Abby joins me on the terrace. Masha is upstairs with Papa and Rosa. Ofelia is in her room. Mickey is somewhere with Lars and Alexei, staring at a computer screen. They seem to all speak the same language, one even Roman is excluded from.

"No." I take the peppermint tea she offers me gratefully. "I think he might . . . need some time to himself after today."

"I can't believe it was Yuri all this time. Or Vera, rather. Dimitry told me," she adds, seeing my discomfort. "But don't worry. I won't let it slip to the children."

"Thanks." I tilt my head to hers briefly. "I don't think they need to know, or not yet, at least. They've had more than enough to deal with."

"Not the greatest wedding present."

I laugh softly. "It's just our life, Abs. I know it must seem crazy to most people. But I was raised in the middle of it. It isn't crazy to me. It's just . . . life." I shrug. "Brutal. Dark, sometimes. But also proud. And loving."

"You're at home in it."

I turn to find Abby looking at me, her blue eyes dark. "This world," she adds. "You're comfortable in it, even knowing how dangerous and unpredictable it can be?"

"Yes," I say. "I guess I am. I'm not sure how good I'd be at the life most people lead. In all the years I lived on the outside, I never really felt like I belonged there. Sometimes I'd meet a man, go for a drink. I'd always wondered what that would be like, to have the freedom to date a normal guy, without security guards all around me and my father vetting his entire family. But the truth was, when I spent time with those men, it never felt right."

"Why?" She stares out over the low stone wall, sipping her wine as the Spanish night comes alive around us. Below, the ground lights turn the holm oaks into a fantasy forest, spread out beneath the high southern stars. I take Abby's hand and lead her over to the chairs, waiting until she's seated before answering her. Something tells me she is asking about more than just my experience.

"Do you remember that British guy, Oliver, who asked me out for a drink when I first started working at the café?"

Abby nods. "Lacoste guy."

I laugh. "Yep. Lacoste guy. Well, I was sitting at this beach-side bar he took me to, sipping a glass of wine. We were talking, the sun was setting; it was all going well. Then all of a sudden, a car backfired in the street beside us."

"Oh, shit." She looks sideways at me.

"Yep." I wrap my hands around my teacup and stare out across the valley. "Oliver didn't miss a beat. I don't think he would have even noticed the noise if I hadn't been so startled that I leaped up from my seat, tipping my glass over. While he was laughing and calling me cute, I was scanning every face for danger and trying to find the fastest exit. I didn't even stay until the end of my glass of wine. I realized that if there had been any real danger, Oliver would have had no chance of helping me. He'd have probably been casualty number one, to be honest. I guess that was the day I realized that normal guys weren't ever really going to be an option for me."

"But isn't it a self-fulfilling prophecy?" Abby is frowning, staring out at the night. "Like if you date danger, then danger finds you. What if you just choose not to put yourself in that environment in the first place?"

"I'm not sure how that works. I never had that option. I was born into the bratva." I shrug. "It's all I've ever known. And no matter what I do, I know that world will always find me. I guess in the end I've learned to embrace it, rather than trying to outrun it." I turn to her. "But you weren't born into it, Abs," I say quietly. "And if you want to walk away from it, you have every right to do that. What happened at Pillars would have rocked anyone."

She shakes her head. "It isn't what happened at Pillars," she says slowly. "It goes back a lot further than that. And I'm not sure I can walk away, any more than you can." Her eyes slide to mine, then away. She pours another glass of wine.

I wait.

"Six years ago," she says eventually, "I wound up in a Colombian prison."

I'm so taken aback, I almost fall off my chair. "You wound up . . . wow. What happened? You don't have to talk about it," I add hastily. "It's totally up to you."

"No. It's fine." Abby sips her wine. "I don't even know why I never told you, especially after everything you confided to me. I guess . . . I was ashamed, I think. I mean, your past is pretty glam, you know? Russian royalty, more or less. Hidden treasures and deathly secrets." She smiles ruefully. "Mine's a lot less fascinating, and a lot more predictable. Dumb, rebellious kid runs off with an unsuitable boyfriend against parental advice. Realizes early on she's made a mistake, but isn't ready to admit it, to herself or anyone else. Gets deeper and deeper into the mistake, until she suddenly realizes she's neck-deep in an illegal cocaine operation that stretches from Colombia to Thailand and Australia."

"Oh, Abby." I cover her hand with my own. "I'm so sorry. And I'm so sorry that I didn't know."

"How could you?" She lifts her shoulders and opens her hands, then lets them drop again. "I never told you. I never told anyone, not even my family. I didn't want my face splashed all over the Australian newspapers. I could just see the headline: 'Amphetamine Abby: How an Aussie Farm Girl Traded Cattle for Cartels.'"

"Abby!" I'm laughing despite myself. It's typical of my beautiful friend that even when she's telling the story of her own downfall, she has to make it humorous. She's laughing too, but she sobers quickly.

"Anyway. The end result was that my boyfriend tried to cheat the wrong people. He got dead; I got prison. And eventually, I got out of prison because I made a deal with the people my boyfriend cheated. Then I ran like hell and didn't stop until I got to Spain."

"God, you poor thing." I squeeze her hand, resisting the urge to go around and hug her. I know Abby well enough to know hugs aren't really her style, not when she's like this. "I wish I'd known. That I could have helped somehow. All this time, we were both running, and I never even knew."

"I never told anyone, until Dimitry." Her eyes cloud over. "He knew something was up the moment I pointed out the Colombians in Pillars that night. It also didn't help that Lance fucking Ryder had gotten a hint of the story. That prick has way too much time on his hands," she says, looking rather fierce.

"He didn't know everything, but he knew enough to be dangerous."

"I'm glad you told him."

"Yeah, well." Abby purses her lips. "The thing is, Dimitry thinks he's fucking invincible." She gives me a sideways look. "I know you guys are Russian, bratva hard-asses and all that. But you don't know what the Colombians are like, Darya. Believe me when I say they're every bit as dangerous as the Russians. And they never forget a betrayal."

"Wait." I look directly at her. "Do you mean you think they're still after you? I thought you said you made a deal?"

"I made a deal with the previous head of the cartel." She runs a hand over her face. "He's dead now. His son has taken over. It was the son my boyfriend actually cheated, hiding a stack of cocaine and lying about it. I told the father where to find some of it, but not all." She shrugs. "I don't know where the rest of it is. But the son never believed that. And even if he did, he has never forgiven the fact that my boyfriend embarrassed him. Those men who came into Pillars with Miguel, way back at the start of all this . . . they're part of that same cartel. I'm pretty sure one of them recognized me. Which means it's only a matter of time before someone comes looking for me. That's why I had to tell Dimitry. I was worried that he'd put a bullet through the wrong person and end up in the middle of my mess. I still am worried about that."

I nod, processing what she's said. "So you're not worried about being in danger because of Dimitry's world," I say tentatively. "You're worried about drawing him into yours?"

"God, I don't even know anymore." Abby takes a large mouthful of wine. "His world, my world—they're both just a shit show."

"So that's why you're going home? To give yourself a bit of breathing space?"

She takes another mouthful, and a long time to answer. "I

haven't been home since the day I ran off," she says eventually. "I sent my parents a postcard from Thailand a week after I landed there. All it said was, *Never coming back.*" She shoots me a rueful look. "I know, right? Super mature. After that, I never contacted them again. At first, I was just being stubborn. Then things got messy. Later, I was in prison, and there was no way I was dragging them into that fuckup. My super-conservative, sweet country parents from small-town Australia? No way in hell was I bringing them into any of this. And then, afterward, it just seemed too late. Too complicated. I guess I just thought they were better off without me."

"For *six years?*" I try and fail not to let my shock show. "Abby, there's no parent in the world who wants to lose their child for six years. I promise you that."

"I know." She glances at me. "Since I've seen you guys, the way you all are together . . . it's made me realize how precious family is. And Dimitry, he's never even had a family. I know I have to go home." She meets my eyes. "I'm just not sure I can bring Dimitry home with me," she says quietly. "I'm not sure how those two worlds meet, or even if I want them to. I can't imagine Dimitry there, amid cattle feed and branding, any more than I can imagine my mother knowing that her daughter used to deal cocaine. I also don't know if I can just go home to that world, go back to being the daughter they lost. But Dimitry is going to be busy for a while now, leading this task force to return all the stuff from the vault, so I guess there's never been a better time for me to find out. So—home I go. And I guess I'll find out if Abby Connelly can become Abigail Chalmers again."

"Wait." I stare at her in astonishment. "You mean you've been using a fake name all this time?"

She rolls her eyes. "I mean, it's not quite Lucia fucking Lopez, but yes. I have. That's why I never registered for residency here. My fake isn't quite the same standard as yours, unfortunately."

"Oh, sweet lord." I sit back in my chair, shaking my head, and then I start to laugh.

Once I start, I can't stop.

My laughter spirals, and after a minute, Abby snorts out her wine, which makes me laugh even more. Then we're both doubled over, howling with laughter until we're both weak.

"Oh, Abs." I straighten up, wiping my eyes. "We are the most ridiculous pair ever."

"And you're also my best friend in this entire world." She grips my hand, hilarity fading to seriousness. "I mean it, Darya. You're literally the only person who knows who I truly am. I don't ever want to lose that, no matter what decisions I make."

"You won't." I stand up and walk around the table, pulling her into a hug. We stay like that for a long time. "I don't care where you go or what you do, Abs," I whisper in her ear. "Just promise me you won't disappear."

She kisses my cheek. "I promise." Then she steps back and holds my face. "And I'm not going anywhere until after I see Roman put that ring on your finger. I threw Molotov cocktails at Russian *vor*. I'm pretty sure I've earned my bridesmaid's dress."

46

DARYA

Roman comes home not long after Abby and I have gone to our respective bedrooms. I'm coming out of the shower when he walks in the room. He stops still when he sees me, his eyes darkening. I reach for my robe and his hand shoots out, grasping my wrist.

"Don't."

I feel the familiar curl of lust spiral up from the base of my spine. "Isn't there some kind of rule against this?" I try not to shiver as he traces one finger down my neck, between my breasts. "We're getting married on Sunday."

Roman's lips curl into the sensual half smile that always has me aching for his mouth on my body. "I think it's a little late to concern ourselves with propriety, don't you, *milaia*?" His hand pauses on my swelling belly. "The real miracle is that your father isn't herding me to the altar with a shotgun."

"Speaking of shotguns." I cover his hand with my own, my eyes searching his face. "Yuri?"

He doesn't avoid my eyes, nor does he step away from me. "Dead."

I nod. "Are you—Was it difficult?"

"Difficult? No." Roman pulls me against him, his hands roaming over the curve of my ass. "It was justice. And now it's done." The hard length of him throbs against me through his jeans, eliciting an instant slick of moisture from my body.

"I want to fuck you." His voice is low with need, and I moan, pushing myself against him. "But before I do, there's something I need to ask you." He puts a hand under my chin, tilting my face up to his. "The children are Stevanovskys. They always will be, and I want them to be proud of that. But when I marry you, I want to do it under my own name. I want our child to know who he is and where he comes from." His eyes search mine. "So what do you say, Darya Petrovsky? Are you happy to be a Borovsky? I know it means you will have a different name than the children—"

"I don't need to share their name to love them." I wrap my arms around his neck. "And I want them to be proud of who they are. From what you've told me, Mikhail was like a brother to you. I want them to know who he was and to associate their name with honor, rather than with that treacherous snake Yuri."

Roman grins. "You're a savage little thing when you want to be, *milaia*, aren't you?"

"I am when it comes to the people I love." I touch his lips with my own, the briefest kiss, but enough to send flames through my body. "And I will be proud to take the Borovsky name," I whisper, trailing my lips down his neck, reveling in his husky groan as my tongue touches the soft place beneath his jaw. Then I pull back, frowning. "Wait."

Roman is already pulling off his T-shirt, eyeing my body hungrily. "Done waiting."

"Changing your name is going to take time. We've got less than two days—"

"Darya." He gives me a wry look as he throws his jeans over the chair. "I just killed a man in broad daylight in one of Spain's biggest prisons. Do you honestly think I'll have trouble getting my name changed on a Saturday?"

"Well, I guess when you put it like that—oh!" I gasp as he lifts me suddenly, wrapping my legs around his waist, and walks me toward the bed.

"You're so hot and wet."

I moan as he murmurs in my ear, his cock throbbing against my slick heat.

"I've been thinking about taking this pussy the entire way home."

I moan again as he pulls me hard against him, still standing, letting me writhe on his palms, squirming with the need to have him inside me.

"Give me your mouth, *milaia*." His kiss is as hot and urgent as his cock against me, driving all coherent thought from my mind. His big hands cradle my ass, his thumb slipping inside me as he kisses me on and on. He groans with satisfaction as he probes my hot depths, then runs his thumb up to my swollen bud. I cry out into his mouth, clinging to him as he strokes me closer and closer to the brink.

"Not yet." He lowers me to the bed, spreading my legs wide and positioning himself between them. His hand slips between us, and I gasp as his thumb presses me again, his long fingers manipulating my entire core. "I think you need my mouth here," he murmurs in my ear. My body leaps in response. He takes each nipple in his mouth as he passes them, making me buck beneath him. Then his mouth covers me, his clever tongue slips into the places only he can find, and my mind leaves the building.

My hands are in his hair, my hips arching off the bed. He

holds me firmly, tonguing me with the slow intensity that drives me insane, but never quite allowing me to reach the peak.

"Ah!" My cries are building with each pass of his tongue.

Then his mouth leaves me. "Oh! Roman!" I grasp for him, desperate with need.

"We need to soundproof this fucking room," he growls, and I giggle between my cries.

Then he surges into me, muffling my scream with his hand as he fills me completely.

"*Blyat*. This pussy," he groans, driving into me with slow, sure strokes, hooking his arm under my leg to allow him better access. "So tight. So goddamn hot."

His mouth finds mine as he surges inside me, building the pace slowly, bringing me with him as he heads for the pinnacle. "I want to hear you come, *milaia*," he says roughly into my ear. "I want to feel that pussy clench around me—ah!"

His words throw me over the edge, my body seized with a fierce grip of pleasure, making me scream into his hand as I shudder against him. He holds his cock deep inside me as I spasm around him, and I can feel the savage control he's exerting.

"The feel of you on my cock," he mutters hoarsely. "The way you come—Christ." I grab his ass, forcing him deep into me, and he finally lets himself hit the hard, fast strokes that bring him over the edge with a roar and tumble me into a fresh wave of sensation.

47

ROMAN

The field beside the finca has been transformed into a wonderland of wildflowers, woven through the wooden chairs and strewn across the carpet that leads to the arch of flowers where I wait, Mickey at my side.

The congregation is enough to give Interpol a heart attack. There's the geek squad, of course, headed by Pavel, wearing a ridiculous suit that should be burned at the first opportunity. All of my men are in attendance, or at least those who aren't working security, including a pale-faced but still-smiling Bryce. The members of Mak's team who fought for us in Miami. Alexei's closest *vor*, all of whom look as grim faced and hard as their *pakhan*.

I invited only a few members of the Mercura board, and not all came. I'm mildly surprised, and a little touched, to see Zinaida Melikov among those faces. As ice-cold and stunning as ever, she nonetheless gives me a small smile of something almost like approval when I pass her in the aisle.

I'm guessing she heard about Yuri's demise.

Off to the side, overlooking the valley, long tables covered in white linen and wildflowers stand in a clearing of holm oak, a seamless blend of comfort and natural beauty. The late-afternoon sun turns everything to a mellow, buttery hue. Later, a sea of twinkle lights will turn it into a magical playground.

I stand beneath the arch of flowers, Mickey at my side, as the cellist begins to play. Masha appears first, clad in a white linen dress and open sandals, flowers threaded through her mass of curls, which have been semi-tamed—by my mother, I imagine—into sweet ringlets that tumble down her back. She looks around curiously at the crowd, then sees Mickey and me, and her face lights up in a beam that makes the congregation sigh. She walks down the carpet, tossing handfuls of pink petals around her.

Then Darya appears on her father's arm, and I catch my breath.

My mother has outdone herself; Darya's dress is a vision of ivory silk and tiny handstitched crimson rosebuds that swirl through the bodice like a romantic storm.

However, it isn't the dress itself, no matter how beautiful, that sucks the breath from my body, but the woman who is wearing it. Darya's eyes blaze topaz as they lock on mine, the raw emotion in them gripping my heart fast. Her curls are piled in a thick mass behind her head, threaded with small rosebuds and star jasmine. Their scent reaches me long before she does, wrapping about me in a sensual seduction. The late-afternoon sun turns her skin the tawny, rich tone that drives me out of my mind. The dress falls from directly beneath her breasts, high-lighting their ripe lushness, and skims the delicious bulge of her stomach.

It's all I can do not to throw her down in front of the entire congregation.

I'm vaguely aware of the admiring whispers as she passes the rows of chairs. There's a ripple of laughter as Masha throws petals in the air that get caught on a slight breeze and flutter back to catch in her ringlets. She turns to Sergei, her face screwed up.

"Taste funny," she says, to another round of affectionate laughter.

Sergei smiles at Masha and nods gently in my direction. "Go to your papa, *myshka*." I'm impressed, but not at all surprised, by his upright posture and sure step.

Masha nods solemnly and comes toward me, her little hand releasing crumpled petals as she stares around curiously at all the new faces.

"Well done, sweetheart," I say as she reaches me. She beams at the compliment.

"Come here, Mash," says Mickey, bending down. His tuxedo makes him appear far older than his years, and from the admiring glances of the younger ladies in the congregation, he's making the tux work for him. Masha slips her hand into his and turns to face the crowd. "Lot of people," she says, loud enough to elicit another round of laughter.

Ofelia, leaning heavily on Alexei's arm for support, comes down the aisle behind Darya and Sergei. She and Abby are both wearing halter-neck indigo silk dresses that fall straight to the ground. Ofelia's boot came off yesterday, but she's still walking very gingerly. I'm touched to see the care Alexei shows in escorting her, seemingly attuned to her slightest hesitation.

Behind them comes Abby on Dimitry's arm. She smiles at me down the aisle, and I smile back. I'm glad she's here.

Sergei and Darya halt a few meters in front of me. Alexei and Dimitry wait to see Ofelia safely supported by Abby off to one side of the arch, then come to stand by Mickey. Dimitry grips my shoulder, his eyes meeting mine briefly as he turns to take his place at my side. "I've got your back, brother," he murmurs, and just for a moment, we're boys again, running through the Miami night.

I'm glad the music is still playing and I have time to compose myself before I have to speak.

Sergei steps forward, drawing Darya ahead of him so she faces me. His eyes sparkle a deep, joyful blue as they rest on his daughter. He leans forward to kiss her cheek, then turns to me and places her hand in mine.

"I am giving my world to you," he says in Russian.

I place my hand over his and answer in the same language. "My world is hers, as is my life."

Sergei nods, then steps back and takes his seat beside my mother. Her hand slides into his, and she rests her head on his shoulder.

I barely notice the words the minister says. There is only Darya's eyes, luminous in the golden sunlight, her scent wreathed about me like a spell, the silken touch of her hand in mine. Then Dimitry is stepping forward with the rings, and I slide the band made by my father's hands onto Darya's finger as I repeat the minister's vows.

You are here, Papasha. You may not be at my side, but you are here with me, forever.

A slight breeze stirs the holm oak above in answer, and I smile.

"You may kiss the bride."

Darya's lips beneath mine are a sweet benediction, the end of loneliness and the beginning of a life I never thought I had a right to. "I love you," she whispers in my ear, and I cradle her against me, my world, my life, my love.

"I love you, too," I say.

EPILOGUE

DARYA

It's a month after I married Roman in a sunlit meadow, surrounded by wildflowers and a sea of love, when we finally make the trip to Miami to open the vault.

We make the trip through the basement tunnels as a group. I was worried the girls would be upset by coming back to the place where they were held captive. But to my surprise, all they wanted to know was if Alexei would be there. Now that we are all here together, Masha is clinging tightly to Papa's hand on one side and Rosa's on the other. Lars, who never seems to leave Alexei's side, has his arm through Ofelia's, gently guiding her every step. Mickey brings up the rear.

Abby has already left for Australia, and Dimitry has been taking care of business in Spain while Roman and I honeymooned in the Greek islands.

I say *islands* like we spent time traveling around them.

The truth is we got to the *Guapa*, which was moored at

Milos island, then spent most of the next month either in bed, naked in the pool, or naked in the sea.

Naked, basically.

We round the corner of the basement, and suddenly there it is. The vault Roman's father built with his own hands. The lethal legacy that binds us to our shared history in love, pain, loyalty, and honor.

Roman turns to me. "Are you ready?"

I nod, then look at my brother. "Ready?"

Alexei gives a curt nod of his head. I'm aware of our father standing behind him, tall and proud. He doesn't try to interfere. This legacy is ours now, the responsibility of a new generation.

My father has carried it for long enough.

Roman presses one of the flowers, and a small panel emerges, lights blinking red as it waits for our fingerprints. He steps up and puts his index finger to the panel. One light goes green. I follow him, and a second one changes color. Finally it's Alexei's turn.

When all the lights are green, Alexei holds up his key. Roman presses another flower, and two panels I never knew were there slide aside, revealing two locks on either side of the door.

Roman and Alexei place their keys in the locks and turn them. There's an audible click. Roman takes hold of the central wheel, and the heavy door swings open.

Lights come on automatically, lighting the dim interior of the vault. It's an entire room, bigger than most bedrooms, with shelves lining the walls and glass shelving cabinets. On every surface, spaced at neat intervals, are the treasures that were once entrusted to the Naryshkin family.

Fabergé eggs, some I recognize as the lost treasures of the Romanov imperial family. Every manner of elaborate jewelry, in every conceivable stone and metal. Gold, silver, diamond, and pearl; the shelves are a glittering array from a lost world. One where women wore tiaras with jewels the size of golf balls and gave their children rocking horses with sapphires for eyes.

Because it isn't just jewelry that the *dvoryanstvo* tucked away for safekeeping. They also put aside their most precious possessions.

The rocking horse might have sapphire eyes, but it also has a worn leather saddle and hair that is thin from being pulled out.

A soft toy doll wears a dress threaded in gold and seed pearls, but one of her diamond eyes is missing, and an arm hangs at a crooked angle from being carried around.

One of the first matryoshka doll sets ever made, hand-painted by Malyutin himself more than a century ago, the exquisite paintwork scarred and battered from little hands banging the dolls around.

Leather-bound family bibles locked with gold clasps, containing entire family lineages. Family paintings.

The vault is a treasure trove of family love, the small things, priceless in both monetary and emotional terms, that make a family history.

Every single treasure has a neatly written card propped beneath it, stating the family name, the last known address of any descendant, and any other information that might matter.

We all stand at the entrance, almost too afraid to enter. The vault feels like a still life painting, a snapshot of another world.

It's Masha who breaks the silence. "Horsie!" she squeals, running through the maze of treasure to the rocking horse with the sapphire eyes. She straddles it without hesitation and begins rocking back and forth, humming a tune of her own making.

Roman and I cross the floor after her, gazing in astonishment at the riches piled around us. He bends down to read the card propped against the horse and gives a disbelieving snort of laughter. "Read it," he murmurs to me, pointing to the card. This one is not written in the same neat hand as the others in the room, but in a childish scrawl of Russian Cyrillic letters.

This horse is called Golden Wind and he belongs to me, Grand Duchess Anastasia Nikolaevna of Russia, youngest daughter of Tsar Nicholas II, sovereign of Imperial Russia. DO NOT TOUCH.

"Oh my goodness," I breathe.

Roman nudges me. "Have a closer look at the hair Masha is clinging to. It's made of pure gold thread." We look at each other, laughing in shaky disbelief.

We spend a long time looking through the vault, being careful not to rearrange the careful order. "My father wrote these cards," Roman says, peering at one. "It's his hand."

"*Da.*" Papa nods, his eyes far away in the past. "Aleksander was meticulous about keeping records."

"He loved writing these," Rosa says quietly, slipping her hand into Papa's. "His father made him memorize every piece when he was growing up in the gulag, and the story that went with it."

Papa laughs softly. "Our fathers used to say that it wasn't the piece itself, but rather the reason it mattered, that was important. Russians value stories, you understand. We learned the story of every piece on winter nights, when the snow fell and there was nothing but stories to keep us warm."

I smile at him, suddenly so grateful that we got here at last, that we saved this legacy from the hands of uncaring, brutal men.

I slip my hand into Roman's. "Was it worth it?" I murmur, out of hearing of the others. "Everything we endured to save this?"

He kisses the top of my head. "I think so," he says, his eyes caressing my face. "You?"

I nod, resting my head on his shoulder. "I know so."

After a time, we turn to leave. Masha reluctantly climbs off Golden Wind, kissing her new friend goodbye when Papa says she can't bring him upstairs with her. She stops at another doll, the one with a missing eye and crooked arm.

"Deda," she says, turning wide blue eyes up to Papa, "tell me about this one."

Papa bends down and scoops her up in his arms so she is looking directly into his eyes.

"That, *myshka*," he says solemnly, "is a story for another day."

Lethal Abduction is the next book in the Lethal Legacy series.

ALSO BY PAULA WALSHE

Travel Memoir

Slow Journey South

Sahara

Sign up to receive more free books and updates at www.fehupress.com.